PENGUI

Mad Abo

Praise for *Pants on Fire*:

'A witty, smart debut' *Daily Mail*

'A glitzy whirl of Tim Tams, tantrums and handsome love-interests'
Marie Claire

'It's fun, funny, feather-light and once started, like a box of chocolate
bikkies, can't be put down until you're full and it's finished' *Sydney
Morning Herald*

'Witty, upbeat, modern romance' *Daily Express*

'Alderson shows a gift for slicing through the daffy bravado of women's
mags' real-life Pats 'n' Edinas and makes a highly entertaining meal
of one woman's search for an Aussie fit for a Pom. Highly entertaining'
Heat

'A witty modern romance . . . much more than a *Bridget Jones Diary*'
Australian Vogue

'Wickedly funny and realistic . . . the perfect read for any girl who's
ever wondered if the grass might be greener on the other side of the
world' *OK!*

'A funny, light-hearted read' *Glamour*

'Entertaining and upbeat' *She*

'This sparky novel bowls along with great pace' *Sunday Mirror*

Maggie Alderson was born in London, brought up in Staffordshire and educated at the University of St Andrews. She has worked on nine magazines – editing four of them – and is currently a fashion columnist with the *Sydney Morning Herald* and *The Times*. Her first novel, *Pants on Fire*, was a best-seller in the UK and Australia, and she was a co-editor of the charity anthology *Big Night Out*, in aid of Warchild. She is married and moves a lot.

Mad About the Boy

MAGGIE ALDERSON

PENGUIN BOOKS

PENGUIN BOOKS

Published by the Penguin Group
Penguin Books Ltd, 80 Strand, London WC2R ORL, England
Penguin Group (USA) Inc., 375 Hudson Street, New York, New York 10014, USA
Penguin Group (Canada), 90 Eglinton Avenue East, Suite 700, Toronto, Ontario, Canada M4P 2Y3
(a division of Pearson Penguin Canada Inc.)
Penguin Ireland, 25 St Stephen's Green, Dublin 2, Ireland (a division of Penguin Books Ltd)
Penguin Group (Australia), 250 Camberwell Road, Camberwell, Victoria 3124, Australia
(a division of Pearson Australia Group Pty Ltd)
Penguin Books India Pvt Ltd, 11 Community Centre, Panchsheel Park, New Delhi – 110 017, India
Penguin Group (NZ), cnr Airborne and Rosedale Roads, Albany, Auckland 1310,
New Zealand (a division of Pearson New Zealand Ltd)
Penguin Books (South Africa) (Pty) Ltd, 24 Sturdee Avenue,
Rosebank, Johannesburg 2196, South Africa

Penguin Books Ltd, Registered Offices: 80 Strand, London WC2R ORL, England

www.penguin.com

First published 2002
This edition published for Index Books 2006

8

Copyright © Maggie Alderson, 2002
All rights reserved

The moral right of the author has been asserted

Set in 11/14.75 pt Minion by Intype London Ltd
Printed in England by Clays Ltd, St Ives plc

This is a work of fiction. Any resemblance to real events or people, living or dead, nice or nasty, is entirely coincidental. Except for the Apollos. They were real.

For Popi

Acknowledgements

To have one fabulous publisher is a blessing – to have two a miracle. Love, thanks and deep respect to (in alphabetical order) Harrie Evans at Penguin UK and Julie Gibbs at Penguin Australia. I'm mad about the girls.

Gratitude and affection in spades to all the other Penguins on both continents. I would be happy on an ice floe with any of you.

Deep appreciation is also due to the wonderful Curtis Brownies: Jonathan Lloyd and Lucy McNicholas in London, Fiona Inglis and Tara Wynne in Sydney.

Thanks also to all my colleagues and pals at the *Sydney Morning Herald*, particularly Alan Revell, Robert Whitehead, Fenella Souter, Phil Scott, Anthea Loucas and Stephanie Raethel. And to Jane Wheatley and Portia Colwell at *The Times*.

Special thanks to all my friends for their support and inspiration, specifically Victoria Killay and Caris Davis for 'mentionitis' and 'Marmite miners', Ruby Millington for the 'buggery' and Paula Joye for 'the time before Monkey'. And a big kiss to Kate Duthie, because she is the funniest, most inspiring babe I know.

1

I've got nothing against gay men – some of my best friends are homosexuals. I just didn't expect my husband to be one too.

Even after he told me it took a while to sink in. We were sitting at the breakfast table one Saturday morning when Hugo suddenly put down the fashion supplement and sent our son Tom out into the garden to play. Then he said, in a perfectly normal tone of voice: 'I've got something to tell you.'

Those are always ominous words, but of the nightmare options that passed through my head – I've been made redundant, we're moving back to England, my parents are coming to stay – a coming out speech never figured.

I didn't say anything, I just nodded and looked at him expectantly. Maybe we were moving to Melbourne. Cool.

'I'm a pouf,' he said.

It didn't sink in at first because I already knew that. Hugo had always been a big girl and that was exactly what I loved about him. He adored fancy-dress parties, he liked choosing curtains, he cried in soppy films, he arranged flowers better than I did. Those are precisely the things that made me fall in love with him when we met, aged nineteen. My friends had always told me how lucky I was to have a husband with such 'good taste'. A man who bought you underwear on Valentine's Day that you'd actually want to wear.

So I just carried on looking at him, puzzled, waiting for him to tell me the big news. He sighed and raked his fingers through his hair.

'I'm a pansy, Antonia. A woofter. A shirtlifter. A bum bandit. A turd burglar. A Marmite miner.'

I still didn't get it. I simply couldn't process what he was saying. Not until he leaned across the table and said:

'I'm *queer*, Ant. I've got a boyfriend.'

Then I got it.

For a while I could only stare at him. I think for the first time in my life I understood what the word 'shock' actually means. It was a typically hot and humid Sydney January morning but I felt really cold. I was shaking and shivering. My mouth hung open, but I could think of nothing to say.

I stared at Hugo Xavier James Heaveringham (pronounced 'heaver', rhymes with beaver, don't ask), the man I had spent the past ten years of my life with and, on the surface, nothing had changed.

He still had the wavy dark blond hair, the high cheekbones, the beautiful pale blue eyes and the expression of a constipated spaniel which I had fallen in love with when we met at our first Medieval History lecture at St Andrews University. I had never before experienced the full beam of aristocratic charm and from that first moment I was smitten. Amazingly, so was he.

Somehow the memory of that meeting flashed through my mind fully formed; at the same time I was trying to process what he had just told me. It was as though I was remembering every moment of our life together, whilst simultaneously wondering what would become of us and how we would tell Tom. Not to mention his mother, the devoutly Catholic Countess of Romsburgh, and his father, the atheist earl.

Then one of the words Hugo had mentioned in his confession came rushing back at me like a rude gesture.

'A boyfriend?' I spat out. 'What kind of a boyfriend?'

In that instant, I realized that the infidelity hurt me a lot more than the gay revelation.

'What kind of boyfriend do you think, Ant?' he spat back. 'A *boyfriend* boyfriend. He's called Greg.'

'Greg,' I said in a sarcastic voice. 'Charmed, I'm sure. Hi, I'm Greg, I'm an Aquarius. What does he do, this "Greg"?'

'He's a hairdresser.'

'Oh, how very lovely,' I said, suddenly understanding the provenance of the rather alarming Caesar haircut Hugo had arrived home with one recent evening.

'How long have you known this hairdresser?' I asked, my heart beginning to pound.

'Five months.'

I counted back to August, trying to remember if there had been any signs of anything different back then. I would have been frantically busy assembling the spring stock for my shop, I worked out, so I probably wouldn't have noticed.

'Where did you meet him?' I asked, my skin beginning to prickle with anger.

Hugo looked uncomfortable. He started stirring his tea noisily in his cup, in a way that I realized had annoyed me for over ten years. Suddenly, I was furious.

'I said – where did you meet this hideous little screamer? TELL ME!'

I was shouting. I was standing up and shouting. I never shout. I'm English. I'm a vicar's daughter.

Hugo was standing too. He had gone all red. Not the bonnie wee laddie rosy cheeks that had so enchanted me when we met, but nasty angry red blotches. It was the physical manifestation of the evil twin side of Hugo's nature, which rarely came out, but was fearsome when it did.

'He's not a screamer,' he hissed. 'He's wonderful. I met him in Brisbane. In a bar.'

I remembered now. He'd gone up to Brisbane to see a client and he'd ended up staying nearly a week. I could clearly remember the phone call saying he had to stay the weekend. The art collection had been 'much bigger than expected'. Right.

I had just thrown my teacup across the table at him, when Tom came back through the garden door. I saw him look quickly at us both, as the cup crashed onto the slate floor.

'Mummy?' he said, his little face crumpling up with confusion. Hugo and I never argued.

I scooped him up and kissed his little pink Heaveringham cheeks.

'Don't worry, Tom Tom,' I said, 'Daddy and I are just being silly. It's just a silly game.'

'Can I break a cup?' he asked, always one to grab the main chance. Just like his father.

I buried my face in his soft neck, blowing raspberries on it and probably getting more comfort from the embrace than he was.

'No, you can't break a cup, but guess what, Tomety?' I told him. 'Daddy's just told me he's going to take you to the park, haven't you, Daddy?' I turned and glared at Hugo, daring him to contradict me. 'And then perhaps you can go over to Nat's house for the afternoon. How would that be? You can play on their beach. I'm just going to ring his mummy.'

'Yes, I can take my noodle,' said Tom, wriggling from my arms. 'I'm going to wear my swimmers under my shorts and take my spade and my backpack and my beach hat and . . .'

He ran upstairs making a verbal list on the way. Tom loved to be organized. Not something he inherited from Hugo's side. The most famous Heaveringham was the one who had lost Wellington's despatches at Waterloo, somehow changing the outcome of the battle – for the better. As the Earl was fond of saying, the Heaveringhams were a bit hopeless, but they were damned lucky.

I looked back at Hugo.

'I'm going to need some time to absorb this,' I said, trying to control an insistent quiver in my voice. He came round the table towards me and I could see he was going to give me a hug. A hug-o, as I used to call them. I put my hand out to stop him.

'No, Hugo,' I said, shaking my head firmly. 'I don't want

your hugs just at the moment. I want you to take Tom and get out, so I can have some time to think. I'll call you and let you know when you can come back and we'll talk some more. Right now, I can't take anything else in.'

Eventually, after the usual pantomime with the lost wallet, mobile phone, sunglasses and car keys, Hugo and Tom made a noisy and encumbered exit and I sat at the kitchen table gazing into space.

Nursing a cold cup of tea – Hugo's favourite teacup, I realized with a jolt, the lily of the valley pattern we'd found at a roadside market in the Blue Mountains – I tried to think and not to think at the same time.

I would forget about it all for a split second and then it would come rushing back again. It was like being one of those people with memory loss who can read the same comic strip over and over again and still find it funny. Each time I remembered it, what Hugo had just told me hit me afresh.

How could he be gay? We had a perfect marriage. We were a perfect couple. Everyone told me that and we'd been in a list of Perfect Couples in *Pratler* magazine, with a picture, so it must be true. And all the time he was secretly gay?

I still felt queasy from the shock and decided some toast would settle my stomach. After four pieces with peanut butter, four with apricot jam and two with Marmite, brought back from home specially, I felt a little better. Ready for some porridge and golden syrup. And some cocoa.

*

At that point – G Day, as I came to think of it – we had lived in Sydney for just over a year. Hugo was the managing director of the Australian branch of Cadogan's, one of London's most prestigious fine art auctioneers. He'd been head of the decorative arts department in London and the Sydney job was a major promotion – the Cadogan's equivalent of a Foreign Office Peking posting (the other profession youngest son Hugo had been considering when we left university).

I'd been quite happy to move to Sydney, thinking it would be a nice sunny place for Tom to run around for his remaining primary school years, before he was banished off to a terrifying public school like all other male Heaveringhams before him. And it was a great promotion for Hugo – still only thirty.

It was also a relief to be several thousand miles away from Hugo's parents. Charming though she was, Margot – the Countess of Romsburgh, Lady Heaveringham – had never quite come to terms with her darling youngest marrying 'a parson's daughter', as I once heard her refer to me, and although he was a dear old thing, I did find the Earl – Freddie – rather alarming. He was so, well, mad.

His great passion was preserving the heritage of English folk music and the most frightful beardy weirdies would turn up at dinner, drinking real ale throughout and singing sea shanties, which Freddie recorded on an ancient reel to reel, conducting with his pudding spoon.

Lady H – 'do call me Margot' – was always witheringly charming to them.

'Oh, you're a heating engineer,' she'd say, her eyes

practically closing with boredom. 'How terribly fascinating. You must meet some very interesting people. More pork?'

Hugo and his hearty siblings didn't seem to notice any of it. Too busy getting their share of the hideous food down the front of their holey jumpers and sneaking scraps to the dogs.

While I found his family a bit much, once I had got over the initial naïve thrill of them being full-on thousand-year-family-tree aristos, I was terribly happy with Hugo. What can I say? From the moment we met, we were best buddies.

He had sat down next to me, a flushed and hectic heap, just as the first lecture of our four-year university career was about to begin, all long legs, scuffed brogues and pink cheeks, with a smile as open and irresistible as a toddler's.

He hadn't had a pen or any paper with him and in the last moments before the lecture started, he'd managed to tease me endearingly about my babyish pencil case full of sharp new pencils and smart rubbers, my new pad of lined A4 and my shiny red folder, whilst simultaneously relieving me of everything he needed.

Afterwards he'd bought me a cup of coffee to thank me for my stationery supplies – indescribably awful coffee in a funny little student café in the basement of the Medieval History department.

'Reckon Pope Pius III ground this coffee himself, don't you, Antonia?' I remember him saying, as he peered into his cup, stirring noisily, then twinkling those ice blue eyes back up at me.

I was lost, hopelessly instantly in love, and I bought him a Wagon Wheel to take the nasty taste away. He was not used to being 'mothered' in that way – Lady Heaveringham had enjoyed her children at the hygienic remove of several nannies and a separate wing – and I didn't realize how much such a tiny gesture could touch him.

By our second term, we were living together. We'd both started off in single-sex halls of residence – Hugo in Sallies with all the other Old Etonians, me in Chatham with all the other old virgins – but after Hugo was caught creeping out of my bedroom for the third time by the fierce lady warden, he announced he was going to find us a place of our own.

Not that we were having sex, or anything. I was still practically a virgin. The very sheltered daughter of a country vicar, I had blown the notion of sexual congress up into being some kind of holy sacrament, not something you did on a Friday night just because you felt like it. I didn't mind snogging and all that, but the actual act overawed me. I wanted it to be 'special' before I would risk it.

The great thing was that unlike my previous boyfriends – a couple of boys snogged at school dances, a Yugoslavian ski instructor and a hunky American I met doing my year out stint at a children's summer camp in Colorado – Hugo didn't mind. (Oh all right, I did actually lose my virginity to the American, because I'd thought I was in love with him, but I was in denial about it. It had only taken about three seconds, it had hurt and then I'd found out about his 'steady' girlfriend, so I'd decided it didn't count.)

Unlike them, Hugo said he was happy just 'to cuddle' and we would lie in bed for hours on the grey afternoons of a Scottish winter, when we should have been at lectures, giggling and singing and playing silly games, until we fell asleep in each other's arms. I thought this was as good as life could possibly get. And you know what? It wasn't half bad.

Using his labyrinthine network of family and old school ties, which meant that he seemed to know, or be related to, half the university from day one – or the ones who mattered, at least – Hugo quickly found us a room in a glorious old grey-stone Georgian house on South Street. A school friend of his was moving out to live with his girlfriend, so we moved in.

Seven other students lived in the house, but we were the only couple, with a huge bedroom all to ourselves. We had an open fire and a four-poster bed, which was Hugo's idea of basic student digs, and it was here that we finally 'did the deed' as he romantically put it.

We'd been going out for several months by then and were an established item around the university. After confiding with one of the more worldly girls in the house, Julia, about my fear of pregnancy (although I didn't let on we weren't having sex yet, I was savvy enough to understand Hugo was a 'catch'), I'd gone to the student medical centre and put myself on the pill.

The big event happened the night after the Apollos had beaten the medics at rugger. The Apollos were a rugby fifteen made up of Hugo and his pals – chosen partly for sporting skill, but more importantly for looks. Their team strip was a pink jersey and their motto was *Omnia vincit pulchritudo*. Beauty conquers all.

The miraculous presence of two really excellent backs and one zippy forward in the team won them the match against the thuggish medics, who had arrived at the field drunk and overconfident about thrashing the arrogant woofter toffs. But the toffs won and we celebrated with a party that passed into university legend.

That night Hugo and I had sex. In retrospect, he must have been so het up after the scrum and the showers that playing hide the sausage (another Hugo ism that pretty much sums up his attitude to our sex life) seemed an attractive prospect – even with a woman. In lieu of the far more sexy Number Eight, I now realized.

I can't say I enjoyed it much, but Julia had lent me a book about women's bits, which had warned me that one's early sexual experiences were unlikely to be the magical awakening of myth, so I was fairly realistic in my expectations.

It did get better after that and although it didn't happen very often, we had a good time in our way. The key thing for us was that we always had a laugh. A good laugh and lots of cuddles. I thought that was what being in a stable relationship was all about and I was very happy.

I got pregnant the night we finished our finals. I hadn't suited the pill and, as we had sex so infrequently, it didn't seem worth suffering, so I got myself fitted up with a contraption called a 'honey cap', which all my girlfriends were talking about. As contraceptives go, it wasn't a bad one, but it didn't work very well in the drawer.

To my amazement, Hugo was delighted with my announcement.

'Marvellous,' he said. 'We always breed young in my family. Parents will be delighted to have another grandchild.' He did a mental count. 'Think it will be their fourteenth. It's July now, so if we get married in early September the foliage will be beautiful around the chapel and the bump won't show too much.'

So we were and suddenly I was the Hon. Mrs Hugo Heaveringham. By April, I was sending out engraved announcements of the arrival of Thomas Frederick Xavier Heaveringham, we were living in the family flat in SW1 and Hugo was working at Cadogan's. The Countess of Romsburgh was eagerly planning the christening and Tom's ranks of godparents were off to Asprey's for suitable silver tributes. What a perfect couple.

Ha ha bloody ha.

2

We'd arrived in Sydney at the height of our Perfect Couple moment. The *Pratler* article had recently come out and I was amazed how many of the people I was meeting at the endless round of parties and dinners, arranged by Hugo's colleagues so he could schmooze the most important (i.e. richest) clients, seemed to have seen it.

'Oh, here's the other half of the perfect couple,' I remember one woman saying brightly to me, through expensive gritted teeth, as I sipped yet more champagne on yet another Point Piper terrace, overlooking Sydney's astonishing harbour.

We weren't living on the water ourselves, although I had longed to. It seemed the whole point of Sydney to me, but Hugo had declared it 'common' the moment we arrived and we were living in a large terraced house in a neighbourhood called Woollahra, which an old school friend had told him was the place to be. It was also around the corner from his office. Hugo knew how to keep his life sweet.

But despite my initial disappointment, I soon grew to adore Woollahra. 'It's Holland Park with New Orleans balconies,' I told my sisters, Sarah and Rebecca, in an early e-mail. It was a perfect little microcosm.

There were really nice delis and cafés in the next road, and divine boutiques and antique shops just a little further up the hill. I could walk to a harbourside park in ten minutes, drive to a beach in ten minutes, or jump into the pool in our own garden in ten seconds. We'd had a pretty good life in London, but this was the stuff of dreams, like being at home and on holiday at the same time.

The other great thing about Woollahra was that so many of the people we were meeting through Hugo's work seemed to live there too, so I would meet someone nice at a cocktail party one evening and then bump into them the very next day, getting a carton of milk. It made making friends effortless.

Sometimes I even used to run into Hugo when I had popped out to get something and he was just coming back to the office from lunch. We would stand on Queen Street – the main Woollahra drag – and giggle like a pair of five-year-olds, we thought it was such a lark. I used to blush when I saw him coming. After all those years, he still had that effect on me. He was so handsome in his beautiful suits.

Our social life had been hectic enough in London, a mixture of boozy drinks parties, dinners and weekends away at friends' houses, combined with a few more glamorous dos that were part of Hugo's job, but in Sydney it was amazing – one long round of designer yachts and catered cocktail soirées.

So much for the fabled laid-back Australian lifestyle, we found people in Sydney much more formal than in London. At home our friends only had caterers for weddings and twenty-firsts. In Sydney people had them for Sunday brunches.

And I couldn't get over the women. Talk about high maintenance. They seemed to get their hair and nails done every day and even the ones who didn't work wore suits all the time – even in summer. Chanel suits, at that.

My own droopy pastel-coloured Ghost skirts and cardigans, all spot-on in London, with a pair of jewelled flip-flops and a mad old Mexican basket, didn't seem right at all among this crowd and in the end Hugo took me shopping for a 'social' wardrobe of sexy little cocktail dresses and stiletto shoes. I always felt like I was dressing up as a grown-up when I wore it, but it was all part of the crazy hoot of it all. For the first year, Hugo and I never seemed to stop laughing, we were having such a good time.

And people were being so nice to me. From the moment we landed I was adopted by a small group of women, who had clearly decided I was their responsibility. Well, that's the way I saw it at the time.

The one I liked best was called Suzy Thorogood. She was a friend of a friend of Hugo's very bossy older sister, Anastasia (we called her 'Stasi' for short and it suited her) and I knew I'd be in terrible trouble if I didn't follow her up as Stasi had ordered me to do.

'Meant to be terribly nice,' she had barked down the phone at me, just before we left London, sounding like one of her own Labradors. 'Some kind of a financial PR. Husband's in insurance or some such. Chloe loves her. Worth giving her a call.'

But Suzy rang me first, when we'd only been in town a week, and invited me for lunch with herself and two girlfriends. It was at a fish restaurant on the water, she'd told me, so I wore a sundress and my flip-flops – well, I didn't know, I thought we were having fish and chips. They were all in Chanel and Armani suits.

I liked Suzy immediately. She was tall with short blonde hair and a very fit, tanned, sporty body, which made her look more like an Olympic swimmer than a corporate whizz-kid. She had a very firm handshake and an open smile and she immediately dispelled my embarrassment about my overly casual attire by joking about it, in a nice way.

'Oh you Poms are a funny lot,' she said indulgently. 'I did my MBA over there – that's how I know your sister-in-law's friend, Chloe – and it gave me a great insight into your race. The scruffier they are, the grander they are,' she said to the others. 'I never quite got the hang of it myself. So you must be very grand, Antonia, turning up here like that.'

She had such a warm, cheeky smile, I took it in good heart and insisted that I wasn't grand at all, just clueless.

'But your husband's grand, isn't he?' said one of the other women, narrowing her eyes, which I noticed were very bright green. Very bright green contact lenses.

'Oh no, not really,' I answered, embarrassed. 'He's the youngest son, so he's not going to inherit anything.'

'But isn't his father an earl, or something?' said the woman, still looking at me in that beady way.

'Yes, he is. But it's a very old title,' I added, which back home might have been enough to convey that the Heaveringhams had been very grand about four hundred years ago, but now were only grandish and rather poor in cash terms. I wasn't sure it got the message across to this one though. She was still looking at me like a dog looks at a biscuit.

I didn't feel so much at ease with either of the other women as I did with Suzy, but she was so nice, I was determined to give them a chance. The one asking all the questions was the youngest of the three and the prettiest.

She had long dark-red hair and the kind of kitten face that reminded me of a young Brigitte Bardot. She must have been astonishingly pretty all her life, I thought. Girls like that don't have an awkward phase, they just go straight from cute to devastating. I could just see her, aged ten, beaming out of a photo frame, doing the splits in a sparkly leotard, all the sequins sewn on by her doting mother.

The conversation had moved on, but she was still eyeballing me as though she was trying to find out something I was keeping from her. But when I looked back questioningly, she just beamed at me with the most radiant smile, like the sun coming out. I couldn't help but smile back. Her name was Nikki Maier.

The older of the three was a very attractive, if hard-edged bottle blonde, called Caroline French. As well as diamond studs the size of boiled sweets in her ears, her engagement ring was the most enormous diamond I had ever seen. Although it was all immaculately set off by a French manicure and a beautiful pale blue Chanel suit, there was something claw-like about those hands that I found repellent.

They were never still, always flicking and picking and

fluttering around, sometimes slapping down on the table quite hard, like a simultaneous sign language translation of her real feelings. Mind you, it was hard to judge what she was feeling from her face. She'd had so much botox and collagen injected into it, it was more like a mask than a human phizog.

But lunch was pleasant enough and as the conversation unfolded it became clear that Suzy had a very serious career, with her own large PR and marketing company, specializing in the financial sector. The other two didn't appear to work, although I heard quite a lot about their husbands' careers. Caroline's owned one of the biggest paint companies in Australia and Nikki's had a large cosmetics empire.

Suzy's husband, Roger, had been the boss of the Australian arm of a huge international insurance company, as well as having numerous other business interests, but now he had stepped down from his job to become an MP in the NSW state parliament, which made it quite clear to me that the Thorogoods were a serious power couple in town. The other two were clearly in awe of Suzy, who happily accepted her role as the most popular girl in school. It sat easily with her.

There were a few questions about Hugo's career and when they asked me what I did, I explained that I had never worked formally, as I'd had Tom straight after university and hadn't wanted to leave him with a childminder.

Nikki, who had two kids herself, looked at me as if I were insane. I found out later that she had two nannies – one for day and one for night – and that her children slept in a separate granny flat over the garages, not even attached to their house.

'I thought Chloe said you were an interior decorator,' said Suzy. 'She said your house had been in *Interiors* and that all the smart arty set in London used you to make over their places. She said you were very successful.'

'Did she?' I asked, amazed that one of Stasi's snobby friends had even noticed I existed. 'Crikey, how nice. But I wouldn't go that far, I used to do houses for friends of friends, for fun really, and people would come to my house and buy bits and pieces. But it wasn't a proper business, I just really enjoy decorating houses and finding interesting old things.'

Well, they loved that, they were all mad about decorators. Caroline used to be one, she told me proudly. She'd done a course. I should go over some time and see her swags. Nikki was more straightforward in her approach.

'We'll have to come and see your place when you're settled in, won't we, Antonia?' she said, her green eyes flashing like traffic lights. 'See if you're any good. I need my house redecorating actually, maybe you're the one to do it for me.'

'I'd be delighted to have a look,' I answered, thinking that people like her were the reason I only ever worked for friends of friends and I didn't count her as one of those yet. Then I had an idea.

'Actually, you three might be able to help me,' I said. 'I'm thinking of opening a homewares shop. Now that Tom is at school, I've got time to do it and it's always been a fantasy of mine to have a proper shop. So I would love to know what you think of my style and whether you reckon it would work here.'

They all promised to help, which was a good thing, because up until that moment, while I'd always dreamed of having a shop, I hadn't seriously imagined doing it. Now, it seemed, 'Anteeks' was going to be a reality.

After that lunch I saw quite a bit of the 'girls' as they called themselves. I could never quite understand why somebody as nice and as intelligent as Suzy hung out with the other two, but I continued to bow to her better judgement and we became quite a little gang.

Nikki, in particular, took it on herself to 'look after me'. Rather as a Rottweiler looks after a postman, I decided later, but at the time, I was glad of the help. She gave me the numbers of the best gynaecologists, acupuncturists, masseurs and dentists, told me the 'right' places to get my hair done, my nails polished and my eyebrows plucked and where to find all kinds of services I'd never heard of, like Brazilian waxing, which sounded terrifying, but which, she assured me, 'men adore.' More inclined to thinking in the singular where men were concerned, I didn't think I'd risk it.

Insisting on picking me up one morning, to take me on a tour of Sydney's best (i.e. most expensive) clothes shops, Nikki practically rammed the front door to get inside when I opened it. It was like a home invasion.

'Oh, this is great,' she said, doing a 360 of my hall. 'Can I have a quick perve? Better check out your decorating, Antonia. See if you're any good.'

With that she was off, going through every room in the house, like an auditor. As she looked round, taking in every detail, that hectic, beady expression I had seen on her face at the first lunch came back. She was particularly taken with anything that looked grand and English.

'Oh, I love that big cupboard, where did you get that? Did Hugo's parents give it to you?'

'The armoire? No, I got it in France at a country auction . . .' But she didn't appear to be listening. She had opened my cutlery drawer and was looking at our silver.

'This is nice stuff,' she said. 'I like the crests. Did you get that in France too?'

So she was listening.

'No, Hugo's parents did give us that. It's got Hugo's initials on it, but in fact it belonged to his great-grandfather . . .'

'I like your chairs, they look good painted that grey colour, what do you call that?'

'Well, it's sort of a Gustavian grey – you know, old Swedish style. I painted them myself actually . . .'

She darted a mean little look at me. Smug pity mixed with raw covetousness.

'Well, I like them, anyway.'

She even commented on Hugo's slippers.

'Oh, he's got those velvet slippers. I've seen those in a catalogue. I've ordered some for David with stags heads on them. These look a bit old though, doesn't he need some new ones?'

I laughed. Hugo adored his old slippers.

'He's had them since he was at school. He really likes them . . .'

By the time she'd finished, I was exhausted. I felt like I'd been strip searched. I tried to get out of it, but she was determined to take me round her favourite boutiques, as planned, where she instructed all the assistants to look after me, because I was going to be a good customer. I had the distinct feeling there was something in it for her – discount, or commission maybe. She was in for a big disappointment there, I thought. I had no intention of ever going back to any of them.

After all that she insisted on buying me lunch and although I found her constant barrage of questions extremely intrusive, I felt she was being kind to me in her way and it seemed rude and churlish not to go along with it all. And I have to admit, there was something rather appealing about Nikki. There was a vulnerability under all that pushiness that I found strangely touching and then she had that megawatt smile. It was captivating. She knew it, but that didn't lessen the effect.

A few days after her home invasion, Nikki rang me and said she wanted me to come and have a look at her place.

'I like your house, Antonia,' she said, as though she were bestowing a very special honour on me. 'It's got a really good English feel to it. It looks classy. I want you to come and take a look at my house' – not 'our house', I noted – 'and tell me how I can get that look here.'

I dutifully went. It was down in Double Bay, which was a neighbouring suburb to Woollahra, with smart shops and the most beautiful little white sand beach, but which was, somehow, much more brittle and showy than our little neighbourhood. The Maiers' house was particularly flashy.

It could be described as 'absolute waterfront' – a local expression I found hilarious – but it actually bordered only about six feet of water, so the house was like a pile of narrow boxes, stacked up, with a series of staggered balconies looking over the expensive liquid view.

The views were magnificent – Sydney Harbour still knocked me out – but the house was horrid to be in. Surrounded way too closely by other piles of concrete boxes, it seemed to be permanently in the shade and smelled strongly of mildew, and you were constantly going up and down dark stairs, between the floors. Worst of all, as far as I was concerned, the whole thing seemed to be marble. There were marble floors, marble walls, marble tables and marble ashtrays. It was like being in a funeral monuments showroom, and a plethora of faded and dusty silk flower arrangements added to the effect.

There wasn't much furniture to speak of, just a couple of very large, very ugly sofas down either side of the main drawing room, with a marble coffee table plonked in the middle, covered in remote controls. In the dining room there was a lit-up bar and a monstrous smoked-glass and brass dining table.

'David says he doesn't know why he bought a glass table,' said Nikki, flashing her devastating smile. 'He can't grope anyone under it without me seeing.'

I smiled weakly.

There weren't any paintings, any real flowers, or any

books, in the whole place – just a few framed posters, including the famous knicker-less tennis babe in David's den. Nikki proudly demonstrated how a marble panel in the same room slid back, at the push of a button, to reveal his collection of videos, which included *Teenage Sluts 5* and *Asian Teens 3*, among much more porno, as well as the more usual *Lethal Weapon* and *Pretty Woman*, although when I looked again I realized it was actually *Titty Woman*.

To make the most of such delightful videos, they had the largest televisions I'd ever seen – and one in just about every room.

Their bedroom was enormous, with a huge bed and, all too predictably, mirrors on the ceiling. There was also a video camera, set up on a tripod, pointing at the bed and linked to the TV. I didn't know where to look, but Nikki clearly didn't give a damn.

Leading off it there was an en suite bathroom the size of our drawing room, with his and hers basins, showers and even loos. The towels had 'His' and 'Mine' embroidered on them, I noticed. The curtains in every room were those horrid vertical blinds, opening and closing electronically. They looked dirty.

Nowhere was there any sign of children, which I found almost sinister. I did my best to keep Tom's toys under control in our place, but his drawings were all over the kitchen, his clay models proudly displayed on the mantelpiece and there were always a few plastic dinosaurs underfoot and Lego works in progress lying around. I liked his child energy in the place. Nikki clearly did not feel the same.

At the end of the tour of this soulless house, I was truly speechless, which Nikki took as a great compliment.

'It is a pretty amazing property, I know,' she said smugly, serving me Diet Coke in an elaborate cut-glass goblet on one of the many cold dark balconies. 'But I'd like it to have more of that classy English feeling your house has, Antonia. What do you suggest?'

Demolition was the first word that came into my head, but I managed to stop it coming out of my mouth.

'I'd have to give it some thought, Nikki,' I said, playing for time. 'It's not the kind of, er, property I'm used to working with. I've always decorated old houses before and old furniture sort of goes in them.'

She gave me one of her assessing looks.

'Second-hand furniture?' she said quickly.

'Well, I suppose it is . . .'

'I wouldn't want second-hand furniture in my house. Someone else's dirty old cast-offs,' she was pulling a 'yuk' face. 'This is all new furniture,' she said proudly.

'I'm sure it is,' I said. 'But if you want the look I have in my house, Nikki, it will have to be old furniture. My French armoire is probably 150 years old, maybe more. I wasn't the first person to own it.'

She took it all in.

'Hmmm,' she said. 'I'd never thought of that. I've just never fancied second-hand stuff. I'll have to think about it. Can't you get new stuff and make it look old? Bang it with a hammer?'

'Yes, you can do that. People do, but it's not what I do. It doesn't have integrity for me. What I like about the old furniture I buy is that it has character and a history – a patina which makes it unique. If you go and buy something new, it's exactly the same as all the other ones.'

She frowned at me.

'But at least you know what you're getting,' she said.

'It's not knowing what I'm going to get that keeps me interested,' I replied.

'So where do you get all that old stuff, anyway?' she said, pouring more Diet Coke. 'Does it all come from France?'

I was not about to reveal my sources to her.

'From France and various other places, here and there,' I said. 'You just sort of come across it.'

She looked deeply unimpressed.

'Well, I like them chairs of yours, anyway. I want some of them. I think they'd look good in there. Can you get me some?'

She was beginning to piss me off.

'No, I can't,' I said, firmly. 'I got them out of a filthy old barn in southern Ireland. They were covered in chicken shit. I restored them and painted them myself, as I told you. I could try to find you something similar. But not with that smoked-glass table. Or your china. Or your cutlery.'

She looked furious.

'What's wrong with my cutlery? That cutlery cost a lot of money. It's a hundred per cent real brass.'

'I'm sure it cost a lot of money,' I said. 'But it wouldn't go with Gustavian chairs and the combination would not enhance my credibility as a decorator in Sydney.'

We glared at each other like two cats having a stand-off. Once again she narrowed her emerald green eyes. They were such a give-away, you could practically see her calculating behind them. I thought if I could just focus on it, I'd see a little Reuter screen in there, blinking as she worked out the pros and cons of various actions and their effects on her stock price.

She clearly decided keeping it nice was the best option at this stage and veered off on a new tack, probing me about Hugo and his family. I just went along with it, making the answers as gnomic as I could, until eventually I had the excuse of collecting Tom from school as a pretext to leave.

The next morning she rang and asked if I would get her some of 'them chairs' if she 'let me' redecorate her entire dining room. Having established I could remove, or at least paint over, the marble and replace the table, the china and the cutlery, I agreed. I had to start somewhere in Sydney.

Big mistake.

3

Once I got stuck into redecorating Nikki's dining room, I began to have a really good time. I'd forgotten how much I enjoyed the chase of finding the right pieces for a space, and the challenge of her ghastly house actually turned out to make it more fun. I also had a tax deductible excuse to drive around Sydney and environs, checking out possible sources – and acquiring stock for my shop, which I was planning to open in a few weeks.

The only problem was that Nikki was always trying to come with me. I'd take her my work-in-progress scrapbooks of swatches and Polaroids of possible items, as I had done with all my clients at home, but she was always telling me how much more 'efficient' it would be, if she just came along with me on my buying trips.

In the end I had to stop answering my mobile, to shake her off. Hugo had to text me when he wanted to get hold of me. Luckily she didn't seem to have the hang of that yet.

But still I couldn't escape her. One morning I went out to Wally's Where House, a seriously grungy used-furniture depot on Sydney's southern outskirts, where I wanted to have another look at some chairs I thought might work for Nikki's dining room, with some major overhauling. I was sitting in the car park, waiting for it to open – dealers always get there before places open – when there was a tap on my car window. It was Nikki.

'What a coincidence,' she was saying. 'I'd heard about this place and I thought I'd pop down here and take a look and here you are . . .'

I just looked back at her in amazement. Considering her attitude to old furniture, I found it very unlikely that a trip to this junk heap would be her idea of a fun day out. Even I – who would happily dodge pigeon droppings from above and rats underfoot, to get into a promising-looking old shed – sometimes found myself repelled by some of the old sofas and mattresses I encountered down there.

I got out of the car and looked her over. She was wearing an immaculately pressed white linen shirt, tied at the waist, and matching pants. No one who had heard of Wally's – and there was a small group of in-the-know regulars – would ever have gone there dressed in white.

Most of the time, I'm pretty wimpy about standing up to people, but every now and again a flinty little core in me comes out. It came out then.

I looked Nikki straight in her contact lenses.

'Did you follow me here?' I asked her.

She looked back at me, doing one of her instant stock analyses.

'Yes,' she said.

I shook my head.

'You're quite a piece of work, Nikki,' I told her.

She took it as a compliment and beamed her famous smile at me.

'I know,' she said, happily. 'I always get what I want.'

'Well, as you're here, I suppose I'll have to let you come round with me,' I said. 'But I don't mind telling you, you have broken a fundamental rule of trust between decorator and client.'

She gave me another shot of the smile. Like everyone else she worked it on, I just sighed indulgently and let her have her own way.

Of course, I was thrilled to see the grin wiped off her face when she saw what the furniture warehouse was like inside. If you don't have the inborn ability to see beyond the desperate shabbiness and the general smell of failure, death and decay, to the potential of a filthy old object, those second-hand barns are like graveyards of broken lives. But to me they were Aladdin's caves, full of promise just waiting to be unleashed – and prices just waiting to be multiplied by a hundred.

And I should say here, I had no qualms about putting outrageous mark-ups on the things I found in those junk dens. I was the one with the eye for it and the stomach for the hunt and, on the whole, my clients were just happy to have a lovely old chair, or kitchen table, without having to do anything for it apart from sign the cheque.

To my great satisfaction, Nikki was totally bewildered by it all. I don't know what she had expected, but this definitely wasn't it.

'Surely you're not going to buy anything for my house in here?' she asked, picking her way between the towering piles, horrified.

'Oh no,' I said, fingers crossed in my pockets. 'But I

might buy stock for my shop.' She turned and looked at me quickly.

'Are you definitely opening a shop then?'

I nodded. 'Yeah. I've taken a space in the south end of Moncur Street, you know, the bit that goes towards Centennial Park?'

'Isn't it a bit dead down there? Couldn't you get something on Queen Street? It would be much better for your market,' said Nikki, with a savvy that surprised me.

'I looked at a great place on Queen Street,' I told her. 'But I couldn't afford it. So I'll just have to hope that word of mouth will bring customers in – like all the people who come for dinner at your place and ask who did the amazing make-over on the dining room.'

I tried flashing my own version of her smile. She looked pleased at the thought of the attention the dining room would bring her and shifty at the same time.

'Is that all it takes to make a shop successful?' she asked.

I laughed.

'I wish. I'll also have to work on getting some press coverage in the good interiors mags and, most importantly, I need to sell things that people want to buy. Like this.'

I held up a filthy little yellow jug, which had some nasty-looking old forks in it. She looked at it, scowling with disgust, clearly mystified why I thought anyone would want such a horrible object. I shrugged. I wasn't going to tell her about the five or six other assorted yellow vases and jugs I had already collected from various motley sources, that would make a wonderful group on a table, sitting on the old linen tablecloth, hand-embroidered with primroses, that I had found the day before in a charity shop in Bondi Junction.

I chucked the forks into a nearby bucket and looked at the bottom of the jug. It was marked $1, but by the time I'd washed it and styled it, I reckoned I'd be able to sell it for $60. Bingo. I made a note to that effect – buy price, sell price – in my trusty exercise book, which Nikki immediately tried to see.

'Nosy!' I told her, snatching the book away, and we carried on around the barn, with me fearlessly diving into sinister cardboard boxes and looking under vile old beds, while Nikki tried not to touch anything. I was gratified to notice that she had about a yard of filthy old cobwebs hanging off her perfect white linen arse as we left.

After that, Nikki stopped asking to come on my buying trips, but she was still very inquisitive about every step of the transformation of her appalling dining room into a rather opulent salon, in a sort of faux St Petersburg style.

It worked in the space, because I had deliberately made it like a camp 1960s filmset version of *Russe luxe*. '*Chic ironique*' Hugo called it, when he came over for a look, which seemed to delight Nikki, although I can't imagine she really knew what it meant. Either way, the room was cute, quirky, warm and very nice to sit in. And she got her grey chairs.

They were the ones from Wally's, which amused me intensely, but she would never have recognized them after

I'd had them stripped in an acid bath and changed the front legs. Then I had painted them my signature grey and upholstered them with a grey and white satin-stripe silk. They were gorgeous. Cost me $10 each from Wally's and $90 each, fully finished. They cost her $3,000 for ten. That's showbiz.

On the day I came to put the final finishing touches to the room – she was having a 'launch party' for it that evening and it meant a lot to both of us that it was perfect – she showed me that the paint on one of the chair legs had been badly chipped. She said the man who'd come to hang the chandelier (I got it from a sale of the fittings from a communist-era Polish cruise ship – it was fabulous) had done it.

I touched it up quickly from the end of a tin of paint I had in the car. Then, while I was rushing to lay the table and arrange the flowers ready for the photographer from *Belle* magazine, who was coming to shoot the room just before the party, Nikki persuaded me to 'jot down' the mix for the grey.

'In case the chairs get chipped again,' she said, and Hugo and I had 'left town'.

I never shared my paint mixes with anyone, but she knew exactly when to catch me off guard and I scribbled it down on the back of an envelope just to get her off my back. Oh, she was a crafty girl.

The party for Nikki's dining room was a great success and the perfect launch pad for my shop, which was opening the following week. I handed my new business cards to everyone there. 'Anteeks – Fine Junque and Objects of Charm', they said, in elegant grey type, with the address and phone numbers and stuff.

The silly name had been Hugo's idea and I liked it, because it didn't sound like I was taking myself too seriously – and with all the proper grown-up antique shops round the corner on Queen Street, I thought I'd better make that clear.

It seemed to work. In no time all the key newspaper sections and magazines had rung up wanting to do features about me and the shop. I was happy to oblige and called Hugo and Tom in as extras on some of the pictures.

The shop looked great – if I do say so myself – and it hadn't cost me much to do it up at all. I had found some great cabinets in an old draper's shop in Newcastle – the one up the New South Wales coast, not the one back in England where the bo-ats come in – and tacked cheap pine trims on the front and painted them all matt white. With a couple of grey-painted salon chairs it was instant Christian Dior goes boho.

Hugo and Tom helped me paint the floor the same pale grey, which was a very funny, messy day, and I made an 'Anteeks' shop sign out of a mixture of old commercial letters I had found here and there, in a funky jumble of colours and sizes. It looked very charming.

The night before it opened, Tom, Hugo and I had a picnic dinner in there and toasted its success with champagne. Tom had drawn me a special advertising notice to encourage customers, using his best felt tips.

'Nice things! Groovy shop! Charming! Good stuff! Tom's mummy!' it said, with a picture of me holding a big yellow and white spotty jug he'd found for me all by himself, hidden away in a cupboard in a junk palace up the Pacific Highway.

I put his poster in the window, surrounded by the display of yellow jugs and vases, Tom's spotty one full of crabapple branches with the fruit still attached. It looked very fine and from the first morning, Anteeks was a roaring success.

Having a shop was just as much fun as I'd hoped it would be. All kinds of people popped in and it was very sociable. Hugo would sneak out from the office and have tea with me some afternoons, bringing me a slice of orange cake from our favourite café, Agostini's, which made it seem naughty and wicked, like a midnight feast.

Used to being master of my own time, I did find it a bit of a juggling act with Tom at first and had to shut up shop whenever I had to go and pick him up from school, or take him to the dentist, which I knew wasn't great for business. Sometimes I had to shut completely for a couple of days while I went hunting for new stock, but it seemed to work out. People seemed to accept that quirky opening hours were just part of the Anteeks experience.

And it all got easier. Once there was a bit of a buzz about the shop the other mothers from Tom's school were happy to drop him off for me and they'd usually stay and shop a bit themselves.

I knew we were really on the Eastern Suburbs social

map when his friend Nat's madly competitive mother, Carla – a dedicated follower of Sydney fads – volunteered to look after the shop sometimes, when I needed to go off and do something. It was clearly a cool place to shop and be seen.

Certainly very few customers left Anteeks empty handed, even if it was just a charming old tea strainer, or a roll of vintage silk ribbon from the huge stash of old stock I'd bought from a country haberdasher's.

One of the first through the door on day one had been Nikki, loudly demanding – in a very full shop – that I give her a discount. While I was serving another customer I noticed her pick up the little yellow jug I'd bought at Wally's. When she saw the price, her eyes snapped open for a second and then narrowed into her most calculating look. At the time, I thought it was funny.

Looking back on it now, those early days of Anteeks were like some kind of golden age. Hugo and I were still in great demand on the social circuit – the success of my shop had made us even more desirable – and the parties were more fun now that we knew more people.

I was really enjoying the challenge of having a proper business of my own and Hugo's job was going brilliantly – he'd just had a record sale at an auction of Australian art. Most importantly, as far as I was concerned, Tom was very happy and doing well at school.

It was into this perfect picture that Hugo had dropped his cluster bomb.

*

On the day of the big announcement, he'd come back from dropping Tom off at Nat's house and was sitting opposite me in the drawing room.

'There is never a right time to tell someone something like this,' he was saying. 'If I'd told you when you were having a bad time, you would just have said – how could I add to your troubles like that? Wouldn't you?'

He was right, but I was just filthy angry with him about everything. After a lot of puffing and blowing and crying, calling him names and threatening to cut his goolies off if he ever brought ghastly Greg into our house, or introduced the foul pervert to our son, I finally ran out of steam and just sat there looking at him. Eventually I found the strength to ask him the one question that was really plaguing me.

'Tell me one thing, Hugo,' I said. 'And I need an honest answer to this . . .'

He nodded, looking very serious.

'Have you always been gay secretly?' I asked him. 'Was our marriage just a cover for you?'

He looked straight back at me and I knew that whatever he told me would be the absolute truth. He wasn't half a Catholic for nothing.

'You are the love of my life, Antonia,' he said. 'From the moment we met, I had eyes for no one else – male or female. Our relationship has brought me nothing but joy.'

He paused and sighed deeply and I saw his Adam's apple plunge as he swallowed nervously. That dear old aristocratic chicken neck.

37

'You will always be my best friend, Antonia, if you'll let me be. But, yes, I think deep inside I have always been gay. But I didn't want to be and when I fell in love with you, I thought I wasn't.'

'So why now?' I whined. 'Aren't we happy? Haven't we always been happy?'

'Of course we have,' he answered, looking so strained I almost felt sorry for him. 'Wonderfully happy, but I'm certain it would have caught up with me one day wherever we were and being in Sydney, where everyone is so relaxed about it and you see men happily holding hands in the street, it all just welled up inside me.'

I remained silent, as I felt he had more to tell me.

'I did go to a gay bar in London once,' he said quietly. 'But I knew immediately it wasn't for me. I'm not interested in lots of casual sex, I'm fundamentally a monogamist, as you know, and coming here I realized I could still have the cosy home life I love, but I could have it with a man and satisfy my sexuality as well – and keep my job. And not tell my mother.'

He looked absolutely stricken as he said it and I felt even worse. I tried to stop them, but tears just rolled down my cheeks. He had shattered my world in a moment and while I knew that he had his tough survivor side, along with all the twinkly charm, he was still my darling Hugo, the big boy I had grown up with and he still trusted me enough to tell me his deepest darkest secrets.

He came over and put his arm round me, wiping my tears with his linen handkerchief. He might have been hopelessly shambolic, but Hugo Heaveringham always had a clean hankie in his pocket. This time I didn't push him away.

'Don't cry, Ant,' he said. 'Please. I'm so sorry. I'm heartbroken too, but I couldn't lie to you any longer. And I want to try living with Greg. It's something I have to do.'

Of course that just made me howl like a dog. The combination of his heartbreaking sincerity and the idea that one day he would not be living with us any more really got to me. But eventually, through my racking sobs, which were soaking his lilac shirt, I managed to choke out what was really worrying me.

'But what about Tom?' I wailed. 'What are we going to tell him? Daddy doesn't live with us any more? He lives with a man?'

'Yes,' said Hugo. 'That's exactly what we have to tell him.'

I just looked at him.

'I'm not the first man to do this, Ant, or woman. Especially in Sydney. I happen to know that there is a girl in Tom's class at school in a similar situation – she lives with her mother and her stepmother. I met them through Greg.'

'Tom's not going to live with you,' I said quickly, my blood racing.

'Don't worry, Ant, I wouldn't do that to you – either of you. I'm going to live nearby. In fact, I've already taken a house just round the corner. Tom will carry on living here with you, but he can come and see me whenever he wants.'

'Is Greg the home-wrecker moving straight in with you?' I asked, my bitterness returning.

'Not immediately. We're going to do it in stages, so we can get used to it and Tom can get used to it.'

'We!' I said. 'Already you and this Greg are a "we". Isn't that cosy? Are you choosing fabrics together? Oh, you have got it neatly worked out, haven't you, Hugo?' I said, really angry again.

'Yes. I have,' he said bluntly. 'I wasn't going to spring this on you in a messy way. I've got the house. I'm moving out. On Monday.'

He had assumed his most patrician expression and was talking in his steely managing director voice. This was the Hugo who had survived a barking mad father, a glacial mother, three merciless older brothers, a storm trooper older sister and a school like an emotional boot camp. The other side of the charming Hugo whom everybody loved – the one who sometimes reduced his junior staff to tears. He could be a real bully sometimes. I knew there was no point in arguing.

I just slumped back into the sofa and put my head in my hands. Reverting quickly to nice Hugo, he put his arms around me and stroked my hair. For what felt like ages, we just sat there in each other's arms. Although he had shattered my world, he was still my best friend. He was the one who had wounded me – but he was also the only one who could really comfort me.

Humans really are weird sometimes.

4

So that's where Tom found us, when Nat's father dropped him off later that evening, curled up together like two puppies in a basket, just how he most liked us. He let himself in with his own key – something he insisted on having – came flying in and jumped on the sofa.

'We went to Nielsen Park and I swam all the way to the shark net,' he was telling us. 'It's really really cold out there and something brushed my leg and I swam like anything in case it was a real shark. Imagine if it had been a real shark and it saw my leg and thought – yum, lunch!'

He was chattering on, while insinuating his wriggling little body between us, as he had done so many times before. Hugo and I just looked at each other. Our lives had been wrenched apart that day, but we still had the telepathic communication of a very close couple.

'Hey, Tomski,' said Hugo, giving his tummy a tickle.

'What?' said Tom, looking up at us with such happy innocence I almost burst into tears again.

'Mummy and I are going to have an experiment. Do you want to know what it is?'

'Is it something about a man called Greg?' said Tom, perfectly calmly.

I nearly fell onto the floor.

'Well, yes, it is, Tom,' said Hugo, making a mystified face at me. 'How did you know?'

'Nat told me,' said Tom carelessly, and he started giving us shark bites on our legs.

Of course, it wasn't all that simple. When it actually came to Hugo leaving the house with a suitcase – which he did two days after springing it all on me – and not being there when he woke in the morning, Tom hated it as much as I did.

In fact, he cried his eyes out every morning and every night for the first two weeks, which was terrible for all of us. He would get very upset when he realized things like Hugo's slippers weren't there any more. So did I. I even missed his noisy tea stirring.

But to give him credit, Hugo did his best to make it easy for us. He took Tom on lots of guilty-father summer holiday outings and would come round after work and put him to bed whenever he could. Sometimes he came over to have breakfast with us too and Tom appeared to be adjusting to his strange new life, the way children do.

Things didn't get really wobbly until the new school year began. At first it was OK, but after a few days there were tantrums most mornings about going, because he said he 'hated' his new form teacher, although he would never say why.

'She's a farty pigbum,' was the most explanation I could get out of him.

This went on for a couple of weeks until his teacher rang me at the shop one morning to say that Tom had been 'very naughty' in class. It seemed he had called her 'Mrs Pigbum' to her face.

Mrs Picton – her real name – was clearly experienced at her job as the first thing she asked me was whether there were 'any problems at home'.

After I explained the situation to her – there didn't seem any point in prevaricating, as she must have been the last person in the Eastern Suburbs to hear about it – she agreed some playing up was only to be expected in the circs and promised to give Tom some special attention. She seemed all too resigned to such life changes occurring among her young charges and said she was going to move him to a different desk, whatever that meant.

At around the same time I started to notice a distinct sliding off in the willingness of Tom's class mates' mothers to drop him off at Anteeks after school the way they used to and when I rang Carla a couple of times to see if she could look after the shop for an hour or two, somehow she was always busy.

I put it down to the novelty wearing off – which I also assumed was the reason for the less frequent mentions of Tom's once great friend and desk mate, Nat, in his running commentary on his own life.

It never occurred to me, at the time, that these shifts were anything to do with the new shape of my personal life.

It wasn't until the approach of Tom's sixth birthday in late March that I finally realized what the problem was. He seemed strangely unenthusiastic about planning his birthday party. After several failed attempts to engage his interest in the subject – Did he want a theme? Did he want to have it at home or go out somewhere? How many friends did he want? Did he want burgers or sausages on sticks? – I finally asked him whether he actually wanted a birthday party. He shook his head very solemnly.

'No, Mummy,' he said. 'I'd just like to watch something funny on the telly with you and Daddy and have oven chips.'

If Hugo had been around at that moment I could quite happily have sunk an ice pick in his head. After that it didn't take much probing to find the cause of Tom's reluctance – he didn't think any of the children in his class would want to come to his birthday party. It seemed a lot of teasing and nasty name calling had been going on, much of it instigated by Nat.

Now I understood Mrs Pigbum's new classroom seating arrangements – and it didn't take long for them to work. One day he brought his new desk mate home for tea – it turned out she was the little girl with two mummies Hugo had told me about. She was called Vita, which might have been a hint to her father, and while they ate their spaghetti hoops, they had a long conversation about the relative advantages of having two mummies and two daddies.

'Of course, Greg's not my daddy,' said Tom firmly, after hearing all about Vita's mummies. 'I've only got one daddy. Greg's just my daddy's special friend. And Mummy is still Daddy's special friend too, aren't you, Mummy?'

'Oh yes, definitely,' I said, trying to mean it. But I wasn't feeling very special. In fact I had never felt so lonely in my life. I would see Hugo when he came to visit or to collect

Tom for an outing, but I didn't see him in my own right any more.

Nothing on earth would have got me through the door of the house where he was now living with grisly Greg and he no longer popped in for afternoon tea at Anteeks. We had both agreed it was better that we didn't see each other too much for a while, apart from when he came round to get Tom, to try to grow some kind of an emotional scab over our wounds. It all sounded very mature and sensible, but in actual fact it was bloody murder.

About ten thousand times a day, I would think, 'Oh, I must show Hugo that . . .', or 'Hugo's going to laugh when I tell him about this . . .' and then it would hit me all over again. No Hugo to show and tell anything to. He was round the corner, hearing all about Greg's day at the salon. I indulged in some very violent fantasies about Greg and as long as Tom wasn't around to see me, I spent a lot of time lying on the sofa watching crap television and sobbing.

Anything rather than go to bed – because, for me, one of the worst things about Hugo's absence was trying to sleep. After ten years of sleeping wrapped in his arms, fitting together like spoons in a drawer, I found it very hard to sleep on my own. I'd never experienced insomnia before and suddenly understood what a hell it is.

I tried everything – hot-water bottles, a pillow in the bed beside me, several of Tom's teddies, camomile tea, aromatherapy baths, relaxation tapes, boring books – but nothing worked. Hour after hour I lay there, wide awake, listening to the World Service and wishing it was Radio

Four. Wishing the pillow was Hugo. Wishing I was dead. It really was some kind of torture and left me as limp as an old dishcloth when the alarm went off at 7 a.m.

Apart from missing the physical presence of my husband and best pal, I also missed our social life. Tom wasn't the only one feeling like Noddy No Friends. Hugo and I had gone out so much from the moment we'd arrived in Sydney and all of a sudden there were no invitations to anything. Well, not for me anyway. I'm sure he still got asked to lots of parties and dinners and he had all his work events to go to, but apart from a few things, like a cocktail do for *Vogue Living*, I wasn't invited to anything in my own right.

It was such a shock. I had really thought all those people were my friends, but now I realized they had just been inviting our perfect couple persona to enhance their party profiles, not us as people. As the boss of Cadogan's – and an earl's son – Hugo was still somebody, but on my own, suddenly I was a nobody.

Even Nikki Maier had stopped calling me. The only person who was still loyal was Suzy Thorogood, who had taken me out to lunch as soon as she heard the news about Hugo, which was later than everyone else, as she had been on one of her business trips to New York when it all happened.

She was really lovely about it, completely straightforward and honest.

'I've just heard the awful news, Antonia, and I'm taking you for lunch,' she had said. 'And I'm not going back to work afterwards, so we can get pissed if you want to. You need looking after. It must have been such a shock for you when he told you. I'm sure you'll survive, but in the meantime, I'm officially offering you my shoulder – it's waterproof.'

We did get pissed, I did cry all over her designer shoulder and it was very helpful. For one thing, she told me that Greg was personal hairdresser to most of the ladies in the canapé set, which explained why Tom's friend Nat had known about Hugo's new relationship before I did. His mother, Carla, was one of Greg's regular 'girls'. So, it seemed, were most of the mothers at Tom's school, which solved the disappearing school-run mystery for me.

And there was another thing about that lunch that made me really value Suzy as a friend. I knew from reading the *Sydney Morning Herald* that her husband Roger had recently been given a post in the NSW state cabinet. After being an MP for a very short time, he was already Minister for Planning and the Environment, which was a great achievement, but she didn't bring it up, she was far too sensitive to brag about her husband while I wept for mine.

To show my gratitude for her thoughtfulness, I did.

'You must be so proud of Roger,' I said. 'It must be thrilling to be married to a cabinet minister. So grown-up.'

She smiled, but even through my drunken funk, I thought I saw a shadow cross her face.

'Oh yes, it's great,' she said, not looking particularly enthusiastic. 'But it does mean he's away from home even more. They work bloody long hours, politicians.'

Then she changed the subject to some diverting nonsense about how drunk and messy someone we both knew had been at a recent charity fund-raising dinner. Silly gossip about someone else was just what I needed to take my mind off myself and Suzy knew it.

As we left, she gave me a present – a double CD called *I Will Survive – The 30 Best Heartbreak Anthems*. It was the most useful thing I'd ever been given and I played it over and over again all those nights I stayed at home, watching telly and wondering where Hugo was with gruesome Greg.

I had finally encountered his Mr Right, bumping into them both in Queen Street one Saturday morning, just after Easter. It was such a shock. I had just nodded mutely at Hugo before dashing into the nearest shop, but in that brief moment I'd had time to register that Greg was astonishingly good-looking – in a clichéd kind of a way. He looked like a model from a Gucci ad, all sleek blow-dried hair and perfect pecs, and he dressed that way too, in tight jersey shirts and bulge-enhancing trousers.

Peering out at them unseen from the shop window I saw to my secret delight that he was wearing a bracelet, which nearly made me shout with laughter, until I noticed that Hugo was wearing one too, peeping out of the French cuff of his Turnbull & Asser shirt. They were matching. How very lovely.

It had nearly killed me, seeing them together, but in the interests of Tom's happiness and my own sanity – and taking sage advice from Suzy – I'd decided that I was going to try to get on with Greg. But guess what? He refused to be nice to me.

When they had been living together quite a while – he'd

moved in almost immediately, so much for doing it 'in stages' – I'd told Hugo I thought Greg and I should meet officially. Hugo was pathetically grateful and I think in a funny way he wanted to show us off to each other. The only problem was the venue. I still wasn't ready to have Greg in my home and visiting them in their homo love shack was definitely out of the question, so I suggested Hugo brought him into the shop one evening after closing.

I was incredibly nervous before they arrived and felt furious with myself as I tidied and restyled everything, so it would look its best. Who was I trying to impress, I wondered, but I had drinks and nibbly bits all ready and I was determined to make the meeting go as well as possible.

Of course, they arrived just as I was lying on the floor trying to reach a spool of ribbon that had rolled under a cabinet. Not a great start. Greg looked down his nose at me, folded his arms and sat on my counter, pushing my carefully assembled plate of crostini out of the way with his hip.

Hugo pulled me up from the floor by my hand and gave me a warm hug. I saw Greg sniff and look away. Then he picked up a little ceramic figure of a pug that I kept by the till because it reminded me of my mother's dog. He looked at it with contempt and practically threw it down again. Hugo didn't seem to notice.

'Antonia,' he said, Mr Manners to the last, 'I would like you to meet Greg Papodopoulos. Greg, this is Antonia Heaveringham.'

I felt my mouth twitch with childish amusement at his

name, but managed to control it. I was about to put my hand out to shake his, when an instinct made me wait to see if he did it first. He didn't. He didn't say anything either. He didn't even look at me.

I looked at Hugo, questioningly. He scratched his head. Then he folded his arms very high up his chest in a posture I knew to be his personal expression of extreme social discomfort. It pleased me to know that it would be a while before Mr Papodopoulos would be able to read him as clearly as I could.

'Now,' said Hugo, trying again, in a tone he had learned in school army cadets. 'I think it's important that we all face up to the situation. It's not easy, but we are all going to bump into each other all the time in Sydney and I, for one, would like to think we could all . . .' – he glanced at Greg as he said it – 'at least be civil to each other.'

'I couldn't agree more,' I said in my most cut-glass voice. Then I waited for Greg's agreement. Silence from Mr Pap.

'How about you, Greg?' I said, eventually, trying to make contact. For Tom's sake, more than anything, I had decided to give him one more chance. He looked up and sighed, like it was the most boring thing he'd ever been asked to do and finally looked me in the eye.

'Sure,' he said, shrugging. 'Whatever.' I could have slapped his spoiled little dermabrased face. Of all the men in the world, I thought, why was my darling husband in love with this one?

'Right then,' said Hugo, delighted with the progress. 'I believe Tom is at Vita's house this evening, isn't he, Ant?'

I nodded.

'So how about we all go out to dinner and you two can get to know each other properly?' he continued in gung-ho mode.

'I'm busy,' said Greg, way too quickly. 'Actually, Hugo, *we're* busy. We're going to Nikki's.'

He gave me a triumphant look as he said it – all of it guaranteed to cause me maximum pain and insult.

Hugo looked as though he'd been winded. I knew this was not how he had wanted it to go. It was his dearest wish that I would come to love darling Greg, as he did – and vice versa – and now he knew it was hopeless. I folded my arms too. My flinty core came out.

'You know, Greg,' I said. 'It's one thing to steal someone's husband and take him away from his home and his child, but it's quite another to then be plain rude to the person you've done it to, who is trying to do the decent thing by you. And as someone who has known Hugo Heaveringham for an awfully long time, I'm going to give you a piece of advice. The Heaveringhams are a family who put a lot of store by good manners, so if you want to stick around one of them you'd better learn some.'

I paused to savour the look on his face.

'Do give Nikki my love,' I continued. 'And have a lovely evening. Goodbye.'

It was a golden moment. I didn't care if I was going to regret it later, it felt so good telling him what I thought. He looked so angry and so surprised, it was brilliant. My cheeks were flaming and my heart was thumping, but it felt really good. He started to storm out, before pausing in the doorway.

'I'm leaving, Hugo, and you'd better come with me,' he hissed and then – get this – he actually spat on my floor.

I just looked at Hugo. Words weren't necessary. I knew Greg was history. Hugo was clearly infatuated with him, but there were some lines I knew you could never cross with a Heaveringham and Greg had just pole-vaulted across one of them. Hugo gave him a cold look and turned to me. He took my hands in his and looked at me, sadly.

'Thank you for inviting us here tonight, Ant,' he said. 'It was extremely gracious of you and I apologize for my friend's behaviour. I'll call you tomorrow.'

Hugo lifted my hands to his lips and kissed them, then he left. As he hit the street, I realized that he was actually running after Greg.

I went home to an empty house.

I got even less sleep than usual that night, turning the evening's events over and over in my head. Surely Hugo couldn't stay with someone as awful as Greg, but if he didn't, would he come back to us? And would I take him?

I really didn't know. It had been over three months since Hugo had come out and moved out, the hardest months of my life, but by concentrating on the shop and on Tom, and with the help of Suzy's CD, like the song said – I had survived. I didn't know if I was prepared to risk it all happening again. Because now that Hugo had come to terms with being gay, if it wasn't Greg, surely it would just be someone else?

I wondered yet again if I shouldn't just move back to London. That had been my first instinct when the whole thing had happened, but when I'd thought more about it, I'd realized it would be much harder for Tom to be separated from his father by twelve thousand miles, than having him living around the corner with a man.

There was also the consideration that I would have to explain why I had left Hugo, to all my friends and relations – not to mention Hugo's lot. There had never been a divorce in the Heaveringham family, as Lady H was very fond of announcing, and it wasn't a precedent I wanted to be responsible for setting.

In fact, I was so frightened of her I was quite happy to go along with Hugo's pretence that we now had two phone numbers at the same house – the 'family number', which was the old number in our house, and his 'personal line', which was actually the phone in his new house. He'd told her it was something to do with the internet and she'd never questioned it. None of them had. They weren't what you'd call a close family.

I was quite happy to keep up the pretence for myself as well. So far I hadn't even told my own parents or any of my friends back home what had happened. I was just too humiliated. I'd only told my sisters, who were both wonderful and agreed I should stay in Australia for the time being, for Tom's sake and my own.

As my elder sister, the ever sensible solicitor Rebecca, reasoned – her legal analysis coming to the fore – it was one thing being a single mother in Sydney, where everything was new and strange, but to do it in London, where there were ghosts of Hugo's and my past on every corner, would be unbearable. Plus, she pointed out, it would mean more upheaval for Tom.

She was right, and apart from anything else, I didn't want to leave my little shop. I loved Anteeks and it was doing really well. I knew I would never be able to afford the equivalent location in London and I just wasn't ready to chuck it all in. Then Hugo really would have spoiled everything for me, I thought. So I stayed.

Hugo didn't ring me the day after my encounter with grisly Greg, which surprised me, but Suzy did.

'Hear your husband's split up from his little bum chum,' she said, straight to the point as always.

'How on earth did you hear that?' I asked, still not used to the speed of the Eastern Suburbs tom-toms, but delighted at the news.

'Had my hair done this morning. Greg wasn't in. Too upset. He was over at Nikki's, being comforted.'

'Oh God,' I said.

'Will you take Hugo back, Ant?' said Suzy. 'If he wants to come?'

I thought for a moment and suddenly the answer I had tossed and turned about all night was clear to me.

'No,' I said, firmly. 'He's gay.'

'Good girl,' said Suzy. 'That's the way.'

And it was lucky I had reached that conclusion, because two days later, I heard that Greg had moved back in with Hugo. I didn't understand what my charming husband could see in such a nasty piece of work, but he was a grown man and had to make his own choices. And it just went to prove, I thought, lust conquers all.

More dull Hugo-less weeks went by and as the leaves fell off the spreading trees in Queen Street and it turned into Sydney's strangely bleak version of winter, I tried to stop thinking about myself and concentrated instead on making sure Tom was happy.

I was also very glad of having the shop to distract me and it was doing better than ever after a wonderful six-page spread in *Vogue Living*. With lavish pictures of the shop and the house, with lots of gorgeous detail shots, it made me and Tom look happy and sparkling – almost a perfect couple in our own right. It cheered me up a lot. I also took up my old hobby of needlepoint, to fill up the long evenings and the quiet hours in the shop.

Tom had his own name for my rediscovered hobby. One quiet afternoon he was 'helping' in Anteeks as he did most days after school and after rearranging a display of old teapots – rather well, I had to admit – he came and leaned on the arm of my chair and watched me stitching.

'What are you doing, Mummy? Is it sewing?' he asked after a few moments.

'It's a sort of sewing,' I told him. 'But it's called needlepoint.'

He watched for a few more moments before making one of his characteristic pronouncements. Tom was a very definite boy.

'Well, I think you should call it filling holes, because that's all it is. You're just filling holes with wool.'

So that's what we called it from then on, filling holes. But however pointless it seemed to Tom, I'd always enjoyed it and I had fun coming up with smart lines to embroider on cushions for the shop.

A pretty pink one with 'Yes' on one side and 'No' on the other was my biggest seller, closely followed by a matching pair that had 'Chairman of the Board' on a navy blue cushion and 'Chairperson of the Bored', on a lilac one. It clearly struck a chord with the locals and was bought in equal numbers by thin women with large diamonds and expensive hairdos and well-dressed young men with large muscles and expensive hairdos, which pretty much summed up my clientele.

So those were my days – sitting in the shop, filling holes – and my nights were spent in front of the television, alternately sobbing at anything remotely sad and eating biscuits. Once I nearly choked on a chocolate chip cookie, I was weeping so hard at a British Airways commercial. It was truly pathetic.

Then one day, when I was really starting to wonder if I would ever go out again, a particularly lavish object dropped through my letter box. It was a large fuchsia pink envelope, lined with tissue and addressed in gold, and it contained quite the most splendid invitation I had ever seen. It was from Suzy, who was having a huge fortieth-birthday party, at their Palm Beach house.

'I did think about having it in town,' she told me the next morning, when we met for brekkie in Queen Street, 'because it is winter, but I want people to make a weekend of it. I didn't have a big wedding, so I'm having this instead.

Five hundred of my closest friends,' she laughed. 'Just a cosy little evening . . .'

And that was what I really liked about Suzy – she did laugh at herself. She was definitely a central figure in the champagne social set and among the 'top end of town' wheeler-dealers in her professional life, but she could see the preposterous side of it all too.

Underneath the Crème de la Mer skin, the head-to-toe black label Armani, the daily blow-dry and the serious rocks, a conscience lurked in Suzy Thorogood.

I reckoned it was left over from her radical student days, when she'd intended to be a human rights lawyer, before getting waylaid by the more lucrative speciality of corporate PR. She'd once let it slip to me that she worked in a soup kitchen every Christmas Day, but she'd made me swear not to tell any of the other 'girls' about it. She didn't want them to think she was a 'goody goody'.

'I'd hate to live up to my married name too literally,' she'd said, grinning.

But while it was good to know that she wasn't as silly as the likes of Nikki Maier and Caroline French, I was delighted that it was the socialite side of Suzy which was planning her birthday party. I was seriously in the mood for some fun.

'The decorative theme is A Thousand and One Nights,' she told me, excitedly. 'I've hired a guy called Antony Maybury to do it all. He's really a dressmaker, in fact he's making my dress for the party, but he's brilliant at styling parties too – especially when the budget is no object.'

She laughed at herself again and somehow when Suzy

said something like that, it didn't bother me. I normally hated people talking about money, but she was proud of her wealth – their wealth – in a way that was somehow acceptable. They hadn't started with much, she'd told me, but between the two of them they had built it up and now they had all kinds of business interests and directorships, as well as their own principal professions.

I had no idea how much money they actually had – apart from people you know are bona fide billionaires, I've never really understood how much money you need to have to be considered 'rich' – but it was obvious from the way the other women on the circuit deferred to Suzy, that she and Roger had more than most.

At first it had amazed me that Hugo and I seemed to know so many rich people in Sydney, but after a while it was quite easy to forget that there was a real world out there as well. In London you were constantly aware of the gulf in fortune that exists in large cities, but in Sydney I rarely ventured out of Woollahra, unless I was going to Palm Beach, or on one of my buying expeditions, and it was easy to start thinking that everyone lived in a five-million-dollar house, had an ocean-going yacht, ate out every night and always flew first class.

I did try to remind myself that the life I was leading wasn't normal, but for the time being I was quite happy to share Suzy's excitement as she planned what she was determined would be remembered as the 'party of the decade'.

And that was another thing I liked about Suzy – funny, kind and self-deprecating as she could be, at heart she was still fantastically ambitious in every area of her life. It wasn't enough for her to be the social doyenne, the most successful woman in her profession, an adoring mother to her two teenage children and very popular, she also had to be a famous hostess and a perfect size 10 – and I was told she was an absolute demon on the tennis court. She hated to lose.

She was certainly determined that her party would be an unforgettable hit.

'We're flying in loads of stuff from Morocco and India, as props,' she told me. 'We've got two hundred carpets coming and hundreds of lanterns and cushions and big painted plates that we're going to pile up with couscous. We've got embroidered tents coming from Rajasthan, musicians from Goa and a chef from Marrakesh. We're going totally overboard on the décor, but it's not fancy dress. I want people to really dress up and look gorgeous. *Vogue Entertaining* are doing a shoot at the party, so you'll have to get an amazing outfit together, Antonia. No flip-flops – that's what you Poms call them, isn't it? – this time, please.'

She looked me over fondly. I knew my hair could do with a wash, I was wearing my usual droopy layers and a pair of old Tod's which were seriously due for retirement. My trusty Mexican basket was at my side.

'I'll lend you some jewellery,' she said.

'That's quite all right,' I said in a mock haughty voice. 'I've actually got quite a healthy collection of jewels stashed away at home, from the Heaveringham vaults. It's one of the advantages of marrying into the aristocracy, you know.

I just don't wear them during the day, like you colonials all do.'

We giggled.

'What? Second-hand jewellery?' she said, pulling a face and pretending to be horrified – I'd told her about Nikki's trip to Wally's Where House.

We laughed some more and my mood got even better when Suzy told me she wanted me to be one of the select few who stayed in the house for the party, coming up on the Friday night on the sea plane, which they had chartered for the whole weekend to ferry guests back and forth from the city to Palm Beach.

I'd been to Suzy's 'beach house' before and it was rather as I imagine the Kennedy compound in Maine must be, all wide verandas, manicured lawns and tennis courts, and more bedrooms and guest cottages than you could count. I could hardly wait for the big night.

Four weeks later, as we waited for the first guests to arrive, looking over the ocean from Suzy's veranda, I felt I looked better than I had since my wedding. I'd certainly never been so well groomed. All the women staying at the house had been given a manicure, pedicure and massage during the day and Suzy had brought up a team of make-up artists and hairdressers to add the finishing touches. I was very relieved that Mr Papodopoulos was not one of them and suspected that Suzy had taken care of that deliberately.

Best of all, I had the most beautiful dress to wear. Her friend Antony Maybury had created it specially for me and it made me feel like a movie star. He'd done something amazing with a hidden inner structure, so I didn't have to wear any underwear with it, but still felt totally confident. It was a draped column of slinky silk jersey, in a rich ruby red, with long sleeves and an unbelievably bare back, the whole thing suspended from a high neck band, with gold chains looped across the back and round my hips, to keep it on me.

'This colour is good with your hair,' he'd said, during the first fitting, frowning at my head in the mirror, as though he was trying to remember a word. 'Sort of dark mouse, isn't it? But it suits you. Funny that.'

He held the bolt of cloth up against me and started cutting it. 'You English girls have beautiful skin. Let's show off as much of it as possible without giving you frostbite.'

With my hair up, a major pair of Heaveringham diamond drop earrings in my lugs and my best Jimmy Choo jewelled mules on my feet, I really felt like a glamorous Sydney girl – which is exactly how Suzy described me.

'You look wonderful, Ant,' she'd said when I came down, sounding like she really meant it, but adding, with a wicked look, 'no one would ever know you were English.'

She looked like Cameron Diaz herself, in a layered chiffon kaftan in different shades of green, through which you could make out the lines of her long slim limbs. She had a serious pear-shaped emerald pendant around her hair, the enormous jewel resting on her forehead. That was her birthday present from Roger, who was looking pretty sprauncy himself in a peacock-blue raw silk shalwar kamcez he'd had specially made in Jaipur.

I stood leaning against the veranda rail looking out over the embroidered tents filled with cushions and carpets, the flaming braziers to keep off the chills, the phalanx of waiters with silver trays of champagne and cocktails, and the enormous flower arrangements like brilliantly coloured birds. The air was heavy with incense and a small band was playing wonderfully exotic sitar music. Antony Maybury winked at me as he bustled past, wearing a turban, making final adjustments to his decorations.

'We're going to have the night of our lives,' said Suzy, clinking her champagne glass with mine, as she went off to greet her first guests.

I thought she was very probably right.

5

Wrong. Among the first guests to come out of the house were Nikki and David Maier – and Greg Papodopoulos. For one gorgeous moment, I thought Hugo wasn't with them, but a few minutes later I heard his unmistakable voice booming out of the drawing room.

'Oh, Suzy,' he was saying. 'No . . . This is all marvellous. Greg has told me how gorgeous this place is, but I had no idea it was the full Hyannis Port.'

I was normally amused by the way he and his family used the word 'no' to express enthusiasm ('Oh, *no*, I love it. Noooo, it's marvellous' was a normal Heaveringham reaction to a Christmas present, for example), but it was the last thing I needed to hear at that point. Especially as I detected a slightly different tone in Hugo's voice that evening. By the time he had got on to the flower arrangements – 'No! These are totally fabulous. We are loving. Divine . . .' – I had worked out what the difference was. *We are loving*? He sounded distinctly queeny.

And, of course, Nikki and Greg had seen me – standing alone – and were making no effort to walk the ten steps to acknowledge me.

I often think there is a lot more animal intelligence left in human beings than we give ourselves credit for. How else can you explain the way that two people both know that the other one has seen and recognized them, without either of them acknowledging it? It must be something to do with anti-pheromones. But I had another basic instinct on my mind at that point – escaping, before Hugo saw me.

Trying not to run, I stepped off the veranda and strolled ever so casually towards the tents, as though there was no place on earth I would rather be. I could swear I felt the fire of malicious eyes on my back as I went although, of course, I could have been imagining it.

But I didn't imagine Nikki's voice when it clearly rang out, 'Hi Hugo, darling. Look, there's your ex-wife, looking like Father Christmas in a red dress and with no one to talk to. Such a shame, isn't it? She looks quite nice, for once.'

I didn't hear Hugo's reply, because I was hiding behind the tents by then. Where I stayed as long as I dared, fuming about it all and particularly about Nikki calling me Hugo's 'ex-wife', when we were still very much married, even if we didn't happen to live together any more.

The evening did not get any better. I knew a lot of people at the party, but the whole thing was marred for me because I was so self-conscious about Hugo and Greg. It seemed as though wherever I went, they were already there – and it wasn't exactly a small space.

Suzy and Antony had divided the garden up into lots of defined areas, almost like a series of rooms, so you always had that feeling there was somewhere else to go and discover, where there might be something marvellous going on.

As well as the huge outside dance floor and various food stations with whole goats roasting over charcoal, great piles of couscous, towering arrangements of exotic fruit and much more, there was a series of different bars serving different kinds of drinks. Then there were all the tents, with chill-out zones for lying around in, stand up and mingle areas for socializing and long tables where groups could gather. All this and still there wasn't enough room for me to escape from the dashing duo, who seemed to be waiting – having a fabulous time – round every corner I explored.

But while I was having a miserable time, I could still see it was a wonderful party and I was very happy for Suzy that it was going so well. Certainly everyone had gone to enormous effort with their outfits – always a great compliment to a hostess – and from very early on people had starting dancing. Those who weren't getting down on the dance floor were constantly cruising around, mingling, and every other moment, great peals of laughter would break into the night.

It was, without doubt, one of the best parties I had ever been to. It was just a shame I was having such a rotten time at it.

No matter how hard I tried, I didn't feel like I fitted in anywhere. I just floated around feeling completely unanchored. The problem was, I didn't have a core group of friends to keep coming back to, and that, I realized, was something I had taken for granted all my adult life. I had always been part of a party posse and now suddenly I wasn't. And worst of all, of course, I didn't have Hugo.

In retrospect, I couldn't believe I had been so thick, but I had been so excited about all Suzy's plans I hadn't thought it through – but this was the first big party I had been to without him, since I was nineteen years old. It was hell and it was made even worse by the fact that he was there with someone else. I hadn't considered that possibility either and I was quite hurt that Suzy hadn't mentioned to me that Hugo and Greg were coming together. It wasn't like her to be so insensitive.

Adding to my general woes, I also had the distinct impression that people weren't particularly thrilled to see me. I tried to convince myself I was just feeling insecure, but it seemed as though I wasn't really welcome anywhere. If I went up to a group I knew, there would be a slightly embarrassed pause and then the conversation would continue, in a way that didn't include me, so I'd melt away again and try another group. The only times I felt happy all evening were when I was with Suzy and Roger, but I couldn't hang around them all the time like a cling on.

I finally knew I wasn't imagining it when Caroline French actually turned her back on me when I went up to say hello to her. I hadn't seen her for a while and was quite looking forward to a chat, but she distinctly turned round and ignored me. I was so astonished I just stood there and I saw the man she was talking to give me a slightly embarrassed look over her shoulder, which confirmed my worst fears. I couldn't believe it; I didn't think people really did that. Not once they were past Tom's age anyway.

That was all ghastly, but worst of all, I had no one to dance with. I love dancing and I couldn't believe how left out I felt. It made me realize, once again, just how lucky I had been all those years, when I could just drag Hugo out to dance, without thinking about it twice.

Once you're on the dance floor, it's fine, there's always someone to boogie with, but it's the first partner that's crucial. I certainly didn't have the guts to go and dance on my own. Maybe if I'd felt a bit tipsy I would have but, on top of everything else, I was having one of those nights where every successive drink just seemed to make me more sober.

Eventually I just gave up even trying to have a good time and sat in a chair, watching other people dance and feeling like some kind of tragic maiden aunt – isn't it lovely to see the young enjoy themselves? I tried to find it interesting on an anthropological level, just to make the time pass.

I'd been there about ten minutes – or was it ten hours – and was starting to wonder if I could creep off to bed without Suzy noticing, when salvation appeared in the form of Antony Maybury, who stood in front of me and put out his hand.

'May I have the pleasure of dancing with your dress?' he asked.

I practically jumped into his arms. At last, I thought, I could start enjoying myself. Antony was a good dancer who interjected the twirls and turns he was putting me through with hilariously bitchy remarks about other people at the party and what they were wearing.

The DJ was playing some great tracks and I had finally stopped thinking about myself, when who should pile onto the dance floor, but the Maiers, the Frenchs and the Heaveringham-Papodopouloses, who all seemed to be having a marvellous time. Hugo had his jacket off and his dress shirt unbuttoned to the waist – all he needed was a medallion, I thought – and was dancing the wild leprechaun leap I knew so well.

Antony didn't seem to have noticed the newcomers to the dance floor, or he just didn't care, so I did my best to keep on dancing, although I suddenly felt desperately self-conscious and had to concentrate to keep moving. The minute you start thinking about dancing, you can't do it and I felt like some kind of badly programmed robot.

I was just about getting back into the rhythm, when Antony released me suddenly from a major spin and I found myself facing away from him and standing right in front of Caroline's husband, Tony. Just as at any normal party, he smiled at me, took my hand and jived with me in a friendly way. Maybe it was going to be a fun night after all, I thought.

But no, suddenly Caroline had put herself firmly between me and her husband, with her back to me once more, so I was left standing in the middle of the dance floor, like a complete prune. I turned round to find Antony and saw to my horror that he was now dancing with Nikki. David Maier had disappeared and Hugo and Greg appeared to be in a clinch. Greg looked me right in the eye and licked Hugo's neck.

I left the dance floor.

I was going to escape to my room, but Suzy and Roger

were sitting on the swinging cane sofas on the veranda and I couldn't get past them into the house without explaining. But I knew I was very close to tears and I just had to be alone.

Already starting to sob, I headed blindly down the sloping lawn away from the house and when I was about halfway down I was very relieved to see a small gazebo tucked away by the garden wall. I headed for it. It was pitch dark inside and I stumbled in. By then I was crying so seriously I didn't see the figure sitting in the corner until he took a deep drag on his cigarette.

It was Nikki's husband, David. We recognized each other at the same moment and he stood up and came over to me.

'Hey, Antonia,' he said, flicking his cigarette through the open window. 'Now what's the matter with you, little lady?'

He came closer and took my arm. I was crying really hard, those painful tears that make your chest ache, and much as I wanted to stop I couldn't. Before I really registered what was happening, David had his arms round me. In that first instance, I was quite touched, I needed some comfort and arms are arms in that kind of situation. Then I felt his left hand stroke my buttock and I snapped back to normal awareness. Just as I did, he slipped his other hand inside my dress – there wasn't much to stop him – and started fondling my right breast.

'David! Stop it!' I squealed, like a teenager, but he took no notice. He pushed me back against the wall and tried to put his knee between my legs. I managed to hold him off, wriggling as much as I could to try to get out of his grasp, but the fact was, he was much stronger than me and I was flat against the wooden wall, with nowhere to go. Suddenly I was really scared.

'Must be terrible, seeing your old man out there pashing that poofter,' he said into my ear. 'Must be very frustrating, a grown-up girl like you, not having a man in your bed, eh? Bet you get really lonely at night in that big house on your own.'

Now he had his hand up my skirt and I was deeply regretting the no-underwear dress.

'Ooh,' said David, clearly encouraged. 'No panties. You must be panting for it.'

He laughed at his own joke and started slobbering all over my face. It was disgusting. I tried to kick him, I tried to scream, but it's not easy when someone has his mouth over yours. It was probably only seconds, but it seemed to go on for hours.

It was like trying to fight off a giant squid. I would concentrate on trying to loosen his grip in one place, only to feel his other hand exploring somewhere else. Worst of all, I could feel his hard-on pressing against my lower stomach, where he was deliberately rubbing it up and down. In the nightmare of it all, I realized he'd managed to undo the top of my dress, so my breasts were completely exposed and then he pulled the skirt up over my thighs. When I heard him unzip his flies I went limp with terror. And that saved me.

The moment he felt my body flop he thought he had his opportunity and he pulled away from me, ready to mount his final assault. I sensed my moment and I kneed him in the balls with all my strength.

'You fucking little bitch, you whore,' he gasped, as he staggered away from me and I ran out of the door and up the lawn as fast as I could.

I kicked off my shoes for speed and was holding my dress up with one hand as I ran past a very surprised-looking couple who were smooching by the garden wall. The look on their faces brought me to my senses and I realized I couldn't blunder back through the party in the state I was in.

I skirted left behind the catering tents and picked my way in the dark, tripping over the guy ropes, to the side of the house. I had to fight my way through some large spiky shrubs, but eventually I made it to the other side of the building, where I knew there was a small door into the house, away from the main entrance. I was very happy to find it open and slipped inside just as I heard Suzy's voice round the corner farewelling some guests.

I ran up to my room and locked myself in. I ripped off my dress, stuffed it into a plastic carrier bag and threw it into the waste-paper basket, then I turned the shower on full blast. Just before I got in it, I looked at myself in the mirror. What a fright. My make-up was smeared all over my face and my hair was like a tangled nest. As I scrubbed the mascara off my cheeks, I realized I was wearing only one of my diamond earrings.

At least I was able to blame my fragile state on a hangover the next morning. The hardest part was joining in Suzy's rapturous party post-mortem. I couldn't possibly tell her I'd had the worst night of my life, culminating in an attempted rape.

'I hardly saw you all night, Ant,' she was saying, as she hoovered up a fried egg sandwich, sitting on the veranda wearing a white cashmere cardigan over a sarong and never taking off her very dark glasses. 'What did you get up to?'

I was amazed at the good front I managed to put on.

'Oh, you know, flitting around, talking to people, dancing, drinking too much . . .'

'I'm so glad you enjoyed yourself, Ant,' she said, patting my leg. 'I was a bit worried about you when I saw Greg walk in. I specifically didn't invite him, you know – he's hardly one of my friends, he just works where I get my hair done. And I did actually call Hugo and ask him not to bring him, which he agreed to. It was Nikki Maier who brought Greg. I am so cross with her. Hugo was really embarrassed when he arrived and saw them on the veranda . . .'

'So they didn't arrive together then?' I asked her.

Suzy shook her head. 'No,' she said, through a mouthful of egg. 'They definitely arrived separately, but coincidentally very close together. Hugo looked really surprised when he saw Greg.'

She paused and looked at me, clearly not sure whether to say more. I said it for her.

'But he didn't seem to mind for long, though, did he?' I sighed.

'No, he didn't. I'm sorry, Ant.'

After breakfast I told Suzy I was going to get some air and braced myself to go back to the summer house. I had to find that earring. They had belonged to Hugo's grandmother and I felt responsible for them.

I picked up my shoes, which were still strewn on the lawn from the night before, and then forced myself to walk towards the little wooden structure. It had seemed such a terrifying torture chamber the night before, but now it looked so flimsy in the sunlight. I felt physically ill when I looked at the corner where David had pinned me, but I got on with searching the floor for my earring. I looked everywhere, but there was no sign of it.

It was the perfect end to a perfect weekend, really.

One particularly chilly morning a few days later, I was in the shop, happy with every passing moment that put the nightmare of Suzy's party further behind me.

I had thrown myself into reorganizing all my stock and was working on my needlepoint cushions like a woman possessed – I'd had some wholesale enquiries about them. It still got to me in the long hours I lay awake at night, when memories of David Maier's slobbery mouth and groping hands came back to haunt me, but during the day, if I kept busy, I could push it all down in my mind.

I was sitting behind the counter stitching while a tall red-headed woman who came in quite often was browsing happily through the old linens, when I saw a very low, very red sports car screech to a halt outside. The door slammed and Nikki Maier came storming in. She saw the other woman and immediately stopped, pretending to be looking at some cutlery.

Eventually the red-head paid for her pillowslips and left. As the door closed behind her, Nikki turned on me. She strutted over to where I was sitting and pulled my earring out of her pocket.

'Do you recognize this?' she asked me, swinging it backwards and forwards in front of my face.

I was so pleased to see it, I smiled with relief, before I had time to think about the implications of Nikki having it. I didn't have her powers of instant analysis, clearly.

'Oh!' I said, delightedly, reaching for it. 'My earring. What a relief . . .'

But before I could take it, she'd snatched it away from me.

'Hang on a minute, you little slut,' she said. 'Where do you think I got this?'

The situation was beginning to dawn on me.

'Well, I lost it at Suzy's party . . .'

'Yes, you did, didn't you? Well, I found it in my husband's pocket and I found your lipstick all over his collar, you whore.'

I looked at her appalled.

'You were seen coming out of that shed where you had been rooting my husband by a friend of mine and then I found this in his pocket. We're on to you, you pathetic English tart. Just because your husband is a fucking pouf, don't think you can go round trying to steal our blokes.'

I could think of nothing to say. She was hardly going to

74

believe me if I told her her husband had tried to rape me, was she?

'Caroline told me you were coming on to her Tony earlier in the evening,' she continued. 'And then you took advantage of my David, when he was drunk. But don't flatter yourself, he'd had so much coke that night he would have fucked a King's Cross whore, so you needn't think of coming back for a second go. He said you were a dud root anyway.'

She laughed coarsely. I opened my mouth like a fish, but nothing came out.

'So watch out, lady muck, we're on to you. I've told Suzy and all the others girls what you've done and you can be sure you won't be welcome anywhere in the Eastern Suburbs now.'

She leaned across the counter and impaled me on her artificial green gaze.

'You're going to regret ever coming to Sydney, you stupid Pommy slut,' she said quietly and dropped the earring into my cup of tea.

6

The weeks that followed Nikki's visit to my shop ranked as the lowest of my life to that date and 1 September may have been the official first day of Australian spring, but it started off as just another typical miserable day in a long line of them.

That afternoon I had sorted my tax receipts, shut the shop early so I could collect Tom from school – standing alone to wait because none of the other mothers seemed to want to talk to me any more, and getting a parking ticket because I didn't know they had re-zoned the street – and had taken him, complaining all the way, to his piano lesson.

Then I bought a week's food from Woolworths in Double Bay, plus a packet of safety pins, to re-fasten my skirt after the button flew off in the Biscuits and Baking Goods aisle, retrieved a still-whinging Tom from his piano lesson, drove home, unloaded the car, put all the shopping away and started the dinner. Then I went to shift the big load of laundry I had put on that morning, into the dryer.

When I pressed the open button, the door of the washing machine – a front loader – flew back and flooded the kitchen with a torrent of foamy water, leaving behind a sopping mass of grey sheets and one stray black sock.

My favourite lime green espadrilles were caught in the deluge.

I sat down next to the washing machine, in a pool of soapy water, and sobbed. At that very moment Tom appeared holding up a copiously bleeding cut finger. He'd been using my best Global kitchen knife to try to prise a CD-rom he shouldn't have been playing with out of the disk drive of my laptop, which he shouldn't have been touching. And he'd carefully bandaged it with my new white linen skirt, which he'd found in a carrier bag in the hall, as yet unworn.

'Look, Mummy, I've turn-the-keyed it,' he said proudly. 'Do you think I need to go to Casualty?' He unfolded the $300 dressing, to reveal a flapping flesh wound.

I actually screamed, like a banshee. A blood-curdling primeval howl. Then the doorbell rang, prompting me to start banging my head against the wall. I couldn't take one more bit of pressure.

'I'll go,' said Tom, running for the door before I could tell him we were not in. I just prayed it wasn't Nikki Maier popping round with a baseball bat, to make me a bit more miserable.

It definitely wasn't Nikki.

'Oh, how marvellous,' said a very fruity voice from the hall. 'A wounded soldier. Was it shrapnel? Shall we rush you to the field hospital? It could be fatal. Where's matron?'

There was the sound of Tom squealing and jumping up and down with excitement and a throaty laugh from the recipient of one of his legendary hugs. Then Hugo's Uncle Percy walked through the kitchen door.

'Mummy, Mummy,' said Tom, holding on to his arm and leaping about like a flea. 'It's Uncle Perky.'

'Has the dyke burst, darling?' said Percy in his unmistakable voice, like a cross between Ralph Richardson and Dame Edith Evans, so ridiculously plummy and 1930s English in style that crowds would gather round him in public places, like the sausage counter in Harrods Food Hall, the number 12 bus stop, or wherever he happened to be making his unique comments on life.

Ten minutes later I was reclining on the sofa, a stiff vodka martini in my hand, the smell of frying onions wafting in from the kitchen and Billie Holiday's velvet tones floating from the CD player, with Percy providing back-up vocals from the kitchen, as he mopped the floor with Tom's help.

'What a strrrrange frrrrooooot . . . That's right, Tom, swish, swish, swish, squeeeeeeeeze. Marvellous stuff. That sticking plaster holding out, is it? Good man.'

Percy's very particular head, with its extravagantly arched plucked eyebrows and mauve-rinsed and bouffant hair, a tribute to his late friend Quentin Crisp, popped through the hatch to observe me.

'All right, sweet pea? Feeling better? The deck's all swabbed and Master Heaveringham and I are well on the way with a mushroom risotto. Need a top-up?'

I shook my head and a tear of sheer relief rolled down my cheek.

Percy cooked the dinner, laid the table, including a small centrepiece of garden foliage, cleared up, put the sheets on to wash again, put Tom to bed, read him a story and then sat me down at the dining table with a bottle of single malt and a carton of Sobranie cocktail cigarettes, straight from his duty free carrier bag.

'Smoke, darling,' he said, waving a bright turquoise ciggie under my nose. 'Sinning will make you feel better. Then tell me everything about that naughty poofter nephew of mine.' He screwed a lilac cigarette into an ivory holder and clamped it between his teeth. 'I hear he's shacked up with a hairdresser.'

'How on earth did you know, Percy?'

'Gaydar, darling,' he said, patting my hand and topping up my glass. 'Drink up.'

He lit his cigarette and blew a plume of smoke through his nostrils that swirled around his purple head like an old film still of Marlene Dietrich.

'I was coming over to Sydney anyway,' he continued. 'For Sleaze Ball, which is supposed to be wonderful, much better than that common Mardi Gras, which is full of parking attendants dressed as Adolf Hitler, which is not amusing or arousing, I may tell you, and it just sort of wafted over the ether that Hugo had decided to be a homosexualist. Nothing wrong with that, of course, life-long member of the League of Dorothy myself, but a bit rough on you and little Tomety, I thought, so here I am. Plus we've had a perfectly frightful summer in the Med this year. Capri was like Aberystwyth, couldn't see the point of it at all.'

A sudden ghastly thought roused me from the Valium calm Percy's extraordinary presence had instilled in me.

'His parents don't know, do they?' I asked suddenly.

'Good GOD, no. That ghastly Margot would split her panty girdle, if she thought one of her precious little sons was a poof. Freddie wouldn't give a damn, of course, we all took it up the jacksie at school, no big deal, but Margot would be horrrrrrified. It's her deeply suburban soul, you see. Father made ball bearings or some such.'

Having known Percy Heaveringham – or Stephen Heaveringham-Taylor, as he was really called – for nearly ten years, his ridiculous appearance (he had been wearing a voluminous white voile poet shirt, fastened with some kind of gypsy sash over dark pink linen trousers, a short tweed cape and mustard-yellow embroidered Moroccan shoes when he had arrived), his over-the-top voice and outrageous statements no longer surprised me.

I had understood right from the start, when I first met Percy, that his entire persona was an overcompensation for his strange upbringing as Hugo's father's illegitimate half-brother.

Percy was brought up with Freddie, Hugo's dad, as part of the family, but his adapted surname was a constant reminder that he wasn't fully of it.

He was the result of a 'forgetful' moment Hugo's grandfather, the fifteenth Earl, had had with an exotic dancer ('Esmé la Rose') during the Blitz. After she was killed in an air raid – wearing nothing but a feather fan and a professional smile, according to Percy – the Earl had felt he should do the right thing by the boy.

So at the age of two Percy was moved from a small flat in Maida Vale to a stately home in Lincolnshire and when the time came he had been sent off to Eton, where he was known as the Heaveringham Half Bastard.

Lesser characters might have been broken by such a childhood, but Percy was a survivor. His charismatic personality was his lifebelt and the more he exaggerated it, the more attention he got. It was hardly surprising he was a little odd.

From the moment we met, we recognized each other as fellow displaced persons. My father was a quite dotty and completely unworldly country vicar (deepest Somerset) who officiated at a very smart girls' boarding school, as well as carrying out his general parish duties. In return for his services my sisters and I had been educated at the school for nothing and, as a result, I had also grown up not quite sure where I belonged.

We were the classic hand-me-down vicar's daughters, yet the village girls would taunt us as 'posh snobs'. At school, the other girls – who all seemed to be jet-set rich rather than the Heaveringham style of impoverished aristos – were perfectly nice to us, but as soon as the holidays came around they would disappear to St Tropez, Mustique, or wherever, and we'd be left mooching around the school grounds and helping Mum make sandwiches for pensioner coffee mornings.

Very early in my relationship with Hugo, I'd met Percy at a terrifying Heaveringham family gathering and he had immediately taken me on as a special project, making me feel much less frightened of them all by telling me his own history.

Never feeling quite accepted among his peers, but a

raging success in college revues, he'd told me, Percy had left Oxford before graduating to pursue a career on the stage in provincial repertory, which was when he'd changed his name.

'Didn't mind Stephen so much,' he'd explained to me. 'But couldn't bear ghastly "Steve". So ordinary. I did try Stefan for a while in New York in the 70s, but gave it up. Too balletic.'

He'd taken the stage name of 'Percy Circus' after the elegant London crescent where he had once lived.

'Thought it was frightfully amusing,' he'd said. 'Percy Circus Esq., 17 Percy Circus, London WC1. Don't you think?'

The acting career didn't last long ('Couldn't bear all those ghastly 60s plays about kitchen sinks – one minute I was coming delightfully through the French window with a tennis racket, the next I had to be a moody miner's son in a bedsit, couldn't be doing with it . . .') but 'Percy' and the theatricality never left him – well, I suppose it was in his blood.

After that it was hard to say what Percy did, he just sort of floated around, staying with wealthy people who enjoyed his company. He kept some things in a forgotten boxroom at Willington, the Heaveringham seat, but he didn't have a home of his own, he was a permanent guest somewhere, with a PO box in Belgravia.

'I'm a life enhancer,' I'd once heard him tell someone at a cocktail party, who'd made the mistake of asking him what he 'did', which he considered the most vulgar of questions. He was certainly enhancing my life. In the few hours he had been with us, I felt transformed from a half-mad single mother back into a member of the human race. And he made Tom so happy.

'Can you stay a while, Percy?' I asked him tentatively, when we were halfway down the whisky bottle and I had told him the entire story of Hugo's announcement, gruesome Greg and the sudden mass refrigeration of the female half of Sydney's social set towards me.

Sharing the full awfulness of it with such a dear old pal – but leaving out the details of the sexual assault, which made me feel somehow ashamed – I realized quite how unhappy I'd been. I was terrified he would disappear as suddenly as he had arrived.

'I'll stay as long as it takes, my darling child,' he said, lighting a bright pink cigarette and blowing the smoke over my head. 'As long as it takes.'

It took barely a week for life with Percy to settle into a glorious routine. He took over the household management completely and was so much better at it than me. Silver was polished, the air smelled of beeswax and spring flowers, there was food in the fridge and ice in the freezer. He even reorganized my linen cupboard, filing it all into sets, tied up with lilac ribbons and springs of lavender, and lining the shelves with stripy wallpaper.

Tom loved having him around and insisted on Uncle Perky taking him to school and collecting him as often as possible, which was a wonderful help for me. I think some six-year-olds would have baulked at being associated with a sixty-year-old man with purple hair, who frequently sported a kaftan as daywear, but Tom was tremendously proud of Percy and conveyed his enthusiasm to the other children, who all wanted to join in the fun.

Not that Percy wasn't having fun of his own, in return for all his good works. After he'd taken Tom to school in the morning he would drop into the shop to chat and tell me what he'd got up to the night before.

'There's this marvellous place called Lady Jane beach,' he told me one late spring day, when the sun was pouring through the shop window. 'Everyone's totally in the nuddy and if you like the look of a fellow, you just tip the wink and off you go. Simple as that. It's even better after dark. Had a daisy chain down there last night. Marvellously well built these Aussie chaps. Large, you know.'

'No, I don't know, Percy, and I'm not sure I want to,' I said primly, although the memory of David Maier's dishonourable member for Double Bay was all too fresh. I shuddered and sought distraction.

'What's a daisy chain, Percy?' I asked in innocent curiosity.

'Oh, it's such fun,' he said, taking a large bite of the bacon sandwich he had just rustled up in the shop kitchen and pushing the plate towards me. 'Remember the daisy chains you made as a child? It's just like that. Lots of beautiful flowers, happily joined together.'

The meaning suddenly dawned on me. All too clearly.

'Sort of a fairy ring, really,' continued Percy, licking a large dollop of tomato ketchup off his chin with an unusually long tongue. Seeing my shocked expression he waggled it at me.

'In a public place?' I squeaked, every bit the parson's daughter.

'Where better?' said Percy, clearly delighted at my reaction. 'Except maybe a public loo . . .'

'Oh God, your sex life is too weird, Percy. Don't tell me any more.'

'Thinking about your husband?' he asked gently.

'I suppose I am, Perce. It's all a bit much to take in.'

I picked up a bacon sandwich and drenched it in mayo, before taking a big bite.

'If it's any comfort, I don't imagine Hugo is patrolling the public lavvies of the Eastern Suburbs,' said Percy, between bites. 'I haven't bumped into him there, anyway. No, I believe he's very much a one-hole man. I'm sure he had never been unfaithful to you until ghastly Greg and his dancing pecs brought all that suppressed homoerotic desire out of him.'

I sighed.

'I think you're right,' I said, still chewing. 'And at least I know he wasn't knobbing my girlfriends behind my back. Because I did sometimes wonder, when we would go so long without having sex, whether he was getting it somewhere else.'

'How long is it now since he told you?'

I counted on my fingers. 'Nine months.'

'And you haven't had so much as a flirtation in that time, Antonia?'

I grimaced.

'I've been groped by other people's husbands, but that was somehow my fault, and invitations have not exactly been pouring in recently. Anyway, I don't feel like going out.'

'That's because you're too fat,' said Percy.

I nearly spat out my mouthful of sandwich. I couldn't believe my ears.

'You've packed on the pounds, Antonia. You must be over ten stone. You used to have such a pretty figure. I've never seen a more lovely bride. Such fine features. But you won't feel like going out ever again unless you do something about those spare tyres. Positively Michelin.'

I looked at him in amazement, I was desperately hurt, but I also knew he was right. I had been stuffing myself ever since Hugo had made his announcement and even more so since the incident at Suzy's party. Sitting at home, night after night, eating ice cream straight from the tubs that I kidded myself I bought for Tom. Sometimes I scooped it out with a ginger nut.

It was almost as though I were deliberately sabotaging myself. I always ordered full-cream lattes and then heaped sugar into them. I had cocoa for breakfast and ate crisps straight from the packet, while making dinner. Tom and I had fish and chips at least once a week, which I always told myself was a treat for him. I usually ended up finishing his off too.

I stood up and looked at myself in a pretty full-length cheval mirror I had found in a junk shop in Newtown, painted matt white, and priced at fifteen times what I paid for it. I realized it was the first time I had looked at my reflection properly below the neck for quite a while. Percy was right. I was enormous.

Even in my new linen skirt – Tom's blood stains carefully soaked out by Percy using some alchemical mixture of baking soda and lemon juice – and a silk knit v-neck top, which had seemed so flattering when I'd bought them (because nothing else fitted), I looked seriously chunky. Not just chubby, or sweetly plump, as I had looked for a while after Tom was born, but actually fat.

I turned my stricken face to Percy.

'I'm the elephant woman,' I wailed at him.

He nodded happily.

'I'm sorry to be so hard, darling heart,' he said. 'But you've got enough to deal with, without being the fat girl on Bondi Beach this summer.'

'But what can I do? I've never been fat before.'

'I know, it's awful. From the moment your puppy fat drops off at seventeen, you don't have to think about it and suddenly you're thirty and you develop all these new fatty pads in places where you never even used to have places. But take my advice, get rid of it now, because when you hit forty, it gets much harder to shift.'

'So how do you stay so trim, Percy?' I asked him. 'You're a bit older than forty, I think, and you're positively lissom.'

'I'm fifty-nine, darling. Fifty-nine and proud of it. My secret is yoga. I've been doing it for nearly forty years and my metabolism is like a finely tuned instrument. And I walk miles. You just blob around in the car and stuff yourself. You'll have to change your diet and go and suffer in a gym. It's the only way. I've got this leaflet for you.'

He rummaged around in the large Kashmiri embroidered holdall he always carried and pulled out a crumpled piece of paper. I looked at it: 'The Carlton Spa – Sydney's Premiere Fitness and Leisure Complex'.

'Oh that place,' I said, pulling a face. 'Hugo has membership to that as part of his work package. He went once and told me it was awful, all smoked glass and pert older women in Jane Fonda leotards.'

'Well, according to my enquiries you are still included on Hugo's "platinum membership", whatever that is, and that entitles you to five free sessions with a personal trainer, so you might as well go and take advantage of it. I'll look after this place for two hours a day and you can go off and get yourself gorgeous again.'

He picked up his plate and headed off to the kitchen. As he passed me, still standing transfixed by my horrifying reflection, he stopped and whispered in my right ear.

'I've made an appointment for your fitness assessment at two o'clock on Thursday, so you'd better go and get yourself some pastel legwarmers.'

Then he whacked me on my fat bottom and flounced off.

7

Percy's frankness shocked me into action and I dutifully went off to the Carlton Spa and had my fitness check. 'Nightmare' does not begin to describe the experience. Not only did the place look like an Atlantic City casino circa 1985, it was full of people I totally did not want to see me in gym gear. And they were playing Enya over the PA.

The first person I saw as I peeped out of the changing rooms, feeling horribly self-conscious in some old leggings, a baggy T-shirt and a pair of startlingly white new trainers, was Caroline French.

She was wearing a matching ensemble of pale pink leotard, tights and jazz shoes – oh, and the leotard was belted. Finishing her look she had her usual peanut-sized diamonds in each ear and the olive-sized one on her ring finger. Her other accessory, I suddenly realized, was a textbook perfect figure – big firm boobs, tiny waist, the lot. I'd never really noticed it before, because she was always togged out in Chanel suits. I wondered why she didn't wear leotards all the time. She looked like Mature Workout Barbie.

'Antonia,' she said, her botoxed face assuming a form of frozen smile. I was slightly cheered that at least she had decided not to ignore me, but the way her eyes went up and down my body was anything but friendly. 'Haven't seen *you* down here before,' she said, smugly. 'Are you coming to Jazz Step? We all do it. Troy's wonderful.'

She laughed coquettishly and put her arm round the man who was standing next to her. He was a ridiculous-looking creature, like an oversized Action Man, with bright orange plastic skin, in a supertight wrestler's unitard and workout shoes the dimensions of small tractors. His face snapped into a rictus grin as dazzlingly white as my brand new Nikes.

'You should come, Antonia' he said, in a voice that sounded like Caroline had just pulled a string in his back. 'We have a great time. You'd love it.'

If it gave me a figure like Caroline's I thought I might risk it, but first I had to be assessed by personal trainer Trent, who was bearing down on me at that moment in preposterously small nylon shorts, carrying a clipboard and a stop watch. His legs were so muscle bound he walked as though he was trying to keep a ping-pong ball between his buttocks.

The assessment wasn't too bad actually – well, not at first. After weighing and measuring me, pinching my skin with strange callipers and making me go like the clappers on an exercise bike, Trent announced that I was about twelve kilos overweight, which sounded like nothing. I was quite cheered. It wasn't until he got out his calculator and told me that in 'my lingo' it was actually close to two stone, I realized how desperate my situation was.

He said my flexibility was average and my aerobic fitness just slightly below desirable for my age, which sounded like a fairly good description of me in general, I thought.

Trent reckoned if I radically changed my eating habits, gave up alcohol, power walked every morning, came to the gym for a session with him five times a week and did regular power yoga, he could have me sorted out in just nine months.

'Nine months!' I squealed. The longest I'd ever been on a diet before was twenty-four hours, when I'd wanted to fit into a really small dress for a really big party. I hadn't realized I was embarking on another pregnancy.

I was so terrified by Trent's findings I decided I was going to go all out and take a class straightaway. And Troy gave me such a friendly wave through the window of the workout dance studio, I thought, what the heck? Why not give it a go? I loved dancing, Jazz Step couldn't be that hard.

I regretted my decision the minute I entered the studio and saw Nikki Maier standing next to Caroline, wearing a turquoise all-in-one that described her every luscious curve. Then I realized I recognized ninety per cent of the rest of the class from meetings across canapé trays in Point Piper. They all looked as though they'd had their hair done especially to come to the gym. But it was too late to back out, Troy was already welcoming me over his Madonna headset.

'And today we have a new Jazz Stepper, let's give a big Carlton Club welcome for Antonia!'

The whole class turned and looked and smirked and clapped weakly, as Troy set up a small podium in front of me that looked like something from an Olympics awards ceremony. I had no idea what I was supposed to do with it.

As he fiddled with the sound system I saw Nikki lean over and say something to Caroline. They both perceptibly turned in my direction and laughed. Not in a nice way.

Then as hideous jazz funk blared over the speakers the class began. I didn't have a clue what was going on. Troy was barking commands over his headset in a foreign language that everyone else in the room seemed to understand.

'Grapevine! Mine all mine!' chorused Troy, like it was the wittiest remark of the century and all the trim little bodies bounced on and off their podia like jumping beans on speed.

'Figure of eight! Don't wait! Down the line! One mo' time!' carolled Troy and off they went, hopping up and down and turning and bobbing and worst of all – clapping.

I can honestly say, as I clapped a split second behind the rest of the class for about the twentieth time, before actually tripping over my podium and landing on my arse, that I have never felt so humiliated in my life. I got straight back up again – but not before Nikki had seen me – only to hear Troy calling out my name.

'That's the spirit, Antonia. Get straight back on that horse and . . . Corkscrew! Why don't you?'

It was all I could do not to call back: 'Fuck you! Why don't you?', but I stuck it to the end. I had to. I couldn't bear to walk out, even though for the last twenty minutes

I was just plodding through the 'moves' (as I imagined they were called) like Herman Munster, praying for the whole terrible thing to be over.

Catching sight of myself in the mirror, I could see my 'baggy' T-shirt clinging to every roll of fat, glued to my frame with sweat. Meanwhile, Nikki's ponytail was swinging perkily from side to side as she cruised effortlessly through the routine, throwing in a few optional high kicks for good measure.

Then at last, it was over. They all clapped themselves. I couldn't make my hands meet, I was so cross-eyed with exhaustion.

'Great class, girls!' cried Troy.

'Great class, Troy!' chorused the girls. I thought I was going to vomit.

Taking advantage of Nikki and Caroline's post-class Troy love-in moment, I staggered off to the changing room and slumped onto the bench by my locker, too exhausted even to think about getting dressed.

Through my curtain of troglodyte hair, I saw Nikki and Caroline come skipping gaily in with towels over their shoulders and heard them laughing and chatting in the communal shower. I distinctly heard the words, 'How about when she fell over?' followed by hysterics and then Caroline saying, 'If I hadn't been so careful with my pelvic floor exercises, I think I would have pissed myself.' More coarse laughter.

I was almost – almost – too knackered to care, but I started caring a few minutes later when Nikki came bouncing into my section of lockers, stark naked, perfect fake breasts defying Newtonian laws, brown body still wet from the shower.

Seeing me slumped there, she made no attempt to cover herself, but stood in a pose guaranteed to show off the curve of her waist and the ripe slope of her peach-half buttocks. She had no pubic hair, except a tiny tuft, carefully trimmed into a heart shape. I tried not to stare, while wondering if she was planning to knife me. But she seemed to be trying another tactic. I was so exhausted, I just sat there and waited for it to happen.

'Hello, Antonia,' she said, with fake sincerity. 'Weren't you brave to do Troy's class? Very daring to go straight into the advanced group.'

Then she turned round and bent over. More information than necessary, is all I can say and she treated me to a lot more porn-show moves as she dried herself luxuriously and rubbed cream into her body with one foot up on the bench. I could have given a gynaecology lecture by the time she had her G-string on.

Even in my fug, it struck me that there was something really peculiar about the way she was carrying on. Obviously she wanted to make sure I noticed quite how much better than mine her body was, but a couple of times I noticed her glance upwards as she slowly rubbed the body lotion over her breasts and buttocks. I followed her gaze and saw she was looking straight at a security camera. Most odd.

Swathing myself in towels I trudged off for a shower. When I came back, Nikki was dressed, fully made-up and clearly waiting for me.

'I'm glad I bumped into you, Antonia,' she said, green contact lenses glinting. 'It will save me posting your invitation to my shop opening next week.' She smiled sweetly. As sweet as a sewer rat. Then she thrust a large cream envelope at me. I opened it to see the words:

'Nikki's Knacks – Homewares of Charm and Chic Ironique for the Discerning Decorator'.

I couldn't believe my eyes. 'Chic ironique' was Hugo's phrase. She'd even used my typeface.

'It's in Queen Street,' she said brightly. 'You know, the main shopping street in Woollahra, around the corner from where you are, back there near the fish and chip shop?'

I just looked at her. I knew exactly which shop she was in. The one on the corner I'd told her I'd really wanted, the one I had recently noticed was being painted my particular shade of Gustavian grey and which was double the rent of my place.

'That's lovely, Nikki,' I said, summoning up my best Lady Heaveringham voice. 'I'd be delighted to come – and I'll bring my friend Percy. He's Hugo's uncle.'

Her acquisitive little eyes narrowed, no doubt imagining a dashing Duke of Devonshire type she could flirt into submission, so she could achieve her aim of swanning around an English stately home, like an Australian Raine Spencer.

'Yes, Hugo's Uncle Percy,' I said, laying it on as much as I could. 'Lovely man. Gorgeous. Single. You'll find him very interesting.'

*

Percy laughed so hard when I told him the story of my trip to the gym – complete with demonstrations, using phone books as my podium – he set off a fit of giggle hysterics in Tom, who ended up jumping up and down on the sofa shouting: 'Grapevine! Mine all mine!' I had to give him some warm milk with cinnamon to calm him down.

Percy was still wiping tears from his eyes half an hour later.

'Oh, Antonia, you poor child,' he said, between shaky breaths as he regained his composure. 'How absolutely awful, when you had been so brave to go . . . but do tell me again about the outfits.'

Percy was just like Tom when it came to stories. When you told him one he liked, he wanted to hear it over and over again and would stop you if missed out the tiniest detail. ('The belt! The belt! You've forgotten the belt. That's my favourite bit.')

While he agreed that the Carlton Spa was not for me, Percy was not about to let up on my fitness programme. The next morning he woke me up at six o'clock, made me drink hot water with a slice of lemon – yuk – then forced me to go on a very long walk round Centennial Park, while he got Tom ready for school.

'Don't come back for at least an hour,' he ordered. 'And keep moving.'

When I trudged back in he had me performing yoga moves in the early morning sun, which Tom found nearly as funny as 'Grapevine! Mine all mine!', his new favourite catchphrase, before I sat down to a breakfast of tropical fruits, cut and placed so beautifully the plate looked like a Japanese flower arrangement.

'Heaveringham's Home Spa,' he announced. 'It will do until we can find a gym you can stand.'

Then he forced me to take about twenty enormous vitamin pills, which he said he took every morning as part of his own regime. After all that he told me I had to walk to the shop every day. No car for anything less than four miles, was the new rule.

By 11 a.m. I was so knackered I could have lain on the floor behind the counter and slept. Plus the vitamin pills were repeating on me something chronic and I was ravenous, desperate for my usual morning snack of a creamy latte and a toasted ham and cheese sandwich – all forbidden. Instead I gagged on a cup of vile green tea and nibbled on the raw carrot sticks Percy had packed up for me.

It was quiet for a Friday morning so I worked on my needlepoint. I was trying out a new cushion for a little girl's room that said 'Mummy's little angel' on one side and 'Devil spawn brat' on the other. Judging by the children of the people I had met recently, I thought there would be a large market for it in Woollahra.

I was soon in the calm, almost trance-like state that only the repetitive concentration of needlepoint can induce, but after a while I became aware of a lot more human traffic than usual going up and down my end of Moncur Street. That was good, I thought, maybe I'd get a few more drop-in customers.

I looked out to see if they were likely types and saw that

it was the same two people walking slowly up and down on the other side of the street, peering intently across at my windows, but trying to look as though they weren't. The man was writing in a notebook.

It was bloody Nikki Maier – with a particularly nasty piece of work called Paul, who was the best buddy and former flatmate of Hugo's ghastly Greg. Oh, they would be chums, wouldn't they, I thought bitterly, but what were they doing? Then I realized – they were making notes about my windows.

Rage rose in my stomach like a cyclone. I wanted to go and shoo them off my territory like feral dogs. I certainly wasn't just going to sit there and let them rip me off, so I went to the shop doorway and waved cheerily at them. I really was glad of all the little tricks I had learned from Hugo's mother. There's a lot you can do with icy politeness.

'Hi there, Nikki,' I called brightly. 'Hello, Paul. Isn't it a lovely day? Getting some fresh air? Always good for inspiration, isn't it? Clears the head. How's the shop going? Can't wait to see it on Tuesday. Bye.'

I went back inside, before either of them could reply. Had she no shame?

Percy was just as excited about Nikki's shop opening as she probably was about meeting him. I'd sent him on a reconnaissance mission of my own, strolling casually past her windows on Queen Street, but she had paper over the glass, so he couldn't see in.

'I tried to sweet-talk this rather handsome electrician,

who was in the doorway,' said Percy. 'Covered in white dust. Quite gorgeous. But I don't think he quite understood what I wanted. In fact, he said, "Fuck off, you old poonce," so I couldn't get my nose in.'

The night of the opening, Tom went over to his new best friend Vita's place after school and Percy manned the shop while I went off to get my hair done. I had to feel confident. I was very likely to see David Maier, apart from anything else, and I needed to be strong.

When I came back, Percy helped me dress and insisted that I hang upside down and muss up my expensive blow-dry a bit, so I didn't look like I was trying too hard.

I didn't have a lot of choice in the clothes area, but even after less than a week on Percy's regime, I was feeling slightly less like Moby Dick. I wore a cream bias-cut chiffon skirt to just above my ankles – 'Very fine ankles too,' said Percy, nodding his approval – with a pale green silk rib-knit cardigan, which seemed to skim over the worst of my fatty pads. The finishing touch was my absolute favourite pair of Manolo Blahnik shoes, which always made me feel like a princess. Hugo had brought them home one day as a surprise. None of my trophy wife wardrobe, as Hugo had called it, fitted me any more – but the shoes did.

Percy had also taken care with his appearance. He'd put a fresh lavender rinse through his hair, rendering it fully purple, and he'd set it in rollers, to achieve a bouffant effect, very similar to Lady H's helmet hairdo (which I didn't point out to him). It smelled of lavender too. He'd had the rollers in all afternoon while he was in the shop, he'd told me proudly, with a scarf tied round them. I hoped Nikki hadn't been past on another snoop, because it would have ruined the impact of Percy's arrival at her party.

But the rest of Percy's outfit eclipsed even his astonishing hair. 'She wants a laird,' he announced. 'So I'm wearing the plaid.' And he was too, a splendid kilt in a quite amazing pastel tartan, in shades of mauve, violet, pink and primrose yellow.

'Do you like it?' he asked, swirling the pleats. 'I had it woven specially. The smallest length they'd make was two hundred yards, so I gave the rest to my friend Horace who lined the walls of his downstairs loo with it. Looks splendid.'

On top he was wearing his customary voile poet shirt and, on his feet, traditional lace-up-the-ankle gillie shoes. His highland socks were the same pink as the plaid. They looked strangely familiar.

'These are Hugo's socks,' he said, when he saw me looking at them. 'From that rugger team of his – the Apollos, was it? Liberated them from him years ago.'

My heart gave a little lurch. Those were the socks Hugo had been wearing the first time we'd had sex (yes, he wore socks in bed, it's cold in Scotland in February).

'Do you think he'll be there tonight?' I asked Percy.

'Almost certainly. That little woofter of his is a great friend of Madame Maier's, isn't he? And anyway, Hugo would consider it part of his job to be at any party where cashed-up types like the Maiers and their friends are going to be. He's a good boy like that. And so am I.'

He executed a perfect pirouette that revealed in gory

detail that he was wearing the kilt in the traditional manner. His mother would have been proud of him.

Percy's appearance had exactly the effect I had hoped for when we arrived at Nikki's party. The room actually fell silent when we made our entrance, followed by a round of applause. Percy bowed deeply like Nureyev, accepting it as his due for his 'Sydney social debut', as he called it.

The expression on Nikki Maier's face when she realized that this freak was her longed-for English aristo, was worth every second of humiliation I had experienced at her hand.

Even better, Percy's charisma – which he had turned up to full volume, a technique he had once explained to me ('Open your eyes wide, look interested in everything and imagine you have just heard the most wonderful secret. Works like a charm . . .') – guaranteed that all the attention of the guests was immediately diverted to him.

Society snapper Danny Green lost all interest in Nikki, whom he had been photographing holding a crinoline lady loo-roll cover when we arrived, and spent the rest of the evening following Percy around.

My personal golden moment came when Danny gathered Hugo, Percy and me together for a family group – with me, beaming, in the middle. I could see Nikki and her business partner, poisonous Paul, glaring at us over Danny's shoulder, as the flash went off.

The funny thing was that, despite the circumstances, Hugo and I were still delighted to see each other. We stood in a corner for most of the night, chatting and watching

Percy wow the crowd. This may seem hard to understand, considering how he had shattered my life, but when you've been best friends since you were nineteen and shared everything from university finals to parenthood, you can't just turn it off. Well, we couldn't. We still loved each other's company. Greg was glowering as darkly as Nikki, but Hugo didn't seem to notice.

'Isn't Percy looking well?' he said. 'It's great to see the old duffer and I know Tom loves having him here. By the way, what's this grapevine thing he keeps going on about? Driving me mad. Bloody hell – Percy's wearing my old Apollos socks. I wondered where they'd gone. They're bloody good socks.'

He looked at me quickly – and I knew he was remembering that night back in St Andrews too.

'It's awfully nice to see you, Ant,' he said gently. 'Are you sure you're OK? I know I gave you the shock of your life and everything, but I just couldn't carry on lying to you.'

'I'm getting better, Hugo,' I said. 'Having Percy here really helps because he's so distracting and so helpful. It's like having a nanny and a housekeeper and a personal trainer . . .'

'And a friend?' said Hugo, with his laser-beam perceptiveness.

'Yes,' I nodded. 'A very good friend.'

He paused for a moment and seemed to come to a decision.

'You know, Ant, I don't want to overstep the mark or anything, because I know I'm the one who caused all the trouble, but I do so miss your company. Now that some time has passed, do you think we could start seeing each other again, sort of socially, as friends?'

I thought about it. I still missed him horribly – and it would be nice for Tom.

'Yes,' I said, trying to believe what I was saying. 'It's a good idea, especially with Percy here. That way we'll both get to see more of him. Perhaps we could have the odd family dinner together. It would be lovely for Tom.'

'That's a wonderful idea,' said Hugo, with his adorable dog-like enthusiasm, spilling half his champagne in his excitement. 'I'm so sick of going out for dinner all the time to pretentious restaurants. All the food comes in piles and you have to go outside to smoke. It's ghastly. I'd love family supper with just a chop and a crumble . . .'

He looked so happy at the prospect, I wanted to feel excited too, but I wasn't really sure I was ready.

At that moment Greg came over and slipped his arm through Hugo's. My stomach dropped like a stone. Would he have to be at the family dinners too, I wondered. At least my English cooking would put him off. I'd make steak and kidney pudding – heavy on the suet – with mushy peas, followed by spotted dick, with extra skin on the custard. I'd make him drink Vimto. Flat Vimto.

'Hugo, darling,' said Greg, ignoring me. 'Nikki and David are taking us for dinner at Catalina after this. Just the inner circle. Be ready to leave in half an hour.'

He sniffed at me and walked off.

'Does he have to be quite so unpleasant?' I asked Hugo. 'I mean, what exactly have I ever done wrong to him?'

Hugo looked extremely uncomfortable.

'I'm so sorry, Ant, he was bloody rude then, just as he was that night at your shop and I will say something to him, but I think he just feels intimidated and insecure around you.'

I snorted with indignation.

'And I suppose my feelings never occur to him? Well, I'm not having him to the family suppers until he gets over it,' I said firmly. 'The onus is on *him*, to get on with *me*. And now I'm going to mingle.'

I kissed him on the cheek and before I could object he put his arms around me and gave me a full-on Hugo hug-o, resting his head into the side of my neck and nuzzling it. My body went limp. That embrace was so familiar, I just wanted to slide back into it and die. At that moment Percy appeared.

'Come on, Antonia,' he said. 'We're going out for dinner. Really fun people. Let go of your future ex-wife, Hugo, we're off.'

And with that he took me by the hand and led me away. The man was a saint.

Percy was right about the fun dinner. He'd found a little group of hilarious people at the party, some of whom I had met before, but hadn't got to know properly. Antony Maybury was there and several of the journalists who had done pieces on Anteeks. There was a big crowd of us – about twelve – men and women, gay and straight, and the best thing of all, they were all screaming with laughter about Nikki's shop.

Oh the shop . . . Remember that crinoline lady she was holding? That was pretty much the standard of everything in there. It was all hideous and her mark-up made mine look tame. There was a ghastly standard lamp I'd rejected myself at Wally's for $10 and she was selling it for $940. Painted lime green. Gloss.

'It's amazing really, isn't it?' said a small woman with a Louise Brooks bob, who was a stylist on a glossy magazine. She'd been into my shop a few times, I remembered, to borrow props. 'It's amazing how completely someone can miss the point. The whole shabby chic thing, which you do so brilliantly, Antonia, is based on knowing which shabby object has fundamental charm – and therefore potential chic – and which one is just simply shabby.'

I beamed at her. She totally got it.

'My favourite thing,' said Antony, 'was the IKEA chest of drawers – one hundred per cent MDF – painted Gustavian grey and finished off with those cut-glass knobs that Antonia sells.'

'She bought them in my shop,' I told them, which caused great hilarity.

'And what about that bubblegum-pink sideboard?' said a man with a beard and close-cropped hair, who Percy told me later was a leading interior designer, in the minimalist style. 'It's quite a nice little mid-century piece, but the colour is so wrong. Diabolical. So what I don't understand is – how did she manage to get that grey on the exterior so right?'

'I used it on quite a few pieces when I decorated her house,' I told him. 'She insisted on having the mix details, in case it ever got chipped. I didn't want to give them to her, but she can be a very persistent lady.'

'A pushy bitch, as we say in Sydney,' said a rather beautiful woman, who was the editor of a famous food magazine.

I couldn't believe it, I felt like I'd taken a reality pill. There was another world in Sydney after all, of real people, nice people, funny people, people who could talk about something else apart from money and diamonds and their husband's latest deal. We had such a laugh.

By the end of the dinner Percy had all their numbers and was setting a date for them to come to dinner at our place. For the first time for many weeks, that night I actually went to sleep quite quickly – and without crying.

8

I wish I could say the same about Christmas – that there had been no crying. But that first one without Hugo was the hardest thing I had endured since Suzy's party. It was so difficult to go through the motions of buying the tree and decorating the house and all the things I had to do to keep it special for Tom, when I had only ever done them with Hugo before.

One very hot and sunny December afternoon, about a week before the big day, I was standing on Queen Street outside my favourite deli, staring vacantly into space as I tried to remember what on earth I'd been going in there for, when I saw Hugo and Greg go past in Hugo's car. The top was down and there was a Christmas tree sticking out of the back seat. A huge Christmas tree. I felt like I had been punched in the stomach.

The rational side of my brain told me that Hugo was really getting the tree for Tom – who I had already heard boasting to Vita that he was having *two* Christmas trees and *two* Christmas stockings this year – but seeing them doing what Hugo and I had done together for so long, was nigh on unbearable. If Percy hadn't been back at the house, to distract and entertain me, I honestly don't know what I would have done. I think I might have harmed myself. I was that low.

Percy made Christmas bearable by taking it over and making it different. With his usual sensitivity he figured out that the morning would be the hardest part for me – no sitting in bed with Hugo, drinking champagne and watching Tom open his presents – so he arranged that Tom would go straight over to Hugo's for breakfast, while we had a celebratory brekkie of our own. It involved a lot of Krug and a lot of smoked salmon.

When Tom came back at lunchtime, dragging a pillowcase of swag behind him, Hugo came too and joined us to exchange presents and make things seem a little normal for Tom. I survived it by a whisker and the minute he left I prepared to take to my bed in a darkened room for the rest of the day. But Percy had other ideas.

'That's good,' he said as he saw me heading upstairs. 'Go up and get your bathing suit on. The limo will be here in a minute.'

I looked at him, bewildered.

'What limo?' I said.

'The one that's taking us to Camp Cove,' said Percy, happily. 'Can't be worrying about tedious things like parking on Christmas Day.'

It was a stretch limo, which meant it had to drop us quite a way from the beach in the narrow streets of Watsons Bay, but apart from that Percy had thought of everything. As well as a huge picnic, we had three umbrellas for shade, two beach towels each – lie and dry, as he called them – and special blow-up backrests to lean against.

We ate buckets of prawns and oysters with our fingers,

with plenty more Krug to wash it down, and he'd bought a whole tray of perfectly ripe mangoes. I ate three in a row, standing in the water, with the juices running all down my front.

Percy strolled up and down the shoreline, checking out the 'local fauna', as he called it, wearing a white sarong and a huge cartwheel sunhat, while Tom and I had great fun splashing in the water, playing with his new boogie board. It wasn't Christmas as I knew it, but it was highly diverting.

And it went on like that throughout Tom's summer holidays, with Percy providing constant distractions, to entertain him and to take my mind off all the things that Hugo and I weren't doing with him as a family.

I closed the shop for two weeks in January and devoted myself to having fun with Tom and Percy. We went to see *Jungle Book* outdoors in the Botanical Gardens, went kayaking in Middle Harbour and out to Cabramatta on the train to have Vietnamese noodles and marvel at all the exotic fruit in the market there. We hired a boat on the Hawkesbury River, had picnics at obscure Harbour beaches I didn't know existed, and all kinds of other jollies. Tom adored it all.

One of the greatest successes was a night-time ghost tour of the old King George army hospital and barracks, which covered a large piece of land over on the north shore of the harbour. I'd never even heard of it, but in his inimitable fashion Percy had researched every possible outing and place of interest within a fifty-mile radius of our house. I thought it sounded a bit yucky – visiting an old disused hospital – and I was worried Tom would be terrified of the ghost aspect, but Percy was adamant.

'No, Antonia, it will be marvellous,' insisted Percy. 'That delightful young Keith down at Cadman's Cottage, where I got the tickets – very attractive teeth – assures me it's absolutely fascinating. It's where they used to put all the mangy new arrivals when they arrived off ships riddled with disease and corruption. Also any of them who had gone tonto on the voyage. It's a miracle I escaped a stay there when I arrived myself, what?'

Percy was right – it was marvellous. I was such an Eastern Suburbs Princess, I'd never even been over to North Head before and it was spectacular. There were amazing views of the Harbour and out to the ocean – and no ugly buildings to get in the way, except for the old sheds and structures of the King George Hospital itself, which were incredibly atmospheric.

Even without the gripping ghost stories that the guide worked up for maximum spook effect, the whole place had a poignant romantic air about it that I loved. Some of the buildings were old stone, others were Victorian brick and there were some in Federation style, but all of them had the same integrity of being worn from use as the things I bought for my shop. There was a real sense of history up there.

The part of it that touched me most was the infectious diseases ward, a single storey weatherboard building surrounded by verandas, right down by the shore, with waves crashing into a little rocky cove and the lights of the City shining across the dark water. It was really sad – so many soldiers had died of flu there, after coming home safely from the First World War – but there was a special beauty in the faded paint and it had an intrinsic elegance.

I was amazed how moved I was by the place, but apart from that the outing followed our usual pattern. Percy fell immediately in love with the guide – 'Oh I do adore a man in khaki, Ant,' he had hissed the minute he saw him in his ranger's uniform – and flirted with him outrageously the whole way round.

Tom started out showing off madly, running ahead and jumping out at me, making ghoulish faces, becoming quieter as the darkness drew in around us, until he was clutching my hand very tightly and saying nothing. By the time we reached the morgue – the scariest part, by far – he had both arms wrapped around my waist, his head buried in my hip, just one wide eye peeping out. All the way home we listened to him telling us how scared he hadn't been, but in the middle of the night he climbed into bed beside me, clutching his special teddy.

As well as the outings there was my fitness regime to keep me occupied – or at least that was the idea. I was fed up with it after three days and started begging for mercy, but Percy would not let up. I went off to the shop each morning – after my mandatory one-hour trudge around the park – with a packed lunch of cottage cheese, two Ryvita crispbreads and a bundle of crudités. My afternoon treat was some thrilling melon cubes. I came home each night to a delicious low-fat, no carbohydrate meal – well, as delicious as food without butter, cheese, cream, pasta and potatoes can be.

Needless to say I cheated. When Percy wasn't around I continued to stuff down muffins and cake in the shop. Sometimes I had fish and chips from the shop opposite, to fill up after my diet lunch, which I had usually consumed by about 10.25 a.m. At home I hid packets of biscuits in my knicker drawer to keep me company on the nights when he went out. Then I'd smuggle the empty wrappers out again. I knew the only person I was cheating was myself, but I just didn't think I could get through a whole evening in alone on celery sticks.

And, of course, I didn't lose much weight. There was no hard evidence of my lack of success, because Hugo – always vainer than me – had taken the bathroom scales with him when he left and Percy said he didn't believe in weighing yourself anyway, because of muscle weighing more than fat and all that. He also thought it was 'suburban' to know how much you weighed – just one of his many unique insights on life.

But even without the empirical proof of the scales, I knew I couldn't get away with it for ever. My retribution came one muggy January morning – almost a year to the day since Hugo's big announcement – as I made my cup of hot water and lemon (just a little palate cleanser for the three full-cream milk lattes I would have in the shop later) in the kitchen at home, wearing only a knotted sarong.

I saw Percy peering at me over his bowl of grated apple, muesli and soya yoghurt and held my stomach in, hoping he wouldn't notice that my silhouette was hardly any more streamlined than it had been several weeks before. No use – I was rumbled.

'You're still incredibly fat,' he proclaimed. 'Tie another sarong around your head and you could pass for the maid in *Gone With The Wind*.'

He narrowed his eyes as he carried on looking at me. Then came the verdict I dreaded.

'You're cheating, aren't you, Antonia?'

Without any hesitation, I nodded. I was quite happy to sneak a packet of chocolate digestives up to my bedroom in my handbag, but I have never been able to tell lies. Like I said, I'm a vicar's daughter.

'So what has it been, fatty?' asked Percy in quite a frighteningly severe tone. 'Currant buns and doughnuts in the shop? Tim Tams by torchlight? Tom has already told me you are hoarding chocolate biscuits amongst your lingerie, which is fine with him when he's feeling peckish, let me tell you, but if you're cheating at work as well, that's another matter.'

I hung my head. When I looked up, Percy had his chin resting on one hand and was looking at me intently with those pale blue Heaveringham eyes, which were so disarming and so very like Hugo's. For a moment I started to laugh, as a kind of nervous reaction, but he just carried on looking at me blankly. I went back to feeling mortified.

'Oh, I'm sorry, Percy,' I gabbled. 'I know you only want to help me and I do want to lose weight really, it's just that food is so nice. It's the only thing that comforts me. I'm already thinking about the next mouthful before I've swallowed the one I'm chewing. As long as my jaws are moving I feel I can cope with it all, but when I'm hungry as well, the big hole where Hugo used to be just seems to become a yawning gap.'

Percy listened to me, drumming his fingers on his cheek. I was terrified he was going to say he was so hurt and disappointed with me he was going to leave. Finally, he spoke.

'Filling holes, eh, Antonia?' he said. 'Like your needlepoint? Is that what it is?'

I nodded. He was right. I was just filling holes. I hadn't thought any of it through until I'd made my confession, but that was exactly what I was doing.

'Well, if you can't give up the comfort eating,' he continued, picking up a huge spoonful of his breakfast and sticking it in his mouth. 'We'll just have to step up the exercise.'

And he opened his mouth wide, to give me a good view of the masticated food inside.

The next evening I found myself in a truly terrifying place. Percy and I were side by side, going nowhere fast on electric treadmills and all around us was a heaving mass of sweaty people punishing their bodies.

There were about thirty other people on the treadmills alone, ranging from a ridiculously tall and thin girl who must have been a model, to an enormous man who looked like Arnold Schwarzenegger's Samoan big brother. His arms were the size of my torso.

Mostly, though, the people on the treadmills, the rowing machines and the vast expanse of exercise bikes next to them, were trimly built men with dark orange tans, very short hair and well-moisturized faces, wearing discreet grey marl singlets and jersey shorts.

'I wasn't going to tell you about this place,' panted Percy, whose treadmill was at a gradient roughly equivalent to the upper reaches of the Matterhorn. 'It's one of my secret little social venues – wonderfully steamy steam rooms . . .' He waggled his eyebrows. 'But because it's still New Year resolution time there are all kinds of deals on, so you can't tell me you can't afford it. Plus there is no risk of you running into any of those ghastly social-blights down here.'

He wasn't kidding. The place was called Muscle City and it was rather as I imagined the gym area at Saint Quentin prison must be. An enormous smelly expanse of brutal-looking equipment servicing an even more brutal-looking clientele. There was no Enya piped over the PA system here. In fact the main sound track was animalistic grunting, with a percussion mix of enormously heavy metal objects being dropped on the floor and the rhythmic thump of feet on the rubber treadmill tracks.

Far more gripping than the television screen over my head, which was showing particularly vapid music videos, was the free-weights area, right at the back, which had the floor space of the average multi-storey car park.

The trim tanned fellows seemed to stay within the aerobic zone, where we were, and around the weight machines. The free weights seemed to be strictly for the tough guys – and there was no missing them.

They wore WWF leotards and fingerless string gloves, and had wide leather belts strapped around their waists. Their massive necks grew out of their shoulders like

Edinburgh Castle rising from Princes Street Gardens and tapered into the tops of their heads, many of which were shaved for added menace.

They walked with their arms crooked because the sheer bulk of their muscles prevented them straightening them by their sides. Their 'lats' – as Percy informed me the muscles on the upper sides of their backs were called – reminded me of the flying buttresses on Notre Dame. Their buttocks looked ridiculously small compared to their enormous shoulders. It was the most fabulous freak show.

My eyes were on stalks. It was better than watching the Discovery Channel and I came to the conclusion that if one of Tom's beloved raptors had come strolling in to pump some iron, it wouldn't have looked remotely out of place among the other pin-head primitives.

I was so fascinated I actually forgot I was doing horrid exercise and was quite surprised, when Percy leaned over and pressed the off button on my machine, to find that I had been power walking for thirty minutes. My T-shirt was wet through.

'Good,' said Percy, looking me over. 'You're glowing nicely. Now I'm going to set you up for tuition on the weights machines.'

As we walked over to a seating area in a corner, which seemed to be populated by a collection of man's early ancestors, Percy was waving and nodding and shaking hands like a minor Royal at a garden party. He seemed to know everybody in the place, although with his appearance people rarely forgot meeting him. More surprising was that this lot all seemed pleased to see him again.

'Now which of you bully boys is going to look after my treasured niece?' he asked the assembled Cro-Magnons when we reached them. He had his hands on his hips, head coquettishly tipped to one side, like Doris Day at a clam bake.

'I need someone tough, but fair,' continued Doris/Percy. 'She's a lazy little trollop and I want her to lose two stone – that's about twelve kilos in your language. I warn you, she doesn't know a dumb bell from a dumb fuck, which is probably a good thing in your cases, but she responds well to threats and bullying. Volunteers please.'

For a moment I thought they might tear him to bits, standing there in his pink singlet and hibiscus print shorts, a scarf tied around his mauve hair, but instead of throwing him through the nearest plate-glass window, their rugged faces split into big grins and they all offered to take me on. I honestly do not know how he did it.

After some serious consideration of their various pros and cons, which gave Percy the opportunity to indulge in a little more outrageous flirting – 'Oh no, Andy, I think *you* are just a little *too* big . . .' and the like – we settled on a bald-headed bruiser with the unlikely name of Tristan, who promised to knock me into shape.

Percy announced he was going upstairs to 'freshen up' – a statement accompanied by a stage wink – and I was left to Tristan's care.

Do you know, it wasn't that bad? Although he had hands the size of tennis rackets and a head like the Loch Ness monster, he was definitely your more gentle breed of Neanderthal and clearly sought to disarm non-physical types like myself with the contradiction between his brutal appearance and delicate manners. He called me 'Miss' and referred to his women clients as 'my ladies'.

It worked for me. He was so polite and earnest I actually wanted to please him – at least, I didn't want to hurt his feelings. By starting me off with a gentle run through all the machines on the lightest weights, he didn't scare me off either, although I did feel intimidated by all the men lining up impatiently to use them.

An hour later I joined Percy in the reception area, where he was looking very rested in his favourite white linen kaftan and Indian sandals, freshly applied mauve varnish visible on his toenails.

He asked Tristan how I had behaved and after I received a good report card he stood over me while I joined the gym, paying a terrifyingly large sum up front for my first fifteen private sessions with Tristan, and wrote the appointments – five days a week for three weeks – in my diary, in black pen.

He also had Tristan witness his promise – taken with his right hand in the Boy Scout salute – to look after the shop for two hours a day for three weeks while I was doing them, so there could be no sneaky ringing up to cancel, using Anteeks as an excuse.

There really was no way of getting out of it.

At the same time as Percy was forcing me into physical hard labour, expanding my social scene outside what the gossip columns called the 'Social A List' – and which he called the 'Social All Pissed' – and educating me about

Sydney's historic sites, I was quietly making another friend.

A very attractive woman, who looked about forty, although it was hard to be certain, with infuriatingly long legs and flame-red hair, had been coming into the shop regularly for a couple of months. She was always immaculately dressed, with a crocodile Kelly bag over her arm, and she would look at everything in the shop with the concentration of an earnest student at the British Museum. Better still, she always bought something – usually a lot of somethings.

She really did have an unusually lovely face, I thought, with creamy skin, high cheekbones and full lips, but while she always smiled sweetly at me as she handed over her credit card, there was something guarded about her manner which stopped me asking the kind of questions that would have developed our relationship. It was a shame, because there was something about her I really liked. And not just her black Amex card.

One afternoon, when she had bought my entire display of pretty mismatched teacups, I threw in a silver filigree tea strainer and a set of embroidered napkins as a grateful bonus. She was radiant with delight.

'That's so nice of you,' she said. 'I don't think anyone has ever given me a freebie in Woollahra before. They're normally too busy trying to get me to spend more.'

'You're my best customer,' I told her. 'I just wanted to thank you for supporting me.'

'I love your shop,' she said fervently. She paused and I could see she was wondering whether to say more. I smiled encouragingly and popped a couple of extra doilies into the parcel I was making up for her.

'It has such a sweet feeling in here,' she said in a rush, as though she was expressing something that had been dammed up inside her. 'I haven't been anywhere with an atmosphere like this since I left Tasmania over twenty years ago.'

She fixed me with her cornflower-blue eyes, which definitely weren't lenses.

'It reminds me of my grandmother's house,' she said very quietly, stroking one of the doilies.

I smiled at her again. Although I didn't know her, I could tell that this was not something she would share lightly. I was touched.

'It reminds me of my granny's house too,' I said. 'I think that's the feeling I'm going for. I'm so glad you like it. Not everybody gets it. A lot of people don't like the idea of second-hand sheets.'

She laughed and I glanced down at the credit card she had handed me. It said, 'T. D. M. Sullivan'.

'My name's Antonia,' I said, holding out my hand. 'But everyone calls me Ant.'

'I know,' she said, shaking my hand gently. 'We've been to a lot of the same parties, but we've never actually met.'

'Oh really?' I said. I was surprised I didn't remember seeing such a beautiful woman.

'I don't mix much at parties,' she said, as if reading my thoughts.

'What does the T stand for?' I asked, indicating the credit card. She was really shy, I realized. It was like bringing out one of the timid children at Tom's birthday parties.

'Dee,' she said and laughed again at my surprised expression. 'Theresa Deirdre Mary Sullivan – née McBride – but everyone calls me Dee, for Deirdre. My mother was also called Theresa, it got too complicated.'

'Well, it's lovely to meet you, Dee, and I do really appreciate your support of Anteeks. Please come in and see me any time you feel like a reminder of your grandmother's house – and don't feel you have to buy something. Come for tea next time you're nearby. It would be nice to see you.'

She smiled at me so radiantly, I almost blushed. And I couldn't help comparing it with the neon brashness of Nikki Maier's famous smile. What a world of difference.

Dee did come in for tea the following week, bringing the most delicious selection of French-style patisserie with her, which I happily gobbled down, feeling virtuous about my new gym routine. She was still shy, but we had a really pleasant time chatting about inconsequential things such as whether we preferred Earl Grey or Lady Grey tea and comparing French tea blenders Mariage Frères with my favourite British tea merchants, Williams & Magor.

Any time I tried to make the conversation a little more personal, asking what I thought were fairly unintrusive questions like whether she had any children, where she lived and what her husband did, she found a way of changing the subject.

I did manage to establish that she knew Suzy and Roger Thorogood – she had also been at Suzy's fortieth it turned out – and now I came to think about it, I thought I did remember noticing a striking redhead, in an amazing sapphire-blue dress, with the jewels to match. But when I asked her if she knew Nikki Maier or Caroline French, she quickly said she didn't, although she knew the names.

That surprised me, as they sort of went together as a group and the Eastern Suburbs set they were part of was so tight everyone seemed to know each other, but I didn't push it. At the time, it didn't seem important.

9

To my own great surprise, three weeks later, well into the humid horror of February, I was still going to the gym. More than that – I was starting to look forward to it. Who-would-a-thunk-it? I thought to myself, echoing Tom's current catchphrase. He loved words and had a new favourite every week.

One sunny Saturday he had been playing with Vita in our garden, when he came running in, loudly asking Percy and me to come outside and see what they had built.

'Mummy, Perky, come and look,' he shouted, waving arms covered in mud up to the elbows. 'Vita and me have made a buggery – come and see it.'

'Vita and I,' said Percy. 'But otherwise that's an invitation I certainly shan't turn down. Shall we go and see, Antonia?'

The buggery turned out to be a house for small beetles, made from an empty kitchen match box. Percy and I laughed about it for days – and I was laughing more, generally. Although I could barely stand to admit it to myself, my sessions with Tristan were starting to make me feel better. Not so much physically, I still had a way to go with that – and I still couldn't sleep – but I felt much better in myself.

After the first week of daily workouts I could hardly move and had to spend an entire Sunday lying on the sofa watching old movies, but once I had got over the 'fatigue hump', as Tristan called it – sparking another phrase craze in Tom, who would say things like 'I can't go to bed yet, Mummy, I haven't reached my fatigue hump' – I began to enjoy the routine and the challenge of it.

I even liked the alien nature of my surroundings at Muscle City. It was so unlike anywhere else I had ever been. Most of my life – the shop, our house, Woollahra – could best be described as 'divine'. All toile de Jouy, witty details and fresh flowers on every flat surface. The gym was gritty, smelly, tough and urban, like the inner city suburb where it was located.

Although it was only ten minutes walk from the centre of town, Percy had told me the neighbourhood was 'vice HQ' and a 'heaving hotbed' of prostitution, junkies and drug dealers, though I could never see any signs of it. There were a few drunken derelicts and scruffy types around, but I just gave them a wide berth.

The only thing I wasn't so keen on at the gym – apart from the unspeakable showers, which I never used – was the surly attitude of some of the regulars. They clearly resented people like me day tripping into their world and if I was too slow on a machine they made their feelings abundantly clear.

One time, Tristan nearly got into a fight with a guy who started giving him a hard time about 'shifting Princess Porky off the bench press', as he delightfully put it. It was very embarrassing – although not as bad as running into Nikki Maier nude in the changing rooms, I reminded myself.

I tried going at varying times of day, to avoid the crowds, but it didn't make any difference, Muscle City was always busy, and I decided I would just have to toughen my attitude along with my stomach muscles, which I was properly aware of for the first time in my life – mainly because they hurt all the time.

After my first three weeks with Tristan I had booked up for another fifteen sessions, but when that was up he told me it was getting hard for him to see me five days a week, because he was in training himself for some kind of he-man beauty contest. It was time, he said, for me to learn the discipline of coming to the gym on my own. I agreed to try it.

The first time I went to Muscle City alone it nearly put me off for ever. By then it was late February and I had never seen the place so packed. I got there at 5 p.m. – leaving Percy to look after the Thursday evening late-night shoppers at Anteeks – and had to wait ten minutes before I could even get on a treadmill.

It was then very hard to concentrate on gradually increasing my pace and gradient, as Tristan had taught me to do, as a long queue of restless men was forming, muttering loudly behind me. In the end, I felt so intimidated, I came off after seven minutes, when I should have done at least thirty.

It was even worse on the weights machines. Without Tristan there to look out for me, I only got onto two of them. I would wait politely for my turn, only to be barged out of the way by one of the army of darkly tanned men in small shorts. It was more like doing 'waits' than weights,

I thought grumpily, and after being gazumped one more time on the leg press I decided to leave.

'That was a quick workout, Antonia,' said the guy at the desk, as he handed my membership card back to me.

'I'm surprised you noticed,' I said, a little taken aback to be addressed by name. 'It's so busy in here today.'

'Well, you are just about the only girl in here, so you do stand out,' he said, smiling.

Rather thrilled to be still a 'girl', I looked at him again. He was wearing glasses and he had a badge, announcing he was called 'James', pinned to his baseball cap. The combination of specs and hat made it hard to see his face, but his smile seemed friendly.

I glanced back into the gym and realized he was right. It was all blokes.

'Good heavens,' I said. 'You're right. What on earth's going on? Is it some kind of convention for tanned men?'

He threw back his head and laughed. I didn't think it was that funny.

'You could say that. It's Mardi Gras on Saturday,' he said. 'Come in on Sunday and you'll have the whole place to yourself.'

I felt so stupid. Of course I knew it was Mardi Gras any minute, Percy was in a right old twitter about it – actually terribly excited about the whole thing, despite his earlier claims that it was 'déclassé'. Now it seemed he had a starring role on a float, which he had spent the last few weeks helping to build, and he thought it was the best thing ever. Tom was nearly as excited as he was. He was going to watch the parade with Vita and her nanny – her mums were in it, on their motorbike.

'Or if you find the crowd in here too intimidating,' continued this James person, 'why don't you come in late? We're open twenty-four hours. There's hardly anyone in here after eleven at night.'

I told him I'd try it, with absolutely no intention of doing so, of course. The enthusiastic lie. Just one of our funny little English ways.

The following Monday night I was down there at 2 a.m. Amazing, I know, but at that strange hour, lying in a hot tangle of sheets, it had suddenly made perfect sense. I'd been tossing around in bed since midnight, going nuts trying to sleep, and the idea just came back to me in a flash. Why the heck not?

Percy was snoring so loudly after his weekend of wild excess I could hear him through two closed doors, so it wasn't like I was leaving Tom alone. Working-out in the middle of the night seemed a brilliant solution to my maddening insomnia – and it would also mean I wouldn't have to leave the shop for two hours in the middle of the day, which would be a relief, because I was never quite sure what Percy got up to in there on his own.

When I arrived at Muscle City the receptionist chap, James, wasn't there, someone else was manning the desk, but he'd been absolutely right, the place was as brightly lit as ever, all the machines were turned on, but there was hardly anyone in there.

There were a couple of the tanned men, looking a

little paler in the face now, chewing gum and flogging themselves on the treadmills – presumably hoping to make themselves tired enough to sleep after whatever exotic chemical cocktail they'd consumed over the weekend.

There was one other woman there, I was glad to see, one of the tall, thin model types who seemed to frequent Muscle City, although Sinew City would have been a better name for them. Her neck bulged out like steel cables as she strained on the lats machine. Over in the scary area two enormous pecasauruses were 'spotting' each other – just one of the little phrases I'd picked up from Tristan – on the free weights. And then there was me.

I was so thrilled not to have anyone menacing me for the treadmill I power walked for over forty minutes and then did my full round of weight machines without interruption. I got home at 3.15 a.m. and went straight to sleep. Bingo.

I felt a bit knackered the next morning, although four hours sleep wasn't much less than I had been getting recently. Percy was in an uncharacteristically grumpy mood at breakfast – he never slept in – nursing day three of his Mardi Gras hangover, and he refused to believe me when I told him he wouldn't need to shop-sit any more because I was going to go to the gym in the middle of the night instead.

'Well, I suppose it's quite a creative way of cheating,' he said, huffily. 'A little more imaginative than hiding Jaffa Cakes among your pants, but do you really expect me to believe that you got up at 2 a.m. and went to Muscle City?'

'Yes,' I said. 'And I can prove it.'

I went upstairs and picked up my sweaty workout gear from the bedroom floor. I walked back into the kitchen brandishing it.

'Look! Nasty sweaty T-shirt. Horrid sweaty leggings. Vile sweaty socks. Want a sniff?'

'Hmmmm,' said Percy, wrinkling his nose and sipping his ginger tea. 'It looks like you really did go. Amazing.'

'If you still don't believe me, you can ring them. Their computer logs everyone who goes in and out and when.'

'All right, Antonia dear,' he said, huffily. 'Don't get shirty. I believe you. And for God's sake put those foul vestments in the washing machine. I'm trying to enjoy my breakfast.'

After he finished huffing, we made a deal. Instead of minding the shop in the afternoons, he would take Tom to school on the mornings after I went to the gym, so I could have a lie-in.

Obviously I wouldn't go to the gym in the early hours on nights when he was still out carousing, so it would work out naturally. He always got up early anyway, so I'd leave my trainers outside my bedroom door if I'd been to the gym the night before. Percy was quite enchanted by the eccentricity of the arrangement, Tom was always delighted to have Uncle Perky take him to school and I was ecstatic at the idea that I might start to get some sleep. Rock and roll.

Apart from anything else, with my new gym regime in place, I was glad to be back at the shop full time. A couple of hours out of it each day had got me out of my routine and I was really happy to settle back into it. For the first few days, I was like a dog turning around in my basket. I gave it a good clean, rearranged all the stock and re-did the windows on an end-of-summer theme, with cushions made from old checked Welsh blankets, a row of 50s Thermos flasks and a big stack of mohair rugs and wraps in wonderful colours. Business picked up.

I was happy to say that the opposite appeared to be happening at Nikki's Knacks. I had to walk past it on my way from home to Anteeks and back, or anytime I wanted to get anything in Queen Street, and to my great satisfaction, there rarely seemed to be anyone in there. Certainly not Nikki.

The first couple of weeks after it opened, she had been in there every time I passed, flitting around with a feather duster and fussily rearranging the ghastly little bits of tat – knick-knacks was the word for them – which were her stock. After that initial flush of enthusiasm I didn't see her in there again, just Greg's horrid friend Paul, sitting behind the counter like a poisonous spider. The sour look on his face would have been enough to put off any potential shoppers, even without the ugliness of the 'objets' on sale inside at their ridiculously inflated prices.

Seeing me swan past used to make Paul's scowl even deeper and sometimes I walked up and down several times in one afternoon just to annoy him.

Now I was in the shop all the time, Dee came in to see me quite often and although she didn't buy something from me every time any more, she usually had several carrier bags with her. She always seemed to have a new outfit on too – in fact I realized I'd never seen her in the same clothes twice.

Although she still hadn't let down her guard completely I had found out a little more about her. She didn't have any children, her husband Frank was a 'businessman' and they lived down at Darling Point. Frankie, as she called him, had a very large boat he was terribly proud of – it had a helicopter on the front deck. She made a little moue that told me without words exactly how she felt about the boat.

That was about as personal as we got. Mostly we talked about the stuff I had in the shop and how Sydney compared with London, Paris, New York and LA – all cities which she seemed to know very well, or as well as you can know anywhere from the back of a chauffeur-driven car.

Most of all, though, she was interested in the shop and how I made it work. Not in the sneaky way Nikki had been interested, but out of genuine respectful enthusiasm for the end result. I was happy to tell her some of the tricks of the trade and she seemed to find it all fascinating. With the things she had bought from me over the months and the comments she made, I thought she had a real feeling for it. Not many people did.

Eventually, when her visits were up to about three a week, I felt emboldened to ask her about the clothes.

'I don't want to be rude, Dee,' I said, as I poured her some more Lady Grey tea – the one we had settled on as our afternoon favourite. 'But I have to ask you something . . .'

She looked alarmed but I continued.

'Do you ever wear the same clothes twice?'

Far from being offended, she giggled like a girl.

'No,' she said, laughing some more. 'I don't really. I have a few things, like my leather coats and my Chanel suits, which I do wear more than once, but mostly I find clothes disposable.'

I must have looked as amazed as I felt. I hadn't really wanted to believe that someone could actually do that – or would want to. I loved my old clothes, they were like family friends. I hated it when anything wore out and had to go. I must have been gawping at her. She turned a little more serious.

'If I didn't shop all the time, Antonia,' she said, a furrow appearing between her perfectly arched auburn brows, 'what would I do with myself? I don't work. I don't have children. Or pets. I don't go out for lunch, because I don't really like eating and I don't like any of the people I know who would want to have lunch with me. I have my hair done every day. I get my nails done three times a week. But it still leaves a lot of time.'

She shrugged her shoulders and crossed one slender leg over the other.

I kept my mouth shut, hoping she would say more and she did.

'That's what I do during the week. I get up, I get groomed – at home, of course, I can't bear all those bitchy hair salons in Double Bay – then I get dressed, and then I go shopping. In the evening and at weekends I do whatever Frankie wants to do, which is usually hosting dinners for his business associates, which I don't plan, or cook, or clear up, or it's entertaining people on his boat, which I don't have to organize either. All I have to do is sit there and look expensive for Frankie. As I say, it leaves a lot of time.'

I couldn't imagine such an empty life.

'But don't you want to do anything else?' I asked.

'Like what?' she said. 'I could do some charity fund-raising – isn't that what idle rich bitches like me are supposed to do? But that would mean being on tedious committees with dreadful people like Caroline French. I'd rather just hand over the money.'

'I thought you didn't know her,' I said quickly, more surprised than wanting to catch her out.

'Oh, I know who she is all right and that nasty Nikki Maier, it's impossible to avoid them in the Eastern Suburbs, as you have probably found out, but I don't know them well and I don't want to. I don't want to know any of those women.'

She almost spat the words out. I hoped I hadn't gone too far. She looked down at her tea for a moment and then raised her eyes again. She had a wistful look in them.

'I wanted to do a degree, Antonia,' she said. 'I left school when I was fifteen and I am all too aware of how much I don't know, but Frankie wouldn't let me. He didn't want any wife of his mixing with scruffy pinko students, as he put it. Not good for business. He said I could do a flower-arranging course, or yoga, as long as the teacher wasn't a bloke, but not a degree. After all, it would make me more qualified than him, wouldn't it? And big Frankie wouldn't like that, oh no.'

I felt really sorry for her. I thought I had a tough break, sleeping alone while my once-beloved husband snuggled up with another man, but at least he had enhanced my life while he'd been around – with a lot more than money. And even without Hugo, I had Tom who filled my life with love, and darling Percy. I was trying to imagine what it would be like to be Dee, when I had an idea. I poured some more tea for us both and presented my suggestion as though I were changing the subject.

'By the way, Dee,' I said, busying myself with the hot water and deliberately not looking at her, 'on Monday I'm going on a buying trip through the Blue Mountains. Would you like to come with me? It will take a whole day. It gets a bit boring doing all that driving on my own, I'd love some company.'

She didn't need to reply. The delighted expression on her face when I looked up was all I needed to see.

10

That evening when I got home from Anteeks, there was a strange man sitting at my kitchen table. He had his back to me, so I couldn't see his face, but he looked quite young. He had very black hair gelled into pointy spikes, a bit like Sid Vicious, and a thick silver ring in one ear. Over a long-sleeved black T-shirt, he was wearing a denim jacket with the sleeves ripped off, with the words 'Recherché Rebel' spelled out on the back in metal studs. As he lifted a glass of water to his mouth, I saw he was wearing a thick studded band on his left wrist and a big silver skull ring on his pinkie finger. I was a bit alarmed.

'Hello?' I said, trying to keep my tone friendly, in case he was a psychotic junkie burglar. At the sound of my voice, the man turned round and smiled. It was Percy.

I dropped my bag of shopping on the floor and made a sound that was halfway between a yelp and a squawk, I was so surprised. At that point Tom came skipping into the room.

'We tricked you, we tricked you,' he was singing, as he danced round his great uncle. 'You didn't know it was Perky, did you, Mummy? Did you? Doesn't he look brilliant? Perky, Perky, show Mummy your face properly.'

Percy had stood up and was striking poses so I could take in the full impact of his new look. The transformation really was amazing. He had another silver ring through one eyebrow and a stud beneath his lower lip. His brows, which had been delicate bleached arches ever since I had known him, were dyed as black as his hair. He was wearing black trousers with all kinds of zips and cargo pockets on them, and enormously complicated boots with laces and straps and thick soles, like tractor tyres.

'Percy,' I exclaimed, not sure what I really thought. 'You look amazing. You look so young.'

'Oh I know,' he said, draping himself languorously over the kitchen counter, the back of his hand to his brow, like a silent film star.

In fact, he looked more like some kind of superannuated thrash rocker, but in a weird way it did suit him. I had loved his old look with the mauve hair and the poet shirts, but I had to admit, the new style had taken years off him.

'Whatever prompted this astonishing make-over, Percy?' I asked him.

'I was feeling so twentieth century, darling heart,' he said. 'I looked at all the young chaps at Mardi Gras and I just thought – what the heck? I've always liked to change my look from time to time and I suddenly realized I had got stuck in a Quentin tribute time warp. Before you met me I had an Eton crop and a monocle and wore only bespoke suits and Lobb brogues, before that it was flowing blond hair, velvet trousers and Hussar coats. This is New Millennium Percy.'

'Well, I think it's great, good for you. What do you think, Tom?'

'I think it's *brilliant*,' he replied, sitting on Percy's knee and playing with his piercings. 'Who-woulda-thunk-it? Can I have my eyebrow pierced, Mummy? For my birthday?'

'No, you cannot.'

'Ohwuh. Pleeeeeease, Mummy. It's so rad and Percy said it didn't hurt.'

'No.'

'Vita's mummy has got her front bottom pierced. Vita drew me a picture.'

'Well, isn't that lovely?' I said, looking at Percy, who I could see was trying not to laugh.

'Ouch,' he said. 'Stop twiddling with that, Tom, it does hurt. I was only pretending when I said it didn't. Now run along and play with your buggery.'

Tom bounded out of the room surprisingly willingly and Percy made us some tea. He looked even more incongruous sitting there like Marilyn Manson's grandad, sipping lapsang souchong from the mauve Limoges cup and saucer I had bought him for Christmas to match his hair, but now I was getting used to it, I could see that this punk-rock-pensioner look really rather suited him.

'I'm not so sure about the piercings,' I said, 'although I know they are all the rage these days, but I really do like your hair like that. Who did it for you?'

'Greg,' he said, looking me right in the eye.

'Greg?' I squealed. 'The horrible home-wrecking, husband-stealing, hairdressing bastard?'

'That would be the one.' He sipped his tea and carried on looking at me, one of his new black eyebrows slightly raised, as if to ask me what I was going to do about it.

'And his friend, Paul, did the piercings,' he continued. 'He used to work at a tattoo and piercing parlour and he has all the gear. He's going to do a Maori symbol of strength around my left bicep next week.'

I just looked at him in amazement.

'Don't look all betrayed, Antonia,' he said.

'But I . . .' I started, but he held up his palm to stop me.

'Before you get upset, hear me out. I wouldn't want to go on a villa holiday with Greg and Paul any more than you would, but after giving it some serious thought, I think it would be better for us all if we could effect some kind of rapprochement between you and Greg. Amazing though it seems to us, Hugo seems to be stuck on him, so we are stuck with him. I didn't think it would last this long, but it has, so we have to change our tack. He has been with Hugo – officially – for over a year now and that makes him, in a way, part of the family. My family.'

I opened my mouth to protest, but he held up his hand again.

'As someone who was welcomed to the Heaveringham hearth despite my own difficult start in life,' he explained, 'and who has remained welcome at it, despite my little ways, I have to honour that family code and do my best to make Greg fit into it too. I hope he won't be with us for the long haul because, frankly, I don't think even I could put him over with Margot the moron, but I think we have to act as though he will be. You know I adore you, Antonia, but you must understand – Hugo is my favourite nephew and I want him to be happy.'

He stopped to have a sip of tea. I was still too shocked to speak.

'Now,' he went on, 'Greg has already shown a reluctance to accept your very noble overtures of friendship, probably because, deep down, he feels so guilty – he's a good Greek Orthodox boy, I have discovered from my new best friend, Paul.'

He raised his eyebrow again, to underline the irony and continued.

'So, I shall be the one to act as an emotional bridge, to bring this very modern little corner of the Heaveringham clan together.'

Another pause, another sip, while I sat and tried to take it all in.

'And above all, in this, Antonia, my concern is for darling Tom. Although he is a very good little boy about not showing you how upset he is, I know he misses his father dreadfully. But the problem is he feels guilty going round to see him at his new house, because he knows how much you hate Greg. Tom feels disloyal to you being polite to Greg and disloyal to his father if he's rude to him. It's tearing him in two, Antonia. So, there is nothing he would like more than a family dinner, with all of you there, at least appearing to get on, once a week, or so. Tom needs you and Greg at least to make a show of being friends.'

I hated the thought of it, but I knew Percy was right. I felt ill to think Tom had been unhappy and I had been oblivious to it, numbed as I was by my own pain.

'How do you know Tom feels this way about it?' I asked him. 'I thought he was over the worst of it.' I had really thought he was coping. Fooling myself, I realized, because I had wanted him to be, so badly.

'I eavesdrop on him and little Ms Vita when they are playing together. They play very elaborate games with a large cast of Barbies, Action Men and GI Joes, which are very amusing and heartbreakingly revealing.'

I sat and thought for a few moments.

'I did agree to start having Hugo here for family dinners before Christmas,' I admitted. 'But I always managed to put him off, because I didn't want to broach the Greg issue. I just couldn't stand the thought of him here, in our house, where Hugo and I had lived together.'

'Yes,' said Percy. 'Hugo mentioned the phantom dinners. So how about this? I will speak to Greg and persuade him it is in his interest to be nice to you and we'll have the first dinner out, so you don't have to worry about having Greg in your home just yet. OK?'

I nodded.

'OK.'

And then Tom walked back into the kitchen. He'd spiked his hair up like a porcupine with copious amounts of gel that Hugo had left behind and he was wearing one of my clip-on earrings on the side of one ear, another on his nostril. He'd even inked in his eyebrows with a black marker pen. He struck a pose. Percy and I laughed until we cried.

Meanwhile, the midnight gym thing was working brilliantly. With Percy taking Tom to school in the morning, I could stay in bed until nearly ten o'clock and still have the shop open by eleven, which was plenty early enough for the kind of business it was.

Falling into bed exhausted after my workout at 2 or 3 a.m., I was actually starting to have seven or eight hours sleep again, for the first time for over a year. It was bliss and I realized quite how wrung out I'd been from zeds deprivation. It had been worse even than when Tom was tiny, because there was no compensating bundle of joy to make up for it – just sad memories and fears for the future.

Some time in the third week of my night-time regime, James was back on the reception desk.

'So, how's it going, night owl?' he asked me, as he swiped my card. 'It seems the midnight shift suits you. This is your twelfth late night visit.'

He looked up at my surprised face.

'It's all on the monitor,' he said. 'I had a look when I came back from holiday tonight. I wanted to see if you'd taken my advice.'

'Well, I have,' I said. 'Thank you very much for the suggestion, James. It really works for me.'

After that, he seemed to be on reception most nights when I got there and when he wasn't, I found I rather missed him. Despite the cap and glasses that obscured his face, there was something straightforward about James that was very refreshing after all the layers of complications that seemed to accompany all my other human relations.

One night, when I was fully into the swing of driving over to East Sydney in the early hours, I didn't get there until 3 a.m. Percy had been out until after two thirty and I'd lain awake since midnight feeling annoyed that I was going to miss a session, so as soon as he'd got in, I'd jumped into my workout gear and headed for Muscle City. James was on the desk.

'Wow,' he said. 'This is late, Antonia, even for you. Welcome to your private gym.'

He nodded over his shoulder. There was no one in there at all, which was a first.

'Couldn't get here any earlier tonight,' I said.

'And couldn't bear to miss one?' he asked.

I nodded.

'You've got the bug, Antonia,' he said. 'You're a fully-fledged Muscle City workout junkie.'

My face must have dropped.

'It's not such a bad thing to be,' he continued. 'If you're going to be addicted about something, better it's exercise than drink or gambling – or work.'

He grinned and I hoped he was right as I went off to the treadmills.

Working-out in a completely empty gym had an interesting effect on me. I found it strangely hard to keep up my enthusiasm with no one else there to 'beat'.

Even if there were just a few other people, all usually hugely fitter than me, I felt a sense of unspoken competition, which kept me lifting, pushing, running, pulling, or whatever it was, slightly longer and harder than I really wanted to. With no one else there, I was just going through the motions.

I was lying on my back on the hip extension machine

gazing cross-eyed at the ceiling and on the verge of nodding off, when James appeared at my side.

'Want me to spot you?' he asked.

'That would be great,' I said, spurred back into activity.

After he'd put me through my paces there we moved on to the other machines, with James counting me down on my repetitions. It made an enormous difference. He kept one eye on the front desk and had to go over to check in a couple of wired-looking fellows, but he came straight back to me afterwards.

'OK, that's seven on the third set, just three to go,' he was saying to me on the kneeling chin-up thing, my absolutely worst machine. 'You don't like this one, do you?'

I pulled a face. 'I hate it.'

'Come on, it's just two more now, don't give up. Try to do it in one smooth move, rather than starting and stopping in the middle, that takes more energy.'

He watched me for a moment and then spoke again, softly.

'Why do you think you hate this machine particularly?' he asked.

'I find it hard to know where the muscles are to do this at all,' I said. 'It makes me feel all small and vulnerable.'

'Well, that's a good start – it's good that you can analyse what you don't like about it. That's half the battle. Do you want to try something that might help?'

'Haven't I just finished my reps on here?' I whined, sounding just like Tom trying to get out of piano practice.

'Only if you want to,' said James. 'But if you can stand

to do ten more I might be able to help you get over your emotional block about this machine.'

'Oh, all right then.'

'OK,' he said, briskly. 'Get off for a minute, I'm going to show you something.'

I clambered off the machine and after adjusting the bench height James got on. He knelt on the pad and reached up for the crossbar. I could see now what Tristan had been going on about, when he was always trying to make me place myself symmetrically on the machines. I could see that James had automatically put himself in the perfect position.

'Put ten more weights on it will you, Antonia?' he said.

I quite liked him taking charge and hopped over to do as he asked.

'Right,' he said. 'It's all in the breathing. Breathe in before you start and make the effort on the out breath. I'm sure Tristan told you all that, right?'

'Yes, he did,' I said. 'But I didn't realize it was so important.'

'The breath is everything,' said James. 'But it's not just when you breathe, it's how you breathe. Watch.'

He inhaled really slowly through his nose and his chest lifted up like a giant soufflé. I couldn't believe how much it expanded up and out and to the sides. I could almost see the air travelling down into his lungs and filling his whole torso. He held it for a few moments, with his eyes closed and then breathed out even more slowly, until gradually his chest returned to where it had started from.

'That's breathing properly,' he said. 'When we're anxious

most of us take shallow little breaths that just make us more jittery and nervous. Breathe like that a few times before you start this exercise and you will feel much more in charge of all your muscles, even the ones you think you aren't aware of. Stay conscious of your breathing the whole time while you're working-out and always make the effort on the out breath.'

I was nodding, trying to take it all in. Then he took another of his mighty breaths and as he exhaled he lifted himself up until his chin was high above the bar. The weights, which were practically on maximum, went up too, like they were cottonwool balls, with perfect control, no surges and judders like when I did it.

He lowered himself and the weights back down without making a sound – they crashed down like cymbals when I was on this machine – and got off.

'OK,' he said, smiling encouragingly. 'Your go.'

I adjusted the bench and got back on it, trying to picture my body from above so I was symmetrical. Then I closed my eyes and took the slowest, deepest breath I could manage. I held it and let it go.

'I feel dizzy,' I told him.

'Don't worry, your body's just not used to having so much oxygen in one hit. Don't try to breathe as deeply as I did at first, you'll get stoned. Work up to it gradually.'

I took another few breaths and then tried the movement again. I couldn't lift myself at all.

'Oops,' said James. 'We forgot to change the weights. I'll just do that. OK, now try it.'

It was so much easier, I couldn't believe it. Using my

breath to steady myself I could do the movement completely smoothly. I finished the ten without feeling vulnerable at all.

'That's really great, James,' I said. 'I can't believe the difference it makes.'

'Breathing is the most fundamental thing any of us do,' he said. 'It is the defining difference between life and death, yet we seem to give it less thought than anything. It's amazing when you think about it. All the ancient practices – yoga, tai chi, chi gong, all kinds of meditation – are based on the breath yet most people never even think about it. But then I'm obsessed with all that stuff, so don't start me, or I'll bore you to death with it. OK, how about getting on to that triceps extension, while I check this bloke in?'

The rest of the session went really smoothly. Concentrating on the breathing took my mind off the dull reality of lifting weights and made it all go much more quickly. Plus, having someone else there, when James came back again, made me try much harder than I ever did on my own. I was really hot by the time I finished.

'Thank you so much, James,' I said at the end, wiping my face with a towel. 'I was getting nowhere until you came over.'

'It's very hard to work-out completely alone,' he said. 'That competition effect is much more pervasive than we realize. That's why I go back to the *dojo* in Hong Kong as often as I can. I need to be pushed by being surrounded by people who are better than me.'

'Isn't there anyone better than you in Sydney?' I asked

playfully, not really having a clue what he was talking about and wondering what on earth dojos were.

'Not really,' he said, and then, with no warning, he jumped into the air, spinning round as he went, his right leg shooting out at a perfect 90 degrees, his arms slicing back and forth like pistons. It must have been over in a millisecond, but it had looked almost as though he paused in mid air, before landing back on the ground without making a sound.

'Bloody Nora,' I said, without thinking, I was so surprised. 'Bruce Lee in specs.'

I felt mortified as it came out of my mouth, but James just laughed.

'Close your mouth, Grasshopper,' he said, smiling his mysterious smile, his eyes hidden by the glinting glasses. 'A tiger might jump into it.'

That evening – and his extraordinary display – seemed to take our rather strange friendship on to another level and after that, as long as there weren't too many other people in the gym, James would always come over and spot me through my routine.

I also started hanging out for a little while after I'd finished my workout, having a bottle of water with him at the reception desk and continuing whatever conversation we'd started on the machines. He turned out to be an interesting fellow.

He'd studied martial arts in Hong Kong for several years and with the Shaolin monks in China's Henan Province. He spoke passable Cantonese and Mandarin. He worked at night, he told me, because his body was so finely tuned from the years of rigorous practice that he hardly needed any sleep. He just got bored if he stayed at home.

'You'll find you need less sleep as you get fitter, Antonia,' he told me. 'Fitness has so many benefits that people don't understand, way beyond a flat stomach and a tight butt.'

I instantly held both mine in.

'Physical fitness will make you more efficient physically and mentally,' he was saying. 'You won't get colds, you won't get those stupid little depressions, and you won't forget stuff. Already the discipline that brings you here each night is mental, Antonia, not physical. It's your mind that gets you through that door, not your legs. Carry on working-out like you are and you'll be amazed at the changes in every part of your life.'

I already was. I didn't know about the mental stuff yet, but I was definitely looking better. I had also lost the compulsion to stuff myself all the time. Now I was getting enough sleep, I didn't need to use sugar for energy hits to keep myself going through the day. And the less I pigged out, the less I wanted to pig out, until I began to slide in the other direction and it became almost a game to see just how little food I could get by on, without feeling faint.

After a couple of months, there was no doubt that the hard-core weight loss combination of eating less and exercising a lot, was working miracles. I was back into all my old clothes and some of them were even getting a little big. My legs, which had always been quite good, or so I'd been told, had a new definition in the thigh area and my upper arms were no longer shameful catastrophes to hide inside cardigans. Percy was thrilled with me.

'Oh my darling girl,' he said one day, when I was modelling a summer dress I'd bought in an end-of-season sale – white broderie anglaise with a handkerchief hem, rather like an old nightie – for him and Tom.

'You look like my own little Tess of the D'Urbervilles again,' said Percy, clapping his hands with delight. 'The Nastassja Kinski Tess, of course. Oh yes, once again I can see the fragile young thing who so enchanted me when I first saw her sitting terrified in the corner of the yellow drawing room at Willington. You were wearing petticoats then too, I remember. I was so taken with you. Isn't Mummy pretty, Tomety?'

Tom nodded and cuddled up to Percy.

'Mind you, Antonia, lose any more weight, darling, and you'll be the full Charlotte Rampling.'

He sucked his cheeks in and made a pained face.

'Who's Charlotte Dumpling?' asked Tom.

Feeling trimmer was also a great confidence booster for the first dreaded 'family' dinner and when I walked into the restaurant I saw Greg's eyes flicker over my body in surprise. I had dressed to show it off, of course, in a simple sleeveless shell top and tight bootleg pants – both black, both new.

That's something for you to tell your friend Nikki, I thought, before reminding myself I had to try to get on with Greg for Tom's sake. But before I could think about it any more, Hugo had grabbed me by both hands and was loudly admiring my new figure.

'Ant,' he said, making me do a twirl in the middle of the restaurant. 'No! You look marvellous. Oh it's good to see you looking yourself again. What a babe. No wonder I married you. I could almost turn back for you.'

Hugo's careless ability to make the most inappropriate remark possible, helped to break the ice and I have to say that Greg was behaving like a different person.

It was clearly the Percy effect. He could communicate with Greg in the international language of camp, in which they were both fluent, so he was an effective conduit to make Greg feel included in the party, even when Hugo – clearly happy to be back among his compatriots for an evening – started talking in his most arcane aristobabble, a kind of secret language only those close to the Heaveringhams could possibly understand.

Nevertheless, I could see that whatever Percy had said to Greg about the big picture had sunk in, as he was making a serious effort to be civil to me. He even told me I looked nice. Amazing.

But the main thing that made the evening bearable for me was that I could see that Greg was sincerely fond of Tom. Percy had artfully seated him between Greg and myself, and I was actually touched when my former deadly foe leaned over and cut my son's steak up for him, in a very natural way.

'You seem to be very at ease with children, Greg,' I said to him. 'Do you have younger siblings?'

He smiled, the most natural expression I had yet seen on his perfectly tanned and tended face, which I was more used to seeing thin-lipped and huffy.

'I'm the oldest of seven kids,' he said. 'I helped bring the little 'uns up. And now I have three nieces and two nephews, all under six, with two more on the way. I love kids. I wish I could have some myself.'

There was a wistfulness in his eyes, as he said it, that really surprised me. Well, blow me down, I thought, maybe there was more heart to the blow-dry king than I had ever imagined.

Who-would-a-thunk-it?

11

My trip to the Blue Mountains with Dee was a great success. She had suggested we took her car and driver, so we could relax in the back, but I insisted on going in my well-used four-wheel drive. I thought it was important for Dee to have a little taste of real life for once. I also told her to dress down as much as possible, or she'd send the prices rocketing.

She did her best, in a pair of jeans, a white T-shirt and pink Superga sneakers, a chunky cotton knit around her shoulders, all of which she admitted had been purchased specially for the occasion. I made her tie back her too-perfect hair in an elastic band, which took some persuading, and I insisted she took the huge emerald studs out of her ears. She wouldn't take off her engagement ring – another monster emerald flanked by two humongous diamonds – but she agreed to turn it round, so at least the stones weren't visible.

Satisfied she could pass as a fairly low-level dealer, like myself, we set off. She got more relaxed and skittish with every mile we drove west. By the time we got past Parramatta, I hardly knew her. She was singing along to the 80s tracks on Mix 106.5 – 'Material Girl' seemed particularly appropriate – and she insisted we stopped at a service station, so she could introduce me to the legendary sweets, or 'lollies' as she called them, of an Australian childhood. We headed up into the hills sucking on strange objects called milk bottles, freckles, bullets, jaffas and jubes – and some very alarming things called 'teeth'.

It was really nice to have some company and at our very first stop she proved herself to be a brilliant bargaining partner. It was rather a precious little shop in Springwood, from which I had never bought anything so far because the proprietor didn't understand trade prices, but I always stopped anyway – it's one of the first rules of what I do. You always have to check it out, because you never know. And boy, was I glad I had.

First of all I tripped over a whole box of old linen curtains in my favourite Sanderson print – the lilac – all beautifully soft and faded from years of wash and wear. Raking through them in a desultory way, as though hoping to find something else, I counted that there were six huge pairs. Crackerjack.

I'd just stopped myself from squealing with delight over them and was feigning my usual indifference, when I noticed a set of three blue-and-white Cornishware kitchen canisters – 'flour', 'sugar' and 'raisins'. I was a bit over them myself, but I knew they were very 'collected'. They'd be expensive, but I could still sell them for more in Woollahra. There were also three 1950s baskets of the kind that walked out of my shop after about five minutes in the window and some cute kindergarten chairs, which were another good seller.

I was looking through some old teacups, when Dee came over and very subtly kicked my leg, gesturing with her head to one side of the shop. She'd left the lid open on an old wicker laundry hamper which seemed to be full of lovely old plaid blankets and plump paisley eiderdowns. It was all I could do not to whimper. It was exactly what I needed for my winter stock and these were things you didn't find very often in quantity.

The question was, how to proceed? I didn't like the woman who owned this shop and she didn't like me. I think she recognized me from the *Vogue Living* article and jacked her margins up accordingly. It was going to take some tactical manoeuvring to get the things I wanted at the right price – and it was my most golden business rule that I did walk away, even from something I loved, if I couldn't get the right ratio between buy price and sell price in my notebook.

'What's your best price on the Cornishware?' I asked her, going straight for the most obvious items.

'$200,' she said, without smiling. 'They're very rare and very collectable.'

'Yes, they are,' I said. 'But the raisins one has a chip on it, so the best I can offer you is $100 for the three.'

'$150 is my best offer,' she said.

I stroked them, trying to look as if I desperately wanted them, which I didn't.

'I'll give you $130 for them,' I finally said, as if I couldn't help myself. 'And $75 for those three baskets.'

That gambit worked. The baskets were marked at $15 each and she thought I hadn't noticed. I'd get $65 each for them at the shop and probably $250 for the Cornishware. The chip was microscopic and I knew how to patch it. It all worked out. And the canisters were only a tactic to get the stuff I really wanted anyway.

'OK,' she said, looking very pleased with herself. She thought she'd ripped me off. I hadn't even begun.

'I'll just see if there's anything else,' I said, deliberately not looking at the blankets, or the curtains. And that was when Dee pulled her masterstroke.

She started looking at her watch.

'Ant,' she said, impatiently. 'We've got to get to Katoomba by eleven. That guy's waiting for us and he's brought all that stuff in specially. We really ought to get going and we can't fill up the car with too much junk now because he told me he had loads. And he said he can't hang around.'

'Oh right, yes,' I said, pretending to be flustered and getting a wad of cash out of my jeans pocket, deliberately letting some of it fall on the floor.

'How about the little chairs?' I asked the woman, whose eyes were fixated on the dollars. I knew women like her, the sight of cash mesmerized them. '$20 for the two?'

'$60 for the two,' she said.

'Come on, Ant,' said Dee, holding the door open. I could have kissed her.

'Oh, OK,' I said pretending to be really in a flap. 'Um, how about I give you $100 all up, plus what we agreed for the Cornishware and baskets, and you throw in that box of stuff and that old hamper as well? I haven't got time to look through it all, but I'll risk it. There might be some pillowslips at the bottom. That's $305, so shall we say a round $300?'

I peeled off the $10 notes quickly – I always get them in small denominations, because it looks like more – and when I saw her lick her lips, I knew I had her.

'OK,' she said, reaching for the money and Dee was out of the door with that laundry hamper faster than an escaping bank robber. She had it and the box of curtains in the back of the car, before the dealer even realized what she'd sold.

But the funny thing was, as we drove away with the curtains and the quilts and the blankets and the baskets and the little chairs and the stupid Cornishware, giving each other high fives as we hit the highway, we were all happy.

The dealer had made $300 on stuff she probably paid $50 for in house clearances, and by the time I sold it on, with the curtains made up into cushions and covering a couple of old armchairs from Wally's, I'd be well up into four figures. On top of that my customers would be thrilled to have a beautiful old thing that none of their friends could get. One hundred per cent satisfaction all round. That was the beauty of junketeering.

Dee proved to be an absolute natural at the whole thing. In all the shops we went to she spotted great stuff that I hadn't noticed and always knew when to pull the 'we've got to go' stunt. She also came up with another great trick, of pretending not to like something and trying to persuade me not to buy it. There was nothing like seeing a sale disappearing before their eyes, to make dealers see sense on prices.

By two o'clock, the car was full and we decided to

head back to town, after tea at a pretty little place in Black-heath.

'Dee,' I said, raising my cup in a toast. 'You're a natural.'

We clinked cups. She was absolutely glowing.

'How on earth did you know how to pull those stunts?' I asked her.

She grinned. 'I used to go shopping with my granny, in Tasmania. She was the most amazing bargain broker you can ever imagine. She was a softly spoken little Irish lady, but she could talk a donkey into giving her his tail, with his ears thrown in for good will, and I learned it all from her. Until today, I'd forgotten about it, but it was lurking inside me all along.'

'Well, thank you, Granny,' I said. 'This is the best day's junketering I've had since I opened the shop. It made such a difference having you with me. Will you come with me again sometime?'

'You bet,' said Dee, leaning across the table towards me. 'This is the most fun I've had for about fifteen years.'

Although Dee was still relatively reserved about her private life and never asked me about mine, it was really nice to have a woman friend again. I spoke to my sisters quite a bit and we e-mailed every day, but it meant a lot to me just to have a girlfriend to hang out with and twitter about things like pillowslips and mascara. Especially as Suzy Thorogood seemed to have gone cold on me.

It had happened quite abruptly. After her party we'd carried on seeing each other at least once a week, and it was always a laugh. Then suddenly she froze me out. I was really surprised, as I had always thought her a superior being to the Nikkis and Carolines of this world, but I started to wonder when she didn't return my calls after I'd left messages on her home and work numbers. I thought maybe she'd been away, but when I finally caught her on the mobile one afternoon in April, just innocently wanting to chat and make a date to meet, she was very distracted and offhand with me.

'Sorry, Ant,' she said, sounding like she was doing something else at the same time as talking to me, something she found much more interesting. 'But I've got a huge work load on at the moment, there's a big takeover bid in on one of my clients, and I'm just flat out. I'll give you a call when things lighten up, OK?'

And she'd just hung up. I was more surprised than hurt and after all I had been through I decided I just couldn't worry about it. If Suzy, who I had liked so much and who had been so nice to me, wanted to weird out, that was up to her. I was in self-preservation mode.

The only thing marring my new friendship with Dee was that Percy had taken against her. I was amazed. I always expect the people I love to adore each other, but Percy was basilisk-faced around Dee from the moment I first introduced them in the shop.

'Oh, hi Perce,' I had said, delighted, as he walked in one afternoon wearing a new pair of leather pants and a tight black T-shirt. 'I'm so glad you're here – this is Dee, who I've been telling you so much about.'

Dee was ill at ease socially in general, but Percy's cold manner rendered her mute.

'Oh yes, lovely to see you,' he said, with a curt nod and no sign of his famous charm and charisma. I'd never seen him like it before.

'Just came in to tell you,' he said to me, ignoring Dee. 'We're having a few folk over for supper tonight. That chap Maybury's quite amusing, so I've asked him again and that nice gal pal of his from *Inside* magazine, what's her name? Daisy. And that decorator chappie, Dominic. They're each bringing someone neither of us has met yet, widening our circle. Tom's going to Vita's for the night. They're coming at 7 p.m. I'm doing mussels and my rose petal sorbet. See you later.'

And off he went. I was speechless. I had never known Percy take so little interest in a human being who was new to him. Normally he was like a dog, delighted to have someone new to sniff and wag his tail at. He hadn't given Dee a chance and – even more amazing – he'd broken one of his own rules of polite conduct, he'd talked about a social event she wasn't invited to in front of her. Normally he would have kept quiet and rung me later to tell me about the dinner or, more likely, he would have invited her too. I just couldn't understand it.

It was quite clear that Dee knew she had been snubbed, but she didn't seem particularly surprised and soon made her excuses to leave. I felt desperately embarrassed and hoped she wouldn't hold it against me.

I rounded on Percy the minute I got home. He was stirring the mussels, wearing one of his old kaftans, now dyed black and studded round the neckline with steel rivets.

'Percy?' I said in a questioning tone. 'What was with you today? I've never seen you like that.'

'Like what?' he said coldly, one hand on his hip, the other holding the wooden spoon in mid air, as though it were a fan.

'So unfriendly – to Dee. What was that all about?'

'I didn't really care for Dee,' he said, sniffing and giving the pot another stir.

'But you've never met her before,' I said, mystified.

'Didn't need to. Don't like the cut of her jib, that's all. I make up my mind very quickly about people, Antonia, as you may remember from our first meeting, and she is not one for me. I'm not sure she's one for you either, but that's up to you.'

And, as he turned resolutely back to the stove, I knew that was that. Just one slightly less attractive side of Percy's eccentric personality.

Despite our earlier little spat, the evening was a great success and the new people Antony, Dominic and Daisy had brought with them were all single men – and apparently heterosexual. I had the strong feeling I was being set up and I didn't mind.

Actually it was incredibly nice to have someone male and hairy to flirt with, who didn't have better nails than I did, and they seemed nice enough chaps. Nick, Michael and John were all there to amuse me and I was quite happy to go along with it, although it did cross my mind that it was odd that three attractive men in their mid-thirties, with good jobs and excellent manners, should be single. They were classic 'spare men' as Hugo's mother would have called them. But what the heck – I was happy to have some attention.

As we were finishing the champagne Percy had served with his rose petal sorbet, he announced he was going to introduce our new friends to one of his favourite after-dinner games.

'Shoot, shag, or marry?' he said to Antony Maybury, who looked somewhat surprised at the suggestion.

'Shoot, shag, or marry . . .' continued Percy, twinkling his most mischievous smile around at everybody, but returning to Antony, whom he really enjoyed teasing. 'Cliff Richard, Clive James, Elton John?'

'Can I shoot myself?' said Antony.

'But that's no fun,' said Percy, prodding him on the arm with the mouth end of his cigarette holder. 'You have to choose. I'll give you an example. If you said that to me, I would say: shoot Clive James, he's way too smug, shag Cliff Richard – video it and sell the tape to the *News of the World* – and marry Sir Elton, just for the title, of course. Get it?'

It was clear by his snorts of laughter that Antony did. Percy looked delighted.

'OK, Antony,' he said. 'Now it's your go. Shoot, shag or marry: Andrew Lloyd Webber, George W. Bush, Ian Botham?'

Antony mulled it over, while the rest of us looked at him expectantly. He had really funny thick black eyebrows that moved up and down independently of each other. They seemed to be giving the answer in semaphore signals as he pondered.

'Shoot Lloyd Webber, shag Botham, marry Dubya,' he said at last.

Percy raised one of his own newly black brows in response.

'Very good, but may we know why, Mr Maybury?' he said.

'OK. Shoot Lloyd Webber,' said Antony, starting to enjoy himself. 'Obviously you'd be doing the world a service, no more of those ghastly muscials. Shag Botham – he'd either be a dirty fuck or fall asleep on the job – and marry Dubya, because I would, of course, love to be First Lady.'

Percy clapped with delight. 'Perfect. I knew you'd get it. Your turn, Mayflower. You have to ask the person to your right.'

It was Nick, the best looking of the spare men who'd been dragged along for my benefit. Antony eyed him up.

'OK, Nick,' he said. 'Shoot, shag, or marry – Gwynneth Paltrow, Kate Moss, Antonia Heaveringham?'

Poor Nick looked thunderstruck – how could he answer without causing offence to me? His cheeks went quite pink and he looked from me to Antony and back with his mouth open like he was watching a table-tennis match. Luckily, Percy's snorts of laughter saved him from social death.

'Oh Antony, you are naughty, but you do totally get the game, you bad boy. Now Nick, you don't have to answer that, it was impertinent, but it's your turn to ask Antonia, because she's on your right.'

Nick turned to me, still looking pink.

'Er, Antonia,' he said. He really was quite attractive when you looked at him properly. Blue eyes, black hair – always a good combo – and he was nice and tall too. 'Shoot, shag, or marry – Michael, John, or me?'

This time it was my turn to blush and I thoroughly enjoyed it. I felt quite girly batting my eyelashes at him and telling him he was awful. He had just dopishly copied Antony's joke, with a lot less subtlety, but it didn't matter. It was just really nice to have somebody paying sexy attention to me in a cute, charming way. Up until then the only straight male attention I'd had since Hugo left, was David Maier's unwelcome assault.

And I was even happier by the time they'd left, because all three spare men had separately asked me for my phone number.

Percy had done it again.

It was past two by the time they'd all gone home and I'd had far too much to drink to drive to Muscle City, so I allowed myself a night off from it. I didn't go the next night either. I went to a movie with Michael, followed by dinner, which was a novelty. An evening out – with a man. I couldn't think of anything to say to him, but it was nice to be asked and especially so soon after meeting him. He'd rung me at the shop the next morning.

I'd been on a date, I suddenly realized, lying in bed afterwards. The first date I'd ever been on really, unless you counted that coffee with Hugo in the Medieval History department cellar. My other dalliances, prior to Hugo, had just sort of happened – on the ski lift, in the camp kitchens – without any formal dates. Now I needed a little black book to keep track of my love life – as both the other spare men, John and Nick, had already rung to ask me out the following week. I felt like hot stuff.

When I walked into the gym at midnight on the third night, James seemed pleased to see me.

'Hey, Antonia,' he said. 'I thought you'd given up on us.'

I stuck my tongue out at him and jumped onto a treadmill. The gym was busier than usual, but then I was there earlier than I usually went. It was amazing the difference even half an hour made at that time of night.

I got on with my thing, but while having more people around helped to keep me focused, I rather missed James's encouraging comments. I sneaked a few looks over to the front desk to see what he was doing and he was always busy checking people in and out and selling them protein drinks.

It surprised me to realize how much I missed chatting to him. It took my mind off the tedium of the repetitive exercises, but it was more than that. I just liked talking to him. He was so different from the other people I knew.

Chatting to James wasn't all wordplay and wit and verbal high-wire acts, it was just, well, talking. He did have a sense of humour, of course, and we laughed a lot, but it wasn't all so highly strung and hysterical as it was with my usual friends.

We were so different from each other, I reflected, trying to remember when to breathe in and out on the seated leg curl. We came from such disparate circumstances and experiences, we couldn't assume things about each other, like mutual references. It made me realize that most of the conversations I had with Percy and Tom, especially with Hugo, and even with the people at Percy's dinner party, were all in some kind of coded language, which was often almost the point of the conversation, rather than what we were actually saying.

Talking to James, I had to think a bit more than I was used to. Like the breathing he had taught me, I had to stay conscious and work at it, but that felt good in itself. And I liked the way his mouth curled at the edges when he smiled.

And after the hurt inflicted on me by Hugo and the let down of the women friends I thought I'd made in Sydney, it was also great, I thought, to have a platonic friendship with a straight man. Well, I assumed James was straight. After Hugo's revelation, I'd never be entirely sure again, but he certainly seemed pretty hetero.

It was funny how I could chat to him, I thought, a rather odd, loner kung fu freak who worked in an all-night gym, but I'd found it very hard to think of anything to say to Michael the Spare Man the night before. I would have thought I'd have had more in common with a stockbroker, I'd known enough of them in London, after all, but in his case we'd ended up having a very tedious conversation which was more like a verbal list of every film each of us had ever seen. Not even very many of them the same. I'd glazed over for good at *Terminator 2*.

I wondered if it would be easier with Spare Men John and Nick, when I had dinner with each of them the following week. John was something in marine insurance, so I rather thought it wouldn't in his case, but it would be a lark, just the same, going on another date. Nick was a journalist though, so he ought to have something to say.

He was taking me to a very fashionable new restaurant that I'd been reading about in the social pages, which should be fun, I thought. I was sitting on the abs machine wondering what to wear to it, when James appeared. He never made a sound when he moved and I would just look up and find him there. He watched me for a while and then adjusted the weights on the machine.

'It's too light for you, Antonia,' he said. 'No wonder you were getting bored with coming here, it's not a challenge for you any more. I think you need to add two kilos to all the machines to keep yourself interested.'

'Oh, I didn't miss coming because I was bored,' I told him, panting slightly at the strain of the increased weight. 'I've been out on the town dating sexy single Sydney men.'

Somehow, over the weeks, I'd told James all about my marital break-up. I wasn't even sure how the conversation had gone that way, but once I'd started I'd just told him the lot. He hadn't seemed shocked or particularly surprised, just pleasantly sympathetic. It had been good to talk about it in a matter of fact way, with someone who didn't know any of the protagonists, except me, and who didn't secretly relish the gossipy scandalous side of it.

I'd also told him all about Tom and the shop and Percy

and he'd taken it all in with interest, without passing any judgements. I suppose he was what they call a good listener.

As he knew all about my disastrous love life, I thought he'd be interested in the bright new turn it had taken. I was rather excited about it, but James didn't look particularly thrilled for me – not that it was ever easy to know what he was thinking under that stupid hat.

'So you're heading into the Eastern Suburbs singles scene, are you?' he asked, leaning against the machine in his usual navy nylon tracksuit pants and white polo shirt. 'That's seven, Antonia. Just three to go. Keep your neck soft.'

'Well, I've been on one date and I have another two next week, so I suppose I am. All these handsome men just keep ringing me up and asking to take me out.'

I knew I sounded silly, babbling on like a teenager, but it made such a change to have something to be silly about.

'Nine, ten,' said James. 'Good. Have a break before the next lot. That's great, Antonia – about the men. I hope you have fun. Not that I'm surprised all these guys want to take you out, you're very pretty, as I'm sure you know. But I must tell you one thing.'

I lay on the machine and looked up at him. I was glad he thought I was pretty. I was turning into a boy magnet. Cool bananas – as Tom had taken to saying. But James was looking quite serious.

'OK, start the next set,' he said. 'One, two, don't forget your breathing . . .'

'So what is this thing that you must tell me?' I asked, hoping it would be something else about me being pretty.

167

'Oh,' said James, looking a bit reluctant to go on, after all. 'I don't want to scare you, but there is a certain kind of man in Sydney, Antonia – especially in the Eastern Suburbs – who preys on single women. That's ten. Let's go on to the adductor.'

He fiddled with the weights and stood politely to the side as I sat there feeling ridiculous with my legs splayed wide open, struggling to bring them back together with the heavier load on board.

'You . . . were . . . saying . . .' I grunted out, still unable to close my legs entirely.

'Take it slowly, I've jacked the weight up quite a bit. Breeeeeeathe . . .'

'Carry on telling me about these men, James,' I said testily. 'I want to hear what you have to say.'

'Oh, look,' he said. 'I'm sure these blokes you're seeing are very nice, but just watch out for yourself, that's all. There are so many gay men in that scene, that any straight guy can start to look like something special and those creeps really play on that. They might seem like "gentlemen", but they collect scalps, if you know what I mean. I know a lot of the girls who come in here and I've heard some really bad sob stories. Single women can be very vulnerable in this town.'

Now I really was annoyed. How dare he tell me that Nick and John and Michael were creeps? He didn't even know them. What a spoilsport. Just when I was feeling good about myself and having a bit of harmless fun, he'd gone all moralistic and was making me out to be some kind of pathetic victim. I was really grumpy with him.

'So what about you then?' I said snippily. 'Maybe it's yourself you're describing, seeing as you know so much about it – and if you meet so many sad single girls in here, perhaps you prey on vulnerable women yourself, eh, James?'

He stood up.

'No, Antonia, I do not,' he said, sounding cooler than I'd ever heard him. 'If you really want to know – I'm celibate. I conserve my chi for my practice.'

He placed his hands together at his chest and bowed to me, before walking away. When I left the gym half an hour later, he was nowhere to be seen.

12

A couple of days later I was in the shop, with Dee helping me to do the new winter window display, featuring the quilts and the blankets we'd bought in the Blue Mountains. It was looking wonderful.

With no prompting from me she'd brought along some beautiful dark red bare branches from her garden, which looked really stunning in a huge green 1940s vase we'd found on our most recent mission to Newcastle.

We'd draped the quilts over the kindergarten chairs, which were yellow and green, and we'd filled the 50s baskets with gumnuts and fir cones. With the adorable woolly animals I had Country Women's Association members across NSW knitting for me, popping up throughout the window, the whole thing looked really cosy. We went outside to admire our handiwork.

'I feel a bit guilty,' said Dee as we stood and gazed at it. 'If I'd seen this window a year ago, I would have come in here and bought the lot. You've done yourself out of your best customer by being so nice to me, Antonia.'

'If you hadn't come on the last two buying trips with me, I wouldn't have most of this stuff,' I said. 'And windows as lovely as this will bring lots of new customers in.'

'They would if you had more passing trade,' said Dee.

'I only came the first time because I'd seen the articles in *Belle* and *Inside*.'

It was the truth. I was doing OK, but I could be doing so much better if I was actually on Queen Street where the action was.

'You're right,' I said. 'But them's the breaks. I have to be satisfied with what I have.'

The phone rang and I ran inside. It was Percy.

'Is that awful Dee there?' he asked.

'No,' I said, crossly. 'But my friend Dee's here. Why?'

'I need to talk to you urgently, but not in front of her. Call me back when she's gone.'

'I will do no such thing,' I replied. 'You're only five minutes away, give it an hour and try your luck.'

He put the phone down.

He was in luck, because shortly afterwards Dee left for one of her twice-weekly facials, so when Percy came creeping along the other side of the street, trying to see if she was there, she had already gone. He came through the door making the air raid siren all-clear noise. He was wearing new leopardskin print jeans.

'You really must get over this Dee paranoia, Percy,' I said. 'I'm beginning to find it very tedious. I really like her and I'm not going to stop being her friend, so deal with it.'

And she's the only girlfriend I've got these days, I thought, although I didn't voice it.

'Oh simmer down, Antonia,' he said, throwing a pile of patchwork knitted blankets onto the floor and settling himself down into one of the shop's armchairs. 'Pass me some needlepoint, I'm in the mood.'

171

I handed him an embroidery frame set up with a new cushion cover I was developing. So far the canvas had the words 'Too Rich, Too Thin' traced on it in pencil, with the outlines of some curly borders. I'd already done the background in navy and was still deciding what colours to do the swirls and lettering in. Percy snorted with laughter when he saw it.

'Very good,' he said. 'You can give one to your dear friend Dee for Christmas. And to that busy little body Suzy Thorogood. I saw her scampering along Queen Street just now, like a nasty little bony crab. You really are a hopeless judge of character, Antonia, but you clearly know your customers, these cushions will sell out immediately. I think we should do the lettering and curlicues in two shades of rich red and a very expensive-looking beige.'

I chucked him my bag of wool and he threaded a needle with dark crimson.

'What were you in such a flap to tell me earlier?' I asked him, as I put some tea into the pot.

'Oh yes,' he said, with great enthusiasm, settling himself in the chair like an old dog. 'I'd completely forgotten. You know that Nick fellow we had to dinner last week – has he rung to ask you out?'

'Yes,' I said, proudly. 'We're going out on Friday, to that new restaurant down at Woolloomooloo, the one that's always in the social blight pages. Pansy's, or Panda's, or whatever it's called. What do you think I should wear?'

'Nothing,' said Percy vehemently.

'Oh, come on, Perce, I'm not that desperate for a snog.'

'I mean,' he said, with great drama. 'That you must *not* go.'

'What are you talking about?' I said. 'I'm really looking forward to it. I haven't been anywhere exciting for months and I think he's rather cute. I love that dark hair, blue-eyed look of his.'

'No no NO!' said Percy at increasing decibels. 'You must call him at once and cancel. I had lunch with Antony today and he told me everything.'

'Everything what?'

'Apparently, he's an absolute rogue.'

He uttered the words with his most theatrical relish. He'd make a marvellous Lady Bracknell, I thought, in this mode.

'What do you mean he's an "apsol-yoot rrrrrrrrrogue"?' I asked him, imitating his pronunciation.

'A total wolf. Legendary throughout the Eastern Suburbs for preying on defenceless women. And – so Antony tells me – there's nothing he relishes more than the chance to spoil a pretty English gel, fresh off the boat, before she hears about his terrible reputation.'

'I came on a plane, Percy. Over two years ago. And I'm hardly a gel – I'm a wife and mother.'

'Oh, don't be so pedantic, you know exactly what I mean. You're new blood in the singles meat market and he's sniffed you out like a cunning old ferret.'

I had to laugh, but at the same time, I was beginning to feel a little uneasy. It all tied in horribly with what James had told me.

'What about the other two spare men who came for

173

dinner – are they wolf ferrets too?' I said. 'Because they've both asked me out as well. In fact I went out with Michael the other night. I didn't tell you, because I didn't want any fuss about it.'

'Was he the dull one?' asked Percy.

I nodded. 'He likes action movies,' I said.

Percy raised his eyes to the ceiling.

'God preserve us. Yes, no, apparently he's relatively harmless. The worst he does is bore women to death. Even very stupid girls tire of him quickly, according to Antony, which is a shame, because he's got pots of money and a huge willy. Antony's always trying to pair him off with his divorced clients, but it never works.'

'So that explains why he's single. What about the other one – John?'

Percy thought for a while, holding his thread in the air, mid-stitch, trying to remember.

'Oh yes, I've got it. He's the stalker. Terrible problems with his mother. Falls madly in love with any woman he thinks mummy might deem "suitable" – she's a frightful cow apparently – and then stalks them like a jealous psycho if they don't respond. Or, if he thinks they're attractive, but not at all suitable, he just chats them up, shags them, dumps them and tells everyone about it, just like that Nick Pollock fellow.'

I sat down and exhaled deeply.

'Let me get this right,' I said. 'You asked Antony, Dominic and Daisy to bring some nice single men to our house for me to meet and that trio of sociopaths was the best they could come up with?'

Percy chortled.

'Antony says they were the only ones they could think of who were single, hetero, relatively entertaining and could be taken out in public. They weren't expecting you to marry any of them.'

'Well, it sounds like they should have come with health warnings attached. Beware: highly toxic.'

'That's why Antony called me for lunch. It had already got back to him that Nick was bragging about you around town and how you were gagging for him, so he thought you should be warned.'

'Well, I suppose I should be glad of Sydney's over-efficient bush telegraph for once,' I said, handing Percy his cup of tea. 'I'm going to cancel those dinners right now.'

I went behind the counter to find the numbers and nearly had a heart attack when Percy suddenly shrieked, 'Oh my GOD!' terribly loudly.

'Whatever's wrong now?' I asked him. 'I nearly had a cardiac arrest.'

'No!' said Percy, in full Heaveringham flow. 'I nearly forgot the other thing I had to tell you. I must be going potty. Guess what?'

'I have no idea and I've had almost enough surprises for one day.'

'No, no, this is good news. Nikki's Knacks is closing. Paul told me. It's been haemorrhaging cash since it opened, as you can imagine, and apparently Nikki's husband blew up and told her she had to close it immediately. He hits her apparently. Isn't that horrid? Anyway, his business isn't doing too well either, at the moment, and he doesn't think it's adding to his image having such a public failure on Queen Street, where all their friends and associates can see it.'

I felt sorry for Nikki if David did hit her, no woman deserves that, not even her, but I was so pleased the shop was going I was jumping up and down and clapping.

'Paul's furious,' Percy was saying. 'Because he left his job at the piercing parlour specifically to work there and of course Nikki is blaming the shop's failure entirely on him. Says he put customers off, which is true, of course, he's absolutely poisonous, but nobody could have sold that dreadful tat, especially at those prices. Not even me.'

As Percy twittered and stitched on, I was beaming with happiness that justice had prevailed, but I was also having another little thought I wasn't going to share with Percy just yet.

If Nikki's Knacks was closing, that gorgeous little corner shop on Queen Street would be up for lease again and if I got Dee on board as a business partner, I just might be able to afford it. And I wouldn't even have to paint the exterior.

I went to Muscle City late that night – to see James as much as to work-out. I wanted to thank him for warning me about the Wolves of Woollahra. He'd been absolutely right and I owed him an apology. But when I got there he wasn't on the desk. Instead it was another, rather burly, hairy fellow I didn't like much. I'd seen him there before, talking to James. I thought he looked like a Hell's Angel and he probably was one, judging by his filthy old Harley Davidson T-shirt and the tattoos on his hands. His fingers said 'LOVE' and 'HATE' and his name badge said 'Spider'.

'James not working tonight?' I asked casually, handing over my membership card.

'No,' said Spider, sniffing contemptuously and punching in something on the keyboard.

He looked up at me.

'You're that chick he's always talking to, aren't you?' he said and chuckled to himself. 'If you really want to know, he's off on one of his mystery jobs. The Inspector Morse of Muscle City.'

'Is he a policeman?' I squeaked.

'Shit no, it's not quite that bad. He's a private dick.'

I must have looked bewildered. I wished Spider would speak English.

'He's a private detective,' he said, slowly, like I was retarded. 'People pay him to poke around where he's not wanted. Hasn't he told you all about it when he's chatting you up on the adductor? I've seen him at it. Not that it'll get you anywhere.' He laughed coarsely, so I reckoned I wasn't the only one who knew about James's elective celibacy.

'Fuckin' kung fu weirdo,' he said, scratching his stomach and smiling to himself. I noticed he had several teeth missing. 'Mind you, I wouldn't wanna be in a fight with him. Here's your card, darlin'.'

I did my routine very quickly and went home. Muscle City didn't seem such a safe place with Spider on the door and even less so when a group of enormous thugs came in at 3 a.m., still wearing their bouncer dinner jackets and dicky bows. I fled while they were still high-fiving Spider and calling each other 'bro'.

I didn't fancy another evening with the bikies, so I got Dee to ring Muscle City the next day to ask who was going to be on the desk that night. I didn't want my Pommy accent to give me away. She did a really good job, putting on a very believable whiny nasal voice and making up some cod story about having to give James back something she'd borrowed.

I had to put my hand over my mouth, to stifle my laughter until she put the phone down.

'You constantly surprise me, Dee,' I said.

She smiled like a naughty cat.

'Granny again?' I asked.

'Yep,' said Dee. 'She used to come up with the best excuses when I didn't want to go to school. She could do a perfect impersonation of the district nurse. I used to put her knitting in my mouth while she was doing it, so they wouldn't hear me laughing.'

'Did you live with your granny when you were little?'

Dee got her nervous look on. My questions were getting too personal.

'Yes. She brought me up. My parents, er, left. Anyway, I'm afraid your friend Spider's on the desk again tonight. They're not expecting James back until Sunday.'

I was at the gym by midnight on the appointed day, but James still wasn't in evidence, there was yet another guy on the desk. At least it wasn't Spider, I told myself, but I felt really deflated James wasn't there, because I'd geared myself up for the big apology. I'd been practising what I was going to say.

About an hour later, when I'd nearly finished my circuit, I was straining on the chin-up machine when I heard that wonderfully deep voice by my head.

'Sure you've got that on the heavier weight, Antonia?' it said.

I nearly brained myself on the crossbar I was so pleased to see him.

'Jim of the gym!' I said, beaming. 'You're finally here. You've been away . . .'

I petered out, not sure if I was meant to know about his other job, or whether it was even true. Spider was probably just making it up to be weird.

'Yeah,' said James, sighing quite heavily. 'I had a job on. How are you anyway? Get back to your reps, Mrs. You can talk while you do it. Where were you up to with this lot? I know how much you like this machine – not – so I'd better keep an eye on you.'

'I've done my first ten – and, yes, it is on the heavier weight and, yes, I am suffering.'

'Good.'

He counted me down through the next set and I didn't really feel up to talking at the same time. Even with my new breathing routine, I still hated that machine. When I'd moved over to lying on my back on the hip extension, I felt a bit more sociable.

'So have you been away?' I asked, trying to sound artless.

'No, I was in Sydney, doing another job I do sometimes,' he paused. 'I thought Spider told you about it.'

He was smiling his secret smile. I grinned back, knowing I was found out. He must be good at his other job, I thought. He was good at tricking things out of people.

'Well, he did mention something about it,' I said. 'But I wasn't sure whether to believe him. I didn't think private detectives really existed.'

'Well, it's nothing like Humphrey Bogart, or Hercule Poirot for that matter, but we definitely exist. There's quite a few of us in Sydney actually, the place is so goddamned corrupt, no one trusts the police here.'

'Yes, I read that thing in the paper about the policeman who sold his badge to a known criminal. I couldn't believe it.'

'Believe it,' said James, getting up and stretching his arms above his head.

'Ooh, I'm stiff,' he said, doing side bends. 'I spent all last night sitting in my car. Gets pretty cold and cramped at 4 a.m., let me tell you.'

He was turning his head from side to side and as his right arm went up to cradle the side of his neck, I saw the muscle on his bicep pop up like a fish leaping out of a river. Something went ping in my stomach. Well, a bit lower than my stomach actually. It wasn't a feeling I'd ever had before. It was like a twinge. A nice twinge.

He didn't seem aware that I was staring at him and as he carried on stretching and bending I looked at him properly, really for the first time. Up until then I had been so distracted by the hat and glasses and the horrid nylon track pants, I hadn't taken the rest of him in. Now I looked properly I saw he was tall, his shoulders were broad, he had a well-developed chest and I could see, through his white polo shirt, that his stomach was as hard and flat as the bench I was lying on. As he bent deeply to one side his shirt came untucked and I had an eyeful of smooth brown skin.

Crikey, I thought. So this is what they call lust.

I was so fascinated by what I was looking at, I'd come to a complete standstill on the machine. James suddenly opened his eyes and looked at me mid-side bend. He held my gaze just for that one beat longer that let me know he'd realized I'd been ogling him. I had another twinge.

'How many's that, Antonia?' he asked, straightening up, with a very small twinkle somewhere at the back of his eyes.

'I've got no idea,' I said.

'Right then,' he said, leaning over and putting another weight on the stack. 'You'll start again then.'

After that he had to leave me to it because there was some kind of commotion at the front desk. I dutifully finished my sets, gathered up my bag and towel and walked to the door. James wasn't there. I didn't want to go without saying goodbye to him and in all my hot and bothered confusion I still hadn't thanked him for warning me about Sydney's sleazy men.

I asked the other guy on the desk if he was still around. He nodded and picked up a phone.

A few moments later James came down the stairs, taking them three at a time, I noticed.

181

'You done?' he asked, smiling. 'Did all your reps? Still breathing?'

I nodded.

'Good girl. Want to have a bottle of water with me, before you go?'

I nodded again. I felt shy now every time I looked at him. I'd never seen such a flat muscular stomach. Hugo was slim, but there wasn't any muscle to speak of, he was like a long piece of pasta. James appeared to be more like a well-trimmed side of beef.

He got two bottles of water out of the fridge behind the desk and we went and sat on the squashy old vinyl chairs by the main entrance.

'So, you never told me what you've been up to, since I saw you last,' he said, screwing the top off his water and throwing it across the room, right into the bin. I threw mine the same way and totally missed.

'Well, nothing actually,' I said. 'And that's what I wanted to thank you for.'

He put his head on one side and blinked at me. Then he did something he'd never done before – he tipped his hat back and took his glasses off. I only caught a glimpse before he put them back on again, because he was rubbing his eyes, but he looked very different without them. Twinge number three. This was getting embarrassing.

'You wanted to thank me for nothing?' he said.

I could see he was really tired. It reminded me of Tom, trying desperately not to look sleepy so he wouldn't have to go to bed. It wasn't the time for deep and meaningfuls, I realized, and suddenly I felt all shy and weird with him anyway. In fact I felt a bit hot and light-headed and wondered if I'd overdone it on the machines, or whether it was just some kind of lust-induced body shock. Either way my mouth wasn't working properly.

'Oh, it was just that I wanted to thank you for warning me about those guys,' I blurted, in a big rush. 'The ones that wanted to take me out. You were absolutely right about them. They were all famous creeps. The guy who introduced them to me told Percy to warn me off them.'

James sighed.

'Was one of them called Nick Pollock, by any chance?' he asked.

'Yes,' I answered, amazed. 'How on earth did you know that?'

'Oh you know, I hear things round and about and I know what he's like. I've been hired twice to follow him – by two different women who thought they were engaged to him at various times. In both cases they didn't like the photographs I presented them with.'

'That bad?' I said.

He nodded. 'Yeah, he really is a supercreep. He's not even smart about it. He was supposedly engaged to these women and I caught him on film pashing other girls in his own car. He didn't even make it interesting for me.' He shrugged his shoulders, holding his hands out like a Frenchman. 'He's not just a creep, he's a stupid creep.'

'Did you know it was him, when I was talking about my fabulous dates the other night?'

'Not for a fact, but I had a hunch it might be. That Eastern Suburbs scene is pretty predictable.'

'I'm sorry I was snippy with you, James,' I said. 'I just didn't want to hear it.'

'That's all right, Grasshopper,' he said, and he stood up. 'You're still learning about this town. See you later, I've got to go and work.'

And he tweaked the end of my nose. Twinge.

13

When I got home that night I dropped immediately into a deep, almost drugged sleep, but I was plagued by strange and disturbing dreams, which were so vivid I didn't know whether I was awake or asleep while I was having them. At one point I woke up with my entire body drenched in sweat. My nightie was wet through and I had to dry the bed with my hairdryer before I could go back to sleep. As soon as I slipped into unconsciousness again, the dreams – or nightmares, I wasn't sure which they were – came back.

Even when I did wake up in the bright morning light, I still felt full of all the strange physical sensations and emotions my subconscious had thrown out at me in the night and I was reluctant to let it all go. For quite a while, I just lay there, trying to stay suspended in that strange place between sleep and wakefulness.

All the dreams were about James. And they were very rude.

Of course, my strange visions were confused and non-sensical, as dreams always are, with graphic scenes of James naked, stretching his body and reaching out for mine, mixed in with Hugo telling me he could turn back for me, Percy telling me I was his little Tess and Nick Pollock's handsome face looming around like a terrifying demon, his black hair peaked into horns, morphing into David Maier and then back into James again.

When I did wake up properly I felt really embarrassed and almost ashamed, like I'd done something dirty. But it was as though my body had made a decision about something that my mind wasn't ready to accept. Maybe it was something to do with getting fitter and really being aware of my physicality for the first time, but it seemed as though my body was acting out what my brain couldn't deal with – that I needed to have sexual contact with someone. Soon.

Although I could analyse that in my head – after all, it had been well over a year since I had even kissed anyone, if you didn't count David Maier and I certainly didn't – I was still confused and disturbed by the graphic nature of my dreams.

Why James, I wondered. I didn't really know the guy and apart from lifting weights, I had nothing in common with him. Spider was right, he was a kung fu weirdo – and a celibate one at that. I'd never even seen him without his hat on and, given his philosophical stand on sex, I was unlikely ever to see him naked. He clearly had a great body, but if I was going to get sent into a frenzy by every flat stomach and broad chest I saw, Sydney was going to keep me busy – it was full of men who were 'built', as Percy called it.

Even once I was up I felt like I was wading through treacle and, though I did it every day, it seemed an awfully long walk from home to the shop. I didn't get there until midday and Dee was waiting on the doorstep. She had her mobile to her ear, which reminded me that I'd forgotten to turn mine on. All I wanted to do was get inside and sit down. Dee looked concerned when she saw me.

'Are you all right, Ant?' she asked. 'I've been trying to call you.'

She looked closely at my face and touched my arm. 'You don't look too well, you know.'

As she spoke to me, reality seemed to dissolve like a Berocca tablet in a glass of water and I fell to the pavement in a heap.

I don't remember how she got me inside, or how long passed but at some point, I saw Percy's face looming over mine and he was dabbing my forehead with a cool wet hankie, faintly scented with lavender.

'It's all right, my little Tess,' he was saying. 'I'm taking you home.'

I don't remember getting there, only waking up in my own bed some time later, with a pounding headache. My head felt like a cracked egg. Percy was at my side, holding my hand. Through a gap in the curtains I could see it was dark outside.

'What happened, Perce?' I croaked.

'Oh darling,' he said. 'You're not at all well. You have a raging temperature and the doctor says you have to rest. Do you remember the doctor coming?'

'No.'

'He says you're completely exhausted. You've been doing too much.'

'But what about Tom?' I said, trying to sit up and just

falling back again. I suddenly felt terribly sick and was relieved to see that Percy had put a bucket next to the bed.

'Tom's fine. He's staying at Vita's for a couple of days and when you're a bit better he'll come back here and I'll look after both of you.'

I was still fretting. My mind wouldn't stop racing.

'But what about the shop? I can't leave it closed, when I've just got the new stock in . . .'

'Your friend Dee is looking after the shop.'

I turned my head to look at him and it felt like a lump of lead was rolling around inside my skull. But even through my fug, I was surprised at his tone. It didn't sound at all contemptuous.

'Maybe she's not as bad as I thought,' he said. 'Now drink this water and then try to go back to sleep. I'm just going to sit here quietly, in case you need me, so you don't need to be afraid.'

I squeezed his hand and my eyes filled with tears. What had I done to deserve a friend like Percy? He squeezed my hand back and passed me a glass of deliciously cool water, holding my head up so I could drink it.

I lay back blinking and when I looked up at Percy I saw he was looking at me with an expression of great concern. Crikey, I thought, I must be terribly ill.

'What?' I said to him. We knew each other so well, one word was often all we needed to communicate.

'Who's David?' he asked quietly.

I was puzzled.

'I don't know anyone called David . . .' I started to say,

then I remembered David Maier. 'Why?' I asked quietly.

'When you were out for the count this afternoon,' said Percy, 'you were ranting and raving quite a lot and you kept saying "David, no. David, stop it." It was quite distressing.'

I did the only thing I could do. I burst into tears. When I had recovered sufficiently, I told him the story of my horrible encounter with David Maier at Suzy's party.

It was hard to tell it and I couldn't look at him while I was doing it, but I felt better when I had. When I finally looked back at Percy I saw that he had tears flowing down his cheeks. He sat on the side of the bed and gave me a big, yet gentle hug.

'My poor darling little Tess,' he said, kissing my forehead. 'I would like to have that bastard killed for what he did to you and if I were more of a man, I would go out and do it myself. But don't worry about it any more. It's all in the past, you're OK and you have Percy here to look after you. I won't leave you until I know you're safe.'

And he held me in his arms, a vague smell of lavender emanating from his black kaftan, until I sank back into a dead sleep.

I stayed in bed for over a week. Although Percy did his best with tempting invalid meals, which he said were straight out of Mrs Beeton, I found it very hard to eat anything and even getting up to go to the loo made me light-headed.

Tom came home and although it was lovely to see him I found his hectic energy exhausting.

'Are you having a fatigue hump, Mummy?' he asked me, lying next to me and gazing earnestly into my eyes. Then he jumped up and trudged round the room in a circle, singing a new song he had made up.

'A hump, a hump, ahumpahumpa hump,' he intoned, his shoulders slumped like someone very tired. Normally I would have found it hilarious, but in my clapped-out state it was all too much.

It was like having Tigger bouncing around the room every time he came in to see me and after a couple of days Percy sent him to stay with Hugo and Greg. Like everything Percy did, it saved the day and was also a very politic move, because I was too knackered to object to him staying there and it was an important milestone for us all to get over.

Hugo came to see me quite often, bringing some very nice flowers and a card from Greg. Dee called in every day on her way home from the shop, with bottles of exotic mineral water, exquisite pieces of fruit and the latest air freight magazines. She had a perfect bedside manner, which didn't exhaust the patient, and knew exactly how long to stay. I could see Percy warming towards her with every visit.

In the second week I felt well enough to get dressed, but not to leave the house. I spent most of my time lying on the sofa watching terrible daytime television. I tried to do needlepoint but it gave me an instant headache, as did reading.

I was starting to eat a little and one night Percy invited Dee to stay for supper with us. I sipped some delicious chicken broth he had boiled up, using two very expensive organic chickens, and allowed the quiet prattle of their conversation to wash over me.

In gentle tones, guaranteed not to stress me, Dee reassured me that everything was going well at the shop and said that she was quite happy to carry on minding it as long as I needed her to. Frankie didn't mind, she said, he thought it was a suitably ladylike activity for her – and he said it kept her out of the other shops in Woollahra.

Then Percy pulled one of his stunts.

'Did you know Nikki's Knacks has closed down?' he asked Dee.

'Well, I had noticed it hasn't opened for a few days,' she said.

'Why don't you two go into business together?' he said casually, as he gathered up our plates. 'With some capital input from you, Dee, the two of you could afford to lease that Queen Street shop, which is bigger than the current place, as well as being in an infinitely better location.'

Dee and I looked at each other, our eyes wide open. It was just what I had planned to suggest to her.

Percy fished around in the pocket of his leopardskin jeans.

'Here's the card of the estate agent who's re-leasing it,' he said, handing it to Dee and walking out of the room.

Dee and I looked at each other again, waiting for the other to say something and then we both spoke together.

'Go on, Antonia,' she said, as we stopped again, laughing.

'Well, would you like to come into business with me?'
I said. 'I had been planning to ask you about it the day I
got ill.'

She looked really happy.

'There is nothing I would like more, Antonia,' she said.
'I had been wondering if I could suggest it to you, but I
didn't know how to bring it up. It seemed a bit cheeky,
but yes, I would love it.'

I put my hand out and we shook on it.

'Once I'm better, we can make it all official with a
lawyer,' I said. 'But from now on I am quite happy to think
of it as our business. I trust you to do what you think is
right, while I'm not there.'

Percy came back in to find us grinning at each other.

'So that's settled then, is it?' he said. 'Jolly good. Now
who would like some nice milk jelly?'

By the third week I felt well enough to go out on small
expeditions and Dee drove me slowly up to the shop
to make sure I was happy with the way she was doing
everything. She'd had to change the window, as most of
the winter display had been sold and I loved what she'd
done instead.

It was all pink and white and red with lovely twigs of
quince blossom arranged in old white china jelly moulds
– and knitted piglets she'd ordered specially from the
CWA, walking around them in a circle. There was a set of
red-and-white 1950s kitchen canisters and stacks of
checked tea towels tied up with stripy ribbon. It was really
charming.

'Percy's milk jelly gave me the idea for moulds. Do you think it works?' she asked shyly.

'It's absolutely brilliant,' I said, hardly able to believe I had found such a perfect business partner – who had immaculate good taste and stacks of cash to invest in the enterprise.

With a little bit of negotiating coaching from Frankie, Dee had done a great deal on the corner shop lease and we were due to move into it in six weeks' time, once all the paperwork was sorted out.

It transpired that Nikki had refused to pay the last two months' rent, claiming the landlord had been negligent about some cooked-up problem with the drains, which she asserted had made a bad smell affecting custom, so it was not the simple handover it could have been. But as far as we knew, she didn't know it was us who was taking over, or I'm sure she would have made it even harder.

It felt good to be out in the world again, but I still felt very weak and woozy. Loud noises startled me and if I did anything too strenuous I came out in a muck sweat and waves of vertigo took me over. I didn't feel safe crossing the road on my own, because I wasn't sure where my foot ended and the world began.

It was a very strange sensation, which my doctor said was caused simply by stress and exhaustion – and working-out in the middle of the night, practically seven nights a week, probably didn't help either when I wasn't used to that much physical activity. He also thought losing weight as quickly as I had would not have been great for my system either. I didn't tell him I'd been practically starving myself. I'd learned my lesson about that.

At the end of the third week, I was lying on the sofa at home dozing when the phone rang. It was James from the gym. I was so surprised to hear his voice the power of speech deserted me.

'Are you all right, Antonia?' he asked. 'I was wondering why you hadn't been in for so long and then I heard you've been really sick. I got your number off the computer here, I hope you don't mind.'

My heart was pounding, as though I had one of my dizzy attacks coming on. I could tell I was blushing and I felt as embarrassed as if I had actually done all the filthy things to him that I had done in my dreams.

'Of course I don't mind,' I said weakly. 'It's incredibly nice of you to call, James. I should have let you know why I wasn't coming in . . . I'm sorry.'

'Hey, don't worry about that, I just wanted to know you're OK.'

'Well, I have been quite ill actually,' I said. 'Nothing fatal, it seems I just collapsed with exhaustion. The last eighteen months or so have been a bit of a strain on my system.'

'Gee, I'm really sorry to hear that, Antonia. I hope I didn't work you too hard on the machines here, but you seemed to be getting really strong.'

'I think my body was getting stronger, but I had overdrawn on my emotional account to such a degree it all just collapsed.'

'You exhausted your chi, Antonia,' said James, getting

194

onto his favourite subject. 'It's precious stuff, as I told you. Well, I wish you better and if there's anything I can do, just call me at the gym. And when you're well enough, come in again and I'll show you some really gentle chi gong moves that will build up your energy reserves again.'

'Thanks, James. I'll do that. And thanks for calling, it was really nice of you.'

'No worries. Oh, and listen – drink a lot of water. OK? And breathe.'

'I promise. Goodbye, James.'

I was really touched he'd taken the trouble to ring and collapsed back onto the sofa. Twingeing slightly. I must be getting better, I thought.

That night Percy arrived home with Tom and Dee in tow. They'd been over to our favourite Thai take-out in Redfern and had brought me some wonderfully fragrant soup. I must have been getting better, because the delicious smell was making my tummy rumble.

Tom came running in and threw himself on the sofa beside me.

'Are you over your hump, little Mummety?' he asked and I told him I was. 'Oh good,' he said, springing up. 'Now I can show you my new dance.'

He capered around the room scissoring very straight arms and legs and making barking noises.

'Do you know what that is, Mummy?' he asked me. I shook my head. 'It's The Biggest Spotty Dog You Ever Did See – Percy taught it me. It used to be on the telly in England.'

'Taught it to me. That's very good, Tom. I like it better than the hump song.'

Dee and Percy came in with the soup and Tom started jumping up and down again. After having him out of the house for a couple of weeks I'd forgotten the sheer impact of his energy.

'Guess what, baby?' he said, striking an Austin Powers pose he must have acquired during his stay at Hugo's house. 'I nearly forgot because I was showing you my spotty dog – we went to Dee's house today and she's got a helicopter in her garden called a chopper and I went in it and Dee said I can have a ride in it one day really soon. Dee's husband is called Frank and he said I can hold the joystick. He's really nice. He gave me a Chuppa Chup. Toffee banana.'

'Good heavens, Tom,' I said. 'What a lucky boy. A helicopter *and* a Chuppa Chup, fancy that.'

I looked at Dee who was smiling sweetly at Tom, but looking a little embarrassed as well. I'd never been to her house, but it seemed Percy and Tom had and I did feel a little cheesed off.

Percy turned round from the dining table, where he was laying the food out.

'You should see Dee's house, Antonia,' he said. 'It's frightfully grand. Has its own beach and jetty. All completely private.'

I noticed he hadn't mentioned Frankie. I was longing to know what the great mystery man was like – and if Tom had met him, Percy must have too, but clearly he didn't want to talk about him in front of Dee. Interesting.

We sat down at the table and Percy filled our bowls with soup.

'Now,' he said, when we were all settled. 'We have a little surprise for you, don't we, Dee?'

She looked a little shy and passed me a set of keys. I looked at them questioningly.

'We both think you need to take a break,' said Percy. 'To go away and have a complete rest from everything, on your own, and Dee happened to mention that she and Frankie have a little beach house up in Byron Bay that would do the trick.'

I looked at Dee. She nodded encouragingly.

'Those are the keys,' she said.

'Tell her about the chopper,' said Tom excitedly, squirming in his seat.

'Frankie wondered if you would like to be flown up there in the chopper,' said Dee. 'It would be much quicker than flying to Ballina. He says it just sits around most of the time and it would be good to give the pilot some practice.'

All I could do was beam with gratitude.

When Dee was gone and Tom was in bed, I insisted Percy tell me everything about Dee's house and the mysterious Frankie. I hadn't felt so excited about anything since I'd fallen ill.

'How on earth did you get in there?' I asked. 'I've known Dee for ages now and I've never got anywhere near her house, or Frankie, she's so cagey about everything.'

Percy waggled his head from side to side the way he

did when he was pleased with himself about something.

'Oh, you know,' he said. 'You just have to be clever about these things. Dee doesn't have children, Dee adores Tom, Tom would love to see inside a helicopter . . . it wasn't hard, Ant, darling. You just didn't try hard enough.'

'Oh all right, you wily old fox, now tell me everything. What's the house like, what's the boat like, what's famous Frankie like? Spill.'

Percy sucked his teeth, relishing the suspense he was keeping me in. Then he leaned over conspiratorially.

'The house is . . .' he paused for dramatic effect. 'Apsol-yootly heinous.'

My mouth dropped open in surprise.

'How can it be?' I said. 'She's got such good taste. You've seen that gorgeous red and white window she's done for the shop and she's bought so much great stuff from Anteeks, I don't see how it can be horrible.'

'Frankie,' said Percy, nibbling a rose cream. He'd discovered a source of his favourite delicacy – rose and violet cream chocolates – in Sydney and one or two after dinner was part of his daily ritual.

'Frankie pankie could make Blenheim Palace ugly just by being in it,' he continued. I waited for him to expand. 'He's what you might call a rough diamond, with the emphasis on rrrrrrough. It's a lovely old house – what they call Federation – but Frankie's taste and Frankie's interests clearly rule. Apart from some lovely flower arrangements, there isn't a sign of Dee in the place. It's all conspicuous consumption of the grossest kind.'

'I want more detail,' I said, reaching for a violet cream myself.

'OK,' said Percy, settling cosily into story mode. 'You arrive and there is an electric gate with an intercom. You buzz and the guard lets you in. All very Lady Penelope. I rather liked that bit. There are signs everywhere with large slavering Alsatians on them. You go down the drive and the first thing you see is a long curving line of garages – about eight of them, all with the doors open so you can see the cars inside. There was a beautiful old open top Roller like my friend Basher Ponsonby had at Oxford and all kinds of pointy red Italian monstrosities.'

I lay back on the sofa, to take it all in.

'The house is what we would think of as the Edwardian style – as I say, Federation – in lovely old stone with Virginia creeper or some such all up the front. Very Sussex, really nice. A maid opens the door and from then on it's shag-pile hell. Dee clearly didn't want me to go in, she was trying to lead us round the side and straight out to the chopper, so I pulled the old loo stunt and then got "lost" when I came out. Always works like a charm.'

He picked up another chocolate and continued between bites. He always nibbled the chocolate casing off first and then slowly licked the fondant.

'The reception rooms have lovely proportions, with big windows looking out over the Harbour – it would really be hard to think of a nicer family house – but the decor defies belief. It's that kind of decorating where an almighty amount of money is spent to achieve an unbelievably cheap effect.

'The light fittings are like something out of a 1980s bistro, all varnished brass curly wurlies and there are three enormous cut moquette sofas. The main *objet d'art* in the drawing room is a television – which had horse racing on it – although there are a few mawkish prints in over-elaborate frames. There's also quite a collection of Lladró on smoked-glass shelves.'

'I can't believe it,' I said. 'No wonder she didn't want me to go there. Now tell me about Frankie.'

Percy paused, clearly looking for the right words to do him justice.

'Imagine every dodgy scrap-metal dealer, tarmac layer, crooked builder and barrow boy you have ever met, multiply them all to the power of *n* and you have Frankie. His face is as craggy as the Peak District. I think he is what the Australians call "as rough as guts". But, of course, fantastically charismatic as well. It was like shaking hands with a crocodile, huge leathery paws, very dry and very strong. Lots of gold jewellery and hair dyed a frisky auburn. He was wearing white shoes.

'But, I have to say, he clearly adores Dee. He's so proud of her. My little queenie, he calls her and he was charming to us. Made Tom a huge Coca Cola cocktail in an enormous brandy glass with umbrellas and pineapple and cherries hanging off it. Sat him up on the bar – which is the full monty with optics, beer taps and the lot – while he made it. Very sweet. Insisted on opening a bottle of Bolly for me, then served it in a wine glass, full to the brim. He's very generous, very warm and would crack your head like a walnut if you crossed him.'

'Crikey,' I said. 'No wonder Dee hasn't introduced me. He sounds terrifying. Do you think he's seriously dodgy?'

'I'm sure he is, but he's strangely decent at the same time. He's not the sort who would ever hit a woman. He'd get someone else to do it.'

Percy paused to laugh at his own joke and then got back to his tale.

'Do you know what he said, when he met me? "So you're the old poonce I've been hearing about. What happened to your purple hair?" That broke the ice. I like people who are upfront.'

'What was the boat like?' I asked, not wanting to miss out on a single detail.

Percy uttered a strangulated cry.

'It is soooo vulgar, like some kind of adolescent James Bond fantasy, but actually so gross, even Goldfinger would recoil. But the helicopter is a very fine thing. I do rather envy you going up in it. Perhaps I'll have a ride with Tom. Frank is the kind who would keep his promise to a little boy.'

I was still puzzled how Dee could have such good taste and live in such an awful house.

'What do you think she did with all the stuff she bought from me?' I said, trying to figure it out. 'Do you think it's all in a store room somewhere, still in the carrier bags? I saw a programme once about compulsive shoppers who did that.'

Then something occurred to me.

'Hey, Perce,' I said. 'Do you think the beach house will be as yucky as the Sydney house?'

'Bound to be, darling. You'll probably have a solid gold Jacuzzi to watch the whales from. Wish I was coming too.'

14

The day before I was due to be airlifted up to Dee's beach house she popped round to see me. She handed me an envelope that contained a map, a note and another set of keys. I looked at her questioningly.

'The chopper will drop you off at our beach house in Byron,' she said. 'But this map shows how to get to another house which I think you will like a lot more.'

I didn't understand. 'What do you mean?'

'The keys you have already are to our official Byron Bay house, but I actually have another house twenty kilometres away, that is my house – really *my* house. This is the key for that.'

She looked down a bit nervously.

'Frankie doesn't know about it. Nobody knows about it, except me – and now you. It's my escape and my safety hatch. I bought it ten years ago, in my maiden name, with money I had saved from my various allowances. I needed something that was just mine. I know I can trust you not to tell anyone about it – and I really do mean *no one*.'

She looked me straight in the eye.

'Frankie wouldn't like it if he knew,' she said quietly. 'But you'll like it much better than the official house, trust me.'

'Won't people notice if I'm not in the other one?' I asked.

'Just leave the lights and some music on. It's very private and that will be enough to cover us. I've cancelled the gardener and the housekeeper for the fortnight, saying I didn't want you to be disturbed. Just make sure you're back there ready for the chopper when it comes to get you. Stay one or two nights there, if you like, and mess the place up a bit, so it looks like someone's been in when the cleaner comes. Then get a taxi into town and hire a car to go out to my house. Don't get one taxi from the big house straight to my house. Byron's a small place.'

She smiled conspiratorially. I knew that she was showing me a level of trust even beyond my asking her to be my business partner. I gave her a really big hug.

The minute I walked into Dee's secret house – which was called 'Gumnuts' – I knew where all the stuff she'd bought from Anteeks had gone. The place was divine.

It was really tiny, with just two bedrooms, a small kitchen/living room and a funny old bathroom, but it had true character. The walls were all panelled with tongue and groove, painted subtle shades of green, and the floorboards were painted cream with large sea grass mats and rag rugs over them. It wasn't right on the beach, but a short walk from it and surrounded by bush, so I could hear the wind in the trees as I lay in bed at night. I knew at once that this was somewhere where I could be happy alone and could really build up my strength.

What a contrast to the other house, which had been,

just as I had feared, a nightmare of hard granite surfaces, gold swan taps and vertical blinds, complete with a very elaborate spa on the deck, just as Percy had predicted.

It had a row of golf buggies waiting at the back door, to save you the chore of walking the few yards to the beach, and I was terrified of the burglar alarm, which was like the flight deck of a 747 and looked like it would call out the national guard if accidentally set off. I hated the place, just as Dee had thought I would, and couldn't wait to leave.

Even though it was right on the well-populated slopes of Watego's Beach, I spent one very nervous night there, feeling like floodlit prey for burglars. I felt so much happier out at Gumnuts, on my own, even though it was in a much more remote location and there was no telephone.

My mobile didn't work very well out there either, so if I wanted to call home for a proper chat, I had to walk half a mile to the payphone at the nearest minimart, which was good for me. I missed Tom a lot, but I needed some time alone, just to be and not to think about anyone else.

On my first day, I realized with a jolt that I'd never really spent any time on my own, in my whole life. I'd gone straight from home to university, via a year in the States, where I had travelled with my best friend from school.

Then I'd met Hugo in my first week at St Andrews and lived with him for the next ten years. When he left I still had Tom and shortly after that Percy had arrived. So spending some time completely alone was a novel and interesting experience.

With space to think about everything that had

happened, I even began to wonder whether Hugo hadn't done me a favour by ending our cosy relationship. We'd been little more than children when we had got together and I began to wonder if I'd had a case of arrested development.

I certainly knew nothing of the world my sisters inhabited. The lives they told me about – of the modern workplace and the dating scene, starting and ending relationships, one-night stands and sharing flats – were like another country to me.

I was like some kind of 1950s bride, the way my life had been until Hugo left, and being forced out into the real world, painful though it had been, would give me a more interesting and rounded life in the long term, I decided. It was good to join everyone else in the twenty-first century.

With every day that passed I felt physically and emotionally stronger. Although it was well into winter, the days were still warm up there and I spent them lying in a hammock on the back deck reading, listening to music and just dozing. I went for long walks along the beach, picking up shells and stones and gazing into the horizon.

It was chilly at night, so I would light the log fire in the sitting room and curl up and listen to my favourite poems on cassettes my mother had sent over to me from home.

When I arrived back in Woollahra two weeks later, I felt reborn, more rested than I'd been for years and much more able to cope with life. Two days after I got back, Percy – ever the canny diplomat – had organized the first family supper at our house, with Greg on the guest list. In my new laid-back beach-bum state, I coped with it just fine, basking in compliments from all of them about how well I looked.

It also helped that it was now over eighteen months since Hugo had left and it didn't seem so much like 'our' house any more, it had become where I lived with Tom and Percy.

'You are looking absolutely marvellous, Ant,' said Hugo, when he walked in. 'You've really got a bloom about you. If I didn't know better, I'd think you were pregnant.'

Now clearly used to such hideous Hugo clangers, Greg rushed in to change the subject.

'How's the gym thing going, Antonia?' he asked. 'Still going to Muscle City?'

'Do you know, I haven't been for five weeks,' I said. 'I haven't gained any weight, thank God, because of being ill, always wonderful for the figure, but I am starting to feel a bit squidgy again, I've lost my – what do you call it? – my definition. I think I need to start going again.'

The fact was, I felt quite nervous about going back there. I didn't want to lose what I'd worked so hard to build up before I flaked out, but equally I didn't want to knacker myself again. But mostly I was shy about seeing James.

I had thought about him a lot more than I wanted to admit, even to myself, while I'd been away, and still hadn't resolved my feelings. It didn't make any sense to me, but just remembering how his muscular, hard body had looked when he stretched, could give me a serious twinge. It was embarrassing, immature and cringe-making, like falling for your tennis coach, or your ski instructor, which I thought I'd got over when I was seventeen.

But was it really him I had a crush on anyway, I wondered, or was he just a focus for my generalized sexual frustration?

In the end I decided I just had to go and see whether I had been imagining the whole thing – which I justified to myself by saying I was merely taking him up on his offer of strengthening chi gong.

To be sure of seeing him, I went back at my old time of well after midnight and there he was – a slightly odd and fully celibate speccy kung fu weirdo, in his godawful nylon track pants and that wretched bloody hat. I was beginning to wonder if he was bald underneath it. His face lit up when he saw me. I'm sure I blushed.

'Antonia!' he said. 'You're back. That's great. You look great too. Really rested.'

He came round from behind the counter and for a terrifying moment I thought he was going to hug me, but he just patted me on the shoulder and shook my hand.

I had definitely been imagining the whole thing, I realized. The glasses, the track pants, that stupid hat – he was a total geek. I looked at my feet in a confusion of shame and self-consciousness. Relieved and disappointed at the same time, that my childish crush had evaporated like steam from a kettle.

I must have been slightly insane from the exhaustion, I thought, with too much time to think. His attitude to me was exactly the same as it had always been, but I felt very differently about him.

'Now, you mustn't overdo it tonight, Antonia,' he was saying. 'Just five minutes on the treadmill and then I'll show you those chi gong moves, if I'm not tied up at the desk.'

'That would be great,' I said, totally dreading it, and shot off to the aerobic zone.

The chi gong wasn't too embarrassing actually. I was worried he would take me upstairs to the dance studio, which would have been way too intense, like a scene out of *Fame*, but as he was alone on reception, we had to do it somewhere he could keep an eye on the door.

It turned out to be just simple movements, with very concentrated breathing, and I did quite enjoy it. When it was over, I promised to come back for more sessions to build up my strength and then bolted for it.

I had parked in my usual spot, in a small laneway, just across from Muscle City and along a bit. There was always a space there and I had started to think of it as my own. Not that night. As I stepped forward to open the car door, a figure emerged from the nearest doorway and grabbed me round the neck.

'Give me your bag,' said a really rough voice.

'I don't have a bag,' I said, truthfully, I only took my keys and my membership card when I went to the gym. The man pulled his arm tighter round my neck.

'Don't play games with me, sister. Feel this?'

Something cold touched my cheek.

'It's a knife and I'm serious, so give me your fuckin' bag.'

I was trying to answer, although I could hardly breathe,

when another figure stepped into the laneway. I couldn't see his face, because the light was behind him, but now I was totally terrified, there were two of them, I didn't have a bag, I didn't have any money – what would they do to me?

'Leave her alone,' said a deep voice. 'Now! Drop the knife, raise your arms and step back slowly.'

The second figure walked further towards us. It was James. He had taken his hat and glasses off – and he was holding a gun. I didn't know which shocked me more, but I was highly relieved when the mugger let go of me and stepped back. Now it was his turn to be terrified. I ran down to the main road.

'I just wanted her bag . . .' he was saying. 'I wasn't gonna hurt her. I just need some money for a fix. Put the gun down, mate, I won't hurt her.'

'Fuck off out of here,' said James. 'And if I see you round here again, you won't get away so easily. I've seen your face now, you piece of junkie shit. Fuck off.'

The mugger ran for it and I just stood there shaking. My teeth were chattering, I was completely freaked out. James came over and wrapped his arms around me. It was like being enveloped in a big warm coat. He stroked my head and said comforting things into my ear, like you would to a frightened dog.

'It's all right, Antonia. I'm here. I won't let anyone hurt you.'

But I was still freaked out – where was the gun? I'd never seen a handgun before in real life. It was almost as frightening as the mugger.

Slowly James turned me round and, with his arm still around me, led me back to Muscle City. His other hand was still holding the gun. I looked down and saw it glinting silver in the streetlight.

He parked me behind the desk, sliding the gun into a compartment under the counter and bolting a door over it. He wrapped a blanket round my shoulders and went to make me a cup of tea. I was still shaking and shivering when he came back with it.

'Are you all right, little one?' he said, bending down with his arm round my shoulder. He still didn't have his hat and specs on. I looked up at him. He had short dark hair, slightly wavy – a full head of it – and almond-shaped green eyes. He was beautiful. On top of everything else it was just too much. I started howling. Really ugly snotty crying.

James roped tissues out of a box and handed them to me, crouching by the chair and putting his arms back round me again, rocking me gently, like a child, which of course made it worse. His arms were so particularly nice. I howled some more. Nearly a yodel.

Before I knew what was happening he'd picked me up, like I was a little rag doll and sat himself down on the chair, with me on his knee. I wrapped my arms around his shoulders and buried my face in the male smell of his neck. It was so delicious, I felt dizzy.

He had one arm tightly round my waist, the other hand was stroking my hair and he was whispering soothing noises into my right ear. I could feel his lips vibrating against it.

It was so heavenly I almost lost consciousness, but I snapped back very suddenly when I realized that I was just about to start licking his neck. His celibate neck. It had been a completely unconscious animal instinct. I pulled away from him and looked into his face again, fully aware that my tear-stained gob probably looked like a monkey's bum.

Those eyes. They were gorgeous. The nose. The forehead. The hair. He had a scar through one eyebrow, which just added to the general effect. It all worked so well together. That hat and glasses combo he wore was like one of those joke-shop faces and completely obscured his looks. I just stared at him. And he stared back. I saw his Adam's apple bob up and down his throat as he swallowed. He bit his lip. Talk about deep breathing, I could see my breasts heaving up and down in front of me. He broke the silence.

'Are you all right, Grasshopper?'

I nodded. 'I feel better now.'

He pulled me back onto his chest again and put his chin on top of my head. It felt quite natural to be there. I had one hand on the top of his arm and I could feel the round shape of his bicep beneath it. I was breathing in his scent with every breath, a mixture of clean shirt and man. I realized I was in some kind of erotic daze, but I had questions I had to ask him. The gun was bothering me most.

'How come you had a gun, James?' I asked his chest. 'Isn't that illegal?'

'We keep it behind the counter here,' he said. 'Just for moments like that. This can be a rough area.'

I sat up and looked at him again. I wasn't sure which I liked better – leaning against his chest or looking at his face.

'But I thought you were a kung fu expert, couldn't you just have Bruce Lee-ed him?'

He looked steadily at me.

'If I'd done that,' he said, 'I probably would have killed him. In the circumstances, the gun was safer. It wasn't loaded.'

I breathed out. It was a relief to know he didn't walk round like the Sundance Kid as a matter of course. Then something else occurred to me.

'How come you were there when it happened?' I asked. 'You were on the desk when I left.'

He reached over to the counter and put his glasses on, then the hat. It was like a light going off. I was still waiting for his answer. I asked again.

'How did you know I was in trouble, James?'

'Like I said, Antonia. This is a rough area. It's late when you leave here. I keep an eye on you.'

I think I would have sat there for the rest of my life quite happily, but two men came in to use the gym. They gave us a very funny look when they saw us sitting there and James jumped up to look after them like we had been caught doing something very naughty. Not naughty enough in my opinion.

At 2 a.m. another fellow came on duty at the desk and James drove me home in his car. I'd come back and get mine the next day, we had agreed, when I felt up to driving again.

I was tense all the way home. I felt so close to James, but at the same time, things were no different between us. It was funny, I thought, unless you actually kiss, nothing has changed. Maybe he would have comforted any girl like that, whom he had just saved from a savage mugging. I felt all jittery and tense, but I didn't want the journey to end either. I liked being sealed up with him in an enclosed space.

But of course, all too soon, there we were outside my house in Holdsworth Street. I didn't want to say goodbye to him. The moment I got out of that car the question mark of possibility would be gone.

'Well, here we are then,' I said, wondering whether I should invite him in for coffee. Isn't that what people did? But it wasn't like we'd been out for dinner. I'd been mugged and he'd saved me. Pass the etiquette book. But I noticed he didn't turn the engine off, which gave me the hint he wasn't planning on staying.

'Well, thank you, James,' I said, to fill the gap. 'You saved my arse. I don't know how I'll thank you properly . . .'

'Just keep coming to the gym, Antonia,' he said. 'Let me teach you some more chi gong. I know how good it will make you feel. And it's boring in there when you don't come in. Just park right outside in future.'

I smiled at him and leaned across and kissed him very gently on the cheek. On his cheek, but close to his lips.

Sort of a two-way bet. He could have moved his head a centimetre to make it a proper kiss. He didn't. I legged it into the house.

It wasn't until he drove off that I realized I had never told him where I lived.

15

I went back to the gym a couple of nights after the mugging – the old getting back on the horse thing – and the night after that too. I went regularly, four times a week and no more. I'd been working-out too much before I got ill and I didn't want to risk that happening again. I also thought some kind of restraint on my visits would help me to cope with my pathetic teenage crush on James, whom I had now mentally renamed Clark Kent.

Over the next few weeks we settled back into a routine, which calmed me down a bit. He taught me some more chi gong, spotted me on the machines, we chatted a lot and he saw me into my car at the end, but there was no more specs off and there was no more sitting on his knee. Dammit.

I told myself just to accept it. He was celibate – he'd told me that – and in any case I could hardly expect him to start groping me in the middle of a public place. But judging by the effect being close to him had had on my blood chemistry, I realized I was going to need to get out and find myself a man – a non-celibate one – sometime real soon. I just didn't know how.

For the time being I just tried to enjoy James's company and sneaked pervy looks at him whenever I could. I still had the odd erotic dream about him, but I managed to keep it under control.

Meanwhile everything else was going swimmingly. Dee and I were now official business partners, all signed up, legal and proper, and we had just moved into our beautiful new shop. It looked absolutely marvellous. With Dee's injection of capital, we were also able to spread our junket-eering net wider than before and we'd had a very successful trip to South Australia, where we had found some more wonderful old shop fittings.

The thing I liked best was a lovely jangly bell, from an old butcher's, that rang every time someone opened the door. It was very chummy and cosy and it rang all day.

I couldn't believe the increase in custom now we were on a major pedestrian thoroughfare. Turnover tripled in the first month and carried on growing. The rent was double, but we were definitely ahead. In fact we were so busy I almost missed the quiet afternoons I used to spend in the shop doing needlepoint and thinking about nothing in particular.

When it came time to do our spring windows – acres of daffodils, knitted ducklings and green and yellow china – we decided to have a celebratory dinner in the shop and it was really fun. We had a long table down the middle and twenty of us sat down to a meal cooked by Percy, all served on mad old mixed-up china and table linen out of the stock room.

Now that the shop was in Queen Street, it was only a minute from the house and Percy rushed back and forth between courses with Hugo in his car to get the next dish. It all added to the general hilarity of the event – which is why he did it, of course.

Antony, Daisy and Dominic came and got on brilliantly with Hugo – Greg, they already knew, of course. The other guests included Tom and Vita, Vita's two mummies, Danny Green, a couple of social pages scribes Percy had been quietly cultivating, and the editors of various interiors magazines. Just to be wicked, we also invited Paul, who was still fairly poisonous, but it was worth it, to get back at Nikki.

To my great delight Dee brought Frankie with her and I really liked him. He reminded me of the stallholders on Portobello Road fruit market, lovable rogues, who would charge you double one day and give you a free bag of bananas the next just because they liked your smile. I wouldn't have trusted him with my handbag, but he was an entertaining fellow to sit next to at dinner. He was full of stories and anecdotes about his days as a bookie and as a builder. He was one of those people who seemed to have done everything and it was very entertaining watching him and Percy trying to out-charisma each other.

'You're not bad for a poonce,' Frankie would say to Percy, getting him in a bear hug. 'I like you. You're a good poonce.'

'And you're not bad for an ignorant old yobbo,' Percy would reply. 'Have you ever slept with a man, Frankie? You should try it. You might like it.'

At one point, they were arm wrestling. Frankie only just won.

I had wanted to invite Suzy and Roger Thorogood as well, because even though I didn't see her any more, Suzy had been so kind when Hugo first nuked me and I wanted to thank her. Plus I thought it might start our old friendship up again, I just couldn't quite let go of that idea. I hadn't seen her for months and I couldn't even follow her busy life in the social pages, because she never seemed to be in them any more. Roger was always there, but no Suzy.

To my surprise, Dee was adamant that they shouldn't be invited. She was very firm about it, so I decided she had her own reasons and just let it go. Didn't bother me that much either way.

I told James all about the dinner, as I did about most things in my life. In fact, I think I rather babbled on when we were together, because it helped distract me from how much I wanted to see him with his shirt off. So I told him all about the great dash that Hugo and Percy had done with the pudding – a Baked Alaska – the night of the dinner, to get it back to the shop before all the ice cream melted.

'Why did he do such a tricky dessert?' said James, who was spotting me on the pecs machine. 'If he knew the kitchen was in another building, why didn't he just do something simple like an apple pie?'

'Is that your special favourite, James?' I asked, unable to resist a small flirt.

He nodded. 'If I ate sugar it would be,' he said.

'Percy does it for the challenge,' I said. 'The chance to

create a drama, show off, be the centre of attention and be praised.'

'Fair enough,' said James. 'We all need a bit of that. That's ten of those. Take a break.'

I came to an abrupt halt.

'Yes, we all need praise,' I said. 'You could give me some right now for doing those reps ha ha ha – but the thing about Percy, which I really admire, is that he creates it for himself. He doesn't wait for it to come along, like most of us do. He seeks opportunities to earn praise.'

I paused for a moment.

'What do you do for praise, James?' I said. 'Apart from saving mothers of small boys from horrible muggers. Do you win very important kung fu competitions?'

'No,' he said. 'I beat myself.'

'Whips?' I squeaked. Maybe he was a kinky celibate kung fu weirdo.

'No,' he laughed. 'I mean that I set myself goals and then I beat them. OK, that's enough rest. Twenty this time.'

I pulled a pleading face and he clapped his hands.

'Come on, chop chop.'

I got back into my rhythm, but still found it hard to be with him in silence. I was never sure my hand wouldn't suddenly jerk out and grab his bum.

'But what about praise and attention from other people?' I said, just to keep talking. 'Surely you need a bit of that?'

'I honestly don't think that's something I'm motivated by.' He stopped and thought, tantalizingly lifting the peak of his cap to scratch his forehead. I wanted to throw the wretched thing across the room. 'I suppose I do like it when clients in my investigative work get the result they want and it helps their case.'

'Is it mainly following errant fiancés and that kind of thing?'

'Oh no, that's bullshit work. I stopped doing that years ago. Now I work mainly for clients I think have a real case of injustice to fight. I don't do tacky industrial espionage, or filming disability pension bludgers digging the garden or anything like that, just stuff I think will actually help people and the community.'

'I'm impressed,' I said, nodding. 'See – there's your praise, James. I think you are a good person. But what sort of thing do you mean?'

'Well, at the moment,' he said, 'I'm doing a job for a conservation group. They want to save some lovely old buildings in a really unspoiled part of town and they reckon the developers will stop at nothing to get their way. I'm trying to catch them poisoning trees and that kind of thing. The conservationists just need some hard evidence that the developers are not doing everything by the book, because at the moment the planning people seem to be protecting them with smokescreens of bureaucracy.'

'That's appalling,' I said, sitting up on the machine. 'That was twenty, James, in case you didn't notice. Sydney's lost loads of interesting old buildings even in the two and a bit years I've been here. It's a real shame.'

'Tell me about it,' he said, sighing deeply. 'They're

destroying this city's maritime history all around us, just to turn a few more filthy bucks.'

I shook my head. I hated old buildings being knocked down, just as I hated old objects being thrown away. Pretty much anything that had been repeatedly used had a history and was worth saving, in my opinion. I tried to explain that to James, how it was the whole philosophy of my shop. He listened quietly and I knew he understood. He looked thoughtful for a moment as I clambered off the machine and then he spoke.

'Well, if you're really interested, Antonia,' he said, 'you can come with me on a recce. I'm doing one tomorrow night, staking out the site where the conservation group reckon the developers are going to pull some dodgy stunt. Start a fire, or something. I've spent a few nights over there already and I'm going again tomorrow to see if I can see anything.'

'What would I have to do?' I asked, thrilling to the idea.

'Just sit in the car with me and wait. It's incredibly boring, but you're welcome to come if you're interested. It would be nice to have some company actually.'

'I'd love to come,' I said, wondering if he knew how much I meant it.

James picked me up from home at 9.30 p.m. I had no idea where we were going but he had told me to wear warm clothes and to bring some CDs, because he was 'bored shitless' with his.

He wasn't wearing his cap. He had glasses on, but they were different ones. The ones he wore in the gym were big, like aviator specs, these were small oblong ones with black frames. He was wearing a puffa jacket, with faded jeans and a black polo neck. Gorgeous. I felt fantastically shy, but told myself not to be so silly. We were going on an important mission. It was hardly a date.

Nevertheless I'd had a total crisis about what to wear. I didn't want to freeze, but I didn't want to look like a total dag – my favourite Australian word – either. In the end I'd gone for a corduroy skirt, my best knee boots and a lilac cashmere sweater. I had a knitted hat in my bag, in case it got really nippy, along with a Thermos of coffee, some snacks and a carefully selected handful of CDs.

'Hey, Antonia,' said James, as I got into the car. 'You *are* a girl.'

I didn't know what he meant.

'You're wearing a skirt,' he said. 'I've only ever seen you in your gym kit before.'

'Well, it's nice to see you without your cap on,' I said.

He rubbed his head.

'Yeah, it's a bit chilly without it, but it can obscure my vision, so I never wear it on a recce.'

I had to ask him.

'So why do you wear it all the time in the gym? And those horrid glasses. These are much nicer.'

'Do I look different without them?' he asked, quietly.

'Totally,' I said, far too vehemently.

'Well, there's your answer,' he said.

'You mean you don't want people to know what you look like?'

'Not more than necessary.'

223

'But you do really need the glasses?'

He laughed. 'Yes. Why do you ask?'

'Just checking. I was just wondering how far you took the cloak and dagger stuff, that's all.'

'You are a funny girl,' said James. 'Just as far as I think I need to. OK?'

'OK,' I said, feeling rather like Tom, for having asked so many silly questions. I resolved to shut up for a while. That didn't last long. We were going through the Harbour tunnel when it occurred to me I had no idea where we were going.

'Where are we going, James? I never asked you.'

'I want it to be a surprise. It's an interesting spot, somewhere that not everyone in Sydney knows about.'

We drove in silence and it wasn't until we were well out of Mosman that I realized where we were going.

'Are we going to the old army hospital?' I asked him. 'What's it called – the King George?'

'Yeah,' he said, sounding surprised. 'We are. Do you know about it?'

'Yes,' I said. 'We took Tom there on a ghost tour in the school holidays, it's totally wonderful. They're not really going to pull it down, are they?'

'They want to,' said James.

I was incredulous.

'But it's amazing. It's one of the most atmospheric and special places I've ever been to. It just throbs with history and the passage of human life, and with the big naval connection it's such a part of Sydney's development as a city . . .' I ran out of words.

'Development's the word,' said James, as we pulled off the road and down a dark track towards the old hospital.

'It may be a historical treasure,' he continued. 'But it's on a prime harbourside site and there's a group of people who think that what's needed here is not wonderful old buildings and natural beauty, but luxury housing, marinas, hotels, cafés and retail opportunities. If they get their way, it will look a lot like Darling Harbour down here.'

I was so upset, I had tears in my eyes.

'But they won't let them, surely?' I said.

James sighed. 'Well, the group I'm working for is trying to stop them and, of course, there are a lot of planning regulations that are supposed to protect places like this, but between all the different interest groups and the red tape, there are gaping holes that things get through. Plus, a huge project like this would create a lot of new jobs and boost the economy. Economic recovery always starts with construction and economic growth gets a government back into power. Something like this goes all the way up and all the way down.'

We'd come to a locked gate across the track. James stopped and got out. I watched him in the headlights. He got a flashlight out of one pocket and something else I couldn't see out of another and, in no time, the gate was open.

We drove through and I hopped out to pull it to behind us. We crept slowly along with James peering out at the dark through the windscreen.

'I'm just thinking where is the best place for us to wait,' he said. 'I'd like to try a different spot tonight. We've got to be somewhere we won't miss anyone coming in, but where it wouldn't be too unlikely for someone who was just doing a bit of mischievous exploring to park. Maybe just here.'

He pulled over to a kind of lay-by beyond the first large set of buildings. We were under trees, so it was very dark, but we could see right across the site, down to the Harbour and to where the waves were breaking by the old hospital. When we stopped, he changed places with me.

'The passenger seat is better for taking pictures. No steering wheel in the way,' he said. He looked at his watch. 'Well, here we are then. It's 22.05 now and we could be here until dawn. Are you ready for that?'

'Sure,' I said. 'I'll try anything once. Would you care for a ginger nut?'

The time went really quickly. We were so used to chatting to each other, we just carried on like we were at the gym. He asked me how the shop was going and wanted to know about Tom's latest catchphrase – which was 'fandabidozee', incidentally, something Percy had taught him.

Then he looked through the CDs I'd brought – after an agonizing selection process – and showed me his prize surveillance equipment, which was a special infra-red camera that enabled him to see and take pictures in the dark. He kept it in a hidden compartment under the glove box. I had a look through it and it was quite eerie how I could suddenly see the buildings clearly and lots of rabbits, happily skipping about, oblivious to the fact that I was watching them.

To pass the time I got him to tell me stories about his *dojo* and the Shaolin monks and how they could hang upside down in trees and stuff like that. I loved hearing about it. I made him teach me how to say hello and thank you in Cantonese and to tell me about the best meals he'd ever had in Hong Kong. With the CDs and the coffee and the biccies, we were having a fine old time. We both loved Massive Attack and we played *Protection* five times in a row.

We were having a singalong to Kylie – or at least I was – when James suddenly stiffened and turned down the music. He put a hand on my arm to quieten me.

'There are people here,' he said. 'I saw a flashlight.'

All the hair on my neck stood up. It was terrifying. I hadn't expected to be this frightened. I hadn't expected to see anyone.

'There, did you see it?' he said and I had. There was a light flashing down the slope, between us, the morgue and the old hospital. Actually, there was more than one light and they were bouncing around quite a bit.

'Just stay quiet and we'll watch,' said James. He wound down his window and cocked his head to listen.

I felt cold all over and thought it must have been the air coming from outside. I rolled my window down and carefully put my hand out. It wasn't that much colder than in the car, but I still felt freezing. I pulled up the sleeve of my jumper and my arm was all goosebumps. I looked at James and saw him shiver inside his down jacket.

'They don't seem to be coming up here,' said James. 'They're just staying down there, moving about. It's weird.'

Then he picked up the camera.

'This is even weirder,' he said. 'I can't see them through the camera.'

We looked at each other. I raised my eyebrows and said nothing. I didn't want him to think I was stupid. He lifted the camera up and down to his eyes a couple of times and then passed it to me. It was true. You could see the lights with your naked eyes, but as soon as you put the camera up, they disappeared.

I gave the camera back to him and we watched the lights for a moment more and then just as suddenly as they had appeared they went out.

We looked at each other again.

'Do you think someone was there?' I asked in a voice that came out very small and squeaky. James opened his eyes wide.

'There was something there,' he said. 'It could have been a group of people walking with flashlights through the trees and that's why they seemed to come and go.'

'They must have been jumping up and down on trampolines as well,' I said, realizing I no longer felt cold.

'You're right – that was just plain weird,' said James. 'And we couldn't see them through the camera. It doesn't make any sense.'

He looked at me closely. 'Did you say you came on a ghost tour here?'

I nodded. 'Yes. We didn't see any ghosts, but there were loads of spooky stories and it was really easy to believe they were here. It sort of throbs with atmosphere, doesn't it?'

'You're not wrong,' said James, rolling up his window. 'Let's put some hearty Christian music on,' he said with mock joviality.

We had some more coffee and played a few games of I Spy – not very interesting in a car – and I tried not to think about the ghost stories the guide had told us. By 3 a.m. I was starting to feel quite sleepy and after jolting back to consciousness a couple of times when James spoke to me, I think he must have let me drift off, because I woke suddenly to his hand gently shaking my leg and his urgent whisper.

'Antonia, wake up. There are people here. It's for real this time. Keep still, stay very quiet and keep watching. Wind your window down a bit, slowly, so we can hear. I'm going to get the camera ready.'

I could make out the sound of cars coming down the track and then they came round the corner into view. There were two large four-wheel drives and they were coming towards us. My heart was pounding and out of the corner of my eye I could see James taking the lens cap off his camera.

'Stay cool, Antonia,' he whispered in his deep, animal-calming voice. 'If they come over to us, let me deal with it. It will be OK, they've got no reason to suspect us of anything. As far as they're concerned it's just a coincidence that we're here tonight.'

To my very great relief, the cars pulled over to the right and didn't come quite to the point where they could easily have seen us. Four men got out. They were holding flashlights. James lifted up his camera.

'Well, well, well,' he murmured. 'I think we hit the jackpot.' He squeezed the shutter a few times. 'Let's just watch and see what they do.'

The men moved off away from us, towards another set of buildings where we couldn't see them.

'Are they getting away?' I asked.

'I don't think so,' said James. 'They'll have to come back to their cars and I'm pretty sure they'll come over this way as well. This is where they want to build the shopping centre.'

After an agonizing wait, we heard their feet coming across on the gravelly path and saw the flashlights playing over the buildings right next to us. James took some more pictures of them, as they looked at the foundations of the old buildings and then out towards the Harbour. Then he passed the camera to me. I looked through it and let out an involuntary gasp.

'Oh my God,' I said. 'I know them.'

'What?' said James, sounding horrified. 'Do they know you?'

I nodded, dumbly. There was one man I didn't recognize, but the others were David Maier, Roger Thorogood – and Dee's husband, Frankie. I felt something like panic rise in my chest and thrust the camera back at James, who very quietly hid it away in the compartment under the glove box.

Then a flashlight shone right into my eyes.

'Shit,' said James. 'They've seen us.'

And before I could say, or even think, anything he turned round in his seat, grabbed me and stuck his tongue in my mouth. Despite my surprise, I was aware of heavy footsteps coming closer to the car. Without taking his mouth away from mine, James managed to speak.

'These guys are really dangerous, Antonia. We can't let them see you, we've got to make this look real. Whatever happens, don't let them see your face.'

I was terrified, but at the same time, I was ecstatic. James was kissing me. And while I knew he was just using me as a cover, he was doing an awfully good job of making it seem real.

He had his hands cupped around my face and his tongue was exploring my mouth, gently but insistently. Then his hands moved down over my body and then up under my jumper. I was moaning involuntarily and so was he. Or maybe he was just acting, it was hard to know, it was all happening at once. Suddenly I heard David Maier's voice near the car.

'Hey, fellas, we've got ourselves a courting couple,' I heard him shout over his shoulder. 'They're pashing. Shame we didn't get here a bit later, might have been something more interesting to look at.'

I heard his footsteps coming closer and it sounded like the others were coming over too.

'I've got to see this,' said another voice, coming nearer. A voice I recognized as Frankie. 'Pashing in the passion wagon. Reminds me of my youth. But we'd better check them out anyway,' he added, his voice hardening, and remembering what a street-smart old fox Frankie was, it suddenly dawned on me what was about to happen.

If they knocked on the window and James had to take

his face away from mine, to acknowledge them, they'd see me. I knew immediately what I had to do. Relying on my hair to cover my face, I pushed James away from me as hard as I could, back into his own seat and then I sank my face into his lap, unzipping his fly at the same time.

I made it just as I heard them stop right by the car and I found something very hard waiting there for me. I put my mouth round it and gently moved my head. James groaned. There was coarse laughter outside.

'Way to go, mate,' said Frankie. 'Get her to give you a headie.'

'Are we next?' said David Maier, which nearly stopped me in my tracks. But not quite. I moved my head faster. James had his hands in my hair and was starting to writhe in his seat. I felt him throw back his head.

'Oh God,' he was saying and this time I didn't think he was putting it on. I certainly wasn't. I rolled my tongue around the end of him, swishing my hair across his lap at the same time.

'She knows what she's doing,' said another voice, who I realized was Roger Thorogood. 'It's giving me ideas. Think we should head home, what do you say, guys?'

'Maybe we should call in somewhere more interesting on the way?' said David Maier and the others grunted in agreement.

Then I heard the footsteps start to move away and the laughter get fainter. Finally the car doors slammed and the engines revved. I didn't entirely want to, but I stopped moving.

'Just stay where you are,' whispered James, breathing

heavily, his voice quivering slightly. 'Just keep your head out of sight, until they've gone.'

His fingers were still twining my hair. Encouraged, I breathed out deeply and ran my tongue over him slowly. He let out a wobbly sigh.

At last I heard the cars drive off and very gently James lifted me up and looked into my eyes. My heart was pounding and I didn't know how much was fright and how much was passion. He was still holding my head in his hands and I thought he was going to say something – something like, Good work, agent Antonia, now we can leave. But instead he pulled my face towards him and kissed me again, gently and insistently, with his sensuous tongue.

And that was it. James made love to me until dawn. I'd never experienced anything like it. I hadn't known what a man could do to a woman until he did it to me. And he did it in the passenger seat, he did it in the back seat, he did it, most memorably, over the bonnet of the car and as the sun came up he did it on the ground, with me lying on his down jacket. The noise I made would have frightened the ghosts away.

I was rendered speechless and helpless by the feelings he aroused in me and was amazed at the things I did back to him, completely out of instinct. I did things to James I had never even heard about – and he seemed to like it.

Without going into too many grisly details, it took me just a few minutes with James to realize I had never really come with Hugo, not properly. With James it happened without me having to think about it, the rush of feeling just took me over like a tidal wave. It was harder to hold it back than to let it happen and it happened over and over again.

And his body was everything it had promised to be under those nasty track pants. Muscular, strong, smooth, supple and mighty well endowed where you'd most want it to be. He took me to another planet. In a solar system Hugo had never even heard of.

As the sun came up, he was lying beside me, nuzzling my ear and neck, his fingers caressing my body, through the tangle of my clothes. I was stretching out in bliss, unable to stop my limbs and hips moving, as long as he was touching me.

'You're so beautiful,' he said. 'I've wanted to do this to you for so long.'

I rolled over and pulled myself on top of him, my legs astride his hips so he couldn't move. I stroked his head with my hands and gazed down at his beautiful face.

'But you told me you were celibate,' I said.

'Do not laugh at the snake,' he said, in his best kung fu voice. 'For he may turn into a dragon.'

And then he made love to me again.

16

By the time we surfaced it was bright daylight.

'Shit,' said James, blinking and looking at his watch. 'We'd better shift ourselves. Those rangers start work really early and I don't want to get caught in here.'

We pulled ourselves together hastily and got back into the car. As we drove up to the gate something occurred to me.

'James,' I said. 'Wouldn't it have tipped Frankie and his cronies off that someone was already there when they found this gate unlocked last night?'

'No,' he replied. 'Those guys are so arrogant, they would have assumed that it was just their luck that it was open. Are you hungry?'

I realized I was more ravenous than I'd been since Percy first put me on a diet.

'I'm staaaarving,' I said.

James smiled and squeezed my hand. He didn't let go of it. In fact he held it, resting on his thigh, all the way back to the Eastern Suburbs, taking his away only to change gear. When we stopped to pay the toll at the Harbour Bridge, he leaned over and gave me one of his slow insistent kisses, until the cars behind us started hooting.

Eventually we pulled up outside a café in Elizabeth Bay and James got out and opened the door for me. As I stepped onto the pavement, he pulled me up, put his arms round me and kissed me again, pressing me against the car.

'I can't keep my hands off you,' he said.

'That'll teach you to be celibate,' I said, realizing that until that night I had been celibate myself since well before Hugo's announcement. What a difference a night makes, I thought.

The café was crowded with people sucking up life-giving caffeine on their way to work, but I was oblivious to all of them, although I noticed James give the room the once-over when we walked in. I also noticed that he sat with his back to it all.

We both had the works – bacon, eggs, mushrooms, the lot – although James didn't have any tea or coffee, just hot water.

'You're playing havoc with my regime,' he said. 'I drank coffee poison with you last night and I never eat this stuff.' He put a large piece of bacon into his mouth and grinned happily.

He held my hand all through breakfast too – eating with a fork in his left hand, picking the bacon up with his fingers. I watched every movement, experiencing one of my now customary James twinges when he licked the bacon fat off them.

'Are you left-handed?' I asked, suddenly and totally obsessed with every tiny detail of him.

'Yep,' he said. 'And I'm left-footed too. I went to a Jesuit school. I think that's why the ascetic lifestyle appeals to me.' He paused and narrowed twinkling eyes at me. 'And of course it makes breaking my vows – chastity, poverty, penitence, no wheat, dairy, sugar, caffeine or animal fats, et cetera – all the more enjoyable. Especially the chastity part.'

I grinned back at him, finding everything about him delicious, delightful, de-lovely and every other cliché of total lust. It wasn't until I was mopping up the last of my egg yolk with a crust of toast that the first prongs of reality prodded me. What would happen next? Would he just take me home and leave me? Was this just a one-night stand? And if it wasn't, was I mad? Did I really want to get involved with another man – ever – after what Hugo had done to me?

I was also beginning to have a sinking feeling about my own behaviour from the night before. What must he think of me? We'd barely kissed and I'd gone down on him like a porno slut – *and in front of other people.* I felt a hot flush of shame as I remembered it. Of course, at the time, it had seemed the only way to protect myself from being recognized, but maybe I actually was just a filthy trollop.

I stared down at the remnants of my fry-up and my eyes filled with tears. It had all seemed so beautiful and special and pure and now I wondered if it wasn't all just incredibly sleazy. I felt James squeeze my hand.

'Hey, Antonia,' he said, softly. 'What's the matter?'

I took a deep breath and forced myself to look up at him. He looked really concerned.

'Are you OK?' he said.

I nodded, swallowing. Then I shook my head.

'What is it? Tell me,' he said.

'It's just – what I did last night – you know, when they came up to the car . . .?'

'Yes,' he said, his eyes twinkling. 'I think I remember. What about it?'

'Well, I don't want you to think that's something I go round doing to people. In cars. With other people there . . .'

He smiled at me so kindly and gently, I felt encouraged.

'In fact,' I said. 'I've never done it before. Ever.'

James grinned at me and leaned over the table to nuzzle my nose.

'Well, I'm extremely honoured you chose me to practise on and let me reassure you – you can do it to me any time you want. Seriously though, Antonia, it was a brilliant bit of quick thinking in the circumstances – and it certainly took my mind off the danger we were in.'

He pulled back and looked at me with his head on one side.

'And I'm glad you brought that up,' he said quietly. 'Because I don't want you to think that last night was a normal occurrence for me either.'

I wasn't sure what he meant. Did he mean that it was a one-off freak accident that would never happen again?

'What I'm trying to say,' he continued, 'is that it was special for me – it *is* special for me. I don't want you to worry about any of that. As I told you, I know all about those shitty guys and what they do to girls in this town and I want you to know that I am not one of them. I was celibate, by choice, when I met you and it was my choice to break it with you. I haven't met anyone who makes me feel like you do for a long time.'

I squeezed his hand. I felt totally reassured and all the fuzzy feelings came flooding back again.

'But . . .' he added.

Oh God, I thought, what was he working up to? I knew there was a catch.

'We're going to have to be really careful,' he said. 'Really discreet.'

I still didn't understand – was he married? Did he mean we'd have to meet in motels?

'What are you saying, James?' I said. 'Just tell me. If there's any problem tell me now.' Before I fall for you even harder than I already have, I thought.

He sighed.

'You said you knew those guys we saw last night,' he said, looking serious. 'Did you know all of them?'

'No,' I replied. 'Only three of them. I know David Maier, Roger Thoro—'

He held up his hand suddenly to stop me, glanced quickly over his shoulder and leaned in closer.

'Don't use their full names, Antonia,' he said quietly. 'Ever. You never know who's around – anywhere. What about the other two?'

'Well, of course I know Frankie you-know-who – he's my business partner's husband.'

James looked horrified.

'Bloody oath,' he said, under his breath. 'I had no idea the Dee you talk about all the time was *that* Dee.'

'Do you know her?' I asked.

'No, but I know who she is. It's part of what I do to know about these people.'

He looked down for a moment and then back at me with his eyes narrowed.

'Do you know much about her?'

'Is this an interrogation?' I asked, only half joking. 'And if so, are you the good cop or the bad cop?'

'I'm a verrry bad cop,' said James, winking at me. 'But it's not an interrogation, I just wondered how well you know her.'

'Well, we're business partners, but we're not super close emotionally, I suppose, because she's quite shy about all that, but I do spend most days with her. I really like her. She's a great girl and she has great taste.'

'Except in husbands,' said James.

'Is Frankie really seriously dodgy?' I asked, my heart sinking, my worst suspicions confirmed.

'Pretty much,' he said, nodding. 'But he's not the worst of that little bunch.'

'Who's the worst?'

'The other guy, the one you don't know.'

'Yeah, who was he?'

He glanced over his shoulder again, leaned towards me and spoke as low as he could in his deep sexy voice.

'Pieter van der Gaarden. He's the really big shark in this town. Those other guys are just pilot fish compared to him. He's South African – Afrikaner. Lost everything over there and came here with nothing, started out driving a taxi, now he's a billionaire. He's completely self-made, completely amoral. Not married, no kids, cares only about money. Well, money and hookers. You don't want to know some of the things he's involved with. I wish I didn't sometimes. He's a total sleaze bucket. Keeps a very low profile, never takes part in that social scene where you met the others, but controls them all – and a lot of other prominent Sydney identities – like puppets. They're all terrified of him and in total awe.'

'Because he's the richest?'

'Partly that, although no one really knows how rich he is. It's more because he's so brutal and so without shame, that he impresses them. They all know that somewhere inside they have a soft centre, a certain point beyond which they couldn't go and they know he doesn't have it. It frightens and excites them.'

I sat and digested what he was saying. I had already suspected Frankie was dodgy and I certainly knew how vile David Maier was, but I was surprised at Roger Thorogood.

'Is Roger dot-dot-dot really as bad as the others? I mean – he's an MP now, he's a cabinet minister . . .' I realized, as I said it, how naïve I sounded and James's face confirmed it. 'I guess he is then,' I added, starting to feel a bit depressed about it all.

'Any cabinet minister seen hanging around with Mr You Know Who – let's call him Mr P – is extremely suspect,' said James. 'Especially the Minister for Planning. Which is probably why they were there at four in the morning.'

I looked back at him, the full weight of the situation finally sinking in. It also occurred to me that this might explain Suzy Thorogood's sudden change of character.

Maybe she knew what Roger was up to and was terrified anyone would find out. I didn't blame her.

'I guess it's pretty serious then . . .' I said weakly.

James nodded. I had the feeling he didn't like having to tell me any of it.

'Those guys are the heavy mob, Antonia. There's nothing Mickey Mouse about Mr P – or Frankie, for that matter. A woman organizing a protest against another site they were involved with – a lovely old terrace street down on the water in Balmain – mysteriously disappeared five years ago and she's not the only one. We reckon concrete over-boots and so do the police – the ones they aren't paying off, that is. Now they want this site developed. They stand to make millions out of it – it's a big scheme even for Mr P – and they will go to almost any lengths to make sure it happens.'

'Especially David you-know-who,' I said.

James inclined his head. 'Why do you say that?'

I lowered my voice. 'Because his business is in serious trouble – he really needs the money.'

'And he's a nasty piece of work, I hear. Beats his wife? Is that right?'

I nodded. I didn't feel ready yet to tell James just how nasty David Maier was, but I had a feeling I would one day.

I finished my coffee and finally James drove me home. As we approached my street he opened the glove box and took out his baseball cap and the horrible big specs I was so used to. Driving with one hand, he put them on.

Reality crashed back down on me like an unexpected wave.

'Are you going to the shop today?' he asked me.

I nodded. 'I'm already late,' I said. 'Dee will be waiting for me . . .'

'Just try to act normally,' he said. 'She won't know anything about what Frankie is up to at the King George and, with any luck, she'll never have to. What we are trying to do is to stop them in their tracks at this stage, using the official channels, before it gets any uglier.'

He pulled up a few doors away from my house and took my hand – after glancing in the rear-view mirror, I noticed. Once again, he didn't turn off the engine.

'I'm sure I don't even need to say this to you, Antonia. But don't say anything about last night to anyone. Not even about what has happened between us. If it does turn nasty, you will not want to be associated with me, believe me. Just trust me on this. OK? It's nothing shifty on my part, I just don't want anything to happen to you.'

'OK,' I said, simultaneously thrilled that he cared and sick that he wouldn't come inside right now and ravish me again.

He leaned over and kissed me very tenderly, nuzzling my cheek with his nose.

'I won't be able to see you for a few days,' he said. 'I have a lot to do, I may even have to go interstate, but I will see you at the gym as soon as I'm back. For the time being that is still the best place for us to meet. Just keep going there. I have your number and you can call me there if you need to find me. I'll always get a message. Your code name can be Jane, OK?'

'You Tarzan, me Jane,' I said lamely, starting to feel totally miserable at the thought of the imminent separation.

He laughed and I got reluctantly out of the car. As he drove off I suddenly realized why all the cloak and dagger malarkey was really necessary. Frankie and David Maier had only seen the back of my head, up at the King George Hospital – but they'd seen James's face. He was a marked man.

17

Percy was sitting at the kitchen table when I walked in from James's car, nursing his cup of green tea and doing the crossword in the *Sydney Morning Herald*. He glanced up at me over his half-moon glasses, which on him somehow looked perfectly at one with a pierced eyebrow and spiky hair.

He said nothing, but I saw a smile flit across his face as he turned back to the paper.

'Have fun, Antonia?' he asked, in an innocent voice, which was clearly anything but. 'Pleasant evening?'

'Yes, thank you,' I said primly. 'Did Tom behave himself?'

'Oh, yes,' said Percy. 'We had a lovely time. We played Boggle and then we played Cluedo. I was Miss Scarlet. Needless to say, Tom – Colonel Mustard – won. Incidentally, he wanted to bring you breakfast in bed this morning, but I told him not to disturb you, as you'd had a very late night and would be awfully tired and grumpy. Let's just say, I had a little inkling that you wouldn't be back last night.'

'Oh really,' I said, trying to sound casual. 'Whatever gave you that idea?'

'I looked out of the window when you were leaving. Saw the driver. I wouldn't have come home either.'

Not trusting myself to keep quiet, I left the room as fast

as I could. Working on my strongly held belief that a secret is something you don't tell anybody, that had to include Percy, although I knew it would be next to impossible to keep him off the trail. He had a retriever's instinct for sniffing out anything you were keeping from him.

As I ran upstairs I could hear him whistling 'Some Enchanted Evening'.

I felt rather filthy after my night of carnal knowledge, much of it spent rolling around on the ground, but I didn't want to have a shower, as it would wash the last traces of James off me. I considered calling in sick to Dee, so that I could just lie in bed all day, smelling him on my skin and luxuriating in the memory of the night before. Little vignettes of the last twelve hours kept popping into my head, causing mass rioting in my gonads and I wanted to enjoy it while it lasted, in case the doubts set in again.

I also wanted some time to digest the implications of seeing Frankie and the other two up there, but I forced myself to bathe, get dressed and go. James had told me to act normally and I knew the sooner I saw Dee and got on with it, the better.

I felt a little awkward when I first walked in. She looked just the same as ever, with her quiet, sweet smile, and so pleased to see me that I felt I was somehow betraying her. But what could I do? It wasn't my fault her husband was a semi-criminal property developer and it was obvious from her cagey ways that she had a pretty good idea how dodgy he was.

Luckily the shop was really busy, with lots of particularly demanding customers providing the ideal distraction. One of my least favourite types were the women who would demand to have an old blanket or basket in another colour, as though I had a warehouse of them at my disposal. 'Have you got this in lemon?' was the sort of thing they'd say and it was all I could do not to reply, 'Try IKEA.' Normally they drove me nuts, but that day I was delighted by the diversions.

Even so, thoughts of James would spring into my head constantly, but I just let them bob around for a moment, before pushing them away and getting back to the work at hand. I was a little dizzy from the rush of it all and my extreme lack of sleep, but mainlining skinny milk lattes, I got through it.

At about five o'clock, when Dee had left for one of her myriad beauty appointments, the phone rang.

'Say it's a wrong number, if you can't talk,' said James's deep sexy voice. I sank down onto the nearest armchair, practically fainting with pleasure at hearing him.

'I can talk,' I said.

'I know,' he said, chuckling. 'I just drove past Dee in Double Bay.'

'Why don't you come over and see me then?' I said. 'You must be round the corner.'

'I am and I'd love to, but I can't. Even this is foolish, but I just wanted to hear your voice.'

We breathed down the phone at each other for a moment, savouring the connection. James spoke first.

'What have you done to me?' he said. 'There I was – a perfectly happy celibate kung fu weirdo in specs and then along comes this little English girl with beautiful sad eyes and seduces me. Next thing I knew I was eating bacon.'

I just giggled. I was so happy I couldn't speak.

'Anyway, naughty little English girl,' he continued, 'I'm on my way to the airport. I won't be back until next week. I'm not even sure which day, but I'll be at the gym as soon as I'm back in town. Just make sure you're there, usual time, OK?'

'OK,' I said, almost weeping at the thought of not seeing him again for days.

He paused again.

'I can still smell you on my fingers,' he said, causing a major earthquake in my lower body. 'That is, the ones that don't smell of bacon.'

I giggled some more. I was a jelly. A useless jelly.

'Bye, Grasshopper,' said James, tenderly. 'Take care.' And he was gone.

I sang all the way home. When I got there, I whisked Tom off his feet and spun him round until he was breathless with giggles. I cooked him and Percy dinner, giving them their favourite chocolate ice cream for pudding and I wouldn't let Percy do any clearing up. I was so happy, I could do it all. Percy watched me with one eyebrow raised and I didn't care.

At about nine thirty, the fact that I hadn't slept at all the night before finally caught up with me and I crashed out. As I drifted off to sleep, the last thing on my mind was James holding my head and that first kiss when I knew he meant it. Oh joy oh bliss oh gorgeous speccy kung fu weirdo sex god. I kissed my pillow.

*

James's handsome face was the first thing on my mind when I woke up the next morning too, but by midday I was starting to feel decidedly flat. Although I'd slept eleven hours straight, I was still aware of every hour of sleep I'd missed out on the previous night. I had serious sleep lag and it was making me cranky.

'Are you all right?' Dee asked, after I'd snapped at a bike messenger who was late delivering something. It wasn't like me at all, but I was feeling so irritable. I wanted to speak to James again, I wanted to see him, I wanted to touch him. I wanted to fuck him. Sorry, but I did.

Every moment that passed made his absence more painful and made me start to wonder whether I'd imagined the whole thing. I'd get little flashes of the way he had made me feel, which were enough to torture me and also to make me wonder if anything could really be that good. Because I was also wondering, deep down, what the hell I was doing getting this involved with someone. The Hugo hurt was still there and I didn't think I could take any more, if James turned out to be a rotter, or gay, or whatever.

'I'm sorry, Dee,' I said. 'I think I've got a bad case of the pre-menstrual blues. I feel really grumpy.'

More like post-coital blues, I thought guiltily, but I couldn't tell her the truth, which just added to my general irritation. I hated lying to a friend.

Dee smiled fondly.

'I thought it was something like that,' she said. 'Why don't you go home? We're not so busy today and I've got nothing on. Go home and lie down and watch daytime TV.'

249

And that's exactly what I did – in between staring at the ceiling and thinking about James, that is. With every minute that passed from our last contact, I felt a little more confused. I would veer from ecstatic swooning that I had met such a gorgeous, sexy and affectionate man, to total bewilderment. I didn't know where he was. I didn't have his home phone number. I didn't even know where he lived. Whenever I'd asked him he'd managed to change the subject. I could see how good he must be at his job – the one outside the gym, that is. He was so very good at disappearing.

On the other hand, I kept thinking, he'd made it clear to me that it wasn't just a one-night stand to him, or even a happy accident. He'd told me, straight up, that he'd liked me for a long time. Just as I had liked him. But it still felt so weird. What would happen next? Was he going to be my boyfriend?

It all seemed back to front. We'd had the most amazing sex and I felt incredibly close to him, but we hadn't done any of the things I thought you were supposed to do, when you were working up to having a full-on sexual relationship with someone – going out to dinner, seeing movies, going round art galleries, meeting each other's friends and all that – but in some ways I actually knew him really well, from all our talking at the gym. I didn't know what we were.

Unlike my sisters I had so little experience of men and 'dating'. They seemed to go through men like tissues, but James was only the third one I'd ever had sex with. It all seemed very complicated, the way they described it.

When I lived in London we had quite often had emergency summit meetings to discuss their latest romantic fiascos. Not that I was much help to either of them, but I was always happy to be a sympathetic ear. And at least my naïve contributions made them laugh.

Now I longed to ring them to talk about James, to ask them what I should do and think about it all, but apart from breaking my secrecy promise to him, there was another part of me that didn't want to tell anyone what had happened, not even them. It would somehow destroy the magic to put it into words. It could sound sordid, to describe our passionate night together, when it had been so, well, beautiful.

With all this sloshing around in my head, I didn't go back to the gym for the first few days. It would be too redolent of James, I thought, and make it all the more painful that he wasn't there. But after four nights spinning on my mattress, I decided that a workout would be a useful sleep aid, just as they had been when I first started going to Muscle City.

It felt good to be back, when I finally walked in, even despite a completely irrational stab of disappointment when James wasn't at the desk. Worst luck, it was scary Spider.

'G'day,' he said, gruffly, not even looking at me, but after he had swiped my card, he looked up suddenly and gave me one of his appraising stares. I felt like a kitten being sized up by a bull terrier. 'Humph,' he said, or something grunty that sounded like that. 'Got a message for you.'

He scrabbled around under the desk and then handed me a sheet from a phone message pad, with the following words on it, in appalling writing: 'Miss ya heaps. See ya soon. Keep breathing. Tarzan.'

I hoped the 'ya's were Spider's spelling and not Tarzan's.

'Bloke rang and left it earlier,' he said. 'Sounded pissed. Guess you'd have to be to leave a message like that. Tarzan . . .' He snorted, with his usual contempt, scratched his belly and went back to the racing section of the paper.

I whizzed through my workout with a big smile on my face, although I was slightly puzzled by the notion of James drunk. He'd told me he never touched alcohol.

I'd been to the gym three more times before I was finally rewarded. After eight agonizing days since he'd dropped me off at home, I walked in to see James on the desk. I didn't even mind the stupid hat and specs, I was so pleased to see him. He flashed me a beaming smile and then went back to getting some sports drinks out of the fridge for a group of men in very tight shorts.

'I'll be right with you,' he said to me, over his shoulder, with impressive sang-froid.

As soon as they'd gone, he turned back to me and leaned over the counter far further than he needed to take my membership card.

'Hello, beautiful,' he whispered and squeezed my hand as he took the card. I just stood there gawping at him, with what I'm sure was a very dumb smile on my face. All my doubts and fears had disappeared. Once I had seen how he looked at me, none of that other stuff mattered.

More people came in behind me and James got official again.

'I'm a bit tied up here, at the moment, Antonia,' he said in formal tones. 'But I'll come and go through your routine with you later, when Bob gets in, OK? Shouldn't be long.'

And he winked at me, causing an eruption in my cycle shorts.

It seemed like about three hours later, but was probably only twenty minutes, when I was lying on the hip extension and heard a deep voice in my right ear.

'Me Tarzan . . .' he said. I giggled and started to sit up, but I felt a firm hand on my shoulder, holding me down. 'Stay where you are for five minutes and finish those reps. I know how you like to get out of them. Then come up to the dance studio. I'm going to teach you some very special chi gong moves.'

And then he was gone on those silent feet.

It felt like the longest five minutes in history, but finally the hand on the clock ticked round and I went upstairs, my heart pounding louder than the tramping feet on the treadmills downstairs.

The dance studio was empty and dark with just a few shafts of light from the streetlamps outside shining through the high windows. It was a bit creepy. I stood in the doorway for a moment until my eyes adjusted and then took a few steps inside.

All I could see was the wall of mirrors, the barre and the piles of exercise mats against the opposite wall. It smelled of sweaty bodies mixed with floor polish. I took another step inside and a hand suddenly grabbed my right arm and pulled me over into the darkness. It was James – real James, my James, bareheaded, barefaced and beautiful.

I started to speak, to tell him how happy I was to see him, but before I could get a word out, his mouth was over mine and he had pushed me back against the wall. There were no slow gentle kisses this time, his tongue invaded me, almost violently, and pinned my head back, while his hands went to work elsewhere. He didn't say a word as he tugged up my top and sports bra with one hand, my shorts down with the other and entered me as suddenly as he had grabbed my arm.

It was rough, fast, brutal and utter bliss.

Afterwards we slid down the wall together and landed in a heap on an exercise mat. We just lay there panting and staring at each other in the semi darkness. He stroked my head.

'I hope I didn't hurt you,' he said.

I shook my head, I was still trembling. It had flashed through my mind as he tore off my clothes, that he was behaving just as David Maier had at Suzy's party, but the difference was that I wanted him to and he knew it. What a difference. He bent over and kissed me tenderly on the lips. Then on the cheeks, the forehead, the nose, the chin.

'I couldn't help myself,' he said. 'I've been going crazy thinking about you. There was no time to be nice.'

'It was nice,' I said. 'Very nice.'

I lifted myself up, pushing him over and pinning his arms down onto the mat. 'So nice,' I said, pulling up his polo shirt and flicking my tongue over his nipples and down his flat, hard belly. 'So nice, you're going to have to do it again.'

And that was how it went on. I went to the gym just as I always had. Mostly James was there, sometimes he wasn't, and when he was we made love like animals – or just like people who were crazy about each other.

Mostly it was in the dance studio – all over the dance studio – but we also found shelter in the ladies' changing rooms, the steam room, the showers, in a cleaner's cupboard and, on one outrageous occasion, very early in the morning, on the chair at the front desk. It was different every time, but it was always divine.

What James had told me about all-over fitness was true, I realized. Along with strengthening the muscles of my back and abdomen, I also seemed to have strengthened the muscles inside. I could make him come without moving visibly.

His breathing techniques made a difference too. I asked him about it and he showed me how I could use breathing to hold back my orgasm, which just made it better. He could hold his back for ages when he wanted to and he often wanted to. In short, he drove me wild. Frequently I would come back to consciousness with my teeth sunk into his hand, which he'd clamped over my mouth to muffle sounds I'd had no idea I was making.

But it wasn't just sex – James had to work after all and he couldn't leave the desk unless one of the other guys was there too. When he had to keep an eye on things I would stay on after my workout and sit behind the desk with him, just chatting and laughing together. The only thing we didn't talk about was the King George Hospital, or anything to do with James's investigations.

'If you don't know something, then no one can trick or force it out of you, can they?' he'd said right at the start. And in all honesty I was quite happy not to have my little dream world shaken by the sordid realities of what James might have been uncovering. It also made it easier for me to be 'normal' with Dee. Most of the time, I did a really good job of not thinking about it.

The other thing we didn't talk about was where James lived, or what his phone number was, but I'd stopped caring. Although he wasn't always there, I saw him often enough at the gym to sustain my sanity and I figured it was all part of his least-known, least-risked professional philosophy. And while I didn't know what most people would consider fairly basic facts about him and had never seen him outside the gym, apart from the night at the King George Hospital, I was getting to know him as a person, very well indeed.

Our backgrounds could hardly have been more different, but we had a lot in common. We were born six months apart in the same year and shared a lot of childhood cultural references, even though I'd grown up in a West Country vicarage and he'd grown up in an Australian industrial town.

He told me it was the way the huge multinational company had got out of paying his family compensation when his father died from asbestos-related lung disease, entirely related to his job – when James was ten years old – that had made him so fanatical about uncovering corporate corruption and injustice in his adult life.

So while the sex had rearranged the heavens for me, it was so different from anything I had experienced before, I loved spending easy time with him just as much. In fact, the more we made love, the more I wanted to talk to him and the more we talked, the more I wanted to ravish him. I hadn't realized how the two worked together before. With Hugo, sex was something that happened occasionally and had very little to do with anything else in our relationship. With James the two were indivisible.

I was walking home from the shop one beautiful September evening, admiring a magnolia tree in full bloom and wondering if I would see him later, when the meaning of that occurred to me. It must be the difference between close friendship and true romantic love, I realized. Hugo and I had been inseparable best friends. James and I were lovers.

I did sometimes get worried that I was obsessing on him way too much, but it was only the second serious love affair I had ever had in my life, so – I told myself – it wasn't surprising I was going a bit silly in the head.

One evening I was in the kitchen at home, stirring a risotto and thinking – guess what? – about James. I was just remembering how his wet body had looked the night before from my vantage point, kneeling on the floor in the ladies' showers, when Percy appeared beside me.

He took the spoon from my hand and tapped the edge of the saucepan. I looked down to see a smoking pan of half-burned rice.

'You put Tom's plimsolls in his lunch box yesterday, Antonia,' said Percy, into my left ear. 'And his sandwiches in with his PE kit.'

I giggled in my new half-witted way.

'I know what's up with you,' continued Percy, still whispering. 'You're spunk drunk. Somebody is rogering you senseless, you lucky girl.'

I turned and looked at him in amazement. How did he know?

He took the ruined risotto off the stove and filled the pan with cold water.

'I'd just love to know who it is,' he said. 'Any chance of a night cap and a cosy chat with Uncle Percy later, when young Tom is in bed? Or are you rushing off to that gym where you spend so much time? Hmmmm?'

I'm fairly certain I blushed. Percy snapped his fingers in triumph.

'Got you!' he said. 'I knew it. You're being given a damned fine seeing-to by one of those fellows at Muscle City. At my gym too! You are a fast learner, you naughty girl. Now, I wonder which one it is . . .'

He paced up and down the kitchen with all his theatrical flair.

'Couldn't be that awful Tristan,' he was saying. 'He'd be far too sentimental. He's the kind who talks about girls as "ladies" and buys them padded Valentine cards. Can't be the dirty biker, I don't think you're that depraved yet, still got a way to go. Although I rather like him, of course. Then there's that very attractive Chinese Malay. Beautiful skin, but I think he's my team rather than yours . . .'

I had the strong feeling he knew exactly who it was and was just enjoying teasing me. Percy could tease for England.

'Perce,' I started, seriously concerned that it had gone far enough, but there was no stopping him.

'I've got it,' he was saying. 'It's that nice chap who wears that silly hat all the time. The cap is very unbecoming, but the body underneath is knock out. Muscled, but not overdone. I believe he's some kind of martial arts champion, am I not wrong?'

He snapped his fingers again. He was having such a good time.

'That's who picked you up here that night,' he cried, triumphantly. 'The time you didn't come home, you filthy girl. That was him without the hat. I can see it quite clearly now. Well, good for you. I've had a big flirt with him myself, got me nowhere, of course, but I thought he was charming. Found me once *in flagrante* in the steam room, rather embarrassing really, but he just laughed. He has a good sense of humour for a muscle man, normally they're frightfully dreary.'

He was quite pink with triumph, standing there with his hands on his hips, his various steel rings glinting as he quivered with satisfaction. I was equally pink with embarrassment and confusion. He reached over and tapped me lightly on my right breast with the wooden spoon.

'Your nipples are hard, darling,' he said. 'Total giveaway. You'd be a useless spy.'

18

Needless to say, I told Percy all about James. I could tell he was quite hurt that I hadn't 'shared my joy' with him (as he put it) sooner and after all he had done for me and Tom, after Hugo left, I felt the least I could do was give him a vicarious thrill with lavish descriptions of James's sexual attributes. I had suspected for a while that Percy's stories about his wild goings-on at Lady Jane beach were largely imagined, or certainly not as frequent as he liked to imply.

'Oh, do tell me again about when he grabbed your arm and *took* you,' he said, pouring himself another brandy and lighting a black Sobranie – he'd abandoned the cocktail variety along with his mauve hair. 'I adore that bit. Tell me how he didn't utter a word.' He shivered with pleasure at the thought of it. 'Oh, I shall never look at him in the same way. It's always the quiet ones, you know.'

He hardly let me get a word in edgeways, he was so overexcited. He reminded me so much of Tom sometimes it was extraordinary.

'Tell me, darling,' he said in conspiratorial tones, grasping my forearm and leaning towards me. 'Is he terribly . . . big?'

I had to laugh. He was so serious.

'Well, I don't have much to compare it with, in all

honesty, Percy, but I think he is more than adequately catered for by all accounts.'

'Bigger than Hugo, eh?' he said, wickedly.

'Yes,' I replied, happily. 'Much bigger than Hugo. And Greg too, I should think.'

'And girth?' asked Percy, in his most genteel voice, creating a round shape with his middle finger and thumb, his little finger coquettishly raised.

I looked at him, puzzled. 'What do you mean, "girth"?'

'It's all in the girth,' he proclaimed. 'Everybody gets hung up on length, nine inches, ten inches, all that nonsense, who cares if it's four inches rampant, it's width that matters. Diameter. *Heft.*'

I suddenly understood what he was getting at and made a hand gesture of my own. Percy's eyebrow ring shot up.

'Mmmmmm,' he said. 'Very nice, no wonder you're smiling. I'm surprised you can walk. Mind you, I do think these Australian fellows are very well equipped, on the whole. No wonder they call it the Lucky Country.'

I felt extremely disloyal to James, discussing him in this crude way, but after Percy had guessed, I knew I had to tell him something, or he'd carry on digging until he found out everything – creating a lot of mess and trouble along the way.

But I certainly didn't tell him the whole story. I told him nothing about James's other life as a private investigator, what we'd been doing the night he had picked me up from home and of course nothing about the hideous complication of Frankie being involved. And I didn't tell him that I strongly suspected I was falling in love with James as well. I wanted him to think it was a purely physical thing.

My only worry was coming up with a plausible reason for wanting to keep the whole relationship secret. I didn't want him involving Dee, to try to find out more, it was all too close and too much was at stake. So, trying to use the kind of psychological tricks Percy loved to pull, I decided to appeal to his love of secret sin.

'All this is strictly between us, of course, Perce,' I said, holding up my glass to clink in a pact. 'As I am sure you will understand, the sneaking around is a large part of the fun and it would ruin it if anybody else knew. I don't want to have to try to explain it to Dee, or Antony, or anyone, they wouldn't understand. Is that all right?'

'Oh, noooo,' said Percy, meaning yes. 'I entirely understand. I had a six-month relationship like that with Halston's Filipino butler. Dear old Roy – that was Halston's name, did you know? No wonder he didn't use it, what? – anyway, he didn't have a clue what we were up to and that was the whole point, sneaking off to the coat cupboard for a knee trembler when everybody else was in the drawing room. Found out later he was doing it with half of the lady guests as well, but it didn't matter in the slightest. No, the subterfuge is the main thing of it.' He tapped the side of his nose and winked. 'Secret squirrel,' he said. 'You can rely on Uncle Perky.'

Having 'fessed up to Percy, I had to do the same to James. To my great relief, he didn't seem that worried about it.

We were sitting behind the Muscle City front desk playing backgammon when I told him. It was two in the morning – just a normal night in the totally wacko life I was now completely used to.

'I hope you aren't cross, Jimbo,' I said. 'But I know Percy. He'd guessed right and he knew it. He can read me like a trashy magazine. If I hadn't confessed, he would have dug away tirelessly until his suspicions were confirmed, which would have been a lot messier. He's not a troublemaker by nature, but he really can't bear being left out. As it is, he is enjoying the naughtiness vicariously.'

'I'm enjoying the naughtiness too,' said James, taking one of my pieces off the board. 'I think you did the right thing. It was a good psychological move.'

I threw the dice.

'But that wasn't a good backgammon move,' I said, putting my piece back on and removing two of his. I wagged my tongue at him and he bared his teeth at me, growling and pretending to be cross. I considered his reaction to my Percy confession for a moment.

'I'm surprised you aren't more concerned,' I said. 'You were so adamant about the secrecy before.'

'Well, that was a while ago.' He looked at his watch. 'Six weeks, three days to be exact.' He grinned at me. 'After that length of time I'm satisfied no one has made a connection between you and me and the courting couple up at the King George, so I think we can relax a bit.'

He paused and looked up at me.

'But I still think you should exercise extreme caution where Dee is concerned,' he said. 'Even if we hadn't seen her husband that night I would have advised you to be careful around her.'

'Well, it does explain something,' I said. 'I could never understand why she was so cagey when I first met her. She was like Bambi, she was so nervous and jumpy. She's still very wary of revealing any personal details and I've never even been to their house. Percy got inside once, through his usual chicanery, but I've never been asked.'

'All makes total sense,' said James. 'When you're playing high stakes like Frankie does, everyone around you gets infected with the paranoia. Dee wouldn't know the details of half of what he gets up to, but she knows enough to be in danger. She can't ever fall out with Frankie – she knows where too many of the bodies are buried, as they say.'

I looked at him, horrified.

'It's just a figure of speech, Antonia,' he said, 'I mean she knows enough to put Frankie and a lot of other people away, which protects her, but also puts her at risk. Men like Frankie always have a beautiful wife sitting around like a flower arrangement at all their sordid little soirées with their business associates. She's his star witness, which makes her very valuable to him – but very vulnerable to other people.'

I thought back to Dee's shopping mania. No wonder she wanted to take her mind off her life – and no wonder she wanted to get as much out of it as she could.

'They pay a high price for their diamonds and their designer clothes, these women, don't they?' I said.

'You're damned right,' said James. 'And I wish more of them understood that before they got sucked into it all.

Mind you, most of them have their own skeletons to hide as well.'

I waited for him to add more, but he got a look on his face which I knew meant the subject was closed for the time being and I went back to thrashing him at backgammon. I was learning a lot from my kung fu guru. A lot about waiting. He'd tell me when he wanted to.

I didn't see James for a few days after that and it gave me plenty of time to mull over what he'd said. If we could relax about our relationship a bit more now, maybe it meant we didn't have to conduct it entirely in a skanky gym in the middle of the night. I had been wondering for a while what it would be like having sex with him in a bed and was getting quite obsessed with the idea of waking up beside him.

I also wanted to see what it was like being out and about with him. I felt closer to him than anyone alive – apart from Tom and I'd only been out in public with him once, when we'd had that breakfast. It hadn't bothered me at first, it was all so amazing and new, nothing like that seemed to matter, but now I began to crave the more normal, mundane experiences with him – staying in with a video and a plate of pasta and all that. I also wanted him to meet Tom.

So I decided to invite him to one of our family suppers, which were now quite regular occurrences. He could meet Tom and Percy – and I could show my handsome hunk off to Hugo and Greg, because although I had come to terms with their relationship to an extent and had even grown almost to like Greg, I still had something to prove.

James didn't seem very keen on the idea at first. I asked him while he was spotting me on the leg extension and I noticed he inhaled very deeply before replying. Probably something Shaolin monks do to maximize oxygen supply to the brain, I thought.

'Aren't you happy with our little scene, Antonia?' he said, after exhaling. 'Because I've got to tell you – I've never been happier with anyone.'

I thought for a moment, trying the breath thing myself, but it just made me feel dizzy.

'Of course, I'm happy, James,' I said. 'You've totally changed my life, but I suppose I want you to be a bigger part of it.'

'Can I think about it?' he said.

I nodded. Like I said, I was learning the waiting game with him. But I didn't wait long – just until after we had sex the next time. We were up in the dance studio about three-quarters of an hour later, sprawled behind a pile of exercise mats. James had recently administered what Percy would have called a damned fine seeing-to.

I was lying in the crook of his arm and I whispered into his ear, without moving.

'Have you thought about what I asked you downstairs?' I asked, nuzzling him as I spoke. 'I know you're wary of changing anything between us, but I do so want you to meet Tom. You two are the most important people in my world and I want you to know each other. Please come for supper.'

I heard the exhale.

'How can I refuse you anything, you naughty girl?' he said. 'You've got me by the goolies. I'll come to your supper, or whatever you call it. But you'll have to pay a price – in advance.'

And he saw to me all over again.

The family supper took place three nights later. Percy had been thrilled when I told him Mr Muscle and I were moving it on to another level and that he was coming over for dinner.

'Ooh, what fun. The great leap forward. I bet he has a special diet,' he said, starting to twitter. 'Find out, Ant – maybe I'll have to order special low-fat organic tofu.

Percy had clearly wound the rest of the family up to fever pitch too. Tom was very excited about meeting Jackie Chan – which is how Percy seemed to have sold him – and he'd been practising kung fu kicks all over the house.

When I got home from the shop on the night of the dinner he had set up some planks in the garden which he hoped James would be able to smash in two with his head. He had also assessed the various trees to see which one would be best for hanging upside down in. I told him not to get too excited about it and asked him not to badger James too incessantly.

Percy and Tom weren't the only ones who were overexcited. Hugo and Greg actually arrived early for once.

'Sooooo,' said Hugo, chucking my cheek in a way I found intolerably patronizing. 'You have a new beau and we're all going to meet him. What fun. He does know we're still married and I'm a pouf and everything, doesn't he?

We're not going to have to stage a mini "Cage aux Folles Down Under", are we? That would be too tiresome.'

'He knows, Hugo,' I said. 'And he's cool about it. But just try not to flutter too much, would you?'

Between him fluttering, Percy twittering and Tom tweeting it would be more like bird watching than dinner, I was beginning to think.

'Of course, darling,' said Hugo. 'I promise to behave immaculately. We'd hate to put him off, wouldn't we, Greg? Percy says he's a babe.'

Although I was becoming highly anxious about Hugo's probable behaviour at the forthcoming event, I couldn't help smiling at the mere thought of James and I saw Hugo and Greg exchange an arch look. Then the doorbell rang and I rushed out to meet the man himself. I had been so keen for him to come and meet Tom – and to show him off to the others – but now I was really nervous.

I didn't have to worry about one thing – he looked his absolutely gorgeous best. He was wearing dark blue jeans, loafers with no socks and a black T-shirt that could have been designed to show off his body. No hat. No glasses – he had his lenses in for a change. He kissed me warmly.

'Hello, babe,' he said softly. 'Nice to see you're a girl again – you know this is only the second time I've seen you out of a filthy T-shirt, don't you? And I fancy you anyway.'

I hugged him and he grabbed my bum – cue entrance Tom.

'Who's that, Mummy? Is it the kung fu man?'

James laughed and shook his head. 'I'm really in for it

this evening, aren't I?' he said amiably and I had a horrible feeling he was.

Tom had run back into the kitchen, before I could introduce them.

'Uncle Perky, Uncle Perky,' he was shouting. 'The kung fu man's here and he's touching Mummy's bottom.'

'The kung fu man,' said James. 'Is that really who I am here?'

'He's only seven,' I said.

Percy appeared – or rather, made an entrance. He was wearing his leopardskin jeans, with no pants underneath, it was all too clear to see, and a black T-shirt rather like James's. He had a jangling mass of silver bracelets on his wrist and his hair was looking particularly black and particularly spiky.

'James, my dear,' he said, mincing along the corridor. 'Percy Heaveringham. Lovely to see you. We've met at the gym, of course, but I may have had lilac hair at the time. It was in the steam room . . .' He smiled like the Queen Mother. I could have beheaded him. 'Do come in and meet the rest of the family.'

He extended one elegant hand towards the drawing room, as though he was displaying the prizes on *Sale of the Century*.

Hugo and Greg were smooching on the sofa as we walked in. Tom was doing kung fu fighting up and down the room. Not bothering to disentwine themselves, Hugo and Greg looked up at James and let their mouths drop open. They looked back at each other and then seemed to have a racc to spring to their feet and greet him.

269

'Well, hello . . .' said Hugo, sounding exactly like Terry Thomas meeting a luscious young staff nurse, but Greg beat him to the handshake and was much smarter in his approach.

'G'day, mate,' he said, sounding like he was off to wrestle a few crocs. 'The name's Greg Paps. Probably seen you down Muscle City, used to lift weights down there meself. Free weights.'

'G'day,' said James. 'Yeah, I think I've seen you down there.' Then he turned to shake Hugo's hand. I turned with him and saw that Hugo had gone bright red around the neck. Never a good sign in a Heaveringham. If any of them saw that particular pigmentation appear on their father, they would flee to opposite ends of the house – and that was quite a long way, believe me.

In this instance I couldn't tell if it was lust, fury, or jealousy that was causing the chemical reaction known as the Heaveringham Hurricane and if it was jealousy I wasn't sure if it was me, Greg or James he was jealous of. All I knew was, we were all in serious trouble.

'So,' he said, sneering at patrician full bore. 'Boffing the wife, are you?'

'What's boffing?' said Tom, leaping into the room. 'Will you show me, kung fu man – I mean, James?'

I'm ashamed to say I fled to the kitchen. It was either that or set about Hugo's head with the poker. Percy found me by the sink doing one of James's breathing exercises.

'Oh, Antonia,' he said, hand to his chest. 'He really is marvellous-looking without that hat on. And so charming. You are a clever girl.'

'What is that fuckwit faggot Hugo Heaveringham doing in there now?' I asked him, hissing with fury.

'Reading the *Spectator*,' said Percy.

After a few more deep breaths, I went back into the drawing room to find Hugo reading as described while Greg was looking out of the window with his arms folded. I went and stood by him. James was in the garden breaking Tom's planks with his head.

'I'm going to have a strong drink,' I said, with icy civility. 'Would you like one, Greg? Hugo?'

'I'll have a beer,' said the newly butch Greg.

'Pink gin,' said Hugo without looking up. If I'd had a soda siphon I would have had at him with it.

I got their drinks and a large vodka for myself and went out to see what my two favourite people on the planet were up to. James was showing Tom a kung fu kick. Tom's face was radiant with joy. At least something was going well.

'What are you two boys up to?' I asked, ruffling Tom's hair.

'Stop it, Mummy,' he said, like a total brat. 'You're breaking my concentration. James says it's all in the mind.'

'Oh, does he?' I said. 'I'll have to remember that next time I'm at the gym.'

James put his arm round me and kissed my head.

'Your husband gets to the point, doesn't he?' he said. He was smiling, to my relief.

'Oh, God,' I said. 'He's normally so charming, but every now and again he gets all complicated. I don't know if he's cross that you are sleeping with me or that I'm sleeping with you, when he thinks it should be him, or because Greg wants to, oh I don't know. But don't worry, he'll get over it and try to win you over with his charm.'

'James, James, watch,' came Tom's little voice. We looked up to see his head descending towards the planks at great speed.

'Tom, stop that!' I shrieked, but before I even had the words out, James had somehow leapt in his direction and scattered the planks before too much damage was done, although Tom did glance his forehead off one of them. Blood trickled down his face. James scooped him up, like a toy.

'Are you OK, little buddy?' he said to him. 'I think you'd better go to your mum.'

But Tom didn't want mum. He clung on fiercely, tightening his grip on James's neck, burying his face in his shoulder and starting to howl. I glanced round to see Hugo staring out of the window, looking even more hatchet-faced if that were possible, and scarlet around the neck again.

'I wanted to hit the planks like you did,' Tom was stuttering out between sobs.

James was talking to him in the same soothing tones he had used to me after the mugging.

'You have to be a big boy to do that, Tom,' he was saying. 'It takes years. You have to start with easy things. When you're feeling better, I'll show you some things you can do now, but don't try any of that hard stuff for the time being. Now, how's that head of yours? Reckon it needs a bandage?'

He turned to me and pulled a 'Help!' face. I took Tom

from him and carried him into the kitchen to clean him up. It was just a flesh wound and he was over it very quickly, eager to get back to his new best friend, James. He ran into the drawing room and leaned on his knee.

'Do you think I'll have a scar, James?' he asked, gazing up at him, rapt. 'Like yours?'

'I'm sure you will, mate. A really big scary one.'

'I do hope not,' said Hugo, with his most icy smile. 'Or I may have to sue you for mutilating my son.'

'Oh, give it a rest, Hugo,' said Percy, in one of his very rare cross moments. 'You're behaving like one of the ugly sisters. Get over yourself.'

There was a deadly pause, then I saw Greg squeeze Hugo's hand. I squeezed James's and the atmosphere lifted.

'Will you show me boffing now, James?' said Tom.

I wish I could say things got better at the dinner table, but they didn't. Percy had clearly forgotten his enquiry about James's special diet and seemed to have prepared the worst possible menu for his regime, which James was far too polite to refuse. We started with stilton soup and then moved on to lasagne, with lots of fatty minced beef and lashings of cheesy sauce.

There were hot rolls with the soup and I tried not to notice when James cut his with his knife, then took the butter from the butter dish with the same knife and spread it straight onto the bread. It was a different country I told myself, with different ways of doing things. But I couldn't stop myself glancing over at Hugo, who had a look in his eye I had seen many times at the Heaveringham dinner table. He'd seen it and he'd clocked it up against James.

Percy had shown surprising restraint at James's request for just water to drink and happily provided him with a large jug, complete with ice and slices of lime. When James was on his third glass or so, I noticed the water was a pale shade of pink. As we cleared the soup plates away in the kitchen, I asked Percy what it was.

'Oh, just a little Campari, darling,' he said. 'I couldn't let the poor boy drink plain water. Revolting. Added a little splash of voddie as well. Much better for him.'

I went back into the dining room and scooped up the jug and glass with no explanation and replaced it with plain water. I saw James rub his eyes a little later and realized that the unfamiliar alcohol was getting to him.

Percy presented him with a groaning plate of lasagne, saying he was sure James had a hearty appetite. He set about it manfully, although I knew it represented just about all the food groups he tried to avoid. And while he was struggling with that, I was struggling with the way he was eating it.

He was holding his fork, prongs up, in his left hand and pushing the lasagne onto it with his knife, then raising the fork to his mouth, with both elbows out. I couldn't help looking and noticing and caring and I saw Percy and Hugo exchange a glance that made it clear they had noticed too. Percy appeared to be warning Hugo not to say anything, but it was bad enough that they'd noticed.

In that moment I really came to hate the English class system and all its stupid little rules. And I hated myself for caring about them. I was trying to tell myself it didn't matter, when I noticed that Tom had stopped eating and was staring at James.

'James is shovelling,' he said, in his most piping tones. 'How come he's allowed to shovel? I'm not allowed to shovel.'

'Be quiet, Tom,' said Percy. 'You say some very silly things for a seven-year-old. Grow up.'

But it was too late to salvage the situation. The damage had been done.

James looked at me and then over at Tom, just as he picked up his knife and fork and started eating exactly as James had been, elbows out like a rower. I saw the realization dawn on James's face and I knew my own mortified expression would be giving me away, but I didn't have any reserves of false jollity left.

James slowly put his knife and fork on his plate – he didn't put them together, I noticed, hating myself all over again. Hugo was smirking and Greg was frowning, clearly aware that something was going on, but not quite sure of the significance of it.

'That was really delicious, Percy,' said James, putting us all to shame with his good manners. 'Thanks, mate.'

Then he folded his arms and didn't say anything else. I can't say I blamed him.

Clearly delighted his handsome rival had been humiliated, Hugo then launched into one of his super vivacious moods, enchanting us (not) with hilarious (not) tales of his recent dealings with Perth's art collectors. The point of all the stories was how common and ignorant they all were and how superior was Hugo's knowledge of the art world and life in general. Percy looked stony-faced as he cleared away the plates.

James politely refused pudding – or sweet, as he called it, causing another flicker across beastly Hugo's smug face. Zabaglione clearly wasn't James's favourite. He sat there quietly as Percy and I attempted to make some kind of neutral conversation and then as we put down our spoons, he looked at his watch and said he had to be off.

Hugo hardly looked up as he left, but Greg sprang out of his chair to pump his hand again, touching his upper arm, all matey like. Tom held onto his hand, begging him not to leave ever and to come back immediately. And as we walked him to the door, I saw Percy grab his bum, giggling like a schoolgirl.

'Ooh lovely,' he said, in what I think was supposed to be a cheeky winning way. 'Just wanted to see if it felt as nice as it looked. Come back soon, James darling. We'd love to see you again.'

He came right to the door with us, so I had to go outside to the car to have a moment alone with James, snapping at Percy and Tom over my shoulder, to stay inside.

James said nothing as he got into the car, but wound down the window, so I could speak to him. He had a totally blank expression on his face.

'You were right, James,' I said. 'That was a total disaster. I hate them all. I'm really really sorry.'

'Not your fault,' he said. 'I had a feeling it might be like that, but what can you do?'

'Please don't let it affect us, James,' I begged pathetically.

He just looked me in the eye and said nothing – and everything. It was quite clear that as far as he was concerned, it had affected us.

'When will I see you?' I asked, feeling panicky.

'At the gym, Antonia,' he said, starting to wind up the window. 'At the gym.'

I leaned in to kiss his cheek before he wound it all the way up, but he drove off, without acknowledging me.

I went back into the house and ran straight up to my room.

19

Of course I went racing off to the gym the next night, desperate to make things right again and, of course, James wasn't there. As always, when I least wanted to see him, Spider was on the desk.

He showed his usual lack of interest as he swiped my card, but as he handed it back to me I plucked up my courage to ask him if he knew where James was. He looked at me with suspicious eyes.

'Who wants to know?' he said.

'I do,' I squeaked, feeling and sounding more like Piglet, than a grown woman. Spider was definitely a heffalump.

'Why?' asked Spider.

'Because I want to speak to him,' I said.

'Well, he's not here,' said Spider, with his customary charm. 'He might be tomorrow. I dunno. If I do happen to see him, who shall I say was looking for him?'

'Antonia,' I said in a very small voice.

I saw him scribble it on a piece of paper and then he went back to his racing form. He was a total farthog, I decided.

James wasn't there the next night either and I was starting to get frantic. I just wanted to sort it out with him and have a proper chance to apologize. Now I realized just how nuts it was that I had never persuaded him to give me his phone number. He had my numbers and my address, so why had I thought it was all right for it all to be so lopsided? I rang directory enquiries to find out if they had a number for J. McLoughlin – but they had over a hundred listings for that name and as I didn't know the suburb, let alone the street, they couldn't help.

The third night I stayed away from Muscle City, because I couldn't stand another disappointment and another smirk from Spider, who seemed to be a permanent fixture behind the desk, where I had become so used to sitting myself. But on the fourth night James was there.

I ran up to the desk like an eager dog, probably with my tongue hanging out. I saw a sad smile flick across his face when he first saw me, but as I got up close, he resumed the cool countenance he had been wearing when he drove off after the family dinner.

There was no bending over the computer to whisper tender greetings to me, he treated me just like another Muscle City regular. Farthog Spider was sitting beside him, I noticed, his feet up on the counter.

'Hello, Antonia,' said James, with no emotion in his voice. 'Good to see you.'

He handed back my card and made no move away from the reception desk. In normal circumstances, with Spider there to cover him, he would have had me up the stairs and pants off by now. I didn't know what to do with myself. My eyes started to sting with tears. I saw him notice and sigh.

'I'll come over and see you later on the machines,' he

said. 'Go on, get on with it. And no slacking.' He smiled faintly, but it was all I could do not to break down as I got onto the treadmill.

Could one dinner really have done this much damage? I asked myself, desperately. I forced myself to carry on trudging and tried to do his special breathing to calm myself. It worked to an extent, but I plodded through my weights routine like a condemned woman, glancing at the desk as often as I felt I could.

James wasn't there most of the time, just farty Spider, so why wasn't he with me? All kinds of crazy thoughts invaded my brain. Maybe he was upstairs wildly bonking someone else. Maybe I was just one in a series of desperate lonely women he shagged at the gym. Maybe I was one of those delusional, sexually frustrated bunny boilers and had imagined the whole thing.

When I was just about finished on the last machine and beginning to feel hysterical, he suddenly appeared and sat down on the metal crossbar by my head. No kiss, just his face near mine, where it was so familiar. Tears immediately filled my eyes again.

'I'm so sorry, James,' I said. 'That dinner was a nightmare. I never dreamed any of them would behave like that. I think I just underestimated how complicated the situation is with Hugo. I should never have inflicted him upon you.'

'It's OK, Antonia,' he said. 'It wasn't your fault. It was just fucked up from the moment I arrived.'

He patted my hand. I had longed for his touch, but this patting was worse than no contact. It was so asexual. It was like something he would do to reassure his grandmother. I started to feel cross. So the evening had been a disaster – but did that have to mean it was all over between us? It certainly wasn't all over for me. I decided to be brutally honest. It seemed I had nothing to lose.

'James,' I said, 'I know you must be offended, but it was only one evening – are you going to let that change everything? I don't think we should give up something so special, just because my ex-husband was rude to you.'

James rolled his eyes and sighed with exasperation.

'If only that was all it was,' he said. 'Don't you get it, Antonia? I'm crazy about you. I think about you all the time, but that night proved something that I have long suspected about us.'

'What?' I asked, reverting to Piglet mode.

'We come from different worlds, Antonia. You're a silvertail, you live in some kind of silver-plated world – sorry, solid sterling – that I don't understand and don't belong in. I'm just a gym junkie jerk, from a steel town, obsessed with martial arts and with controlling my life, so I don't end up like my dad. Dead at fifty.'

He put his head back and sighed deeply. I could see he was in serious distress. I longed to run my tongue along his throat.

'Look,' he continued, 'we have something great between us – but it only works in here, because it's nowhere land, and in the middle of the bloody night it might as well be never-never land. It's not real life. It wasn't real life at the King George either. That night was amazing, like being in a movie. It was, as they say, "unreal", which means it is not reality. And when you try to mix reality into something like this, it just disappears.'

He snapped his fingers.

Now I was fighting tears very hard. I just blinked at him.

'I didn't know you at that dinner, Antonia,' he said, squeezing my hand with something that felt much more like his usual touch and frowning. 'I looked at you and I thought, this is the woman I love, but she's got a weird mask on and I don't know her.'

I was still fighting off the sobs. He'd never told me he loved me before and now he was telling me and it all seemed to be over.

'Do you know what I did after that dinner?' he continued.

I shook my head.

'I went and got shitfaced. I have hardly drunk for over ten years and I left Q Bar off my face at 4 a.m. That's how upset I was.'

'Spider said you were drunk when you left that Tarzan message,' I said, completely irrelevantly.

'Uh?' said James. 'Oh, that. I was putting it on, so he wouldn't know it was me.' He shook his head in confusion. 'What are we talking about that for?'

'I think I was trying to distract you,' I said, as the first tear escaped and rolled down my cheeks. Then they wouldn't stop rolling. I buried my face in my hands.

'Oh, don't cry, Antonia,' said James, pulling my hands away from my face and wiping away the tears. 'Please don't cry. I can't stand it. I never wanted to hurt you, but that dinner was such a reality shock. That's why I didn't want to come to it. Why didn't you listen to me? I knew it would be like that. I've met your poofta uncle in here before. He's a funny old bloke, I like him, but I knew what it would be like at your place from meeting him. All bloody silver spoons and bollocks. Your world is not my world – don't you get that?'

'Maybe it was just the wrong thing for us to do first,' I said. 'Maybe we should try something else, like just going to a movie, or out to dinner . . .'

He thumped the padded seat of the machine so hard, I nearly fell off it. He looked absolutely furious.

'You just don't get it, do you?' he said. 'I'm a peasant to you lot. Don't you remember – I *shovel*.'

I felt sick. He hadn't missed any of the ghastly nuances of that wretched dinner. He glared at me for a moment, then he threw his glasses on the floor and put his face into his hands, rubbing his eye sockets hard with his palms. When he took his hands away I could see there were tears in his eyes.

'The last thing I want to do is to hurt you, Antonia,' he said. 'But if we carry on the way we have, I don't know where it will end, because it can't go anywhere but here.'

He sighed a wobbly sigh. I started crying again. I knew what he was going to say.

'I'm not going to see you for a while, Antonia. It will be better for us both. I'll take a break from the desk, to give us a chance to get over it, and when I come back, we can just be friends like we used to be. OK?'

'No. It is not OK,' I said, my voice rising hysterically.

'Well, I'm sorry,' he said. 'But I've made up my mind.'

He bent down to pick up his specs and I thought for a moment he was going to kiss me. But he straightened up, looked at me for a moment and then just walked away. I started to get up to run after him, but something stopped me. I knew if he'd made his mind up I couldn't change it. If a man with his sex drive could be voluntarily celibate for two years, which is what he'd told me, I knew he could steel himself against any entreaties I could make. I knew I had to walk away like he just had – and could only hope I would come up with a brilliant idea of how to bring him back.

I took some deep breaths, gathered up my things and launched myself towards the exit, feeling like the life was draining out of my body with every step. At least James wasn't there to see me go. He'd disappeared again. Spider Spewface was *in situ*, of course, and I studiedly ignored him. But as I pushed through the turnstile he leaned over and put his hand on my arm.

'Don't worry, darlin',' he said, in his gruff voice. 'He'll come round. The silly bugger likes you too much to let you go for good. I've never seen him so daft about a sheila. Trust your old mate Spider on that.'

And he winked at me like a kindly uncle. I was so surprised I made it all the way home without crying.

When I got into bed, however, I couldn't stop crying. I just couldn't believe James would let one bad evening destroy the beautiful thing we had between us. If this was dating, I thought, I understood why my sisters complained about it so much.

I had wondered occasionally if it had all been too good

too soon to be true with James and now my worst doubts were confirmed. I was doomed to rattle from one failed relationship to another for years, as Rebecca and Sarah seemed to. In between fits of sobbing, I slept restlessly and had a lot of bad dreams.

At about 10 a.m., when I would normally have been getting up, there was a knock on the door and Percy came in carrying a tray.

'I've brought you breakfast,' he said, putting the tray on the bed and pulling a chair over. He'd brought me a glass of freshly squeezed orange juice, one of his beautiful fruit salads, like a Matisse on a plate, and a big pot of Earl Grey. There was a cup of green tea for himself.

'It's a peace offering,' he said, taking in my red eyes. 'I'm so sorry about the other night, Antonia. We all behaved appallingly. I hope it hasn't spoiled things between you and James.' He paused. 'But I fear it has.'

He squeezed my hand and tears began rolling down my cheeks again.

'Oh dear,' he said. 'You were crying when I arrived in Sydney and now you're crying again and I do feel to blame. I should have read Hugo the riot act before James got here that night, but I was so excited about it all I wasn't thinking straight. I thought everything had worked out like a lovely Doris Day film. I watch too many musicals. I'm afraid I was a bit unrealistic.'

'So was I,' I said, wiping my eyes.

'Is it really hopeless?' he asked, looking sincerely concerned.

'Yes,' I said. 'Utterly hopeless. James says it will never work because we come from different worlds.' I laughed bitterly. 'He told me I was a "silvertail". It's ironic, isn't it? I spent the first five years of my relationship with Hugo fretting that I wasn't posh enough for the Heaveringhams and now James says it won't work between us, because I'm too posh for him.'

Percy looked as grave as I had ever seen him.

'So what are you planning to do?' he asked me. 'Never go back to the gym and just let him go?'

'What choice do I have?' I wailed. 'He's told me it won't work and he's made his mind up. He has fearsome self-discipline, you know. If he's decided he's going to live without me, he will. He's dedicated most of his life to overcoming the limitations of physical pain and human weakness, through strength of mind, so this will be just another challenge for him. He's probably hanging upside down in a tree as we speak.'

'Don't tell, Tom,' said Percy, his twinkle returning. 'He'll try it.'

I smiled weakly and poked my fruit around with a fork. I didn't feel remotely like eating. Percy sat and nursed his tea, gazing into the distance.

'I don't think you should just let him go,' he said finally.

'Well, good for you,' I said, irritated. 'How exactly am I supposed to not do that?'

'Go back to the gym, find him and convince him.'

I opened my mouth to protest, but Percy held up his hand to stop me.

'I saw the way he looked at you, Antonia,' he said. 'He's

286

besotted with you – as he damned well should be – but it was a lovely thing to behold. Give him a few days to miss you and then go back and claim him. I think he will want you to, deep inside. Whatever he's running away from with all this kung fu nonsense, I'm sure he wants to be persuaded out of it, at heart.'

He might have a point, I thought. Percy's psychological analyses were usually so spot on, it might be worth a try. He'd given me a tiny grain of hope to hold on to. I might actually be able to get up and get dressed, I thought.

Picking up a bit of papaya with my fingers, I looked fondly at my dear old pal, Hugo's mad uncle. What an amazing person he was. He'd had an extraordinary life from the moment he was born and he'd made it even more so, through sheer force of personality. I'd always thought he was like some kind of real-life Zelig, as he always seemed to have been in the key place at the key moment, with the key people.

He was always coming out with things like: 'When I was at the Actors' Studio . . . When I was studying mime with Lindsay Kemp . . . When I was hanging out with Brian Jones . . . When I was with Cecil at Broadchalke . . . When I lived in Topanga Canyon, next door to Joni Mitchell . . . When I was in the ashram with John and Yoko . . . When I was in Marrakesh with Talitha . . . When I was on Mustique with Margaret and Tony . . .'

At first, I'd thought he must be bullshitting, but Hugo had assured me he wasn't. He'd been staying with us in London once and in the same week he'd had a postcard from Nan Kempner and a call from Giorgio Armani's assistant, inviting him to his private island for a summer break, so I had realized it was all true.

People just loved his company – but why wouldn't they? I did – and, as he explained to me, once you had proved yourself to be a trustworthy friend to one famous person and were declared 'good value', you got to know them all.

When I'd known him about a year – and he had been fantastically kind to me at several terrifying Heaveringham events – I felt bold enough to ask him how he lived. I knew enough about the family finances to guess he wouldn't have an enormous private income. He said his secret was not being burdened with possessions or a home of his own.

'I'm a professional guest,' he'd told me. 'It's what I do. I know when to arrive – and much more importantly, I know when to leave. And I'm constantly entertaining while I'm there. Very wealthy people are usually very bored. They love clowns like me who distract them from thinking about their guilt at being loaded.'

'But how do you know how not to outstay your welcome?' I'd asked him. I was a very nervous house guest myself, usually getting up at the crack of dawn in case my hosts had early breakfast and too frightened to have a bath in case of using too much hot water.

'Staying with people is an art form,' Percy had told me. 'And quite complex. First you must never appear needy. I have just enough dough for clothes and air fares and day-to-day guest expenses, such as dinners out, theatre tickets, lavish flowers, the latest books and other charming and amusing gifts for my hosts – and their pets. Very important, the pets. Every now and again I make a bit extra on the horses, which comes in handy.

'Secondly, you have to know when to come forward and dazzle the company and when to retreat. Sometimes you have to make yourself scarce and if the exchequer doesn't run to an evening out, you can disappear, quiet as a mouse, into your room. I always travel with a water-heating element, my Swiss Army knife and my hip flask, so I can have quite a little picnic in my room with no one knowing.

'Then you get dressed and slip out at about 10.45 p.m. smoke a few ciggies round the corner and come straight back in, to amuse your hosts with anecdotes about your hilarious evening out and the ghastly drinks party with no food. Even the most steely hostess is usually inspired to whip you up an omelette. Or to ask cook to.'

Percy claimed that – along with yoga – his very particular lifestyle was the secret to his extraordinary insight into human character.

'I don't have any possessions,' he'd told me. 'Apart from a few clothes and I don't hold on to them for long. Possessions clog the mind, dull your perception and limit your life. The only thing I would be sad to lose is my address book.'

But it had occurred to me, that while he had legions of devoted friends, Percy never seemed to have any long-term romantic relationships. I had wanted to ask him about it for years, but sensed a veil of privacy over the subject, which had stopped me. But now, I thought, was the moment I could bring it up.

He was still gazing vacantly ahead, lost in thought, his teacup loose in his hand. I waved a piece of mango under his nose to get his attention.

'Can I ask you something, Perce?' I said.

He nodded, snapping back to consciousness.

'Of course, darling girl, anything.'

'You've given me such good advice about my romance,' I said. 'Yet you never seem to have any love affairs yourself. Do you think they clog the mind as well, like possessions? Is that why?'

He looked back at me with a strangely blank expression, then he started whisking up the tray and teacups.

'Oh yes,' he said, briskly. 'Far too constricting, get in the way terribly. Drive you mad. I'm going out for a walk, see you later.'

Unusually, after listening to Percy, I didn't believe a word of it.

20

Life carried on – although I didn't particularly feel like living it. I thought Percy's advice to go back and get James was probably good, I just wasn't ready to activate it yet. I didn't feel strong enough for another knockback, so I decided to bide my time – using the new zen patience I had learned from him – and to devote my energy to the other important things in my life, like my son and my shop.

When I got to Anteeks one morning a few days after my breakfast with Percy, Dee disappeared into the kitchen and re-emerged with an enormous bunch of flowers, which she said had arrived for me moments after she'd opened the door. They were gorgeous – all different colours of roses from yellow, through mauve to dark pink.

I tore the envelope open. They were from Hugo.

'I'm a beast. Please have coffee with me this morning. Your deservedly soon-to-be ex-husband, Hugo the Horrible.'

As I stuffed them carelessly into the nearest vase, it occurred to me that the witty charm that had once delighted me so much in Hugo now jarred like the sound of a stuck CD. What was the point of being so adorable afterwards, if you couldn't control your mood when it really mattered?

I decided to let him stew, but shortly afterwards he rang. Unfortunately it was me who picked up the phone.

'Ants pants?' he said in what he thought was his most appealing little voice. Once it would have melted my heart, but not this time. 'Do you really hate me?' he said.

'Yes,' I said. 'More than you can possibly imagine.'

'Oh Antsy,' he went on, making me feel more steely with every whining wheedling word. 'Please don't be cross. I'm so sorry, I was just a stupid jealous old Hector. I would have rung you sooner, but I've been in Melbourne all week. Come and have coffee with me and I'll make it better. I'll buy you some orange cake.'

'Why don't you buy me a balloon as well, Hugo?' I said. All my anger and frustration with him from the last eleven years, for all the times when he had let his spoiled, nasty, snobbish, self-centred side win over, boiled up inside me.

'If only you could make it all better with cake,' I hissed at him. 'Maybe if you'd done all this straight after the dinner, it would be different, but it's too little, too late. And they do have telephones in Melbourne, I believe.'

He tried to butt in, but I carried on talking over him.

'You were so rude and hideous that night, Hugo, I couldn't believe it. It would have been bad enough in any circumstance, but when you consider what I have put up with from you since you walked out and the efforts I have made to be nice to your new friend, I think you could have been a little nicer to mine.'

There was a very loud silence from his end.

'Well, if you can't accept an apology, that's up to you,'

said Hugo, now sounding as cold and huffy as I had sounded angry.

'Yes, it is,' I said. 'Fuck off.'

And I put the phone down.

Dee was making a sympathetic face. I had to tell her something. An explanation that did not involve details of my 'friend'.

'Problems with my future ex,' I said. 'I wish he already was my bloody ex. The sooner we actually get the divorce, the better, although of course, that might mean Hugo having to tell the truth to his parents. The family solicitor will have to be involved, you see. All our assets are tied up with the family money somehow. I've never really understood it. But I know it will be quite complicated with trusts for Tom and all that. That's why Hugo hasn't hurried the process through. His father won't care, but his mother will have a blue hairy fit – there's never been a divorce in her family, let alone an out homosexual – and you should see her when she gets going.'

I rolled my eyes.

'That does sound messy,' said Dee. 'But then I suppose divorce always is.' She paused and laughed bitterly. 'Or anything involving men for that matter.'

I was beginning to agree with her.

After lunch she disappeared off to one of her endless round of beauty appointments – she was having her eyebrows shaped with lasers or some such nonsense – and I had some welcome time alone. It was a quiet afternoon and I picked up my needlepoint.

At the height of my crazed sexathon I had come up with some saucy new cushions, the best selling of which was: 'A hard man is good to find.' I'd actually given one of those to James. God only knows what he would have done with it. I couldn't really imagine him living in a needlepoint-friendly environment. He wasn't the chintzy kind.

In a particularly soppy moment I'd come up with a popular tennis themed one, with a crossed-rackets motif that said 'Love All', and the rather lame 'All things come to those who (lift) weights', which hadn't gone down in a big way in Woollahra. Maybe I should give them all to Spider for his bouncer friends, I thought.

That particular afternoon I didn't feel like doing any of those and doodled around with new ideas on the theme of heartbreak, loss and disappointment. I was well into stitching the words 'One swallow does not a summer make' and was in that familiar brain-in-neutral state, when the bell over the door tinkled.

It was James. James holding a bunch of red roses, interspersed with white gypsophila. I was so surprised, for a moment I just sat there. He stopped in the doorway and I threw the needlepoint down and ran over to him. He wrapped his arms round me and picked me up off the floor.

'You win,' he said. 'I had to see you.'

He put me down and held my chin in his free hand, looking at me intently.

'Do you know, you're the only thing in my whole life I haven't been able to give up?' he said.

As usual, Percy had been absolutely right. And Spider, come to that.

James handed me the flowers and I saw him notice Hugo's much larger bunch on the dresser by the till.

'A pathetic peace offering from Hugo,' I said, grabbing them and dumping them into the bin. Then I took the cellophane from James's flowers and arranged them in the vase with the utmost care. I hated baby's breath and wasn't overly keen on red roses – too obvious, I normally would have said – but these were the most beautiful flowers I had ever been given.

'I take it Dee's away for a while,' he said, as we stood and hugged in the middle of the shop. 'I saw her in Double Bay again, just now. That's how I knew it was OK to come.'

'She'll be under her facialist all afternoon,' I said.

'I wish you could be under me,' said James, biting my ear. 'But I'd better not hang around here too long. Too many windows.'

I dragged him into the stock room, in the hope of recommencing our sex life as soon as possible, but the shop bell rang and I had to leave him there while I served a customer, who was quickly followed by another. When they'd gone I locked the door and turned the sign to 'closed'.

Making whoopee on a pile of old blankets in the Anteeks stock room wasn't much more comfortable than Muscle City's various venues, but while it was still thrillingly naughty, it all felt noticeably different. The passion was still there, but it was much more tender and loving. When we finished, I found I had tears rolling down my cheeks. James kissed them away.

'You are such a sook,' he said, smiling sweetly. 'I wonder what it would be like to make love to you in a bed.'

I smiled back at him. I had been wondering the same thing for so long.

'Would you like to find out?' he asked me. I nodded vigorously. 'Good,' he said. 'A friend of mine has a place up at Byron we can go to. Would you like to go up this weekend?'

'I'd love to,' I said, with Tom-like enthusiasm and fervently hoping Percy would be able to look after him, so I could go.

'Well, that's a relief,' said James. 'Because I've already bought the air tickets.'

Those five days in Byron were probably the best I had ever known. James's friend's house was a very simple structure right by a long deserted beach, with hardly any furniture and a big outside deck. We couldn't see the ocean because of a large sand dune, but we could hear it, and best of all, no one could see us.

We spent the first twenty-four hours in bed, getting up only for the occasional swim and to make cups of tea and plates of fruit. We slept all wrapped up in each other and waking up with him, that first morning, to see his eyes already open and gazing into mine, was as perfect as I had always dreamed it would be. It turned out he spent a lot of the night downstairs reading – unable to sleep –

but he always made sure he was back in bed with me when I woke up.

After that we settled down like any loved-up couple on holiday – going for walks, swimming, reading, listening to music, going into town for fish and chips and just sitting together on the deck as darkness fell. On our second night, we saw a shooting star.

On the third day it poured with rain and we spent the entire afternoon in a funky old pub called The Railway, drinking beer and watching dog racing on the television. We got really pissed.

'You are a terrible influence on me,' said James, weaving back with our fifth round of drinks and giving me a beery kiss.

'Sorry,' I said happily, holding up my glass to clink with his.

'The terrible thing is,' he said, 'I love being corrupted.'

'Cheers,' I said.

'Up yer bum,' said James.

The next day we both felt a little fragile and James announced that he was going to make a 'healing meal', as he called it. He disappeared off to town and I curled up with my needlepoint anticipating a large plate of bacon and eggs, washed down with Coca Cola. But he came back with bags of ingredients I had never ever seen before, all from the wholefood store.

It was macrobiotic food, he explained as he put it on the table and I was distressed to see that, despite promising smells while he'd been cooking, there wasn't a fried ingredient among it. There was steamed brown rice, grated mooli radish, weird yellow pickles, steamed greens with toasted sesame seeds and steamed tofu in a light soya sauce, with grated ginger, and bowls of strange brown miso soup on the side. When I looked down at my soup it seemed to be moving on its own. Weird stuff.

I'd never eaten anything like it before – I'd never really got to grips with sushi even – but apart from some really revolting things called umeboshi plums, which were salted, it was delicious. I was amazed.

The only problem was that he had laid the table with chopsticks and I was hopeless with them. I watched him pick a tiny piece of spring onion from the top of his rice and put it into his mouth in one delicate gesture. It was all I could do to balance a piece of tofu on my sticks and lift it gingerly to my mouth, while he seemed to be able to pick up separate rice grains. Mine just fell all over my lap.

I saw him notice and his eyes crinkled up with amusement. Without saying anything, he got up and came back with a fork.

'Go on,' he said, handing it to me. 'Shovel.'

I cried when he dropped me off at home – or rather, the usual four doors away – on the Tuesday afternoon. Our time together had been so blissful, I couldn't bear the thought of going back to what I was beginning to think of as 'Sydney rules'.

'I'm going to have to get a new washer for your tap,' he said, wiping my tears away. 'It's always dripping.'

'But I'm going to miss you so much,' I said.

'I'll miss you too,' he said. 'My bed's going to feel so big and empty, but you know that's the way it is. I can't stay with you and you can't stay with me.'

'Why not?' I asked like a petulant child.

'You know why not,' he said. I wasn't sure I did any more, but he had his no-arguing voice on and I didn't want to end our beautiful trip on a sour note.

'I'll tell you what though,' he said. 'There's a pen in the glove box, can you hand it to me?'

He scribbled something on the back of a petrol receipt.

'Here's my mobile number,' he said, handing it to me. 'So you'll always be able to find me. It's the only phone I have, apart from at the gym, of course, and I'll be back there tomorrow, so you know where to come.'

'And where to work-out,' I said, determined to keep it sweet, and kissed him goodbye.

After that we settled back into our bizarre routine, seeing each other four or so times a week at the gym, having sex where and when we could and chatting away behind the desk, but after spending some 'normal' time together I didn't find it enough.

And it seemed James felt the same way, because a couple of weeks after the Byron trip I arrived to pick Tom up from school and found James already there, talking to him at the gate.

'Mummy,' said Tom, excitedly, 'James the kung fu man is here, he's come to see me.'

'Isn't that nice?' I said. 'Hello, James. How lovely to see you.' I pecked his cheek and he grinned sheepishly at me.

'Thought I'd come and see how Tom's kung fu moves are developing,' he said.

'Mummy,' said Tom impatiently, clearly convinced that James was his special friend, 'James says he'll teach me how to catch a Frisbee. Do you want to come with us?'

'Well, I'd love to come, if James doesn't mind,' I said.

'That would be great,' said James, winking at me. 'She would be very welcome, wouldn't she, Tom?'

But Tom had completely lost interest in me.

'Which is your car?' he asked, tugging on James's sleeve, and insisting on riding with him up to Centennial Park. I followed behind, feeling quite misty seeing their two heads – or what I could see of Tom's – together. I wondered what they were talking about. When we stopped at a red light, I could clearly see James's smiling profile, as he turned to listen to something Tom was saying and then I saw him throw back his head and laugh.

We had great fun in the park – Tom even allowed me to join in sometimes – and similar impromptu outdoor outings became a new feature of our lives, as spring moved on towards summer. Although, of course, with James being the man of mystery he was, impromptu was the word – he'd never say when he was going to be there, he'd just turn up at the school gate.

His justification was that by the very nature of his work he never knew where he was going to be on any particular day and it was better just to turn up, than to make promises and disappoint a child. I couldn't argue with it, but in between his appearances, Tom drove me – and Percy – insane, asking when James was coming again.

'Between the two of you,' said Percy, one night, when Tom had been particularly insistent with his enquiries, 'I am beginning to wish I had never heard the name James. It's James this, James that, James thinks, James says, James does, James eats, James poops. I'd say you both had a bad case of mentionitis.'

It must have been the success of the Tom outings that inspired it, because one night at the gym James amazed me by asking if I would like to go out with him and some of his friends one evening. I was gobsmacked. Two major revelations at once – going out *and* meeting friends.

'What brought this attack of normality on?' I asked him.

He shrugged.

'We had such a good time up at Byron and I really enjoy hanging out with you and Tom, so I just thought we should give life outside Muscle City another go. It didn't work at your place, but maybe it will work in my world.'

Being a very stupid girl, once again my first reaction was to obsess about what to wear. I had no idea where we were going and didn't know whether to wear jeans or a cocktail dress. In the end I rang his mobile from the shop, while Dee was out getting us some sandwiches.

'James,' I said, nervously.

'That's me.'

'You know tonight?'

'Would that be tonight when I am picking you up from home at 7.30 and we're going out to play some pool?'

'Ah,' I said. So that's what we were doing. I still didn't

have a clue what to wear. I'd never played pool in my life. All I knew about it was from Paul Newman in *The Hustler*.

'What about it?' said James, sounding amused.

'Oh nothing, I just wondered what we were doing . . .'

'Were you wondering what to wear by any chance?'

'No,' I said, feeling stupid. 'Yes.'

'Wear anything, we're only going to a bar. You won't need your tiara.'

As I rang off, I wondered whether he knew I actually had one.

Endeavouring to get into the laid-back cool scene I imagined we were going into – and with Percy's encouragement – I wore a low slung jeans skirt and a T-shirt Percy had given me as a jokey apology present for the disastrous family supper. It had 'Rich Bitch' written on it in rhinestones.

As part of his ongoing efforts to make me dress in a more up to date 'edgy urban' way – in other words, the way he dressed now – Percy insisted on 'customizing' my outfit. This consisted of cutting the sleeves off the T-shirt and hacking about six inches off the bottom of it, trimming the hem of the skirt and pulling the loose threads, so it went all frayed.

He said he was 'styling' me.

I was lying in the bath while he was busying around with my sewing basket and I could hear him humming happily to the song he had put on the stereo. The unmistakable strains of 'Mad About the Boy' came floating in to me. I sang along too.

Also on Percy's instructions I put some kind of gunk in

302

my hair while it was still wet, to make it go all tousled and rough-looking. It worked, but I hardly recognized myself – it made my hair look almost black. The savagely-cropped T-shirt kept riding up to show my tummy and I felt really self-conscious about the whole rig-out, but Percy was delighted with the effect.

'Ooh, marvellous,' he said, when I came downstairs, tugging at the bottom of the T-shirt. 'You should get that tummy button of yours pierced, you know. Draw attention to your abdomen, now it's lovely and flat. You could have a tattoo round your ankle too.'

'You must be joking,' I said. 'I already feel really stupid in this outfit.'

'You look fabulous. Much more modern.'

He wanted me to wear high-heel sandals, to complete what he called my 'look', but I insisted on my old Indian flip-flops for security.

James's eyebrows shot up when he saw me. He was wearing the same dark jeans and T-shirt he'd worn to dinner.

'Gosh,' he said. 'You look different.'

'Don't you like this?' I asked, uncertainly. 'Percy made me wear it.'

'Hmmm?' said James. 'Of course I like it, you look gorgeous. You always do. You just look different. Mind you, I am used to you in a sweaty T-shirt and not a lot else.'

The pool hall was above a pub in Darlinghurst. It was dark, dingy and smoky. I couldn't say it was the kind of place I would have chosen for a night out, but at least my outfit was right. All the girls were wearing very low-slung skirts, or supertight hipster jeans, with tiny little tops – many of them backless – and most of them had pierced navels. Percy was clearly much more *au fait* with what cool young Sydney women were wearing than I was. And they were all wearing amazingly high heels. I felt like a Telly-tubby in my flats.

To my great relief, James held my hand tightly as we walked in. As we crossed the crowded room, weaving our way between the pool tables, I noticed quite a few girls check him out and then look me over very coldly. One or two of them said hi to him and he nodded hello in return, which caused my stomach to clench with jealousy. Were they all his ex-girlfriends? The women he'd slept with before the celibate period?

He stopped and kissed one of them – a particularly tall and attractive blonde in very tight jeans and practically no top, who was chalking the end of a pool cue – and introduced me. She looked at me like I was a used tampon, said 'Hi' and turned back to her game.

I was beginning to have an idea how Hugo had made James feel.

We headed for the far back of the room, where there was a corner banquette.

'That's our spot,' said James, squeezing my hand. There was quite a crowd of men and women there already and Spider was sitting in prime position, his back to the wall, surveying the room over his belly and a bottle of beer. A small woman with long dyed black hair, an eyebrow ring like Percy's and tattoos all over her arms, was sitting next to him. I wished I felt more pleased to see Spider. He had been nice to me that one night, but he wasn't someone I had ever imagined socializing with.

'Hey, Jackie Chan,' said Spider, in the warmest tones I'd ever heard from him. 'My main man.' They high fived each other and Spider waddled off to get drinks for us, barely giving me a look.

James introduced me to his friends and, of course, I forgot all their names immediately. They were a mixed bunch, but there seemed to be a lot of dyed hair, a lot of black clothes and silver jewellery and quite a lot of piercing – it was a shame Percy hadn't come with me, I thought, he would have fitted in perfectly.

They were all friendly enough, although I noticed some of the women looking at me with particular interest, especially when James put his arm round me and pulled me close, kissing me on the forehead. Two of them, wearing the tiny backless tops that seemed to be the uniform of the place, exchanged an unmistakable 'look'. Mind you, he was the best-looking man in there, I thought, no wonder they were jealous.

What struck me most about James's friends, was how laid back and relaxed they all were. There was none of the frantic competitive conversation I was used to from my old crowd, or even from the new friends Percy had made for us in Sydney. Quite a few of them, like Spider's lady friend, didn't say anything at all, just sat there, quietly contemplating their drinks, their cigarettes and the room, seemingly happy to let it all just wash over them.

After a while, Spider and James got up to have a game

of pool with a couple of other guys – I'd already told him I didn't know how to play and it was obvious that this was not the place to learn.

'Come over and watch,' said James, so I did. But wherever I stood I seemed to be in the way of someone's 'shot' and James was concentrating too hard to take much notice of me, although he did put his arm around me from time to time. In the end I went and sat down again.

Still at the table was a particularly stoned-looking guy, who had hardly said a word all night, along with Spider's girlfriend, who I had now established was called Stacey, and the two girls who had exchanged looks over me. They were involved in an animated discussion that patently excluded anyone else and the other two were just gazing vacantly into space. And that was my evening.

The only other moment of note was when the tall blonde we'd seen on the way in, sauntered over to where James was leaning over the pool table and squeezed his bum. It was all I could do not to spring to my feet to punch her out – and I saw the two girls glance at each other and then at me when it happened. They were really starting to piss me off.

I decided just to let it unfold. James had stood up sharply when he felt the touch and turned round smiling – although he looked surprised when he saw who it was. I realized with satisfaction that he had probably thought it was me. The girl was smirking at him, wagging her head like a nodding dog and chewing coquettishly on her little finger.

Spider's Stacey spoke to me for the first time.

'Reckon that skinny bitch is making a move on your man, Toni,' she said, without even looking at me. 'Are you gonna sort her out?'

I pondered it seriously. I would have liked to have broken a bottle over her head, which was presumably the kind of thing Stacey had in mind, but I didn't think James would have been impressed.

'No,' I said. 'I'm going to leave it up to James. He seems to know her, he can sort her out.'

The blonde moved closer towards him, sticking out her ample breasts, but I saw with satisfaction that he stepped back and folded his arms over his cue. His face was friendly enough, but I could see from his body language he wasn't interested. Good. Mind you, the folded arms made his arm and chest muscles pop out divinely. Not good.

'You trust him then,' said Stacey.

'As much as I trust any man,' I said, slipping into her patois. She turned to look at me appraisingly, taking a big pull on her beer bottle.

'He's a bloody good-looking bloke, your James, but I reckon you're OK,' she said. 'Spider says he's silly about you.'

I was beginning to like Spider more all the time, but my happiness was short lived.

'So how long have you been seeing James?' said the prettier of the other two girls, lighting what must have been about her five hundredth cigarette since we'd been sitting there.

I did a mental calculation back to the night at the King George Hospital.

'About four months,' I said.

'Oh,' said the girl. 'That must have been right after he stopped seeing Jasmine then. Or nearly, anyway.' She laughed as though it was the greatest joke.

'Who's Jasmine?' I asked, stupidly.

'That girl who's talking to him now.'

Well, that capped my evening off. We all sat and watched the sideshow together, until I was relieved to see James gradually edging further and further away from Jasmine, as I now knew she was. Eventually he had the excuse of his turn at the pool game to move away from her. She sloped off – squeezing his bum again on the way.

I could no longer even keep up the front that I was having a lovely time. I knew I was looking bored and miserable when James finally came back – all smiley because he and Spider had won both games and made $50 each in the process. I couldn't believe they were playing for money. How tacky.

'Hey, babe,' he said, squeezing in beside me. 'Sorry, I left you so long. I'll sit this game out.'

Stacey got up to go and stand with Spider at the bar. James looked round to see who else had been with me and I noticed a dark look flash across his face when the two backless-top girls grinned knowingly at him. They got up and went off to the loo and I pulled a face at their bare brown backs.

'So,' he said to me. 'Have you been getting to know Stacey?'

I looked at him in bewilderment. Did he really think Stacey was someone I had anything in common with?

'Oh yes,' I said. 'We've been having a very interesting discussion about how best to disfigure women who crack on to your man and your two friends over there have been filling me in on your past love life. How is dear Jasmine?'

'Oh God,' said James. 'Those two are such little stirrers. Jasmine is fine. She's still blonde. She's still a wannabe model. She's still a nice girl. I met her at the gym and I took her out a few times, before I met you, OK? Is there a law against that?'

'No,' I said. 'Except you told me you were celibate before me.'

'I was, Antonia,' he said, clearly getting pissed off. 'Why do you think she's still harassing me like that? She thinks we have unfinished business.'

'Do you?' I knew I was being stupid, as I said it, but I'd had such a boring time and I just couldn't help myself.

'OK,' he said, getting his closed look on. 'I'll take you home. I wouldn't mind shooting some more pool and you're clearly bored shitless and you're being really silly. So I'll drop you off and come back.'

'Back to Jasmine?' I said. Why was I doing it? I knew I was behaving like a fuckwit, but hearing she was a model had made it even worse.

James rolled his eyes.

'For God's sake, Antonia,' he said. 'What soap opera are you getting this from? Do you really think that of me?'

'No,' I said. 'But you're so damned secretive with me, sometimes I don't know what to think.'

'Oh boy,' he said, running his hand over his head. 'Reality check number two. James and Antonia go out in public and everything gets fucked up – the sequel. Let's go.'

We walked out together, but this time James didn't hold my hand – and of course we had to walk right past Ms Sydney Blonde Beauty, who wished him a cheery farewell.

'Bye, James honey,' she sang out. 'Call me.'

I turned round and gave her the finger. Stacey would have been proud of me.

21

We were silent all the way home. I sat there cursing myself. I knew I had behaved stupidly and I was really hoping I wouldn't start crying again, because it was getting a bit embarrassing.

When James pulled up in front of the house – or rather a few doors down, a routine I was really tired of – I made to get out straightaway, but he put his hand on my arm.

'Aren't you going to invite me in for coffee?' he said, softly.

I just carried on looking at him, like an idiot. Was this some kind of a joke? He never came in.

He shrugged.

'I've been thinking all the way here,' he said. 'Tonight was not the greatest success, but what are we going to do? Just give up again? I came back after the last disaster, Antonia, so I'm not going to give up after one more hiccup. It's two steps forward, one step back with us, but we're still going forward. And it's still early – you're not usually even at the gym by this time.'

I was still looking at him, amazed. He'd actually turned the engine off.

'Did you really mean it about coming in?' I asked.

But he was already unhooking his seat belt. He came round and opened the car door for me.

Percy was still up. He was dressed in his favourite 'pulling' outfit, as he called it – the leopardskin jeans and no undies combo. As we walked in he was peering into the hallway mirror applying black kohl pencil to his eyes.

'Ah, James,' he said, in an almost normal manly voice, turning round and shaking his hand. 'How good to see you again. I'm glad you're back, Antonia, because I'd like to go out myself. I was assuming you wouldn't be going to the gym after your evening out.'

He smiled at us and picked up his keys.

'Well, I'll be off then,' he said. 'You can take Tom to school tomorrow, can't you? OK. Toodle-oo.'

I was speechless for the second time in five minutes. He was being so butch. He hadn't batted his eyelashes at James once.

James didn't just stay for coffee – he didn't even have any coffee – he stayed the night. He was still there when Tom came bouncing in the next morning.

'Percy's not there, Mummy,' he was saying as he ran in. 'So . . . Hey, kung fu man!'

He jumped on the bed, in his little pyjamas, striking a Bruce Lee pose, absolutely thrilled to see him.

'You've come to see me at home, James, how nice,' babbled Tom. 'And you slept in Mummy's bed. Daddy used to sleep there. I hope you were comfy. You can always sleep on the spare bed in my room, you know. Would you like some breakfast? I have Cocopops. Do you like Cocopops? Would you like to see my room?'

James fished his underpants off the floor and managed

to wriggle into them just before Tom pulled the covers off and he was dutifully dragged off to inspect everything of interest in Tom's room. I left them to it.

By the time I was showered and dressed they were at the breakfast table. James was still in his undies, but Tom was ready for school. He was having fruit on his cereal, because James did. James smiled at me.

'Tom says I can take him to school this morning,' he said. 'Is that OK with you?'

'That would be lovely,' I said. 'But you might want to get dressed first.'

'Mummy, please can I have chicken's breasts for lunch today?' said Tom. 'And brown rice with mung seeds in it. Can I?'

'Well, not today,' I said. 'Because we don't have any, but I'll buy you some later and you can have them tomorrow. Why exactly do you want chicken's breasts?'

'You need a lot of protein to build muscles,' he said, with the supreme confidence of a seven-year-old who has very recently acquired a new fact.

I made Tom's usual lunch – white bread Vegemite sandwiches (he liked it better than Marmite, the little traitor), carrot sticks and a tub of peach yoghurt – while he bombarded James with more questions, even following him up to my room when James went to get dressed.

'Well, we'll be off then,' said James, coming back into the kitchen and picking up Tom's lunch box. 'I won't be at the gym tonight,' he said. 'I've got something on. But I'll be there tomorrow. I'll see you there.'

He put his arms round me and kissed me tenderly. Over

his shoulder I saw Tom watching with a raised-eyebrow expression I was more used to seeing on Percy. As he and Tom walked out of the door I heard that piping seven-year-old voice again.

'James,' he said. 'Do you love my mummy?'

'Yes,' said James. 'I do.'

'Oh, that's good,' said Tom, taking his hand. 'So do I.'

I really couldn't have been happier. I had everything I wanted. The excitement was still there with James, but now it seemed he was prepared for us to lead a more normal life together as well. I just had to let him come round to things at his own pace, I realized.

The trips to the park had come out of nowhere and become a regular thing, so I had no reason to think that staying over wouldn't become part of our life as well, when he wasn't working all night at the gym. Best of all, Tom loved him and James didn't seem to mind. I purred with satisfaction. It was a warm November morning, the jacaranda trees were out all over Woollahra. It was going to be a great summer.

The only thing that marred my happiness was a strange call from Dee that morning at the shop. She didn't sound herself at all.

'I won't be in today, Antonia,' she said. 'Actually don't count on me for a couple of weeks, OK? I'll call as soon as I know when I'll be in again.'

'Sure, but are you all right, Dee?' I asked. 'You sound a bit stressed. Is there anything I can do for you?'

'No, yes, I'm fine, but I just can't come in for a while.'

She paused and then spoke very quickly. 'I've managed to get an appointment with a surgeon I've been trying to see for over a year. A plastic surgeon. I'm going up to the Silver Springs afterwards to recuperate.'

I was nearly speechless. There was nothing wrong with Dee's face and I hated the idea of her being sliced open unnecessarily, but it shouldn't have surprised me really, from someone who had at least two cosmetic treatments a week, not counting the run-of-the-mill manicures, pedicures, blow-drys and waxings, which were as much part of her daily life as reading the paper was of mine.

'Are you sure you don't want me to collect you from the clinic, or something?' I said.

'No, no,' said Dee, sounding like she wanted to get off the phone. 'I'll be fine. Really.'

'Well, where is this Silver Springs place? Can I come and visit you there?'

'No, they don't let you have visitors, or even phone calls there, that's the whole point – it's a sort of health retreat, in Queensland. Really, I'll be fine. I'm sorry it's such short notice, Ant, but it's practically impossible to get in with this guy, so I can't miss the opportunity. I'd better go – OK?'

'OK,' I said. 'And good luck.'

'Thanks, Ant,' said Dee. 'You're such a good friend. Oh and don't forget to ring that man in Orange, he said he has some old hotel china we might be interested in.'

And she rang off. Apart from the odd extended appointments for botox and collagen, Dee had hardly missed a day in the shop since we'd gone into business together, but everybody was entitled to time off – I'd had more than my share after all. For a moment I worried about her and her baffling obsession with perfecting her already gorgeous looks, but then I just got on with my day, which was going to be much busier, now I didn't have Dee's back-up.

Between organizing Percy to collect Tom from school, arranging delivery of a consignment of summer stock that was coming on spec from our new agent in Western Australia – a very clever decorator discovered by Dee on a business trip to Perth with Frankie – seeing the man about the hotel china, despatching props for various magazine shoots and serving a non-stop flow of customers, I was run off my feet all day.

James would pop into my mind from time to time and I would allow myself a moment of pleasure, thinking about him, before getting on with the task at hand. It all felt so much more settled between us now and my obsessive preoccupation with him had calmed down.

Grabbing a moment between customers in the afternoon – the great spring weather seemed to have put all of Woollahra into a shopping mood – I rang his mobile just to say how lovely it had been to have him stay over. His phone was switched off, so I reckoned he must be caught up doing whatever it was he was doing that day – James McLoughlin, international man of mystery. I wasn't bothered because I knew I was going to see him the next night anyway. I hugged the thought of him to myself for a moment and then got on with my life.

*

That evening Tom, Percy and I went out for dinner. We were all in very good moods, although Tom's mentionitis was reaching a peak.

'Guess what, Percy?' he said, simultaneously shovelling a huge spoon of ice cream into his face.

'Now let me see . . .' said Percy. 'Could this be a fascinating fact about James by any chance? And could you stop eating like a Visigoth, please?'

'Yes,' said Tom. 'It is about James. That was a clever guess. *Dix points.* Anyway, he loves Mummy. He told me. And he slept in her bed. With no clothes on. I saw him. He's got lots of muscles.'

He held his puny little arm up in an attempt to make his biceps pop up like James's. Percy stuck a bread roll up the sleeve of his T-shirt.

'Is that more like it?' he said, winking at me.

'Yeah, cool.' Tom poked at his bread muscle and then tried moving it down to his chest, then his stomach, while Percy and I put our hands over our mouths to stifle giggles. I could see he was wondering whether he could get away with putting it down the front of his shorts, when Percy snatched it away from him.

'That's quite enough of that, young man,' he said, turning to me. 'Where does he get it from, do you think, Antonia?'

I just shook my head and collapsed into laughter. Tom looked at us both, frowning and oblivious to what we thought was so funny.

'Anyway, Mummy,' he said. 'About James . . .'

'Oh God,' said Percy, sinking down in his chair. 'I'm losing the will to live.'

'Do you think he will soon come and live with us all the time?' said Tom. 'James, I mean. The way Greg lives with Daddy? Is James your special friend now?'

'Well, he's certainly *a* special friend,' I said. 'But I don't know if he's going to come and live with us.'

Not yet, I thought, but maybe one day. It was looking better all the time.

James wasn't on the desk when I arrived at the gym the next night, it was the Chinese guy Percy liked. I wasn't concerned because I knew my darling man would turn up later. I liked it when he crept up on me, it added to the general naughty thrill of it all.

I did my twenty minutes on the treadmill with a big grin on my face, anticipating how good it was going to be to see James when he did turn up. I was going to tell him about Tom and the bread roll muscles. How he'd laugh.

When I was about halfway through my weights and he still hadn't appeared, I started to wonder what was going on. Maybe he was planning a really big surprise, but it seemed odd, when he had definitely said he would be there.

He still wasn't around by the time I finished, so I went up and asked the guy on the desk if he knew where he was.

'James not here tonight,' he said, helpfully.

'Yes, I know that,' I said, trying not to sound irritated. 'But he said he would be. Do you think he's coming later?'

The guy shrugged, he really couldn't have been less

interested. I left James a note – signed Jane, for old time's sake – asking him to call me as soon as possible, and went home.

I tried his mobile when I got in – it was just so weird for him to say he'd be there and then not be – but it was turned off again. I decided not to leave a message. Didn't want to sound too needy.

By the next afternoon, when I still hadn't heard from him and he still hadn't answered his mobile, I was feeling extremely needy. Between Dee and James both doing disappearing acts, I was beginning to feel quite abandoned.

After a few hours of agonizing I rang Muscle City at 5 p.m. to ask if James was going to be on that night. A woman answered the phone and sounded friendly enough.

'I'll go and have a look at the roster,' she said. 'Won't be long.'

She came back shortly after.

'Yep,' she said. 'He'll be in at 11 p.m.'

But when I got there at midnight, James wasn't there. The Chinese guy was on the desk again and was as uninterested as before in my questions.

'He not here,' he said. 'He on roster. He not here.' Shrug.

I was beginning to miss Spider, who seemed like Mr Congeniality compared to this bloke.

'Did he get the note I left last night?' I asked.

The guy had a desultory look under the counter and brought up a few pieces of paper.

'One of these?' he asked.

'Yes,' I said. My note was still there and had clearly never been unfolded.

I went home. I tried his mobile. There was no answer.

I didn't know what to think. Had he gone off the whole idea again? We'd had that dodgy night out, but it had all turned out fine in the end. He'd specifically said he wasn't going to let it bother him, and he'd stayed over for the first time. It had all seemed better than ever, but then he hadn't turned up at the gym as he'd promised. It didn't make any sense. Once again, lying on my boiling mattress, ridiculous possibilities coursed through my brain.

Maybe it had been too cosy at my place, too domestic. Maybe taking Tom to school had freaked him out – too much like being an instant dial-a-dad. Maybe the beautiful Jasmine had called him and he'd decided she was less bother than a neurotic weeping woman with a seven-year-old child, a mad poofta uncle in residence and an insanely jealous gay husband round the corner. We must seem like the Addams Family, I decided, to the outside eye.

It was the same story on the third day. James's mobile was turned off. James was rostered on at the gym, but when I went in James wasn't there. There was a different man on the desk that night, an older chap I hadn't seen before. I didn't bother with my exercise routine, I just went straight up and asked him.

'Is James coming in tonight?' I said brightly.

'How would I know?' said the man. He was wearing a thick gold bracelet and one of those nasty rings with a gold sovereign in it. I looked at his name badge, it said 'Sam the Man'. James had mentioned him to me, he was the big boss of Muscle City and a bit of a 'character'.

'I was told he was rostered on tonight,' I persisted. 'But he's not here . . .'

'I know he's not bloody here, sweetheart,' he said rudely. 'That's why I'm bloody here. He hasn't turned up the last three nights, so he needn't bother turning up again ever. The last thing I need in my night staff is unreliability.'

'Where do you think he is?' I asked, stupidly.

'Probably cracking bricks with his head,' said Sam. 'Fucking kung fu weirdo, they're all cranks those blokes. Good riddance to him.'

He swiped my card and went to hand it back to me.

'You can keep that,' I said. 'I won't be coming back to this gym.'

'Suit yourself, darling,' he said and threw it in the bin. 'And if you see your friend James, give him a message from me – get fucked.'

'Get fucked yourself,' I said and walked out.

I didn't go back to Muscle City, but I did keep calling. I even asked for Spider a few times, but he wasn't there either. In the end the nice girl who answered the phone in the afternoon told me – kindly – it probably wasn't worth bothering to call any more.

'I don't want to be rude,' she said. 'But I don't think James will be back here. He really pissed Sam off not turning up three nights in a row and he's been sacked. Sam threw all his things in the bin.'

'Isn't there some kind of staff record, with his home number on it or anything?' I asked. 'You've been really nice to me. I'm sure you understand how it is. I really need to find him.'

'I understand,' she said. 'You're the girl he's been seeing, aren't you? The one with the little boy? I've heard he's pretty gone on you. Spider told me. I'll go and have a look for you.'

She came back a few moments later.

'I've got a phone number,' she said. 'But there was no address on his file.'

It was his mobile number.

'Well, thanks anyway,' I said. 'And thanks for being so nice over the last few days. I really do appreciate it. What's your name, by the way, in case I ever come by.'

'Jasmine,' she said.

22

Now I was totally baffled. It was more than five days since James had said he would be at the gym. He hadn't answered his phone the whole time and I'd had no word from him. I had been steadily working through the well-documented stages of grief and at this point I hit anger.

I could think of no plausible reason why he shouldn't have rung me – unless something awful had happened to him, but surely they would have known at the gym if he was in hospital or something. I'd been over it all in my head a million times and it didn't make any sense. The only possible explanation I could come up with was that he had finally – and for good – cooled off on the whole idea of me.

For all I knew he might already be back in Hong Kong at his *dojo*. Maybe he'd finally decided that my corrupting influence was not worth it after so many years of rigidly sticking to his practice. I'd had him drinking alcohol, eating junk food and squandering his precious chi in countless orgasms – everything a kung fu weirdo shouldn't indulge in.

But would he really put his precious bloody 'practice' before his feelings for me? I started to feel furious with him for mucking me around – if spending one night at my place had convinced him he had been right all along and we were from 'different worlds' why hadn't he just told me? How dare he discriminate against me and call me a silvertail. It was just snobbery reversed. He was as bad as Hugo, I decided.

Meanwhile, Tom was driving me insane asking me when he was going to see James again. How could I explain to him that the lovely kind man who had taken him to school the other day had decided we were upper-crust boneheads and had disappeared off my radar completely? On the morning of the sixth day, I'm afraid to say, his nonstop barrage of questions was just too much and I screamed at him to stop pestering me. I felt awful afterwards.

Later that day Percy dropped into the shop.

'Dee still waiting for her wounds to heal?' he asked.

'As far as I know,' I said. 'I hope she's OK, but she said she was going off to a spa to recuperate and not to worry.' I shrugged. 'God knows what she's had done to herself, but it's just her little obsession, I guess.'

Percy was pulling a very strange face – sticking his tongue right out like an All Black mid-*haka* and stretching his jaw and neck like an old tortoise.

'What are you doing?' I asked him, as he pulled his mouth up into a rictus smile like Jack Nicholson as the Joker.

'My facial exercises.' He went over to the mirror and patted his jawline with obvious satisfaction. 'If Dee did these every day, as I do, she wouldn't need a surgical facelift.'

I just shook my head and smiled. Having Percy around

was like watching a twenty-four-hour comedy channel.

'Anyway,' he said, clearly satisfied that his regime was working, 'I thought I'd come and help you out here, in case you needed to pop out for anything.'

He looked me straight in the eye with his unblinking Heaveringham gaze.

'And I thought you might like to pick your young son up from school today, because I heard you being vile to him this morning.'

'Oh God, Percy, I feel awful about that,' I said.

'You haven't heard from James, have you?' he said, quietly.

I bit my lip and shook my head.

'No,' I said. 'He seems to have done a bunk.'

Percy thought for a moment.

'After that awful dinner I was hoping perhaps you could just look on the whole thing as a good dose of lust anti-biotics to get you over Hugo,' he said. 'But it went a bit further than that, didn't it?'

I nodded, welling up, as usual.

'I thought it had,' I said. 'And he seemed so fond of Tom.'

'Not to mention Tom's feelings for him,' said Percy. 'Reminds me of how I used to feel about the Willington game keeper when I was a boy. Marvellous in his gaiters, and all that blood and killing was so thrilling. So what are you going to do? Just let him go and hope he'll come running back like last time?'

'Well, I'd like to have it out with him,' I said. 'I think it's appalling behaviour to lead someone on and win their trust and go away with them and become part of their life and then just *drop* them . . .'

I was working myself up into a lather of righteous indignation.

'Mind you,' I continued, 'I should have known he'd behave badly in the end. Remember how he ate that night he came over for supper?' I snorted. 'All elbows and shovelling. Ghastly. It was like having dinner with a Viking.'

I looked round expecting Percy to agree and to make some catty remark that would make me laugh, but he was looking at me with a serious expression and narrowed eyes.

'What?' I said.

'I can't believe my ears,' he said. He stood up, picked up his tote bag and walked over to the door.

'I am so disappointed in you, Antonia,' he said, in grave tones. 'The one thing I have always loved about you is that you seemed to be so non-judgemental and open minded and now I discover that at heart you are just another shocking little provincial snob. You're no better than the Anteeks customers you despise so much because they look down on anyone who drives a car more than a year old and think "chint" is the singular of "chintz". If that's the kind of person you really are, then that lovely James is too good for you. I think he's made a lucky escape.'

I just stared at him in amazement.

'You've taken on the very worst of the Heaveringham snobbery, Antonia,' he concluded. 'And with precious little basis for it. Good day.'

And he flounced out.

That was when I hit rock bottom. Dee and James had both done a bunk. Hugo and I weren't speaking. I'd been horrid to Tom. The so-called friends I'd made when we first got to Sydney had long since dropped me and now Percy hated me too. I got through the afternoon in a daze of self-pity. I'm sure anyone who came into the shop that day thought I was a halfwit, but on top of the other abandonments, Percy's outburst had left me in a state of shock.

The only things that roused me from my stupor were two strange men who came into the shop just after lunch. They attracted my attention because they were so unlike my usual customers. For one thing, they were men – my clientele was overwhelmingly female, plus a few glamour boys – and when 'real' men did come in it tended to be at the weekend, in golf clothes, following up some well-dropped hint for a birthday present.

These two were both wearing cheap suits and had a furtive air about them. They picked up a few things and I noticed them glance at me and then at each other. It was a bit spooky, but I was so generally shell shocked I couldn't get worked up about it. I just kept an eye on them in case they were shoplifters. After about ten minutes they exchanged another look and left.

About an hour later, two more men came in, dressed in what you might call exclusive leisure wear. One of them was wearing a huge gold watch, but apart from outward appearances they behaved pretty much the same way the other two had.

After a few minutes one of them came up to the counter

with an embroidered lavender bag. As I wrapped it for him I could see him peering over me into the back room. I straightened up and looked him full in the eye. I wasn't in the mood for bullshit from anyone.

'Are you looking for something?' I asked, icily.

He shuffled his feet and pushed up the sleeves of his leather jacket.

'I was just wondering if the other lady was here,' he said. 'Dee.'

I didn't like this man.

'Not at the moment,' I said. Remembering what James had told me about Dee's paranoia being valid, I felt extremely cautious.

'Are you expecting her later?' he said.

'Yes,' I said. 'That's $30 please. Would you like to leave her a message?'

'Er, no, you're all right,' said the man.

But was he, I wondered. I left a message on Dee's mobile telling her about the two men and asking her please to ring me and let me know she was OK. I didn't know what else to do. Between her and James, I was getting quite expert at such messages.

Percy wasn't in when I got home and had left no note, so I did my best to make it up with Tom, taking him to a movie at Fox Studios and letting him have the very largest bucket of popcorn. He snuggled up to me during the film and – God love him – didn't mention James once, even though it was a kung fu action picture. Children were so forgiving and so perceptive, I thought to myself.

There was no sign of Percy at breakfast either – was he

going to disappear on me too, I wondered – and working on automatic pilot I took Tom to school and then trudged to the shop.

As I picked up my needlepoint, working on 'A good man is hard to find', to go as a pair with my incredibly successful 'hard man' cushions, I felt I was right back where I had been when Percy had arrived over a year before. Alone and lost. It was only a matter of time before I headed to Agostini's for orange cake and two full-fat lattes.

As I sat there filling holes with brightly coloured wool, I wondered whether that was all my affair with James had been. Just using sex and imagined romance as another way of filling holes, as I had used food before.

I was still thinking about it when I was startled by a roaring sound outside. I looked up to see a huge motorbike pull up. The door opened and a terrifying person walked in. His head was bald, but he had a thick black beard almost to his waist. He was wearing a leather waistcoat which revealed arms and a chest entirely covered in tattoos, which went right up his neck and onto his shaved head. He had an enormous silver ring through the middle of his nose, like a prize bull.

After the four strange men who had come into the shop yesterday, I was beginning to feel extremely disturbed by the turn my clientele was taking. Maybe they had been casing the joint and he had a sawn-off shotgun down the leg of his filthy jeans.

'I'm looking for someone called Antonia,' he said, wiping his nose with the back of his hand.

'You're looking at her,' I said, terrified, but trying not to sound it.

'This is for you,' he said.

He handed me a piece of paper. I looked down to see the following words: James McLoughlin, Unit 6, 32 Waratah Street, Bondi Beach.

It was written in blue biro, in really bad handwriting that I knew I had seen somewhere before. Suddenly I got it – it was Spider's writing. I looked up to see the biker climbing back onto his enormous bike. I ran to the door. He already had his helmet on.

'Wait,' I said. 'Did Spider give this to you?'

'Maybe,' he said, revving up.

'Did he, or didn't he?' I shouted over the din.

'Did,' said the biker and roared off.

Fifteen minutes later I was ringing the doorbell at 32 Waratah Street, Bondi Beach. So this is where he lives, I thought. In one of those old deco blocks just off Campbell Parade. Now I knew, it seemed like exactly the place where James would live. I should have guessed.

There was no answer from the buzzer, but I kept pushing it anyway and after a few minutes I heard a voice calling me from above. I looked up to see James leaning out of a window. He was grinning.

'I can't believe it,' he said. 'You found me. Come up. Third floor. Watch out, I'm going to throw the keys down.'

I ran up the stairs, let myself in and walked into the flat to see James propped in an armchair, with his feet up on a large pile of books. Both legs were in plaster to the thigh. I ran over to him.

'Oh my God,' I said. 'What on earth has happened to you?'

'I'd ask you to sit on my knee, but I haven't got any any more,' he said, pulling me down onto the arm of the chair and bending my face down to his. He gave me one of his unbearably sexy slow kisses.

'God, it's good to see you,' he said.

I had so many questions I didn't know what to say first.

'So why didn't you bloody ring me then? It's been a week!' I practically yelled at him, feeling the same kind of desperate loving anger that overcomes a mother when she is reunited with a child who was briefly lost. The only time I had ever smacked Tom was when I had lost him once, for five minutes, at Disneyland.

'I was too ashamed, Antonia,' he said. 'After all my carrying on about security and then I got bloody done over. So much for the kung fu man.'

'Who did this to you?'

'Frankie Sullivan's goons – I think. They didn't introduce themselves.'

'I don't understand why you didn't call me, I've been worried sick – with good reason, I now see.'

'I didn't call because I was worried about you,' he said. 'With your friend Dee and everything, it was all a bit too close and I didn't want them making the connection between us. They're capable of anything. I was lucky they didn't kill me. I think they wanted to, but they were disturbed.'

We just looked at each other. I was overwhelmed by feelings. Relief and joy to see him, fury at what had happened to him and a sense of amazement that I was finally in his home. I got up and walked around trying to collect my thoughts. The flat was beautiful. A completely pristine white space, with the most amazing views of the ocean.

Even the floor was white and the only furniture, apart from the chair he was sitting in, was a large futon. It had my needlepoint cushion on it. Otherwise the only decorations were more books, an orchid in a pot and a photograph of me stuck to the wall with masking tape. I wondered where on earth he'd got it – he'd never asked me for a picture. Then I realized it was the photo from my gym card enlarged.

'I'll have to get you a better picture than that,' I said, marvelling at how porky my face had been. He smiled and looked a little bashful.

'You weren't supposed to see that,' he said. 'Secret boys' business.'

I went over and kneeled beside him, with my head on his lap.

'Oh my poor darling,' I said. 'What have they done to you?'

'They've smashed my knees with a baseball bat.'

I kissed them through the plaster.

'Will you get better?'

He shrugged. 'I've probably got a better chance than most people, because I was fit when it happened. But it's going to take time. I'll be Mr Limpy for a while.'

'I'll look after you, Mr Limpy,' I said, firmly. It didn't feel like it was the time to prevaricate. 'I love you, James,' I said. 'I nearly went mad when I didn't know where you were.'

He stroked my cheek.

'I love you too, Grasshopper,' he said. 'I've been sitting here all these days wondering how could I bring myself to ring you and tell you what had happened and agonizing over whether it was too risky.' He stopped and frowned. 'How the hell did you find me, by the way?'

'Spider sent me a message,' I said.

James punched the arm of his chair.

'Good old Spider,' he said, grinning and shaking his head. 'He knows me better than I know myself. God, he's a good friend. Best mate a man could have.'

I was still bemused by this friendship, but it wasn't the time to pursue it. I had a million more questions to ask him, but he was looking at me in a way that made my internal organs dance the Macarena.

'Help me up, will you?' he said. 'And pass me my crutches.'

I helped him out of the chair and he put the crutches under his arms.

'It's OK,' he said, smiling at me. 'We're not going far.'

After about four steps, he threw the crutches down and collapsed onto the futon.

'Get over here,' he said. 'And show me a good time.'

So I did.

23

'I rather like having you in my complete control,' I said to James afterwards, lying on top of him.

'I always knew you were a pervert,' he said and, grabbing my hands behind my back in one of his, he rolled me over and pinned me down with one plastered leg. I pretended to protest.

'Now what were you saying about control?' he said.

I went to push him away and caught sight of my watch.

'Oh my God,' I said. 'It's nearly three o'clock. I'll have to go and meet Tom.'

'Can't Percy get him?' said James.

I shook my head.

'Percy's not on speakers with me,' I said.

'Oh dear, with me in hiding and Percy not speaking to you, you must have been a lonely girl.'

'You don't know the half of it, James,' I said, thinking about Dee holed up with her stitches at the Silver Springs, but I had to sort Tom out before I told him about all that. I couldn't find Percy, but after a couple of calls I managed to get hold of one of Vita's mummies and she said they'd be delighted to take Tom home to stay the night.

I lay back down and looked at James some more. I never tired of looking at his face. It was like some kind of miracle to me, the way everything was in just the right place, even the scar. He gazed back at me. What a pair of sops.

'Will you stay with me tonight, Antonia?' he asked quietly.

I nodded.

'Good,' he said. 'But first, will you go and get me some food? I've been living on miso soup for a week and you've just sapped the very last of my energy.'

I went out and got a feast of a Thai takeaway and we ate it sitting on the futon, James propped up on the pillows, me cross-legged opposite him.

'You know what you were saying about me being lonely?' I said. He nodded, biting the tail off a tiger prawn.

'Well, you and Percy weren't the only people I've been missing.'

His put his head on one side, questioningly.

'Dee's disappeared too,' I said. 'Well, she hasn't disappeared like you did.' I slapped his plaster cast. 'I know where she is. She's had some kind of stupid facelift and she's hiding out at a spa in Queensland called the Silver Springs, until she can be seen in public again. Of course, she's perfectly entitled to some time off, but I wish she could have given me a bit more warning. Mind you, she chose a good time to make herself scarce, because some really creepy guys came looking for her yesterday. I didn't like the look of them at all.'

'What kind of creepy guys?' said James, narrowing his eyes as I told him about them.

'Let me get this straight,' said James, looking very serious. 'There were two shifty blokes in suits and then two shifty blokes in leather jackets.'

I nodded.

'The second lot of blokes – did one of them have George Michael stubble and a big gold watch?'

I nodded again.

'Was the other one a really ugly short arse?' he said.

'Yes,' I said. 'Do you know them?'

'Shit,' said James, exhaling loudly through his mouth. 'Those are the creeps that did me in. At least they were looking for her and not you, but I hate to think of them being anywhere near you. Fucking mongrels.'

'Oh my God,' I said. 'I thought they were dodgy. Why do you think they were looking for Dee?'

'They work for her husband. They must have been looking for her for him.'

'But surely he knows she's at the Silver Springs,' I said, bewildered.

'If that's where she is,' said James. 'Have you spoken to her there?'

'No,' I said, starting to feel really stupid. 'I left a message on her mobile, but she said they didn't let you take calls up there.'

'I think we should call her,' said James.

He was drumming his fingers on the futon. I could see his mind was racing. So was mine.

'Who were the other two guys who came to the shop then, James?' I asked.

'Cops probably,' said James. 'We've suspected they were

on to this for a while. It's probably a good thing – as long as they're the right cops.

'Can you lend me your mobile?' he said suddenly. 'I can't use mine at the moment. Security risk and all that. We've got a few calls to make.'

First we rang the Silver Springs. They said Dee wasn't there and hadn't been there for over a year, since her last visit. At which point I started to feel sick.

Then he called Spider.

'Hey, Spiderman,' he said. 'Yeah, she's here now. You cunning old bastard. Yeah, thanks. I owe you, man. Big time. Look, it's really heating up with the four stooges. Mrs Sullivan's disappeared and those goons that did me over have been in to Ant's shop. It sounds like the cops have been in too and I don't want any of those people anywhere near her. So I don't think we can wait any longer. I'm going to call O'Hara. We can't do any more of this undercover, it's too dangerous.'

I could hear Spider's expletives coming down the phone. James held the handset away from his ear.

'I know he is cop cunt scum, Spider, as you so delicately put it, but two dangerous men have been in to see my woman and I am not risking it. We've got enough on them now to make the case stick. I'll call that guy at the *Herald* too, just in case O'Hara shafts us, OK?'

There was another volley of profanity from Spider and James rang off, laughing.

'Is it all to do with the King George Hospital still?' I asked.

'That and about three other beautiful sites they're trying

to cover in concrete. Your friend Mr Thorogood is up to his neck in it and I think we've got enough to nail them all.'

I noticed the 'we', but said nothing. James was already on the phone to O'Hara, whoever he was. He certainly seemed to know James and appeared to be listening while James gave him a potted version of the story so far, including his concerns for Dee Sullivan's personal safety. James made an appointment to see him first thing in the morning.

Then he rang a journalist from the *Sydney Morning Herald*, whom he had told me about before. He was one of the good guys, James said, and having him on the story, at the same time as the police got all the information, would make sure it came out in public. He arranged to see him the next day too. The only thing he didn't tell him about was Dee.

'The cops have a better chance of finding her if Frankie – and the others – don't know they're looking for her too,' he explained.

After all that he called Spider back and gave him the update. Then he sank back onto his pillows and sighed.

'Is it all nearly over?' I asked him.

'When we find Dee,' he said. 'She may well be recovering from her surgery somewhere else, but I just want to be sure. Then I hope I can take a break from all this until those bastards are in the dock, when I will be delighted to give evidence against them.' He paused for a moment. 'You might have to as well, you know, Antonia,' he said. 'Are you OK about that?'

'Blimey,' I said. 'I'd never thought of that, but I suppose so. Eeek. Gosh, how terrifying. I've never been in a court.'

'Don't worry,' said James, squeezing my hand. 'I'll get Spider to coach you. He's had plenty of experience of them, as you can imagine.'

'Do you work with Spider on this stuff?' I asked.

'He doesn't really approve of it, actually, too close to cop work for him, but he backs me up when I need it. Like I told you, he's my best mate.'

I looked at him, not knowing how to take it any further. I still didn't understand that relationship.

'You don't like Spider, do you?' said James quietly.

'I love him dearly,' I said, 'for giving me this address. And he was nice to me about you at the gym once too, but I've just . . . never met anyone like him before.' I was searching for the right way to say 'filthy biker scum'.

'He's a sentimental old bastard at heart,' said James. 'But I suppose you wonder why my best friend is a filthy old biker?'

'Something like that,' I admitted.

James sighed.

'I'm going to have to tell you something that is hard for me, Antonia. But I've had a lot of time to think over the past few days and I think you will understand me more if I do tell you. It might change how you feel about me, but at least you will understand.'

'OK,' I said, feeling sick. What was coming? Were they lovers?

'Spider is my best mate,' said James. 'I met him in

prison. We did time together. You get close to people inside.'

I just stared at him. I'd never knowingly met a criminal before and now I realized I'd been sleeping with one for several months.

James laughed wryly.

'I know what you're thinking,' he said. 'But I'm not a bank robber. Spider was, but I'm not. I was protesting about a toxic-waste dump they were building in a National Park. I firebombed the developers' offices and then I sabotaged the diggers and earth-moving vehicles at the site and I'm afraid I assaulted a security guard who tried to stop me. I'm not proud of hurting him – he was just doing his job – but I am proud of the reason I did it. I got five years. I did nearly three.'

I didn't say anything. I didn't know what to say.

'Spider was the big man inside,' continued James. 'He was doing ten for armed robbery, not his first sentence either. He didn't take any notice of me at first, but one day I happened to walk past when a really nasty guy with big ambitions had him cornered with a blade. I kicked it out of his hand, breaking his wrist. Spider looked after me from then on, like a brother. It was really rough in there and I don't know what would have happened to me without Spider's protection.'

He looked at me and seemed satisfied that he could tell me more, without me running for the door.

'I got out first,' he said. 'And when Spider got parole a couple of years later, I did what I could to help him to stay straight. It was a promise I'd made to him. His daughter was born a year before he went in and I found him crying in his cell one day, because it was her first day at school and he hadn't been there to take her. That was when he swore he was never going down again and I promised to help him. I got him the job at the gym. So that's why he's my best mate. We look after each other. I know he's rough, but he has a really good heart – as you found out today.'

I just looked at him. It was a shock, but it did explain a lot – the secrecy, the mystery, the years unaccounted for. I felt around my feelings, rather as you probe your teeth with your tongue to find the sore one. Did it change the way I felt about him? No. So he'd been to prison? So what? It wasn't like it was for rape or extorting money from old ladies.

'Would you do anything like that again?' I asked him. 'Blowing things up?'

He shook his head. 'Definitely not. That was youthful folly. I still feel really strongly about these people who want to build everywhere for profit without giving a damn about what they are destroying, but I know violence is not the answer. Now I work only with bona fide conservation groups and try to catch the bastards out with the law. I had allowed my anger to pull me down to their level and I will never make that mistake again.'

We looked at each other silently for a moment. He spoke first.

'So does it put you off me, knowing that you have just been pashing an ex-con?' he said.

I could tell by his expression that it was a serious question.

'Not in the slightest,' I said.

'That's good,' he said, clearly relieved. 'Because I honestly didn't know how you'd react. I felt like I was being dishonest with you before, but I was so scared of losing you if you knew. Do you understand now, why I thought our lives could never merge? You come from that fancy social set and I hang out with former armed robbers. I didn't see how our worlds could ever mix.'

'Well, you've made it clear to me that the "fancy" set I used to hang out with are no better than Spider,' I said. 'The only difference between him and Roger Thorogood and the rest of those thieves in designer suits is a few million dollars.'

'And a few bars of soap,' said James, grinning. 'But what can you do?'

The first thing I thought when I woke up the next morning – after I had got over my usual amazement at the gorgeousness of the man lying beside me – was about Dee.

I woke James up by kissing him gently all over his face. He stirred, moaning slightly, and tried to climb on top of me, until he realized he was pinioned to the bed by his plaster casts.

'Oh shit,' he said. 'I'd forgotten about my leg irons. Climb aboard, will you, Midshipman Ant?'

'You really are the unstoppable love machine, aren't you?' I said. 'But hang on a minute. It's all very well us cavorting here, but I'm rather more concerned about Dee. She could be tied up in a car boot somewhere and don't forget you have those appointments this morning.'

'Dammit,' said James, shaking his head. 'You're right. For a blissful moment there I'd forgotten about all that. It was a big night last night – all those true confessions – and I think I'm a bit dazed.'

He looked at his watch.

'I'm seeing O'Hara in an hour. You'll have to dress me,' he said, smiling his naughtiest smile.

'Well,' I said, 'it makes a change from undressing you.'

It took us a while but I finally got James down into my car, with various carrier bags of photographs and video tapes.

'What's the plan?' I asked him.

'I need you to take me to the Police Centre in Surry Hills. They will want to speak to you as well, about Dee, but I'll tell them to come and see you at the shop later on today. OK?'

'What will I tell them?' I asked, feeling a bit panicky about it. I'd seen too many TV cop shows to feel happy at the prospect of a police interview.

'The truth,' said James. 'The simple horrible truth, exactly as you see it. You have nothing to hide.'

I glanced in the rear-view mirror at him, propped against one door, his plastered legs across the back seat.

'How on earth will you get home from this police place?' I said.

'O'Hara will be so thrilled with what I have to show and tell them, he'll probably send me home in a limo.'

'Will I see you later?' I said, trying to sound casual, but not liking the vagueness of this reply.

'Don't worry, there'll be no more disappearing,

Antonia,' he said. 'I'll be able to put my phone back on after I've spoken to O'Hara, because his mob will be watching out for me, so you can call me whenever you want to.'

It wasn't the first time I'd heard that.

'Promise?' I said in my Piglet voice.

'Promise,' he said.

Later that morning the two men in cheap suits came back into the shop, with a lady police officer in tow. They waited until a couple of customers had left and then came straight up to the counter and showed me their warrant cards.

'We're looking for Dee Sullivan,' they said.

'So am I,' I replied. 'I haven't seen or heard from her for over a week and I'm really worried.'

I put the closed sign up, made the three of them some tea and then I told them the whole story – how I had met Dee, her wary manner, how we had gone into business and right up to her last strange phone call about the last-minute plastic surgery appointment and her absence from the Silver Springs.

When I finished the police woman asked me if there was anything else I could tell them about Dee, anything at all.

'It might not seem relevant to you,' she said. 'But the smallest little detail can help us.'

I told her about all Dee's regular appointments for beauty treatments and gave her the names of some of the beauticians and salons she went to. But there was one thing I didn't share – I didn't tell them about Dee's secret house up at Byron, because as I was talking to them it had dawned on me, that could be where she was.

After about forty-five minutes the conversation seemed to be over and I thought they were going to leave, but then one of the men – he said his name was George – took me by surprise.

'What can you tell us about Suzy Thorogood and Nikki Maier?' he asked me. 'Have you seen them recently?'

'Don't tell me they've disappeared as well,' I said.

They glanced at each other.

'We're just trying to build up a profile of each of them,' said George, non-committally. 'In relation to another case we are currently investigating.'

I told them everything I could think of, including Suzy's strange behaviour, when she had suddenly dumped me after being so nice. They were very interested in that and wanted to know exactly when it had all happened. I saw them exchange another glance when I said she had cooled off around April. Must have meant something to them, but it was lost on me.

I rang James immediately after they'd gone and was almost surprised when he actually answered.

'Hey, beautiful,' he said. I could hear voices and traffic. He clearly wasn't at home, or at the Police Centre. 'I'm with Spider and the boys,' he said. 'We're having coffee in Victoria Street. It's so great to be out and about again, even if I can't walk, although Spider didn't really appreciate me arriving here in a squad car.'

I could hear snarling noises in the background, which

were no doubt the Spiderman's responses. Whatever he'd said, it certainly seemed to amuse James.

'Anyway, darls,' he said. 'I can't really talk with these hooligans around. I'll tell you all about it when I see you later. I've got to speak to the guy from the *Herald*. He's coming here in a minute.'

'Where will I see you?' I asked, pathetically. I still wasn't quite able to believe he wasn't going to disappear again.

'Well, I thought I'd come and stay at your place for a while,' he said. 'If you don't mind.'

'I don't mind at all,' I said. 'And Tom will be ecstatic.'

I could hear coarse laughter from 'the boys' in the background.

'Hey,' I said. 'Put Spider on. I want to tell him something.'

There was a bit of a kerfuffle and more male banter, then I heard an unmistakable grunt.

'G'day,' said Spider's rough voice.

'Hi, Spider,' I said. 'It's Antonia . . .'

'Oh yeah, Jackie Chan's old lady. How ya doin'?'

'Very well – thanks to you. You really did us a favour, Spider. Respect and all that.'

'Argh, get out of here,' he said. 'Just looking after me mate. He's a prick sometimes.'

'Well, he's my prick, thanks to you, and I won't forget it.'

He roared with laughter and as he hung up I distinctly heard him say, 'Silly cunt,' in tones of great affection.

Percy was in when I got home. Noisily chopping up vegetables and apparently still not talking to me. Tom was glued to a video of *Monkey* on the television – reciting the entire opening speech, starting with 'In the time before Monkey . . .', was his new party piece – so I took my chance to clear the air with Percy. I sat down on one of the stools at the kitchen bench where he was chopping and handed him a carrot.

'Can we talk, Percy?' I asked him.

'It depends what you would like to say,' he said, still not looking at me.

'Well, I'll start with sorry,' I said.

He looked at me.

'Accepted,' he said. 'Talk away.'

I searched for the right words to explain it.

'What I said the other day about James,' I started. 'You must know I didn't mean it. I was just so bewildered that he had abandoned me, I was trying to find ways not to care.'

'I understand,' he said. 'I'm sorry too. I overreacted. You unwittingly hit a very sore point. Now tell me, any news of James – or Dee, for that matter?'

'Yes on both counts,' I said. 'I'll get us some wine, this might take a while.'

I told him the whole story. Right from the King George Hospital and why we were up there, to the visit from Spider's friend, our Bondi reunion and my visit from the police that afternoon. The only thing I didn't tell him about was Dee's beach house. I'd promised her not to tell anyone and I intended to stick to that promise – and I was still deciding what I should do about it.

For once Percy sat and listened, without making fey

comments and asking for more details on the sexy bits. I ended with the announcement that James – and his plaster casts – were coming to stay with us for a while. He reached over to the bag and took out three more carrots.

'He'll need feeding up,' he said. 'I'll make him some healing chicken soup as well.'

I went to stand up, but Percy put his hand on my arm.

'I have something to tell you,' he said. 'I want you to know why I reacted like that when you mentioned James's shovelling.'

I sat down again and poured us both a fresh glass of wine.

'I was in love once, Antonia,' he said. 'When I was at Oxford. When I was very young and very silly. I'd gone straight up to Trinity from Eton and I was an arrogant little shit, but when I first encountered Jack in a tutorial, I knew I had met my match.'

He took a long sip of his wine and I settled myself to listen.

'Jack was a working-class boy from Salford,' he said. 'Doing Classics on a full Exhibition. Despite my own unusual beginnings, I was there on pure privilege and, like all my old school cronies, I was frittering my time away, caring far more about parties and dining clubs and appearing in witty revues than I did about essays. Jack – a miner's son – properly appreciated the opportunity he had been given and he wasn't wasting a moment of it.

'He was gorgeously handsome – blond and tall, with

strong shoulders, but I knew a lot of pretty boys. That wasn't the thing. The thing about Jack was that he had the most brilliant mind I had ever encountered.

'Despite all my class prejudices – which you must remember ran deeper in me, because I wasn't really secure in my own position – I became besotted with him and amazingly, he seemed to feel some affection for me.

'We had a passionate affair. Poetry in Greek under each other's doors, punting down the river together – the whole lot. When I see your face after you have been with James, it reminds me how I felt with Jack in those precious days. I was mad about the boy.'

He nodded sadly to himself and lit one of his black cigarettes. I lit one too. Percy had never shared anything like this with me before.

'From the perspective of today,' he continued, 'when things are all much less rigid, it's hard to understand my behaviour back then, because I'm quite sure I could have been happy with Jack for the rest of my life. But I did a terrible thing, Antonia.'

He took another sip of wine. So did I. I was unconsciously mirroring him, I realized, I was so keen not to put him off.

'I was part of an elite dining club called The Blaggards. It was quite the smartest set at Oxford at the time and I was terribly proud of myself for being part of it. Some chaps, who were rejected, left College, went down. Couldn't stand the humiliation. You had to be related to a peer of the realm even to be considered and you had to compose a bawdy poem in iambic pentameter that amused the club sufficiently to allow you membership. Absolute crap, but it seemed terribly important to me at the time. We were all queer, but you didn't go on about it then, it was just understood.

'Anyway I was staggering along the High with my Blaggard buddies one evening after one of our dinners – needless to say, we were all plastered – and Jack came along the street. One of my number cried out, "There's the miner's son that Heaveringham's in love with. Go on, Beaver" – that was what they called me – "proclaim your love for him."

'I made up an impromptu verse on the spot, in Latin, the general gist of which was that Jack was just a pretty catamite – a sodomite's slave, in case you aren't familiar with the term. All my friends thought it was frightfully amusing. Jack just looked at me like a wounded dog and walked away.

'In my arrogance I really thought he would see the wit and humour of the situation and that all would be fine when next we met. I actually thought he'd think I was clever. I was so wrong. He never spoke to me again. And those marvellous dining companions, whom I had thought such special friends, dropped me as well. Such an open declaration of homosexual love was not permitted, even in that perverse company.'

He took another sip of wine and sighed deeply.

'I'm going to show you something,' he said and digging around in his kelim bag he brought out his wallet, from which he took an old black and white photograph. It was of a beautiful young man, of the Rupert Brooke type, but

350

a bit more butch, lying in a punt holding a bottle of beer and smiling blissfully at the camera.

'That was Jack,' he said.

'Oh, Percy,' I said, almost whispering. 'I'm so sorry. I do understand now why my snobbish remarks offended you. What happened to Jack?'

'He got a starred double first. He never spoke to me again, but the day I was leaving – I went down early, you may remember, never got my degree, now you know the real reason – he left a note in my pigeon-hole. A poem in perfect iambic pentameter on the subject of what happens when you try to move outside your world. Marvellous images of oil and water and the like. Sadly, I destroyed it.'

'Did you never see him again?' I asked.

'Oh, I've seen him plenty of times,' said Percy, laughing bitterly. 'But he still never speaks to me. Jack runs a multinational publishing company – he's terribly important, never out of the *Financial Times*. Quite often we've been at the same parties, but Jack always turns his back on me and, frankly, I don't blame him. The last thing I heard, there was talk of him being knighted. A New Labour queer peer. Ironic, *non*?'

I went round the kitchen bench and hugged him.

'Oh, my darling Percy, that is the saddest story. I'm so sorry.'

He patted my hand, rather absently.

'Never mind, my dear, all in the past. Long ago and faraway. It's just made me allergic to snobbery, that's all. Now I'm going to make your James a lovely apple pie.

351

That's just the sort of thing that will make him feel better.'

He tied on his frilly apron and set about making pastry like a dervish.

24

James arrived – lying along the back seat of a taxi – in time for dinner and we ate it together as a family in the sitting room, with him reclining on the sofa, Tom somehow perched between his legs. To Percy's great satisfaction James had three helpings of apple pie.

'Am I holding my spoon right, Tom?' James asked playfully and Percy caught my eye and smiled.

'Oh, do have some more pie, James darling,' he said. 'I made it specially for you. There you are – just one more little sliver. And a dab of cream so it won't be lonely.'

'You lot are going to be the death of me,' said James. 'Feeding me up when I can't exercise. I'm going to get all fat and flabby and then none of you will like me any more.'

'I'll always like you,' said Tom. 'Can I write on your plaster? My friend Hermione had a broken arm and we all wrote on her plaster. I wrote "bum" on it, when she wasn't looking. She kept it afterwards. Can I keep yours?'

'No, you can't, that's a disgusting idea, but you can write on them,' said James. 'But nothing rude.'

'I'll draw a picture of you doing kung fu,' he said, brandishing a purple felt tip. 'So people will know how it happened.'

We didn't disillusion him.

*

Getting James up and down the stairs was a challenge – as was persuading Tom he had to go to school the next morning, when he felt James needed him around to 'help' – but it was a total joy having my beautiful man at home with me. I kept feeling as though I had to pinch myself that he was there all the time and I didn't have to worry about when I was going to see him again.

Percy said he'd look after the shop and I had James to myself all day. We played backgammon until we were practically cross-eyed, drank endless cups of tea (herbal for James, Earl Grey for me) and just lay around talking. I also gave him a very amusing 'blanket bath'.

But while I was wallowing in my contentment with James, something was nagging at the back of my mind. Dee. We still hadn't heard anything from the police about her. After turning it around in my head I finally decided I had to go and see if she was at her secret house.

I had just been pondering how I was going to explain to James that I needed to go away for a couple of days when I realized he was looking at me intently.

'It's your throw, Ant,' he said. 'But you're miles away. What's on your mind? Tell me.'

I exhaled loudly.

'You know when you've made a promise to someone and you really feel you have to keep it?' I said.

James nodded. 'Sure do. I've got more of Spider's filthy secrets locked away in my brain than I care to think about.'

'Well, I made a promise to someone – and I might have

to go away for a couple of days to keep it. I can't tell you where or why. Is that OK?'

He looked steadily at me.

'Probably. But just tell me this – is it something to do with Dee?'

'Maybe,' I said reluctantly.

'You think you know where she is?'

'Maybe maybe,' I said.

'Well, that's good, but are you sure you don't just want to tell the police? Remember, it was her husband's henchmen that did this to my legs. I'm not going to let anything happen to you.'

'I'm 99.9 per cent certain they don't know where she is – but I think I might, and I must go and see.'

'And you won't tell me?'

I shook my head. 'I made a promise.'

'Well, go then, although I'm not entirely happy about it.' He thought for a moment and then grasped my hand. 'You must promise to call me every hour on the hour while you are away.'

I must have looked incredulous.

'I mean it, Antonia, they're dangerous people.'

'OK, I'll ring every hour. I'm going to go first thing tomorrow.'

I went upstairs to book my flight and as I put the phone down I thought I heard the tiniest little tinkle from the phone downstairs.

Next morning there was a knock on the bedroom door just after my alarm went off.

'Come in,' I called out.

Percy came in with two cups of tea, which he put on the bedside table.

'I just wanted to make sure you were awake,' he said. 'And I thought you might want to see these.'

He threw the papers onto the bed and went out again. There was a monster headline on the front of the *Sydney Morning Herald*: 'Environment Minister In $20 Million Developer Fraud' over a picture of a scowling Roger Thorogood. Down the page, there was a smaller picture of Frankie looking like thunder.

The *Telegraph* was similar. 'THOROBAD!' it said in huge type. 'Environment Minister Sells Sydney Harbour For $20 Million.'

The accompanying news stories went on to describe how a police investigation had uncovered an illegal financial agreement between the Minister and 'property developer Frankie Sullivan', in which Thorogood promised to get Sullivan's planning applications approved in return for payments adding up to $20 million.

'A police investigation?' I said to James, outraged. 'It was you who did all the work – and look at the price you paid for it.' I tapped on one of his plaster casts.

'That doesn't matter,' he said. 'All that matters is that Sullivan and Thorogood are nailed and those hideous developments won't happen. I don't want any medals – I just want the King George left alone.'

I read further, but there was no mention of Pieter van der Gaarden anywhere in the extensive coverage and none of David Maier.

'Why don't they mention Mr P?' I asked James. 'He was in on it, wasn't he?'

'Yes, but even the cops are scared of him,' said James. 'This is how he works – he's Teflon man. Nothing ever sticks to him. Even up at the King George that night I never got him on film – I got the other three clear as day, but he was too smart ever to come in range of the car. That sideshow you were putting on was enough to make those other idiots abandon all caution. And me, for that matter.'

He winked at me. I think I blushed.

'So why isn't that creep David Maier in this story either?' I said.

'He's small fry. Frankie was the one they really wanted and Thorogood went down with him because he's a greedy bastard. Remember that guy O'Hara I went to see – the cop? He's been after Frankie for years. I really made his day when I took those pictures in and a lot more damning evidence that you don't need to know about.'

He went back to studying the *Telegraph* and after he'd turned a few pages, he laughed suddenly and handed it to me.

'Here's your friend David Maier,' he said. It was a small story at the back of the news section.

'Powder Puff Playboy in Bikie Battle' said the headline.

'Go on,' said James. 'Read it out to me. I want to enjoy it.'

He leaned back on the pillows with his arms behind his head.

'Socialite cosmetics mogul David Maier . . .' I read, 'bit off more than he could chew when he argued with bouncers at a King's Cross lap dancing bar on Tuesday night. Maier, who has recently filed for bankruptcy' – gosh, I didn't know that – 'refused to go quietly and punched one bouncer in the face. Unfortunately for the Double Bay playboy, who has recently split from his wife Nikki' – oh my God, I didn't know that either – 'the bouncer's bikie friends saw the incident and came to his aid. Mr Maier is in a stable condition in St Vincent's Hospital with a broken jaw, severe bruising and two smashed knee caps.'

I looked at James with wide eyes.

'Talk about karma,' I said. 'He really deserved that. What a creep. Remind me, when I get back from my trip, to tell you what David Maier did to me once.'

'I already know,' he said, quietly.

'What?'

'He tried to rape you.'

'How on earth do you know that?' I was incredulous.

'Percy told me. He thought I'd want to know and he was damn right.'

I looked down at the newspaper again. Bikies. I looked at James with one raised eyebrow. I didn't even need to ask the question.

'Spider?' I said, quietly.

He shook his head.

'Not Spider,' he said. 'But friends of Spider.'

I put my face in my hands. This was all getting too much. Smashed kneecaps and vigilante beatings.

'Don't worry, it wasn't arranged to avenge you, Grass-hopper,' he said, pulling me close. 'It was just a happy accident. Maier had pissed off a lot of people and he was going to get it anyway. He owes money to all kinds of people in this town you don't want to owe money to. You don't try to rip off your cocaine dealer, for example, if you want your face to stay the same shape, but he seemed to think he was above the rules in any situation. In business he never paid his suppliers and for fun he's been known to rape prostitutes. He used to book girls, treat them really badly and then not even pay them. What's a working girl going to do in that situation? Cry rape? Go to the police? He is a truly abhorrent human being. I'm just glad you managed to get away before he did his worst to you. You were lucky.'

'I'll drink to that,' I said, raising my teacup.

I was more nervous than I'd expected as I waited at the airport lounge for my flight later that morning. James had given me a crash course in private investigator skills before I left. It was a shame Tom wasn't there to join in, he would have loved it. But I was laughing so much I didn't really take it in.

First he made me take his spare phone battery for my mobile, as well as my own, plus a phone card and lots of change, in case I went out of range. Then he taught me some techniques for making yourself as inconspicuous as possible, which was a kind of reverse of Percy's charisma technique, interestingly.

'You can kind of think yourself invisible, if you try,' he'd said.

'Yes, I know,' I'd told him. 'I used to do that in Latin

at school, so the teacher wouldn't ask me to decline a subjunctive verb.'

It had all been hilarious in the sitting room at home, with me doing Humphrey Bogart impersonations and James throwing cushions at me, but now I was out in a public space I felt really vulnerable and self-conscious. I kept looking round to see if anyone was following me, but I decided that James had just made me paranoid and made a deal with myself that apart from the hourly phone call home I would just try to relax about it all. Why would anyone be following me? Nobody knew where I was going.

I felt nervous in a different way as I pulled up outside Dee's house in my hire car. Was I breaking her trust by going to see if she was there? Was I interfering in something I really couldn't understand? I sat in the car, boiling in the bright sunshine, biting my lip and wondering what to do. At least I hadn't told anyone else about it, I thought, and if she was there, at least I could convince her it would be a lot better if she rang the police and told them she was all right.

I rang James – my hourly call was due – and told him as well as I could with the bad reception up there, that I had arrived. Then I decided the only thing to do was just to get on with it, so I walked round the side of the house, picking my way carefully through the thick summer undergrowth, to where I figured she was most likely to be – and there she was, reading a book in a hammock on her back veranda.

'Dee,' I said quietly and she leaped to her feet as though someone had thrown cold water over her.

'Don't worry, it's only me – Ant,' I said. 'I'm alone, no one knows I'm here.'

She was darting looks all around.

'Are you sure you weren't followed?' she said.

'Pretty sure,' I said. 'As I say, no one knew I was coming.'

She looked so different. She was wearing no make-up and her hair was quite wavy without its usual blow-dry. She had it roughly pulled back in a ponytail, with loose strands falling onto her face. She was wearing white shorts, an old shirt splattered with paint and no shoes. She looked so much more beautiful than she did all done up, but there was strain around her eyes. There certainly weren't any stitches to be seen.

'I had to make sure you were OK,' I said. 'Nice face-lift.'

She looked sheepish and not sure if I was joking.

'It's OK, Dee,' I said. 'I know all about it.'

I handed her the *Herald*.

'So they finally got him,' she said.

I nodded.

'I knew it was coming,' she said. 'That's why I came up here.'

'I thought that was probably it. Half the NSW police force is looking for you. They think you've been kidnapped and I think you might have been, if you hadn't had this place to escape to.'

'We'd better go inside anyway,' she said. 'And I should tell you – I'm not alone.'

We stepped into the house and there was Suzy Thorogood, sitting at the kitchen table, with a laptop in front of her. She sprang up when she saw me, ran round the table and gave me a huge hug. I was speechless.

'Oh Antonia,' she said. 'It's so good to see you.'

She pulled away and I saw there were tears in her eyes. I glanced at Dee, who was smiling wryly.

'I've felt so bad about you, Ant,' said Suzy. 'I'm so relieved I can tell you everything now.'

We sat down at the table and Dee handed Suzy the newspaper. I wondered how she'd react. After all, that was her husband there in full-colour shame and disgrace on the front page. She stared down at it for a moment and then up at Dee. The look that passed between them was like something ancient. A mixture of simultaneous pain and relief. A look that could only pass between two women who were in some terrible way connected by their men.

'So they've got them,' said Suzy quietly. Then she jumped up and punched the air. 'Good!' she shouted and then she hugged Dee, the two of them doing a triumphant little dance.

Suzy turned round to me, grinning wildly.

'Don't you see, Ant?' she said. 'Whatever happens now, we're free from the bullshit, free from the lies. Free! The lies were killing me – why do you think I stopped seeing you? I couldn't keep it up, I was so ashamed and now I don't have to live with that any more. And wherever I end up – even if I go to jail myself as an accessory – it will be better than living that lie.'

I looked at Dee, who nodded in agreement, smiling sadly.

Dee made us some tea and we sat down together at the

table. Suzy pushed her laptop out of the way, laughing again.

'I've already started my memoirs,' she said. 'You know me – Action Jackson. What the hell, I might as well make some money out of the hell I've been through. I'm going to sell my story to the *Women's Weekly* and bugger the lot of them.'

'So you both figured out this was about to happen?' I asked them.

'Dee did,' said Suzy. 'So much for the savvy financial PR. I was so confused and freaked out by what Roger was up to I didn't even see it coming. She tipped me off and we ran up here together. I didn't even know she had this place.'

She leaned over and chucked Dee on the cheek. I looked at Dee, so quiet and so deep.

'I didn't even know you knew each other that well,' I said.

They both laughed.

'We've been good friends for years,' said Suzy. 'But apart from the odd air kiss on the cocktail party circuit, we're discreet about it. We didn't want our respective blokes to use our friendship to chummy up together, because we know what they are both like, but it turned out they didn't need our help, did they, Dee?'

'No,' she replied. 'They were perfectly capable of fucking things up on their own. I rang Suzy the minute I realized Pieter van der Gaarden was on the warpath. He was furious because he thought Frankie was trying to take him down with him and Roger – and that puts us in danger. Do you know who Pieter van der Gaarden is?' she added.

I nodded.

'Yes,' I said. 'And one day, I'll tell you how I know – it's quite a long story. But how did you know what was going on?'

'I keep my eyes and ears open and my mouth shut,' said Dee. 'I always have. I've done it for so many years that Frankie forgets I'm there. Anyway, one night just over a week ago I heard him and Pieter having a huge row and I knew it was time to split. I know everything about all of them and that's why I had to come up here. It's Pieter I'm hiding from as much as Frankie.'

'Me too,' said Suzy. 'And I also didn't want Roger to expect me to be the loyal wife, because I'm not the Hillary Clinton type. I knew what he was getting into and I begged him not to. We already had enough wealth and glory, but he just couldn't resist that extra $20 million, could he? And do you know why?'

I shook my head. That kind of money meant nothing to me, she might as well have been talking about chocolate buttons.

'That extra $20 mill,' said Suzy, 'cleverly invested for a while, would be just enough to tip us over into the billionaire category. Roger really wants to be a billionaire.' She took a deep drag on her menthol cigarette and then added, with her brilliant timing, 'He's got a small dick.'

We all shrieked with laughter. It was a welcome break from the tension.

When we'd calmed down again, I turned to Dee.

'Can't you come back now it's all out in the open?' I said. 'Frankie's in custody and the police will protect you from Pieter van der Gaarden, surely.'

'I suppose I can,' she said. 'But I'm not going back to live at that house – ever. I hate that place so much.' She spat the words out.

'Why did you stay with Frankie so long, if it made you so unhappy?' I asked her. 'Surely it wasn't just the money.'

'I couldn't leave,' she said. 'He has too much on me.'

She looked at me with those cool green eyes as if she was considering how much to tell me. Then she lit a cigarette – the first I'd ever seen her smoke. She'd given up years before, she'd told me – too ageing for the skin. She saw me looking at it and waved it in the air.

'Nuts, I know, but I took it up again. It's been pretty tense up here – and with fag ash Lil there,' she nodded at Suzy, who blew a smoke ring at her in response, 'it's easier to join her than to beat her.'

We sat there, with Dee blowing smoke and staring into the distance. Then I saw her look questioningly at Suzy, who nodded gently. Finally Dee spoke.

'You've been a really good friend to me, Antonia,' she said. 'You've done far more for me than you can possibly know . . .'

I opened my mouth to make the usual English protests to a compliment, but she held up her hand to stop me.

'As you trusted me so implicitly, right from the start, when I have been so cagey with you, I think it's time I repaid your trust by explaining my behaviour. There's a reason I don't let anyone get close to me, Antonia, and it's the obvious one – I've got something to hide. Suzy knows my story, she always has, but now I think I owe it to you, to let you in on it too.'

Between her and James and Percy, I was beginning to feel like some kind of mother confessor, but I did desperately want to know what was behind Dee's unusual reticence.

'Well, if you really want to . . .' I said.

She nodded. Suzy squeezed her hand.

'I met Frankie when I was seventeen,' she started. 'I'd just arrived in Sydney from Tasmania. I was a hooker. You know, what they call a "high-class call girl"? Well, there's nothing high-class about it, let me tell you. Sure, you get paid more than a street walker, you get to wear expensive clothes and you get taken out to nice places, but when it comes down to it, you still end up sucking the dick of some hideous man you hate.'

I sat there gawping. I felt slightly sick.

'I imagine a girl like you has never met a hooker before, is that right?' she said.

I nodded. A convicted criminal and a high-class hooker in a matter of days. My horizons were widening.

'Well, the thing is,' said Dee, leaning towards me, conspiratorially, 'you have, but you just didn't know. There is so much of it going on, Antonia. Not just in Sydney, but everywhere. The most surprising people are involved.'

She blew out a long plume of smoke and ashed the cigarette. I noticed her normally perfect nails were bitten off.

'How did you get into it?' I asked.

'Well, you know my grandmother brought me up, I told you that much. I never knew my father. My mother was eighteen when she had me and shortly after I was born she ran away, left me with my granny. Never contacted either of us again. She was wonderful to me, my gran, she'd lost one daughter, so I became her second one, but when I was sixteen she died. I didn't have anyone else and I was really naïve. Then I met this kind man, who was great fun and seemed to want to look after me. Next thing I knew I was looking after him – and all his sleazy friends. Once I was into it and used to the money, I didn't know how to get out. He broke me in, in Hobart, and then he brought me up to Sydney and pretty much sold me on to a madam. That's when I met Frankie.'

She looked so tired.

'Do you want to hear more of this?' she said.

I nodded, dumbly. I didn't really, but I felt she needed to tell me. Suzy went to the fridge and got some mineral water for us all. Dee took a long drink and then continued.

'Oh Suzy,' she said. 'You tell her this bit. I'm sick of it.'

'OK,' said Suzy. 'Now, Antonia, brace yourself for a heavy shower of sleaze. Ready?'

I nodded.

'Right,' said Suzy. 'There's a small group of men here in Sydney who are into "girls" in a big way. They are sort of the high rollers of hookers. They're all married, but "girls" are their hobby. When a fresh piece of meat arrives on the scene, they all have a go with her, before she can be released to the general sweaty mass. It's prestigious to be the first with a new girl. Both our delightful husbands are in that little group.'

She looked at Dee, who raised her eyes to the heavens.

'Frankie was the first – in Sydney – to have me,' said Dee. 'Back when I was seventeen – and he liked it so much he decided he didn't want anyone else to have a taste. He made me his full-time mistress and eventually, against all odds, he married me. He needed a corporate wife with a past – so he could blackmail me with it, not to reveal any of the shit he gets up to.'

'Well, bully for him,' I said. 'But why did you marry him?'

She looked me straight in the eye.

'Money.'

'Really?' I asked, like the naïve twit I was.

'Yes. I didn't grow up with much and having shit loads of money is really nice, Antonia. You've probably been reasonably comfortable all your life, but you can't imagine what it's like to be loaded. It's another world. And I was able to delude myself that Frankie's dodgier dealings didn't matter, because he would give me thousands to donate to charities and that sort of thing. Over time I really fooled myself that I was some kind of society dame, although deep down I knew I was as dirty as Frankie, for having anything to do with it.

'That's why I had to work so hard keeping up appearances. I was terrified if I let one little crack show, it would all come tumbling down. You're lucky that you don't know how great having loads of money really is, Antonia, because once you've had it, it's very hard to do without.'

Suzy nodded, sighing deeply and suddenly looking very old.

'It's addictive,' she said. 'Just like smack and Roger and Frankie just OD'd. They always have to have that one last hit, men like them, that last big deal that's finally going to be enough for them, but it never is enough. So here we all are.'

I was feeling really shaky from all the revelations and I made some more tea, just so I could have a break from it. As I was waiting for the kettle to boil, I remembered Frankie and Roger up at the King George that night and David Maier's suggestion that they should go 'somewhere more interesting' rather than home to their wives in their horny state.

'Did Frankie carry on with his interest in "girls" after he married you?'

Dee snorted derisively.

'Of course he did,' she said. 'I think they invented Viagra with Frankie in mind. He's worse than ever and now he has a new band of sleazy pals to play with . . .'

'Which includes Roger?' I asked Suzy.

'Oh yes,' she said. 'He was well into it. He wasn't when I first met him, I think he just got involved to be part of the big boys' club. He so desperately wants to a "big man", as I told you. Pathetic. He thought it was so great to be part of that sordid little gang.'

'Is David Maier one of them?' I asked.

'God, yes, he's the worst,' said Dee.

'How do you think he met Nikki?' said Suzy.

My eyes popped open.

'Was she . . .?' I stuttered.

'Still is, as far as I know,' said Suzy. 'God, how I loathe that woman. I was only friends with her because Roger insisted – he was buddy buddy with David, because David introduced him to Frankie and Pieter van der G, so I had to play along.'

'I was a bit surprised that you were friends with her,' I said. 'Were the Frenchs in on it too?'

'Totally,' said Suzy. 'Caroline's another ex-hooker and Tony's part of the sleazy bunch, although he's not involved with their dodgy property dealings as well. He's not quite that stupid.'

'So that was why you were friends with those two?' I said, relieved to find that my initial judgement had been spot on.

'Yes,' said Suzy. 'Do you think I would have spent a minute with Nikki bloody Maier if I hadn't been forced to? I'm just sorry I inflicted her on you. I suppose I was so used to hanging out with those deadheads by then, I didn't think about it any more. It was such a relief when I met you.'

She shook her head and lit another cigarette from the end of the last one.

'You know,' she said, 'I was surprised when Nikki actually married that creep Maier – they lived together for a while first, but she forced him to marry her. I was surprised because I thought she was holding out for someone bigger, someone much richer. But I reckon she thought if she could get into the social scene with David she might find husband number two the legitimate way – you know, stealing someone else's. She's sucked Roger off loads of times,' she paused and glanced at Dee. 'Frankie too, I imagine, Dee?'

'Oh God, yes,' said Dee. 'She laid it all on for Frankie and lord only knows who else, but it never worked for her, because they all know where she came from. The difference with me was that they didn't and that was the hold Frankie had over me. He was the only one who knew how he met me and, as a result, I held on to the pathetic belief that I could leave it all behind. But I couldn't. I was always looking over my shoulder. And I still am – look at me, holed up here like a terrified fox hiding from the hounds. I can't live like that any longer so I'm glad you both know about my past. I feel less ashamed now I've told you, Antonia. It's nothing to be ashamed of really, I don't know why I was so hung up about it.'

She sighed deeply, looking very sad, but then she perked up suddenly and looked at us both, grinning.

'And you know what?' she said. 'I am *stoked* that Frankie's going down – because I am so getting out.'

'Me too, babe,' said Suzy. 'Gimme a high five, baby.'

And they smacked hands like a couple of basketball players.

We sat and talked about what they were going to do when it was all over. Suzy said she didn't really think the two of them would be charged with anything, but the trials would still be pretty traumatic – they'd have to give evidence.

Dee said she wanted to do the Fine Arts degree she had always dreamed of doing, but she'd also like to carry on with Anteeks – if I didn't mind being associated with the wife of a soon-to-be-convicted criminal. Which I thought was pretty funny, considering what James had recently told me and I looked forward to telling her all that one day.

'I would be heartbroken if you didn't carry on at Anteeks,' I said. 'And think of all the free publicity the trial will bring us.'

Suzy said that after she'd finished her memoirs and her kids were safely packed off to uni, she was going to shave her head and backpack around India. Considering what they both had been through, I thought, they were inspiring to listen to.

I was just making us all a third cup of tea, when there was the most incredible commotion from outside. There was a tremendous roar followed by lots of ugly male shouting, right in front of the house.

'Hide,' I hissed at Dee and Suzy, who were already on their way to the bathroom.

I ran over to the front window, flattening myself against the wall and peeped round the edge – just as James had shown me. There were about twenty-five bikies outside. Some of them were still on their 'hogs', as I'd learned their motorbikes were called, the others were viciously kicking two men, who were writhing on the ground.

As I watched, horrified, one of the bikies broke away and came up to the front door. Just as I was about to join the other two in the loo, I realized it was the tattooed bald guy who had come to the shop and given me James's address. He hammered on the front door and I opened it. I reckoned he was probably on our side.

'You all right?' he asked.

I nodded, glancing over at the two men who his mates were now holding pinned down. They had blood pouring down their faces. The tattooed man gestured at them with his head.

'You were lucky,' he said. 'They were just about to break in and find you. Is your girlfriend here?'

'Who wants to know?' I asked him.

'Your old man, among other people. Because if she stays up here, they'll just send in another team of goons to find her, so you'd better tell her to get out now, while she has us as an escort.'

I swallowed.

'OK, I'll get her – actually there are three of us. Is that OK?'

'Sure, just get a bloody shift on, will ya?'

I took a couple of steps and then turned back.

'How the hell did you know where to find us?' I asked him.

'Apparently, you haven't rung home for over three hours,' he said. 'We're just acting on instructions.'

'But how did he . . .?' I started.

'Just go and get your friends, would you? We don't have much time.'

I went and knocked on the bathroom door.

'Dee, Suzy, let me in, it's Ant, it's OK.'

Dee was white-faced when she opened the door.

'We've got to leave, now,' I said. 'They've found us.

There were two guys out there, who were just about to break in, but . . . um . . . some friends of mine came along and they're going to get us away from here.'

'Shit,' said Suzy, striding out of the bathroom. 'I'll get my stuff.'

Dee was less convinced. 'Who's out there?' she said, looking anxious.

'Look, I can't explain now,' I said. 'It would take too long, so you will just have to trust me.'

She was shaking. I put my hands on her arms.

'Have I ever given you reason not to trust me, Dee? I really believe your life will be in danger if you stay here. We must leave while we can with protection. Please?'

'Come on, Dee,' said Suzy, reappearing with a small weekend bag. 'Let's get out of here now.'

Dee seemed to snap to her senses.

'OK,' she said, 'I'll come right away. I don't need to pack anything.'

She locked the back door and put the key in her pocket, picked up her handbag and a jumper and shrugged at me.

'Let's go then,' she said.

'There's just one more thing I should tell you both,' I said, as we walked to the front door. 'Try not to be put off by how my friends out here look. They're on our side, honestly.'

When I opened the door the bikies had their hogs lined up in formation, like a flight of Spitfires. The two thugs were slumped at the side of the road. Tattoo man revved his engine and gestured to us with his head.

'Get a bloody move on,' he said.

Suzy grinned at me and headed for the nearest bike.

Dee looked at me momentarily in complete shock and then she threw her head back and laughed.

'They can't be worse than Frankie,' she said and jumped on behind tattoo man like it was the most normal thing in the world.

25

'But how did you find us?' I asked James, as I paced around the drawing room much later that night. Dee sat quietly in an armchair, nursing a strong vodka and tonic. James was in his usual position on the sofa.

Suzy had gone straight home, head up, to face the TV crews and reporters who would be waiting on her doorstep. She said she was ready for the media – she had already put a call to the *Women's Weekly* editor, to negotiate the fee for her story, in the car from the airport.

I was still waiting for James to tell us how he had known where to send his pals to rescue us.

'Well?' I asked him, getting impatient.

'Grasshopper,' said James, holding out his hands in exasperation, 'I don't know why you're surprised. It's what I do. I find out where people are when they don't want me to.'

'But tell us how?' I whined. 'It was weird, wasn't it, Dee?'

'It was wonderful,' she said. 'Thank you, James. I think you saved my life.'

He tipped his imaginary hat at her.

'All part of the service, lady,' he said.

I couldn't contain myself, although I knew I sounded like Tom going off on one.

'Please, James, pleeeeease,' I said. 'Just tell us how.'

'OK,' he said. 'First, I listened in on the downstairs phone when you made the plane reservation, so I knew where you were going.'

'I knew it,' I said triumphantly, snapping my fingers. 'I heard it tinkle. But how did you get back to the sofa by the time I got back downstairs?'

'I can shift quite fast on these crutches when I want to, but most of the time I prefer to let you help me, because I can feel you up while you're doing it.'

He grinned at me. Dee giggled into her drink. She'd been quite skittish since our ride to the airport as bikie molls. It had been quite thrilling actually, especially as we weren't wearing helmets and were totally illegal. It was the most illegal thing I had ever done.

I still wasn't satisfied with James's explanation. I paced around with my hands on my hips.

'OK, so you knew where I was flying to,' I said. 'But how did tattoo man find the house, and at the right time?'

'OK, Miss Marple,' said James. 'I checked out who I knew who was up in Byron and it happened to be him. I've got quite good contacts up there – remember that beach house we stayed in that time?'

I nodded.

'What's that got to do with it?' I said.

'It's actually my house.' He grinned like a naughty little boy. I wondered how many more fascinating facts he had to spring on me.

'Anyway,' continued James, clearly starting to enjoy himself. 'So I found out Bald Matt was up there – that's his name, by the way, the fellow you call "tattoo man" – and he followed you all the way from the airport to Dee's house, and you didn't notice. Not a very good pupil, are you?'

I pulled a face at him.

'Continue,' I said, in a schoolteacher voice.

'Oh, I love her when she's angry,' he said to Dee.

'You were saying, Mr McLoughlin . . .' I said imperiously.

'OK, hold your horses. Bald Matt followed you to the house and then he went round the corner and called his buddies for back up and then they waited. And when I hadn't had a call from you for over three hours, I sent them in.'

'Oh shit,' I said. 'I completely forgot to call you.'

'I rest my case,' said James.

'But how come they got there just as the goons found us?' I asked, warming to my lady detective role.

'That, Grasshopper, was pure luck. You both need to thank your lucky stars about that one and please, Antonia, my darling, I have saved your arse twice now and I don't ever want to have to do it again, so if I tell you that something is dangerous in future, please listen to me. OK?'

I hung my head and nodded like a guilty child.

'And now I'd like one of those drinks Dee's having. If I'm going to live here, with curtains and sofas and other people, I might as well be completely corrupted by your bourgeois lifestyle,' he said. 'And while you're at it, stick this in the video.'

He chucked a video tape at me. There was nothing written on the box.

'Trust me,' he said. 'You'll both find it fascinating.'

I came back with drinks for us all and put the video on. I nearly snorted vodka down my nose when the first frame came into view. It was Nikki Maier, naked but for a white lace G-string, sitting on a bench with her legs wide apart and . . . well, it was disgusting anyway. Let's just say it would have been a good commercial for her Brazilian waxer.

The tape was roughly edited and very poor quality, but as it carried on in the same vein, with the odd change of outfit and position, I suddenly realized what I was looking at.

'Oh my God,' I cried out. 'It's the changing room at the Carlton Spa.'

I looked at James. He was smiling broadly.

'This is a good bit,' he said, nodding at the screen just as Caroline French came into view. She sat down next to Nikki and they started performing as a double act. I watched frozen for a moment, then glanced at Dee who was shaking her head, knowingly.

'Can you turn that filth off?' I asked James. 'Where did you get that?'

'It's the tape from the security camera in the ladies' changing room,' said James, pressing stop on the remote.

'Oh, no,' I said, remembering Nikki massaging body lotion into her breasts that time I'd been in there with her. I'd thought it was weird at the time. 'So they knew they were being filmed?'

Dee snorted with laughter.

'I told you she was after a bigger fish,' she said. 'You know who owns that gym, don't you?'

I shook my head.

'Pieter van der Gaarden,' said Dee. 'I think we were just watching Nikki's idea of a first date.'

'Whatever she had in mind,' said James, 'Spider's making a fortune with these tapes. Maybe she'd like to marry him.'

Dee stayed with us for a while, until she found a place of her own near the shop. With her and James in residence, it was a full house, but at least it took a while for the reporters to find out she was there. They had the shop staked out from day one, but I just said 'No comment' every day on my way in and on my way out, until one of them was smart enough to follow me home. Then we were rumbled.

It was weird having them camped outside, but we just got on with life – which for Percy meant having a flirtathon with a couple of rather handsome cameramen – and eventually they lost interest.

We even had a party – to celebrate the removal of James's plasters – mixing all of our weird friends together. Percy and I invited Antony and that little gang, Dee brought all her beauticians, hairdressers and manicurists, Tom had Vita and her mummies and Suzy came on her own. James invited all his pals, including Spider and Stacey – and Jasmine, whom I had really come to like. I should have known that James wouldn't have gone out with someone horrid, I told myself.

I watched the evening unfold with a sense of wonder.

Antony Maybury chatting to Stacey, who became quite animated with his playful banter, Percy and Spider comparing tattoos, Suzy, Daisy and Dee squealing with laughter over some private girly joke and Jasmine playing Cluedo in a corner with Tom, Vita and Bald Matt. It was a great night.

Hugo and Greg came too, as, after our big row, we were back on speaking terms. It had been necessary really, to clear the air between us and, as time passed, I'd even grown quite fond of Greg – in fact it had been he who had engineered the rapprochement between Hugo and me, making us both see that our stand-off was unfair on Tom. Even more amazingly, Hugo had actually started the divorce proceedings.

When the party was at its height, he came and found me in the kitchen, where I was mixing up a few more jugs of margaritas to keep it going with a swing. He came up and put his arm round me, squeezing my shoulder.

'I'm so glad you're happy, Ant,' he said. 'That James of yours is a really decent chap and Tom clearly adores him, which is marvellous.'

'Thanks, Hugo,' I said. 'And I'm glad you're still happy with Greg. At least you haven't left the one you left me for, as the song goes.'

'No, we're pretty solid.' He paused and scratched the top of his head in a gesture so familiar I felt a tiny pang – a very tiny one.

'Yeah, taking Greg home to meet the folks next month, actually,' he said.

I nearly dropped the margaritas I was so astonished.

Hugo laughed. 'Amazing, isn't it? I've actually told the parents. Did it on the phone, which was a bit tacky, but just had to get it over with. Didn't like myself much, living a lie like that. That's why I was such a shit for a while. It was getting to me. Sorry about that.'

I shook my head.

'Blood under the bridge, Hugo,' I said. 'All in the past. How did Margot react?' I asked tentatively, dying to know.

Hugo bent down and leaned in towards me, propping himself on the kitchen counter in one of his characteristically ungainly postures.

'Do you know, she didn't seem to mind at all,' he said.

'Are you serious?'

'Deadly. She's been doing some kind of a counselling course or some such bollocks and it's changed her attitude on a few things. It was almost as though she were pleased I was a poofter. Now I can be a holy project of forgiveness for her. Plus she said she didn't want any more grand-children and she never liked you anyway . . .'

I set about him with a tea towel. I knew he was joking about the last bit. Well, I hoped he was.

After all the excitement and action it was good to settle down to a relatively normal life again, at least until all the court cases started. Roger and Frankie were in jail on remand and Dee and I were back in the shop. We saw a lot of Suzy, who had given up her job – she had quite enough money of her own to live on, without touching Roger's tainted millions – and was devoting her time to writing her memoirs and doing the chat-show circuit. She was a TV natural, it turned out.

James's career was taking a new direction too. He had set up as a motivational management consultant, working with large corporations to help them develop team spirit and something called 'transparent lines of communication'. Working, in short, to dismantle – in a constructive way – the kind of impersonal big business culture that had killed his father. He'd called it Grasshopper Consulting.

He was helped on his way in his new venture by Hugo, who had been so impressed with the story of how James had saved the King George, he had made Cadogan's Grasshopper Consulting's first corporate client. Then he did a very good job of promoting James's skills to all his CEO chums.

Tom was happy too. James had given up his Bondi flat and we were living together officially, which made Tom quiver with delight. One day I overheard him boasting to Vita that he had one mummy, three daddies and a great-uncle, which I thought was pretty good.

One afternoon in March, a few days after Mardi Gras – Percy had featured on another float – I had left Dee in charge at the shop while I dropped Tom off at a birthday party. Then I'd nipped home, hoping to catch Percy by himself. I had something important I wanted to tell him without Tom around to earwig.

When I walked through the door, the house had an empty feeling to it. Percy was clearly out and about. I'd have to catch him another time.

I went into the kitchen to see if there was any post and saw there was a huge vase of peonies on the table. Next to it was a note.

Goodbye, my darling girl.
Thank you so much for having me. Had a divine time. Have gone to Paris to stay with Karl. Will write. Stay happy, darling heart, and look after your two beautiful boys.
Your loving friend,
Percy H xxx
PS You can call the baby after my mother.

And so we did. Esmé Spider McLoughlin.

PANTS ON FIRE

Maggie Alderson

*'I knew what happened to English gels who went to Australia.
They met marvellous men with strong forearms who tipped
their hats, saved your life and then took you off to live on a
farm as big as Wales. I could hardly wait . . .'*

When Georgia Abbott walks out on her cheating fiancé,
she's left feeling as bleak as the London sky in February.
Until someone tells her about a job on *Glow* magazine in
Sydney. That's Sydney, Australia – where the welcome is
as warm as the weather and the men look like Mel Gibson,
but taller. What's she got to lose?

So Georgia packs up and ships out Down Under. At first
things seem promising, as she's swept up in a whirl of
A-list parties, dancing and debauchery. But while Australian
water may go down the plughole the other way,
Australian men are – oh dear – starting to look all too
familiar . . .

'The perfect read for any girl who's ever wondered if the
grass might be greener on the other side of the world' *OK!*

0–141–00374–X

refresh yourself at penguin.co.uk

Visit penguin.co.uk for exclusive information and interviews with
bestselling authors, fantastic give-aways and the
inside track on all our books, from the Penguin Classics
to the latest bestsellers.

BE FIRST

first chapters, first editions, first novels

EXCLUSIVES

author chats, video interviews, biographies, special
features

EVERYONE'S A WINNER

give-aways, competitions, quizzes, ecards

READERS GROUPS

exciting features to support existing groups and
create new ones

NEWS

author events, bestsellers, awards, what's new

EBOOKS

books that click – download an ePenguin today

BROWSE AND BUY

thousands of books to investigate – search, try
and buy the perfect gift online – or treat yourself!

ABOUT US

job vacancies, advice for writers and company
history

Get Closer To Penguin . . . www.penguin.co.uk